In His Control

NINA BRUHNS

Published by Cajun Hot Press

ISBN 13: 978-0615991184

IN HIS CONTROL
All rights reserved
Copyright © April 2014 by Nina Bruhns

Visit Nina Bruhns at:
www.NinaBruhns.com

Cover art designed by Fiona Jayde.

Third edition
Cajun Hot Press
April 2014

Formerly published as:
The French Detective's Woman – 2012
The Paris Caper – 2013

◙ 1 ◙

Ciara Alexander felt naked without a disguise.

Sliding into the darkness of the swanky Club LeCœur, her heart pumped fast to the hard beat of the rock music as she scanned the crowded dance floor. She didn't know what had possessed her tonight, coming as herself. Recognition would be disastrous.

But for some reason she'd felt reckless all day. Anticipatory. She had an irrepressible feeling something was going to happen tonight. Something big.

Something that would change her life forever.

Little did she realize how right she was. Nor just how disastrous things could really turn out.

But at this moment she felt incredible. Invulnerable.

Not that she was an adrenaline junkie. That time going in the second story window at Baron Palchow's Strasbourg chalet and running into a German shepherd had nearly given her a heart attack. And the job she'd pulled at Le Mans during the famous race and there been cops everywhere...that one had shaved a few years off her life, too.

No, she didn't enjoy the feeling of danger roiling in the pit of her stomach, knowing she was about to risk life and limb and years of freedom. Frankly, anyone who did was a fool. However, she had no choice. It was time, and the job had to be done.

Joining the dancers on the floor, Ciara lifted her arms and closed her eyes in pleasure. This she *did* enjoy.

Moving her feet and her body rhythmically, she felt the driving music clear to her toes. It didn't bother her that she had no partner. She'd find

1

someone eventually. Or maybe she'd dance solo all night. No matter. She could lose herself in the throng and dance for the sheer love of it.

Aside from which, being on the dance floor would bring her closer to her target—the jet-setting Dutch middle princess, here in Paris on her annual million-euro shopping spree.

That was something else Ciara didn't get. Shopping. The need to possess all that...stuff. Stuff was transitory, here today, gone tomorrow. You got attached to it, but anyone could come along and take it away from you. Who needed the grief? Besides, stuff was irrelevant if you had a million euros in the bank.

Money. Now there was something a person could rely on. Money kept a person safe.

Someday Ciara would be safe. If she just had patience a little longer.

It was difficult. But what was she supposed to have done when CoCo had approached her shortly after Etienne's death, far wiser, even then, than her tender eleven years, wanting to escape her seemingly inescapable life of crime? Ciara hadn't hesitated for a second. Nor had she with the four other street kids she'd taken under her wing during the eight years since. So tonight she must swallow her fear and the niggling guilt, and do what must be done.

Looking around the club she didn't see the Dutch princess, but she was there somewhere, or would be soon. Davie had said so, and Davie always had the inside scoop. Plus, the evening tabloids had been closely following the young princess's every move for the last week, and paparazzi were lined up outside the front doors. The princess would be at Club LeCœur and stay till the wee hours of the morning, no doubt about it.

Patience, Ciara, and all things will come.

The first song blended into the next, and then the next, as she worked her body to the music. She'd been in LeCœur before, so the trendy black and silver décor, the pink marble bar with gleaming crystal glasses hanging in racks over it and a multitude of bottles lined up behind, the canopy of white fairy lights twinkling above the dance floor, were all familiar in their posh ostentation. It was the perfect gilded cage in which to trap her avaricious young pigeon.

The patrons were as pretentiously showy as the furnishings. With their self-consciously chic and expensive designer clothes, they were not regular Parisians, but the countryless jet set habitués of international society. The masses of jewels heaped around their wrists and necks—diamonds and emeralds and rubies—sparkled and glittered in the darkness of the club like bright stars in a black sky.

Perfect.

A tiny bead of perspiration trickled down Ciara's neck and as she danced, she reached back to lift her hair off her nape, momentarily glad for her decision not to wear a wig in the warm summer night.

Suddenly she noticed a man watching her, leaning against a pillar at the edge of the dance floor. Tall and dark-haired, he had broad shoulders enhanced by an elegantly tailored jacket—Helmut Lang, if she wasn't mistaken. His smoldering eyes followed her body's every move. When their gazes collided, it was all she could do not to stop in her tracks and stare back at him.

She turned away, irritated.

This *wasn't* what she was here for. A man like that was a one-way ticket to disaster. Distracting. Hell, downright dangerous. The kind of man who could start a woman to fantasizing...

But fantasies weren't real. Ciara knew that. Only the job was real.

Two large, strong hands surprised her, brushing over her hips from behind and holding her lightly. "*Voulez vous danser avec moi?*" a smoky male voice whispered in her ear.

Making a pretense of moving to the music, he pulled her back against his torso. It was firm, muscular. All male.

"No," she answered, suddenly tongue-tied, her usually flawless French vanishing into an awkward patois. "I don't want to dance with you."

But for some reason her feet refused to move away from him. *God, he felt good.*

"You are American?" he asked softly, not letting her go.

"Yes," she answered without thinking.

Instantly, she regretted telling the truth. She didn't want this man—or anyone—knowing anything about her. The truth could be traced.

Still, her nerve-induced accent had probably made her nationality obvious. A dangerous slip.

"You don't like dancing with Frenchmen?" he murmured, sliding his impertinent hands up to her waist. His fingers gripped her a shade tighter; he pulled her a shade closer. Her heart pounded a shade harder.

"I like dancing alone," she said firmly.

She could smell him. Musky. Masculine. She fought not to enjoy it, and the feel of his large hands on her.

He chuckled, the sound rich and savory in her ear. "In France we think it's more fun with two people."

"In America we like to choose our own partner."

"So do we," he said, and lowered his voice. "I choose you."

Her stomach zinged. Under other circumstances she may have considered taking him up on his not-so-subtle offer. The man was sexy as hell, and it had, after all, been quite a while. But not tonight. Tonight she had no time for hooking up. No time to indulge her fantasies. Or her loneliness.

Intent on sending him on his way, she turned in his arms. And caught her breath.

He wasn't handsome. Not even close. His face was a conglomeration of sharp angles and harsh features, his dark eyes more penetrating and intense than any she'd ever seen. But something about his look was so compelling a shiver spilled through her entire body.

He didn't smile. Didn't cajole. Just reached up and traced a thumb along her jaw. And murmured, "Dance with me."

She licked her lips. As if that were answer enough he drew her close and put his arms around her, sliding the fingers of one hand into her hair.

Her will to resist slipped completely. He felt too good. Solid and built, and...oh, so male. His voice oozed power and confidence. Not the prissy French of the upper class, but the coarse accent of the Paris *banlieue*—the rough and tumble melting-pot 'burbs. A little wild, a little uncivilized. *A little like Etienne.*

It had been a long, long time since she'd lost Etienne, her first and only love. And ages since she'd given in to any other man. Her lifestyle since his untimely death hadn't been conducive to anything more than a brief affair, so she'd passed up most opportunities for masculine company. Something so shallow wasn't worth the hassle, or the memories, or the heartache of wanting more.

But this man... Lord, this man was damn tempting.

"Okay," she found herself saying, and the corners of his lips curved up. "But just dance."

He tipped his head in graceful acquiescence.

She wound her arms around his neck and let him guide her out into the middle of the throbbing chaos of the dance floor. She didn't care that they were the only couple doing it the old fashioned way, cheek to cheek. The music was loud and his body hot and hard; the feel of it moving against her nearly drove everything else from her mind.

Damn. She struggled to remind herself of the reason she was here at the nightclub. She could *not* lose focus.

Taking a long steadying breath, she glanced around again. Okay, change of plan. If she played her cards right, this could work out even better than being on her own. She could use him as a decoy. Not to mention an alibi... She just had to be careful.

The only question was what she would do with him when she had to make her speedy exit. She knew what she'd *like* to do. But that might not be possible. And definitely not smart.

All at once she spotted the princess, dancing a few meters away. Wearing a Dries van Noten cocktail dress and Balenciaga heels, she made Ciara in her borrowed black Ungaro look positively boring. Distinctive Cartier diamonds bounced around the woman's ears, jumped at her throat and jingled around her wrist as she danced. Diamonds worth a fortune.

Just one of those bracelets would pay most people's bills for a couple of months. Certainly Ciara's, even with the Orphans.

She felt the heavy kick of nerves she always got just before the lay-down.

Easy does it, she told herself. Best not to rush things. The most important part of any job was setting it up. Moving ever closer. Picking her moment.

So she kept the haughty princess in her line of sight, maneuvering her own dance partner into optimum position. Ready to strike when the time was right.

Except he didn't want to be led. Naturally. It figured a man like him wouldn't dance to her tune. Instead he pulled her body closer still, and spun her away.

She should have been annoyed, but it was impossible to concentrate on anything but how amazing it felt to be in his arms. Her breasts pressed against his chest and her knees tangled with his, lacing their thighs together like lovers. Slowly, he stroked up and down her back with his fingers, skimming the bare skin above the low cut of her dress, sending shivers along her spine. His arousal grew thick and hard between them. He did nothing to hide it, but didn't force attention to it either. So like a Frenchman. Comfortable with his sexuality, but not making a big deal about it. She liked that. Damn, she liked *him*.

"You smell nice," he murmured, burying his nose in her hair as the music slowed to a soft, romantic ballad. His warm breath tickled her ear. By now they'd danced about six or seven songs straight through, and he showed no signs of relinquishing his hold on her. Which was fine. She was enjoying him too much to want to let him go just yet. The princess would wait.

"So do you," she whispered back, and slid her arms under his jacket and around his waist. She hummed out a sigh of pleasure as she brushed her hands over his lean hips and slim waist. Damn, the man's body was fine.

Suddenly, her fingers hit something hard at the back of his waistband. Square and made of leather, it was threaded onto his belt.

She froze in disbelief.

"My handcuffs," the man said, pulling back to gaze down at her. His lips curved into an enigmatic smile. "Does that worry you?"

She snapped her gaping mouth shut, her mind in a whirl. "That depends on what you intend to do with them."

His smile twitched. "I am open to suggestion, but...the official answer is that I'm a cop."

Her eyes widened. "A— *A cop?*" *Ohgod.* The man was a cop. *Un flic, un poulet.* In other words, *un désastre*—a disaster.

"Is that a problem?"

From the corner of her eye, Ciara saw the princess dance closer. She swallowed down a powerful urge to laugh hysterically. *Hell.* The only man in living memory she'd been this attracted to, and now— *Double hell.*

"You planning on arresting me or something?" she asked, only half-joking. Her pulse hammered.

His brow rose. "For dancing? Or...is there something else about you that I am unaware of? Your tourist visa has expired, perhaps?"

This time she did laugh. She couldn't help it. But at the last minute she tried really hard not to sound desperate. "Student visa. Good indefinitely," she lied.

"Well, then," he said, and drew her into his arms again, replacing hers around his neck. "I guess there's nothing to worry about."

If only he knew.

Or, maybe he *did....*

"So," she asked, hoping he couldn't feel her heart beating like a jungle drum against his chest, "Are you here at the nightclub for business, or pleasure?"

She felt him smile against her temple. "So far it's been all pleasure." And just like that he lifted her chin and kissed her.

She let out a tiny gasp. He took advantage, flicking his tongue over hers. Then he pulled back.

Her mind reeled out of balance as the erotic taste of him washed through her mouth. At the same time the princess danced back into her line of sight, arms draped over the shoulders of her escort. Sparkling diamond bracelets dangled within a hair's breadth of Ciara's fingers.

Oh, God, this was it! There would never be a better time. *Or a worse one.* But she had to do it. Now. *And possibly end up in handcuffs...* Or wait for another day. *And possibly end up in this cop's bed.*

Oh, God.

No choice.

Working by touch and pure instinct, she shifted her fingers a fraction of an inch, singled out the bracelet with the biggest diamonds and deftly unclasped it from the princess's wrist. It slithered into Ciara's palm, cold and sharp and glittering like a row of icy snake-eyes.

She closed her hand around it, tilted her head and pressed her mouth to the cop's...as she deliberately dropped the bracelet into his jacket pocket.

🔲🔲🔲

Commissaire de Police Judiciaire Jean-Marc Lacroix was not expecting the woman in his arms to kiss him back.

But when her lips met and pressed into his, criminal detective superintendent Lacroix couldn't resist the temptation to quickly take it to the next level. He grasped her chin and tugged it down, sweeping his tongue inside her mouth, tasting her, plumbing her depths until she moaned long and low, responding with equal fervor. Just how he liked it.

Merde, he shouldn't be doing this. *Mais, bon Dieu*, the lady could kiss.

Jean-Marc hadn't meant to kiss her at all. He had just meant to use her as a way to get onto the dance floor, to be less conspicuous in his surveillance of the flashy Dutch princess and her damned jewelry-dripping entourage.

But he should have known it would come to this. The moment he'd spotted the young woman out there on the floor in that low-backed, clingy little black number, dancing all by herself and enjoying the hell out of it, he'd been a walking hard-on. Now he was a dancing hard-on. And if he had anything to say about it, very soon he'd be a fucking hard-on.

He might be a cop, but off-duty he was only a man—and no better than he had to be. He was here at Club LeCœur strictly on his own initiative, not on the clock. Working a hunch that the guy rapidly stealing his way up the French National Police's *Office Central de Lutte Contre le Trafic des Biens Culturels*—or OCBC's—most-wanted list might show up for such easy pickings as the high-profile princess. As lucky as he was clever, the slippery jewel thief known as *le Revenant*—the Ghost—had been on the OCBC's radar for two years. Now the guy was starting to make media headlines, and they wanted the *fils de pute* behind bars. The officer in charge of the case, *Commissaire* Saville, was good, but somewhat unimaginative. As a *commissaire*, normally Jean-Marc didn't work investigations himself, he delegated and ran things from behind a desk. But he thought he might score some much-needed brownie points with his and Saville's boss, *Commissaire Divisionnaire* Belfort, if he managed to bring down the thief himself. Besides, he missed field work.

Jean-Marc had been to a half-dozen clubs over the past week following the princess and her ostentatious jewels along with the tabloid paparazzi, but *le Revenant* had yet to put in an appearance. Maybe he wouldn't turn up tonight, either.

Which would leave Jean-Marc free for other pursuits. Such as the pretty blonde in his arms.

Donc, he was smart enough to recognize a rationalization when he heard it, but at the moment he didn't give a shit. They had stopped pretending to dance and were now kissing in earnest in the middle of the crowd like a couple of teenagers.

"*Viens*," he murmured, lifting his mouth from hers when people started to stare. He grabbed her hand. "Come on."

Before he even knew where he was going, he trotted down the stairs to the basement level where the restrooms were located, towing her by the wrist. Bypassing the *hommes* and *femmes*, he spotted a door marked "no admittance" and jerked it open. A startled waiter glanced up from unpacking a box of wine and started to protest.

Jean-Marc whipped out his *carte de requisition*, which identified him as a police officer, and ordered, "Out. *Vite.*" The waiter scrambled to his feet and scrammed. The door jerked closed.

The light in the room flickered dimly and the place smelled musty, like old cardboard. But the scent of the woman's perfume clung to him, and she was all Jean-Marc needed to see.

He turned to his captive and pushed her up against the door, setting the lock with a swift flick of his thumb. *He was so ready for this.* He desperately needed to lose his frustrations in the hot passion of a willing woman, to thrust away his anger and annoyance in the blissful forgetfulness of her sweet body. *Bon Dieu,* he needed this. With every fiber of his being he wanted to be inside her.

"*Je veux te baiser,*" he growled, and took her mouth in a savage kiss.

She moaned, undulating her body beneath his as he kissed her over and over, touching her, learning her, urging her on with the blatant language of sex. She reached for his belt buckle.

"*Attends,*" he said, grabbing both her wrists. "Wait."

He eased out a harsh breath, grappling for control. Of the situation. Of himself. He held her there as she panted, watching her breasts rise and fall beneath her silky dress.

He wanted to see them. He wanted to taste them.

He let her go and scraped her dress straps off her slim shoulders, peeling her bodice to her waist. Her bra was black, made of the sheerest lace, and did nothing to hide her breasts. They weren't large, but full and round, tipped with pretty nipples of rose, peaked and eager for his attention.

"*Mon Dieu,*" he murmured. "You are beautiful."

He popped the front clasp and they fell into his hands, warm and silky-soft. With a groan of pleasure he bent and took one in his mouth, sucking in the firm nipple. He licked and suckled her, feeling the tension slowly seep from his shoulders and down to fill his heavy groin. *Bon Dieu.* This time he didn't stop her when she groped for his belt.

He almost detonated when she touched him, taking him boldly in her hand.

"*Non,*" he gasped, pulling her away. With one hand he raised her wrists above her head, with the other fumbled in his inside pocket for his wallet and the protection he always carried. All the while kissing her, deep and hard.

He found the packet and placed it on a nearby shelf. Then snagged the hem of her dress and dragged it up, twisting it into a knot at her waist. How he wished he could just rip the whole damned thing off! He wanted her completely bare. He wanted her naked and open, trembling for his touch.

Suddenly, he noticed she *was* trembling. He jerked back and met her gaze. *"C'est bien?"*

Her long blond hair was artfully mussed, her eyes slumberous and half-lidded; she was a sensuous fallen angel gazing up at him like she would do anything he asked. Anything at all.

"Mmm-hmm," she hummed, "wonderful," and his arousal thickened.

"Do you want me to stop?" he asked hoarsely, just to make sure lust wasn't coloring his perception.

"No. Don't stop," she whispered.

Filled with an inexplicable sense of power, he ran his free hand lingeringly down the curve of her hip, pausing at the lacy edge of her barely-there black panties. Trailing his fingers over the small triangle of fabric, he watched her eyes darken. They were green, the color of a forest at midnight, and pooled with desire.

He slipped his hand under her panties. "Spread your legs," he said, licking at her mouth, his pulse pounding with excitement.

She obeyed and he slid his fingers into her wet heat, seeking her center. She quivered at his exploration, and gasped as he sent them deep inside then out again. He found her bud and worked it, sliding his thumb back and forth, round and round, until she shook with need.

"That's right," he urged roughly. "Come for me, then I'll make you come again, *à ma queue.*"

She moaned, closed her eyes and shattered.

He let her wrists go and sheathed himself one-handed as he coaxed every last shiver and whimper from her. When at last her face was a portrait of bliss and her eyes fluttered open, he took hold of her panties and ripped them off.

She gave a yelp of surprise, her eyes widening as he stuck the ruined panties in his jacket pocket.

"To remember the occasion," he murmured with a wink, then grabbed her thighs, lifted her to his waist and plunged into her.

She cried out, clutching him around the neck, clinging to him as he thrust deeper and deeper. *Exquise.* She was all he needed and more. So much more. She was perfect, young, hot and tight with inner muscles that gripped him like a vise.

He gritted his teeth and marshaled his self-control, wanting it to last as long as possible. Again and again and again he drove into her, until he was a living agony of need to release, until she started uttering the sweet noises of a woman close to completion. He held on for three more hard thrusts, then she swallowed a scream, her fingernails digging into his back. With a roar he let himself plummet over the edge. It lasted forever, the almost unbearable pleasure of releasing his seed deep inside her.

NINA BRUHNS

After the final shuddering spasm he felt purged, renewed, exhausted.
Happy.

Hell, he was in love.

He took her face between his hands and kissed her, both of them
shaking and on the verge of collapse. Her legs slid down his hips but she
clung to him and managed to stay on her feet.

"That was absolutely incredible," he said between sucked-down breaths.
"You are—"

The loud chirp of his cell phone startled him out of his intended litany
of compliments.

"*De merde*," he softly swore, and reached into his inside pocket for it. He
looked down at his newest lover apologetically. "Sorry. I have to answer.
It's probably headquarters."

She nodded. He could tell she was trying to look nonchalant as he
disengaged from her and flipped open the phone, but for a brief second she
looked distinctly nervous.

"*Commissaire* Lacroix," he answered, and her eyes flared even bigger. He
gave her a wry smile and lifted a shoulder as he tried to make out through
the static who was on the other end of the line.

"*Jean-Marc, tu es là?*"

"I'm here," he told his second-in-command, *Lieutenant* Pierre Rousselot,
whose voice was breaking up. "What's up, *mec?*"

"Where the hell are you, buried in some basement somewhere?"

"Club LeCœur," he said a little louder, casting about for a wastebasket.
"They must have thick walls."

"Club LeCœur? Then you know about the robbery, *oui?*"

He straightened, immediately alert. "What robbery?"

"Your Ghost. He's struck again."

A sharp spike of angry frustration swamped over Jean-Marc. God *damn*
it. God *fucking* damn it. It was like the bastard *knew* exactly when he'd
stopped watching.

He paced away from the woman, who'd begun to rearrange her clothing.
"The princess?" he asked, cutting to the chase.

"Just as you predicted," Pierre said. "Say, I thought you were doing
surveillance on the Dutch mob?"

"I took a break."

There was a meaningful pause on the other end. "Ah, *pardon*. Well, you'd
better finish quick. In three minutes the place will be crawling with
gendarmes, the OCBC, and the Dutch secret service. Apparently the victim
has made quite a stink."

Jean-Marc swiped a hand over his sweaty forehead. *Dieu*. He had to get
hold of himself. Any second now his boss, CD Belfort, would be calling,
demanding to know if he'd caught the thief—even though Belfort and

Saville had denied Jean-Marc's request for an official police team to follow the princess's every move. They hadn't believed the chances of *le Revenant* showing up were high enough to warrant that kind of expense. So Jean-Marc had done it on his own time.

And now he'd fucked up.

He glanced at his lover, who was looking around at the boxes on the shelves, pretending not to listen to his conversation. And just like that his anger evaporated.

Damn. She had been *so* worth fucking up for.

"When will you be here?" he asked Pierre.

"I'm parking now."

"Meet you at the entrance in two," he said, and hung up.

He turned to the woman and opened his arms. "Come here, *mon ange.*" His green-eyed angel.

She hesitated, looking uneasy. "You're a *commissaire?*"

He nodded. "*Commissaire de Police Judiciare.* CPJ Lacroix. But don't let that worry you. It has nothing to do with us. *Viens ici.*"

She came haltingly, but she came, stepping into his embrace. As he took her in his arms, she let out a nervous giggle. "I can't believe I let a detective superintendent of the National Police fuck me in a storage closet."

He smiled and kissed her. "Next time I'll do it in a more romantic place, I promise."

Her surprised gaze held his for a moment before it slid to the buttons of his shirt. "Do you have to go now?"

"I'm afraid so. There's been a robbery. Here, at the club."

"*Here?*"

"It's all right. I can vouch for your whereabouts, so you won't have to hang around for questioning." He tipped up her chin and gave her another kiss, then softly asked, "Before we go, I want to know your name."

Her lips parted for a second before she answered, "Ciara."

"I'm Jean-Marc," he said. He wanted to kiss her again, and keep kissing her all night. But their time had run out. *For now.* Pulling a business card from his wallet, he wrote on the reverse and handed it to her. "My cell phone number's on the back. I want you to call me."

She stared down at it. "Really?"

"Tonight. I should be finished here in a couple of hours."

Disbelief flitted through her eyes as she looked back up at him. "I, um—"

"I want to see you again." He took her face in his hands. "There's something between us, Ciara, I can feel it. Let's explore this thing, whatever it is."

Her tongue peeked out then disappeared. "I— I'd like that."

"*Bon.* Good." Relief washed through him. For some reason he'd had the crazy notion she would turn him down.

He placed her hand on the crook of his arm and led her out of their private sanctuary, up the stairs and back into the chaos of the main club. As Pierre had warned, police were everywhere, taking down names and addresses of the impatient club-goers and wait-staff who had all been herded into a group in one corner to await their turn for questioning. To the side of the hubbub stood the snooty princess and her entourage cursing at the two uniformed cops preventing them from going anywhere until they'd spoken to a detective. Until Saville arrived, that meant Jean-Marc.

He figured they could wait a bit longer.

Flashing his *carte du requisition* at the guards, he guided Ciara to the front entrance, where they met Pierre, who took one long, appraising look at her, and said, "*Oo-la-la, mec. Très sympathique.*"

"Shut up, Pierre," he said good-naturedly. Even *le Revenant* slipping through his fingers tonight wasn't going to spoil his mood. No way would Pierre's infernal, inevitable teasing.

"CD Belfort is on his way. We better get to work," his lieutenant said, giving Ciara a shrug. "The boss."

"Walk me out?" she asked Jean-Marc with a shy smile.

"I'll put her in a taxi and be right back," he told Pierre, and they walked out into the warm, black Parisian night.

An explosion of camera flashes went off from the clutch of paparazzi at the entrance, catching them both by surprise.

"*Merde,*" he muttered, shielding her eyes with his jacket lapel. "I'd forgotten about those vultures." Jean-Marc hated reporters. Especially the unscrupulous barrel-scrapers who worked for the sensationalist tabloids.

A few reporters recognized him and shouted questions. He growled, "No comment," at them, pushing through the throng to the curb. Wisely, they moved back. An empty cab sat across the street, and Jean-Marc led Ciara over to it.

"I'll be fine," she said, giving him a hug. "You better get back."

"This guy's timing really stinks," he muttered.

"Who?"

"The thief, this bastard *le Revenant*. When I catch him, I swear I'll make him pay dearly."

She seemed to go pale for a moment, but it must have been a quirk of the light because she hugged him again, then dug around in his jacket pocket with an impish smile. She pulled out her torn panties. "I better take these so you don't get in trouble."

"Ah, *non.*" He snagged them from her and tucked them back into his pocket. "These are mine now. I'm going to put them under my pillow so I can dream of you whenever you're not sharing my bed." He bent to take her mouth one last time. "Which I surely hope will not be the case tonight."

"You are a very naughty man, *Commissaire* Lacroix," she whispered.

"Count on it," he assured. "You'll call me? In a couple of hours?"

She kissed him back and hummed out a sigh. "*Mmmm.*"

"Say it," he demanded softly. "Swear to me."

"I'll call," she said. "I promise." Then she got into the taxi, watching him the whole time it pulled away. Just before she was lost in the flow of traffic, she blew him a kiss. The last thing he saw of her was her smile.

But it was a smile so bleak it suddenly struck him square in the gut.

She had lied.

She had no intention of ever seeing him again.

◙ 2 ◙

Ciara felt sick to her stomach as she lost sight of Jean-Marc standing at the curb with his hands in his trouser pockets staring after her. She turned forward and told the taxi driver a corner where he could drop her, close to her apartment on rue du le Chat qui Piche.

Oh. My. God.

She'd just had sex with a CPJ, one of the very men who'd publicly sworn to hunt her down, send her to jail, and throw away the key.

Not that he knew it was *her* they were after. Thank God, everyone still thought *le Revenant* was a man. But *she* knew. As soon as she'd felt those handcuffs at the small of his back she should have taken off like the Roadrunner at the scent of coyote.

But no. She'd gone ahead and had *sex* with the man. And what's more she'd loved every hot steamy second of it. Even worse, she wanted to do it again. So much so, for a second she'd fooled herself into thinking she could actually make that phone call she'd sworn to him to make.

How had she let this happen?

She covered her face with her hands. And groaned. They smelled of him; musky, erotic, virile. She yanked them away, crossed her arms and stuck her hands under her armpits. But there was no escaping. His scent clung to her everywhere: her hands, her face, her breasts...between her legs. It was like he'd marked her. *His.*

There was also no escaping the hard lumps of the diamond bracelet poking into her arm from the hidden pocket in her dress. *They* marked her as his, too. *His quarry.*

"Jesus, girl, what were you thinking?" she whispered. Hadn't Etienne's death taught her anything?

Why hadn't she worn a disguise?

At least she hadn't told him her last name.

She'd have to lie low now. In France, anyway. Her next few jobs she'd do outside the country. Expenses would be a bit higher, but at least she wouldn't have to worry about running into her new lover, *le commissaire*.

She squeezed her eyes shut and drew her tongue over her parched lips. And tasted him. Deep inside she felt a sharp tug of desire. Her stomach sank even further. If she ever did meet up with him again it would be her downfall for sure. Which would spell ruin not only for her, but to the Orphans as well.

She couldn't let that happen. Jail was simply not an option.

The taxi pulled up at the entrance to the walking street rue de la Huchette. At the heart of the Latin Quarter, the street was filled with restaurants, shops, students and tourists, but she liked living here. It was cheap, and she blended in well. As soon as she got out, she was assaulted by Davie and Ricardo, two of her Orphans. They'd been waiting for her for some time, judging by the worried relief in their faces as they ran up and grabbed her arms.

"Ciara! *Grazie a Dio!*" Ricardo said rapidly in Italian, a sure sign he was über-upset. Ricardo was seventeen, tall, lanky and the second runaway she'd adopted. Innately cheerful of disposition, a perpetual smile had graced his face ever since five years ago when she'd spirited him away from a distant relative using him for unpaid labor in his Paris construction firm.

But Ricardo was frowning now.

A knot of fear tightened in her already jumpy stomach. "What's happened?"

Davie tugged at her arm. "It's Sofie. You have to come with us."

"Sofie?"

The youngest of the Orphans, and the most fragile both emotionally and physically, Sofie Hassan had run away from home at thirteen, from a horror Ciara couldn't even contemplate. She had survived working the Pigalle doing whatever she must, until Ciara had found her one day and persuaded her to join them. But her experiences on the streets, and previously with her father, had left her meek and damaged. She was just coming out of it now, two years later.

"Oh, God, is she hurt?" Ciara asked.

"Yes!" Ricardo said, at the same time Davie said, "No. Well, not too badly."

Ever the pragmatist, sixteen-year old Davie's conservative aristocratic upbringing had clashed violently with his early discovery that he was gay, but had left him with a level head in a crisis. Ciara leaned on him far more than the others. Far more than she really should.

"Tell me what happened," she said, herding them back into her taxi and giving the driver the address of the apartment on rue Daguerre that Ciara kept for the Orphans—Davie, Ricardo, Sophie, CoCo, and Hugo. Part of the reasons these kids had all ended up on the streets was an overabundance of adult control. Ciara had earned their confidence by trusting them to live on their own, with her help but not her interference and a minimum of rules.

"It was Beck," Ricardo said. "He beat up Sofie."

Ciara's heart went cold. *Brigadier* Louis Beck of the Paris *Préfecture de Police* was another on the long list of good reasons one should never get involved with a cop. First Etienne. Now Sophie. It always ended badly with cops. *Always.*

Having worked the infamous red light district for thirty years, Beck was as corrupt as they came, a vile specimen of everything evil in a man. But he'd never actually hurt Sofie before. Ciara should have known that would change.

"How bad?"

"A few cuts on the face," Davie said grimly. "A lot of bruises. She's gotten quiet."

"She won't tell us anything. *Niente,*" Ricardo said, with his expressive Italian gestures. "She just cries."

"She'll talk to you," Davie said.

"Hopefully before Hugo goes after Beck with a switchblade," Ricardo added.

"That's all we'd need," Ciara muttered. Hugo would do it, too.

The three of them arrived at the rue Daguerre apartment and clattered up the half dozen flights of stairs to the attic story, which was the only place Ciara could afford that had two bedrooms and a landlord who consented to look past the youth and tenuous backgrounds of his tenants.

"Oh, sweetie," she softly said when she saw Sofie, bruised and battered, curled into a ball on the sofa. "Baby, what has he done to you?"

She gathered the girl in her arms, relieved when Sofie hugged her back.

"I'm okay," she sighed out, wiping tears with a tissue CoCo handed her.

"She's feeling better now," CoCo said, sitting on the edge of the sofa. "We iced her face and gave her a couple of aspirin."

CoCo was the mother hen of the group, albeit a tough one. Having taken care of herself for nearly all of her nineteen years, as well as big brother Hugo and their cousin Etienne before he married Ciara, CoCo was brash and outspoken, but loyal to a fault. It had been an eleven-year old CoCo who'd brought Ciara back from the brink after Etienne's death, cajoling and shaming her into giving a damn about her life again by asking for help in changing hers. CoCo had been Ciara's first Orphan, but there had been many a time over the past six years that she had wondered exactly who'd been adopted by whom.

"Sofie still won't tell us what happened," Hugo growled from the other side of the living room, pacing back and forth like a tiger on a leash.

Ciara glanced at him and tamped down her anxiety. Hugo had joined the Orphans at the behest of his sister at the ripe old age of fifteen. He was now twenty and the oldest of the group. Hot headed like his cousin Etienne, Hugo's waters ran much deeper. Not an easy mix. For now she set aside Hugo's agitated state and turned back to Sofie.

"Sweetie, you need to tell us. Why did Beck do this?"

The girl glanced up, and suddenly broke into sobs. "Oh, Ciara, What am I going to do? How am I ever going to pay him? But if I don't, he says he'll go to my father and—"

"Whoa! Slow down. What do you mean, pay him?" Ciara asked.

"*Nobody's* going to your father," Hugo said angrily, stalking over to the sofa. "I'll kill the rat bastard first."

"Quiet, Hugo! Let the girl talk," CoCo upbraided, taking Sofie's hand and pressing a kiss to it. Davie and Ricardo came to sit on the floor at their feet. Hugo continued his pacing.

"Start from the beginning," Ciara urged.

"I was going to the market. We've no milk for the morning coffee," Sophie explained. Ciara bit back her impatience, letting the girl take her time. "I was counting the coins to be sure I had enough money, and wasn't watching where I was going. He was there, *Brigadier* Beck, waiting for me outside the door."

Hugo growled again, low in his throat, and CoCo muttered angrily, "Why does he keep after you? The man should be castrated."

The brigadier was a longtime beat cop and had he'd met Sofie almost immediately after she'd run away from her abusive father. She was working the streets and he'd gotten used to enjoying her favors in exchange for "protection." He hadn't liked it when she quit turning tricks, and he'd been harassing her ever since, trying to pressure her into renewing their arrangement.

"He'd been drinking," she went on. "When I wouldn't have sex with him, he hit me. I was stupid. I called him names and told him exactly what I thought of him. He lost his temper."

Ciara winced.

"*Fils de pute*," CoCo said. The fucking bastard.

"But that's not the worst part."

"*Chérie*, what could possibly be worse than that?" Davie asked sympathetically.

"He said if I didn't pay him ten thousand euros, he'd tell my father where I am."

"Ten thousand euros!" Outrage spurted through Ciara. Over twelve thousand dollars.

"I will kill him!" Hugo repeated even more vehemently. "It's what Etienne would have done."

"And Etienne is dead," Ciara snapped, surprising them all. She took a breath and turned back to Sofie. "Where does he expect you to get that kind of money?" There was no way.

"He doesn't," Hugo spat out furiously. "He expects her to fuck him, whenever he calls."

"I won't!" Sofie cried. "I'll leave Paris! I'll go to London, or somewhere else. Anywhere else. So he'll never find me."

"No!" Ciara shook her head. "You can't leave. What about your studies? You're so close to finishing."

Ciara was taking care of all the Orphans financially right now, except for Hugo, paying for the apartment, their food and tuition. She had few rules, but one of them was that each start a course of study that would give them an income and independence when completed.

When she was a girl, she'd seen a movie once where one of the characters had said, "Give a man a fish and you feed him for a day, teach a man to fish and you feed him for a lifetime." That had struck her as very wise. She'd begged her mother to stay in school, but that would have meant feeding her for three more years. And keeping her around. By then her mom had needed every cent she had for drugs. Ciara found herself out on the streets shortly thereafter, but she'd never forgotten that movie, and never stopped wanting to go back to school.

She was determined her Orphans would all learn how to fish.

To that end, Hugo had already graduated from his auto mechanics course, and started contributing to the family coffers. Sofie was a talented artist—a painter—but making a living at that was next to impossible, so she was at cosmetic school, with only a year to go.

Desperation crept into Sophie's tone as she murmured, "But what else can I do? None of us has that kind of money. You have to steal just to pay our rent!"

They all stared at each other for a long moment. Ten thousand euros. And Ciara had thought she'd soon be able to give up her life of crime.

Now she despaired of ever being able to quit. Unless...

"We should go to the police," she announced.

"*What?*" they all exclaimed in a chorus.

"You've got to be kidding!" Ricardo said, leaping up.

Ciara waved her hands, trying to calm down the explosion of protests. "I met someone tonight. From the DCPJ. He seemed—"

CoCo and Davie looked horrified. "The *police judiciaire?*"

Hugo looked equally furious. "No!" he insisted. "*Pas le keuf!* Are you that naïve? Beck is a cop, too. There is no way they'll take our word over one of their own. Just see what happened to Etienne!"

"But Beck's in the Paris *préfecture*. The *judiciaire* is a completely different division—"

"Doesn't matter. They'll end up investigating us instead, and social services will split us up. And you, *you'll* end up in jail!" he said. "Is that what you want?"

"Of course not." Ciara jetted out a breath. She saw his point.

The unfairness of the situation burned at her like acid. The ones who needed the police's protection most of all, the weak, the young and the oppressed, were often the ones who were most victimized by them. It was the same the world over. It's what had taken Etienne from her. She was not about to let it happen to the Orphans, too.

Ciara had liked Jean-Marc, but he was undoubtedly the same as any other cop. What he'd done at the club with her did not exactly put him in the best light. Would he have stopped if she'd told him no in that storage closet? Maybe. But maybe not.

"Okay, you're right," she reluctantly said to Hugo. "We take care of this ourselves." To the others she said, "We need a plan to make Beck leave Sophie alone. Everyone think about what we can do. In the meantime there's little option. We must pay him off."

"But how?" Sofie whispered. "It's so much money."

"Same way I always do. Speaking of which..." She pulled the diamond bracelet from its hidden pouch at her waist. "This must be worth several thousand. That's a start."

"Oh, Ciara!" CoCo exclaimed, taking it from her. "It's gorgeous! Did you slip it right off the princess's wrist?"

She made a face. "Yep. While I was dancing with my cop, too."

All five jaws dropped. Even Hugo's eyes widened before narrowing. "*That's* how you met the *flic?* While you were robbing the princess? Didn't he get suspicious?"

She shook her head. "No. I'm good at what I do." She sighed. "And luckily for us, there are plenty more rich people out there with jewels and paintings and silver that other people want. I've been doing this for almost ten years. Another few robberies isn't going to make much of a difference."

She knew her lifestyle was wrong. She'd known it from the start. But she'd been so young when her mother had kicked her out...she hadn't seen any option—other than selling herself on the streets, which she refused to do. She'd seen what a few years of that had done to her mother.

Then when Etienne had found her and swept her off her feet...well, Etienne was a thief. It wouldn't have done to question how he made a living. Besides, back then the seamier side of life was all she knew.

But that had been fourteen long years ago, and with Etienne she'd discovered there was more to life than simply fighting for survival any way you could. Etienne was dead now but she was still stealing. Each month she told herself, just a little while longer... But months had turned to years. And now...it was too late.

She sighed and shoved aside her fruitless thoughts. "Sofie, I'll get Beck's money, never you worry. We're not letting you go anywhere."

"Or letting that blackmailing pig touch you, either," CoCo added firmly, her eyes blazing.

"That's right." Davie and Ricardo both gave her hugs, and Davie turned to Ciara. "I just heard something that might come in handy. The Countess Michaud is having a big end-of-summer soiree next week. Everyone who's anyone will be there."

Ciara smiled. Outcast aristocrat Davie was her pipeline to the pampered and privileged upper-class world where she currently made her living. Although his father had kicked him out at thirteen, to society, *Monsieur le Comte* de Figeac pretended all was well in the family. Without Davie's tips, her life would be much more complicated and difficult. Ciara had the skills, but Davie had the info and the entrée to the jobs that paid well. Even his coursework in portrait photography had brought in useful contacts.

"There, you see? Everything will be fine," she said, smiling reassuringly at all five of them.

These kids were all the family she had, all she would ever have. She'd do anything for her Orphans. To see they got the chances she had been denied.

And if that meant she had to steal more to pay off that bastard Beck, so be it.

◘ ◘ ◘

"Ah! The most famous bracelet in France," *monsieur* Victor Valois said with a grin as he took the diamonds from Ciara.

It was the next morning, and she was visiting her friend and mentor in his fashionably shabby antique store, *Valois Vieilli*.

Standing behind a glass and gilt Louis XV jewelry display case, he winked. "And the most famous thief, as well. Congratulations! I saw the papers this morning. I was expecting you."

"Are you sure you want to deal with me?" Ciara said, grinning back at the portly, balding old man for whom she had a huge affection. Valois had taken her in as a protégé when she'd brought him her first antique silver piece, accidentally stolen along with a purse on the *métro* during her first year living in Paris. Had it really been eight years ago?

"Surely, you jest! My star pupil? I haven't taught you everything I know just to let *le keuf* intimidate me."

"The cops?" she asked, clued in by the righteous indignation that suddenly flavored his words. "Have they been here?"

"*Mais, bien sûr.* They were waiting for me when I opened." His grin returned. "One would think I was first on their list of suspected fences for stolen jewelry."

Which, of course, he was. And paintings and antiques, as well. Those items were his specialty. His antique store was filled to the rafters with scrupulously legal wares: tons of old furniture and art pieces, rugs and marble, knick-knacks and bric-a-brac. The store had been in his family for generations. Ciara often thought that some of the things crowding the overfilled rooms must have been bought new two hundred years ago and simply gotten lost in the clutter.

But the items he was fencing were well-hidden, in a tunnel under the shop which his father had discovered during the War, part of the ancient Parisian sewer system below the city.

She knew she was in good hands. M. Valois was nothing if not careful. The police had never gotten a single shred of evidence against him. As ruthless as he was loyal, no one ever betrayed the old man. Ciara herself would go to jail in a heartbeat before breathing a word against him. Because she knew he would do the same for her.

"This time it was one of the *commissaires* who visited me. CPJ Lacroix. Angry as a hornet, he was."

"Jean-Marc?" she asked uneasily. "He came here?" *How the hell...?* This was too close for comfort.

Valois peered at her over the rim of his jewelers loupe, brows raised. "Jean-Marc?"

She suddenly realized her mistake. *Lord.* She gave a nervous laugh. "Yes, well, I actually met him last night at the club." She cleared her throat. "We danced. Before I realized he was a cop, of course."

Valois pursed his lips and slowly regarded her. "A very attractive man, *non*? In a rough sort of way."

She picked up a paper-thin Limoges porcelain teacup from the counter and examined it so she didn't have to meet his eyes. "I suppose."

"Lacroix appears regularly in the tabloids. I'm surprised you didn't recognize him from his photos. Before you danced with him."

She carefully set down the delicate cup. "I don't read the tabloids, Valois."

He chuckled. "Sure you don't. And you don't love how they're treating you as the new Robin Hood. Robbing from the rich..."

She rolled her eyes. "Yeah, yeah." Over the past few months, the evening papers had grown quite fond of the infamous *le Revenant* and his daring exploits against the spoiled and privileged. But Ciara didn't like the publicity. It only forced the cops to concentrate harder on catching her. "Why would a police *commissaire* be in the tabloids?"

Valois made one of those Gallic clucking noises with his tongue. "A rather unsavory business several years ago. He was lead detective on a case involving a high end car theft ring. The ringleader was clever. A suspect, he played the helpful citizen to perfection and deliberately befriended Lacroix during the investigation...then betrayed him. Set him up to look corrupt and take the fall. Got away with a few million euros before Lacroix realized what was happening. Then the thief disappeared without a trace, and Lacroix went through hell trying to prove his innocence. The tabloids had a field day with him. They still like to give him a hard time."

"That's awful," she said. She might be a thief, but she always went out of her way to choose wealthy targets who could afford the loss. And she would never implicate another person for her thefts. "Whatever happened to honor among thieves?"

Valois gave her a fatherly smile. "*Commissaire* Lacroix is the law. The enemy. Best not to forget that, *ma petite.*"

"I know. But it was still a fucked up thing to do, and the papers should leave him alone."

"His face on the front page sells copies." Valois tipped his head and studied her. "Ciara, you haven't developed *un penchant* for the man, have you?"

Her mouth dropped open. *Was she that transparent?* "Me? God, no."

"Letting your guard down around him could prove very dangerous. Don't let Lacroix's masculine allure or his bumpy history blind you to how good he is at his job. The man is *formidable.* One slip and he'll be on your tail quick as a viper's strike. *Because* of his history."

Her friend's words sobered her. "Yes. I'll remember that. What did he want with you this morning?"

Valois lifted his shoulders expansively. "The usual. Threatened that anyone who helped *le Revenant* would go down for even longer than he did, when he was caught."

She relaxed a smidgen. "Well, I'll be more worried when they figure out they're chasing a woman."

Valois chuckled. "I'd like to be a fly on *that* wall."

"How much is the bracelet worth?" she asked, after he finished examining the piece and stowed it in a velvet bag.

"About seven thousand euros. I can give you three."

It was about what she'd expected. He took a hefty cut, but then, he did a lot of prep work before being able to sell the diamonds and the melted-down setting. He took a lot of risk. His position as middleman was even more exposed than hers. She didn't begrudge him a single sou.

"Good," she said, tucking two-thousand-seven-hundred euros into her purse. That amount would pay for food, rent and tuition for the coming month or two. Unfortunately, it didn't make much of a dent in Beck's blackmail. "Can you transfer three hundred into my Swiss account this time?" she asked, handing him back three of the bills.

Nine years ago she had opened her Swiss bank account because the Swiss were notoriously immovable to legal enquiries about their account holders. At the time she had planned to build up a nest egg to see her through the completion of her education. She faithfully put ten percent of every job into the account, but it was still pathetically small. Some days that bothered her more than others. Some days she felt she would never break free of the cycle she'd been trapped in her whole life.

"Of course," he said, nodding.

"What do you know about the Countess Michaud?" she asked, shaking off the uncharacteristic self-pity, and recalling Davie's tip. "Does she own anything anyone is looking for? Something in my league?"

Valois glanced at her with a frown. "The soiree next week? What are you planning Ciara? Isn't it kind of soon for another job? Especially in France, with Lacroix sniffing around."

She leaned a hip against the counter and relayed the incident with Sofie and Beck. Valois was a good friend and was invited to the attic apartment on rue Daguerre for supper regularly. She knew he approved of what she was doing to get the Orphans on their feet—it was one reason he was still so ready to help her even though her work was starting to attract unwanted attention. He might make the bulk of his living illegally, but he hated unnecessary human misery as much as she did.

He swore softly. "Louis Beck is scum. Shooting is too good for him. I see how he has you cornered. But I agree with Hugo. There's no way you can go to the police with this. Well, let me think...Countess Michaud..."

He pondered for a few moments, then riffled through a stack of auction house catalogues until he found the one from Dufour and opened it. He turned it toward her and she saw a full page spread of a painting. She whistled.

"A *Picasso*?"

She'd stolen a few small paintings for Valois before, but never anything this valuable. In fact, she'd never stolen anything at *all* this valuable before. Nor did she want to. "I said *in my league*, Valois. This must be worth a million or more!"

"One-million three-hundred-thousand is what it sold for at auction two years ago to the Michauds. As I recall, the bidding was lively, and one of the losers was from overseas and quite disappointed. I'll make some inquiries and see what I can do." He gazed at her intently. "But only if you're absolutely sure you want to make this jump into the big-time."

She knew what he was saying. The bigger the theft, the more intense the investigation and the greater the punishment--which was exactly why she'd always stuck to the smaller stuff.

If she thought the law was after her now, just wait until the Picasso disappeared. That would make international news, not just the Paris evening papers.

But it would be just this once....

"I'm sure," she said. "I have no other option. And if it's as valuable as you say, this can be my last job. My cut will be enough to pay off Beck and take care of the bills until the kids are all able to support themselves."

"What about you?"

Her whole body lit up at the thought. "Maybe I can finally finish my studies, too. Leave this life behind and become a translator or interpreter, as I've always dreamed." Then she thought of the small white business card propped up on her dresser, and smiled.

The old man reached over from behind the ornate jewelry counter and took her hand. "Nothing would make me happier, Ciara. But I beg you, consider this job carefully."

"There's nothing to consider," she said, squeezing back. Maybe when all this was over, just maybe she'd be able to make that call, after all. "You've taught me well. I'm ready for this. Set it up, Valois."

▣ 3 ▣

"Make the call," Pierre urged, plopping down in the standard-issue wooden visitor's chair across from Jean-Marc's desk on the third floor of the DCPJ, or *36 Quai des Orfèvres*, as the headquarters of the *Police Judiciaire* was known by everyone in France and beyond. "You know you want to call her."

Jean-Marc stabbed a hand through his hair and struggled with the irrational need that had been pumping through his body all day. He'd had a gut feeling Ciara wouldn't call him last night, and sure enough, she hadn't. But Pierre was right. Regardless of her inarguable rejection of his pursuit, he had an acute physical craving to see her again.

He'd been fighting a losing battle all day, snapping like a turtle at anyone within shouting distance. Pierre'd finally had enough.

"It would be official police business," his lieutenant continued reasonably. "You need to track her down because she's a possible witness."

True. It had been a real mistake not getting her statement last night. *And her address.* "I suppose she might have seen something useful. Despite being a bit distracted." He made another stab at his hair.

Pierre grinned. "*Mon ami*, you really have it bad this time."

"No worse than usual," Jean-Marc insisted. *Yeah, right.*

"*Non?*" His friend puffed out a skeptical breath. "May I point out, all morning *and* all afternoon you've been testing the patience of every person at 36 Quai des Orfèvres unlucky enough to run into you?"

"In case you'd forgotten, another robbery was added to our growing workload last night," Jean-Marc retorted.

He wasn't the *commissaire* in charge of *le Revenant* case, but lately everyone in the OCBC had become involved in the investigation. It wasn't so much the value of the jewelry he took but the spectacularly audacious way in which he stole it that was making him high profile in the media and annoying the hell out of the cops.

"Belfort is breathing down our necks," he went on. "The Dutch consulate is parroting the princess's vitriol to the news media about the inefficiency of the French National Police. And now we have to worry about where this fucking thief will strike next. I think I have ample reason to be testy today."

"Yeah, except those reasons have nothing to do with why you are."

Jean-Marc ground his teeth in resignation. The man knew him too damned well. "All right, fine. I'll admit it. I fell for this one."

"*Mec*, you fall for *all* of them. What's different about this woman?"

"She doesn't charge by the hour?"

Pierre gave an ironic bark of laughter. "Admittedly, an improvement."

His friend had stuck with him through thick and thin, biting his tongue when Jean-Marc's divorce had sent him into the arms of paid escorts rather than deal with real emotions for the past four years.

A man had his needs. "What can I say. I'm a romantic kind of guy."

Pierre's brows went into his scalp.

"Okay. I'm a horny kind of guy. She was a knock-out. Sweet and affectionate. Nice sense of humor. And *Merde!*, so incredibly hot. My throat aches just thinking about touching her."

Pierre gave him a commiserating look. "Young..."

"Not *that* young. I don't understand what went wrong. She seemed to like it as much as I did."

"Until she found out you were a cop?"

Jean-Marc gazed at him. "Maybe."

Could that really be it? Usually it worked the other way around. Lots of women were turned on by a man with a gun. Or thought you would do them a favor in exchange for sex, get them out of a stack of parking tickets, that sort of thing.

Unless they had something to hide. Then they might run in the other direction.

"Maybe *she's* the thief," Pierre suggested with a broad grin at his discomfort.

Jean-Marc rolled his eyes. "Ah, *oui. Bien sûr.* While she had her tongue down my throat she miraculously nabbed the bracelet. And then managed to hide it while I stripped her practically naked." He thumped himself on the forehead. "Gee, why didn't I think of that?"

Pierre's grin never faltered. "Find the woman and ask her, *mon vieux.* Seems like the perfect solution. Go on, make the call to the American Embassy."

Jean-Marc snorted. "The embassy? You've got to be kidding."

"The law enforcement liaison posted there—"

"Couldn't find his ass in a paper bag. Remember that kidnapping case two years ago? We'd found the girl and sent her home to mama before they'd even gotten through their red tape to start an investigation."

Pierre pursed his lips expressively. "Yeah. Okay. So try the university."

"Which one? She only said she was a student. Not where."

"Call them all."

In the end, he threw up his hands and did just that. As it turned out, it was ridiculously easy to find her. Thank God for computers. The only American student named Ciara in all of Paris was conveniently enrolled at the Sorbonne. Ciara Alexander. Born thirty-one years ago. Sounded about right. He'd figured her to be about ten years younger than his own forty-three. Pushing it, but... Ah, well. A man was entitled to a midlife crisis wasn't he? At least she wasn't *twenty*-one.

The registrar had no qualms handing over her current address to a cop.

"Phone number?" he asked.

"Sorry, none listed."

"Can you fax me over her application? Including her picture?"

"Certainly, *Commissaire*. What did she do?"

"*Rien*. She's just a possible witness to a crime and I'd like to speak to her. Nothing more."

When the fax machine spit out her grainy photo, his body gave a leap of excitement. Definitely the same woman. So much for having something to hide. If that were the case, she'd never have given him her real name.

Now all he had to do was go to her place and ask for a repeat performance of their amazing sex.

Beg if he had to.

Pierre poked his head in the doorway. "Find her?"

"I did."

Pierre's eyes went reverently skyward. "*Merci Dieu*. So I won't expect you in till late tomorrow. Hopefully in a better mood." He ducked out, then right back in. "Oh, I almost forgot. There's a nice snap of you two in the evening rag." He tossed a rolled-up newspaper onto Jean-Marc's desk. "Just the right touch for your already legendary reputation, I thought."

With that he disappeared again. Jean-Marc glanced at the clock as he plucked up the newspaper. Past quitting time. He spread the roll flat, and stared at it in shock.

On the front page was a photo of himself with his arm around Ciara Alexander as they emerged from Club LeCœur. He was looking down at her with a secretive little smile, and she was smiling back, her lips just puffy enough and her hair and dress just disheveled enough to look as though they'd been doing exactly what they'd been doing.

Then he read the headline: DUTCH PRINCESS ROBBED! And the caption under the photo: COMMISSAIRE LACROIX TOO BUSY TO FOIL LE REVENANT!

He pinched the bridge of his nose between his fingers and cursed.

"*Putain de merde.*" This was just what he fucking needed. More negative publicity. Thank *God* he wasn't the lead detective on the case. Because if he had been, it would be like a bad flashback—to the nightmare that had been his life five years ago. The nightmare that had sent him into the tailspin that lost him his wife and very nearly his job. And had made him the emotionally mistrustful bastard he was today.

He straightened, tossed the newspaper into the trash and took a deep, cleansing breath.

Non. Thank God for small favors. He was not in charge, so this thief would not be getting the better of him. Not this time. That *wasn't* going to happen again.

But he would not tempt fate, nor add fuel to the fire, by seeing that woman Ciara again, either. He had enough to think about, enough to do, without obsessing over getting laid.

He could live without her. There were other women. Plenty of them. Ones who didn't disappoint or betray a man. Ones who only sought to please you...for the right price.

Mind made up, he determinedly stuck the faxes of her photo and Sorbonne application, along with the paper he'd written her name and address on, under the heavy leather blotter on his desk.

And sat back glowering at the ceiling, trying to come up with a new strategy to catch the troublesome Ghost. But his imagination had deserted the case for greener pastures.

Resignedly, he leaned over and fished the newspaper back out of the wastebasket and ripped off the front page. And for a long time he stared at the photo of himself with Ciara.

Alors, He straightened his spine, stuck the news page under the blotter, too, and slammed his hands on the desk.

Done.

One all-too-tempting woman gone from his life. For good.

▣ ▣ ▣

As soon as he arrived at 36 Quai des Orfèvres the next day, Jean-Marc was called into CD Belfort's office.

This couldn't be good.

He strode down the gray second-floor hallway wondering what he was going to be chewed out for this time. Despite having one of the best arrest records in the OCBC, he could never seem to please his boss. "A loose cannon," Belfort called him. "Can't tell the difference between you and the goddamned bad guys."

Bon, whatever worked.

He ran into Belfort coming out of an incident room with Michéle Saville, lead detective on *le Revenant* case. Saville marched after their boss with his hands clasped behind his back like an idiot, looking smug.

"What the hell is *this* all about?" Belfort demanded when he spotted Jean-Marc. He halted and snapped open a copy of last evening's tabloid in front of his chest. The one with the photo. And the damning headline. "You were there *before* the robbery?"

He could tell it was going to be one long, fucking day.

"*Oui*, I was there all evening. On my own time," he added, matching Belfort stride-for-stride as he resumed his march down the hall toward his office. Saville was forced to follow behind. "I believe I told you he'd go after the princess's diamonds," Jean-Marc reminded them pointedly.

Belfort's jaw worked. "If you were there watching, why isn't *le* goddamn *Revenant* behind bars?"

"I'm only one man, boss," Jean-Marc said, striving for equanimity. "You may recall I did ask for a team to back me up, and my request was denied."

Belfort whisked over to the espresso machine behind his secretary's desk and brewed himself a cup. The burnt smell of too-strong coffee wafted through the air. "So it was. *Alors*, from now on I plan to listen to you more carefully." He pointed a finger at Saville. "As of now, you are relieved of *le Revenant* case. I'm giving it to Lacroix."

Jean-Marc came to full attention as Saville lodged a loud protest. "Sir, I object! I've been working this case for—"

"Far too long," Belfort interrupted, adding hot milk to his coffee. "Time someone else took over."

"Let Saville keep the damn case," Jean-Marc said emphatically. "I don't want it."

"I don't give a shit what either of you want. *I* want this bastard caught. The *préfet* is starting to get calls. Which means *I'm* starting to get calls."

Belfort's secretary pretended not to listen to the CD's rising voice, but several other officers milling about the common area weren't so subtle in their observation.

"The *préfet?*" Jean-Marc asked in surprise. "About a common thief?"

The *préfet* was the overall head of *la Direction Central*, Belfort's boss's boss. He didn't normally concern himself with such trivial matters as one lone criminal, unless it was a serial killer or terrorist.

"There is nothing common about *le Revenant*," Belfort refuted, turning on a heel and heading for the frosted glass of his private office. "He's thumbing his nose at the OCBC—hell, the whole DCPJ—and the press is making a mockery of us because of it. The insurance companies are complaining about the money they're losing. The nouveau riche don't feel safe showing off their expensive baubles in public. The aristocrats are angry because he's breaching their security at home so easily. They are all becoming annoyed."

They weren't the only ones. Ever since the OCBC realized that the escalating wave of high-end jewel thefts throughout the country could be attributed to one person, Jean-Marc had tried to convince Saville he was going about the investigation the wrong way. Traditional methods weren't going to cut it. The thief was smart. He never struck in the same place, nor in quite the same way. From the crowds of Le Mans to isolated castle fortresses, no setting had daunted him, or deterred him from pulling his clever heists. He never took old or distinctive pieces that could easily be identified, or new ones that had serial numbers etched into them. He stuck to expensive, but unremarkable stones. And he was getting ever more daring. Last night he'd known he was being watched, but hit anyway, against a highly-guarded public figure. Right under Jean-Marc's nose.

Saville hadn't listened to him. However, the last thing Jean-Marc wanted was to head up the case.

"Truly, sir—"

"And if that weren't bad enough," Belfort continued as though he hadn't spoken, sailing through the door to his office, "the bastard is building up a legend around himself, thanks to the media. Becoming a fucking folk hero to the working classes. A goddamned Robin Hood. We're losing our credibility out there, Lacroix. I don't like it."

They'd all been chagrined when tabloids had dubbed the thief *le Revenant*, a play on words referring back to the famous Belgian cat burglar from the fifties—*le Fantome. Le Revenant* also meant phantom, or ghost, but one that walked the earth again, for the second time. It sounded almost romantic. But there was nothing romantic about crime.

Jean-Marc followed Belfort in. The office smelled like red ink and new carpet. "Still, I'd rather not—"

Belfort rounded his desk and sat down with a decisive surge backward in his fancy suede-covered office chair. "This case could make...or break...a man's career," Belfort said, effectively putting an end to the argument.

Because Jean-Marc knew exactly whose career he was talking about.

Belfort disapproved of him. He knew that. Because of his background. Jean-Marc had grown up in *les banlieues*—the projects—the only French kid in his high-rise tenement, sucked into the fringes of crime at an early age. He'd only managed to extract himself from the quicksand of his surroundings because he'd excelled at math at school and attracted the attention of a nurturing teacher. That teacher had probably saved his life. Definitely changed it.

However, his early years did give him an insider's perspective on crime and criminals—one reason he now excelled at his job. Many of his peers frowned on his unorthodox methods—especially *CD* Belfort. But you couldn't argue with numbers, and Jean-Marc's closed-case record spoke for itself.

"A win on this one could make that mess five years ago go away. Permanently," Belfort said, giving him a level look.

And a loss could make *him* go away permanently, he thought. Which was what Belfort was hoping for, no doubt. Record or no, the man did not like him.

"Get out of here, Saville," Belfort told the other *commissaire* with a dismissive wave. "Go and show me I made a mistake by relieving you."

One of the things Jean-Marc liked least about Belfort was his tendency to encourage rivalries between his officers.

"Am I in charge, or is he?" Jean-Marc demanded softly. "Because if I am, nobody will do anything on this case without my say-so. *Nothing.*"

Above the hum of the secretary's copier, silence hung thickly for a moment between the three of them. Then Belfort puffed out his cheeks angrily. "*Bon.* Wait for his orders." He jerked his head at Saville to leave. When he'd gone, Belfort said, "Better get yourself a plan, Lacroix. Fast. I'm through—"

"As a matter of fact, I already have one. Is that all, sir?"

Belfort's mouth thinned. "Yes, that's all. Don't screw up, Lacroix. It's both our heads if you do. But yours will fall first and farthest."

◉ ◉ ◉

On the way back to his own office, Jean-Marc found Pierre and brought him along.

"Better sit down, *mec*," Jean-Marc said, taking a seat and motioning to the visitor's chair, which Pierre spun backwards and slid onto. "We are now officially in charge of *le Revenant* case."

Shock flashed across Pierre's face. "*We?* You're joking."

"Well, me. But you're my second-in-command, so that puts you in the hot seat, too."

"*Merde!* How the hell did that happen?"

"Belfort's getting pressured. He wants a fall-guy for when things go bad."

Pierre made a noise of disgust. "*Poulet.*"

"Yeah, well, I don't plan on going down for anyone, so we better get busy."

"Any ideas?"

Jean-Marc leaned back and swung his feet up onto the edge of his desk.

His chair squeaked in protest.

"Near as I recall, we began getting reports on this guy about two years ago. But he must have been doing jobs before that, *non*? Lesser stuff, maybe, that the local *préfectures* would have taken care of. Not big enough to involve us here at headquarters. Especially when he was just starting out."

Pierre nodded. "Right. But why do we care?" he asked, adding his own feet to the clutter on the desk.

"The OCBC does good police work. We use witnesses, forensics, we find patterns, we find outlets, and all of that leads us to the subject and if we're lucky we make an arrest."

"But...?"

'None of that is working with *le Revenant*."

"True enough."

"Witnesses agree on nothing, he leaves behind no evidence, the fences are mute, and the only pattern that has emerged is that there seems to be no pattern to his work. Other than what he steals—jewels."

"Which means we have to dig deeper."

Jean-Marc nodded, folding his hands over his stomach. "Exactly. His early thefts might tell us where he lives. Criminals work in patterns, within a comfort zone. But this guy has already moved beyond that now. He's a seasoned veteran. His pattern looks random and he's comfortable all over France. If we can find out where and how he got started, we might learn something useful. Something that could lead us in the right direction."

Pierre's brows rose. "You're talking about *profiling* a *thief*?"

"Why not? Hell, nothing else is working."

"You predicted his last target."

"Yeah, but that was a gimme. A flashy princess dripping with diamonds is too obvious to miss. Next time it won't be so easy, trust me."

"Even the best criminals eventually make mistakes," Pierre offered.

"But how long will we have to wait for that to happen? We don't have that kind of time."

"So, what are you suggesting?"

He dropped his feet back on the floor and leaned forward. "Start with what we know and work backwards. We need to get inside his head. Find out what makes him tick. That's the only way we're going to catch him."

Pierre shot him a glance. "I think that FBI seminar you took last year in the States has you brainwashed. Besides, you already think far too much like a perp. It'll only get you in trouble with Belfort again."

Jean-Marc gave a half smile. "Perhaps."

After a short pause, Pierre said, "You know, Marc, you have nothing to prove. Everyone has forgotten about that incident."

His smile faded. "Belfort hasn't," he drawled. "And neither have I. But this has nothing to do with that."

A lie. His wanting to solve this case had *everything* to do with screwing up on that other one five years ago. He'd been made a fool of, the object of pity and jokes throughout the whole division.

This thief was his ticket to redemption. One way or another.

Pierre sighed. "*Bon.* Please just don't start obsessing. Treat this like any other case."

"I'm not obsessing. I'm determined," Jean-Marc said. "There's a difference."

Or so he told himself.

His friend regarded him, then sighed. "*D'accord.* So, where do we start? *Putain,* there have to be thousands, *tens* of thousands, of petty thefts every year. How do we know what to look for?"

Jean-Marc got up and started to pace behind his desk. "We'll need to map his patterns of behavior. Tendencies such as time of day he prefers to work, days of the month, venues, anything else that stands out as statistically significant. When we add that to what we've already established about what he steals, we should be able to follow him back in time, concentrating on the unsolved cases that match."

"It won't be easy," Pierre said, stroking his chin. "This guy does his research. His jobs are obviously carefully targeted, as opposed to crimes of opportunity."

"At least now they are. Which is good. Totally random would be much harder to follow backwards."

"I suppose."

"The other thing I noticed is, the value of the jewelry has been steadily rising. I'd like to know why. Is his confidence rising, or is it his need that's rising for some reason?"

"Drugs, maybe?"

Jean-Marc stopped pacing and shook his head. "No. He's far too organized and contained for an addict. Which is why I think we have a real shot at figuring this out. *Something* is driving him. When we find that, we'll have the bastard."

Pierre rose as well, flipping the chair back around. "In that case, we'd better get to it."

Jean-Marc grabbed a short stack of files off his desk. "First stop, the archives. To order up all the unsolved robbery cases from all over the country for the past five years."

Pierre choked on a laugh. "Jesus, that's going to make us popular."

Jean-Marc snickered. "Hope you're not still trying to chat up what's-her-name down there? Nicole?"

Pierre made a pained face as they walked out together. "Guess I can kiss her goodbye, eh?"

"*Désolé, mon vieux.*"

"Sure you're sorry. Speaking of which, how did it go last night with your latest female obsession? You were in awful early this morning."

Jean-Marc ignored the involuntary curl of anger in his gut at the mention of Ciara. "I didn't speak to her."

Pierre looked surprised. "But why? I thought you were in love!"

"She's not."

"You don't know that."

"She promised to call me. She didn't. Besides, I don't need the distraction. Especially now, taking over this damn case."

Pierre lifted a palm. "Well, I hate to burst your bubble, but after we're done in the archives, you'll *have* to call her."

Jean-Marc halted at the elevator and stabbed the down button. "Oh? And why's that?"

"Because you took over this case. She was a witness to the robbery last night. We're in charge now, *mon ami*, and I don't intend to lose my job just because your male ego got bruised. She may have seen something. We're interviewing her, and that's that."

Jean-Marc ground his jaw. He really hated it when his partner was right. They couldn't afford to ignore a single witness. Especially one who'd danced as close to the robbery victim all night as they had done. He may have had eyes only for her, but obviously she didn't share his blinders.

"I don't have a phone number," Jean-Marc said, still looking for a reasonable way out.

"Then we'll go to her place."

His stomach tightened at the thought. Could he see her again without doing something monumentally stupid? He sincerely doubted it. But Pierre was correct. She had to be interviewed. Even if it would strain his self-control.

"Okay, fine," he gritted out. "But *you're* asking the questions. If I open my mouth I'm liable to get us both in trouble."

◙ 4 ◙

Every time there was a knock at her door, panic skimmed up Ciara's spine. This time was no exception.

Firmly, she pushed the fear into the far corner of her insides where she normally kept it at bay. She'd already taken the diamonds to Valois. There was no reason to panic, regardless of who was knocking.

Nevertheless, she swept a quick glance over her tiny living room, making sure nothing incriminating was lying out in the open. No stolen goods. No bits of elaborate disguises. No maps, floor plans or notes for her next job.

"Who is it?" she called.

"*Police Nationale,*" came a loud male voice.

Panic tore back through her veins, this time for real, riding on a burst of adrenaline. *How had they found her?* The police had never been to her apartment before. Never!

What should she do? *Fight or flight?*

Neither. *Answer the man.*

"*Oui?*" she called. The word cracked in half and she had to clear her throat. "What do you want?" she asked in French dosed with a deliberate American accent.

"Open the door *madamoiselle, s'il vous plait.*"

With a final check around, she took a steadying breath and plastered what she hoped was an innocent expression on her face. Then she opened the apartment door.

And froze. A familiar man in a suit stood there in the cramped hallway, holding up a credentials wallet. It was Jean-Marc's friend from Club LeCœur. A holstered gun peeked out from his jacket, tucked under his arm.

"Sorry to disturb you, *mademoiselle*, but we need to ask you some questions about last night."

Oh, sweet Jesus.

"We?" she croaked, for some reason homing in on the pronoun he'd used. She fought to get her brain back into working order. Surely, Jean-Marc hadn't—

Her heart stood still as her lover emerged from behind the central stairwell. *Oh, God.*

"You remember *Lieutenant* Rousselot," Jean-Marc said evenly. "And me, *peut être?*" His eyebrow flicked up infinitesimally.

She made herself say, "Of course."

Lieutenant Rousselot stepped forward again, insinuating himself into the small space between them. He smiled pleasantly. "Good. Then you won't mind if we come in and talk for a few minutes?"

"Well, actually, I—"

Too late. Rousselot was already walking past her. Jean-Marc also stepped through the narrow doorway, silently crowding her into the tiny living room with his towering bulk. His eyes were hot, volatile, as he shut the door firmly behind them and leaned his back against it. Trapping her.

She smoothed her hand down her thin blue skirt, suddenly wishing she were wearing something a lot more substantial than the flimsy camisole she'd put on hoping to beat the summer heat.

"Why are you here?" she asked, trying hard to keep her voice steady.

He didn't answer, but flicked his gaze to his partner.

"We need to ask you about last night," Rousselot said, his smile widening. It seemed incongruously genuine. "We want to know exactly what you did at the club." He looked at her expectantly.

This couldn't be happening. "I, um..."

"Yes, I know you were—" he made one of those expressive Gallic gestures with shoulders, hands and face "—busy...with *Commissaire* Lacroix, but we hoped you might remember something. Anything. You two were dancing close to the princess before the bracelet went missing. Any little detail you could recall would help tremendously."

Help?

She regarded him for a moment, letting the sweet rush of relief sink in. He was treating her as a witness.

Not a suspect.

Her gaze stuttered to Jean-Marc for a brief second. His face was expressionless, except for his turbulent eyes... He stood like an angry statue guarding the door. Clearly, he had a different agenda than his partner.

"Naturally I'll try, *Lieutenant*," she said, gathering her wits.

"Please. Call me Pierre."

She gestured to the miniscule main room of the apartment, which suddenly seemed even more dwarfed, filled to bursting by these two giant men. "Won't you sit down...both of you? Something to drink? Coffee? Iced tea? Beer?"

Ignoring her offer, Jean-Marc folded his arms across his chest and studied the apartment, such as it was. The Latin Quarter had been built in the Middle Ages, and the size of the apartments hadn't grown since. Her entire space was maybe two-hundred square feet, on a really hot day.

"*Merci, non,*" Pierre said, but he sat down on the sofa.

Nervously, Ciara took a seat in the mismatched easy chair. Both pieces of furniture were old, probably Victorian, and not really her style. But they'd come with the apartment, along with the two bedroom pieces. Someday she'd buy furniture of her own, but this surprise visit reminded her vividly of why she hadn't, yet.

"I don't know what I can tell you," she said as calmly as she could under the circumstances. "I wasn't really paying attention to anything except—" She darted a glance at Jean-Marc, and felt her face go hot.

Thank goodness he was still ignoring her, now perusing the collection of books on her one shelf and the few paintings on her walls—mostly interpretive copies of well-known artists, done by Sofie.

Pierre gave her a grin. "I understand." He reached inside his jacket and produced a manila envelope, from which he extracted several sheets of glossy paper with rows of photos printed on them. "Perhaps you can look through these, tell me if you recognize anyone."

She leafed through them, recognizing several people from the club last night. Presumably the photos were taken from a video surveillance camera at the entrance.

"Tell me what you remember about them," he urged. "One at a time."

One thing Valois had taught her well, always stick to the truth as far as you can. Cops were real sticklers for detail. If you lied unnecessarily about something small, they'd be all over it like sharks on blood, circling in for the kill.

So she told the truth about everyone and everything, including about her and Jean-Marc. With the one small omission—that she was the thief they were looking for. It took her over half an hour to go through everything, making sure to occasionally stumble over her French. Her flawless language skills were a big part of her usual disguises; a vital fact to keep from the police.

As she spoke, Pierre wrote in a pocket notebook and Jean-Marc continued to prowl wordlessly around, examining everything in sight. At one point she heard him open the door to her bedroom, which was behind her, and go in. Her pulse skittered. What was he doing in there? Would he find anything? No. She was always careful to put things away.

As she told Pierre the part about her and Jean-Marc having sex, she didn't dare look up from her hands. She could feel her lover's eyes bore into the back of her neck from inside her bedroom. Pierre just nodded and took more notes.

Breaking off in embarrassment, she fanned her flaming face with the photo sheets. Paris wasn't usually this warm, even in the dead of summer. "I'm sorry it's so hot in here. No air conditioning."

Suddenly she felt the whisper of fabric against her shoulder. Startled, she realized Jean-Marc had taken off his suit jacket and tossed it over the back of her chair. His scent lingered on it, curling around her like a python, robbing her of what little breath she had. Reminding her of being in his arms. *Of him being inside her.*

She shook off the memory. "Are you sure you wouldn't like some iced tea?" she asked Pierre.

"Well, maybe—" But just then his cell phone rang. "*Excusez-moi,*" he said, and answered it, listening for several moments before saying, "*D'accord,*" then hanging up. He stood abruptly and gathered up the photo sheets from her. "My apologies, but I must go." He glanced at Jean-Marc. "*Commissaire* Lacroix will finish the interview. *Au revoir, mademoiselle.*"

Before she could think to protest, he'd swept out of the apartment, leaving her alone with Jean-Marc.

She jumped to her feet, starting for the rapidly closing door. "You should go with him. There's really nothing else to—"

Jean-Marc grabbed her arm. "*Arrête.*"

She swallowed a gasp. And peered up at him. His eyes blazed with...anger? Could he really be *angry* about her not calling?

"Listen," she said, "about last n—"

He cut her off with a swift shake of his head. His fingers dug into the flesh of her arm as he tugged her nearer and grasped her other arm, holding her fast in front of him.

The dark brown leather of his shoulder holster stood out in stark contrast to his crisp white shirt, as did the black stubble on his jaw. His suit trousers, expensive navy blue worsted with subtle pin stripes, covered athletic, muscular thighs. He looked cool and elegant, as he had last night...and incredibly dangerous.

Her heart skipped a beat, then sped out of control. She tugged uselessly at her arms.

"You are afraid?" he asked, his voice low and guttural.

She thought of Sophie, and Etienne, and said, "Yes." Then she thought of last night, and shook her head. "No." She gave up trying to hide her confusion. "I don't know. Should I be?"

His mouth was cruelly beautiful, sculpted and smooth, a sensual slash of cold disapproval. She remembered it sliding over her body last night, insistent, demanding. She shivered. She wanted it on her again.

His eyes dipped to her breasts. "Your body is not afraid. I can see your nipples through your top. They're hard. Like I am."

He started to walk her backwards into the bedroom. She tried to resist, really she did. This would be a bigger mistake than last night. One that could not be undone.

He was dangerous. Wrong for her.

But she wanted him even more now than she did then.

He halted in front of her dresser, low with a big, round mirror. From the corner of her eye she could see the bed with the blue Hand of Fatima design Sofie had painted on the wall above it, palm out, like a warning against the folly of what she was about to do with Jean-Marc. Their profiles reflected back in the mirror, him with his merciless grip on her arms, her with a look on her face she'd never seen before—somewhere between terror and breathless anticipation. She attempted to pull away again, but her limbs were strangely powerless.

"Tell me, Ciara," he demanded. Pulling her closer still.

"Tell you what?" she asked, befuddled and distracted by his legs tangling with hers.

His breath was hot in her ear. "Tell me why you're afraid of the police. Tell me what you're doing that's illegal."

Shock welded her to the spot. She stared at him openmouthed.

No. *He couldn't know.*

She shook her head. "Nothing. Why would you say that?"

He let one arm go and slid a hand over her breast. She sucked in a breath. He squeezed her slightly, his thumb toying with the stiffened tip.

Giving in to the sensation, she groaned softly.

"You want me," he whispered.

He didn't ask. Didn't equivocate. Merely stated the obvious. Keeping his hand on her breast, he turned her toward the dresser and the mirror. Stood with his hard-ridged front pressed into her yielding backside. She started to tremble.

"When you didn't call, I thought maybe you'd lost my business card. But you didn't lose it."

Because there it stood, canted up against her hairbrush, right in the middle of the dresser. Impossible to miss. Rife with implication. Damning in its blatancy.

"There's no sign of a man anywhere in your apartment, so I'm guessing it's not a boyfriend. So why? Then I remembered, you are a foreigner, on a student visa, with no visible income." He leaned down, closer to her ear. "And at the club, when I told you I was a cop, your reaction was...unusual. Suddenly you were frightened of me, and to get involved with me. Why?"

She licked her lips. "I—"

"I'm an excellent detective, Ciara. And I'm also damn good at math.

Two plus two always adds up to four. Now, tell me what you're involved in. Drugs? Prostitution? I'll help you if I can."

She closed her eyes against the chaos trying to break through in her mind. Prostitution? Was he kidding?

No. She'd be all right if she just came up with a plausible reason...

Think!

"You're wrong," she said past the dryness in her throat. "I'm not afraid. That's not why I didn't call you."

In the mirror his eyes met hers as she forced them open. His hand moved across her breast, going for the top button of her camisole. He slid it open. "I'm listening."

Her pulse zoomed.

He slid open the second button.

"It's not that you're a cop," she said in a rush. "It's that you're a *commissaire.*"

His brow went up and his fingers paused on the third button.

She quickly went on, "You're right about me. I'm a foreigner. A student with no money. Look at how I live!" She swept a hand around at her miserably shabby apartment and the threadbare furniture she didn't own. The lack of adornment, the few items of clothing in the tiny armoire. The pitiful state of her life. "But you...you're older than I. An important man. We're from two completely different worlds, Jean-Marc. Why start something when it will never work? I'd never be welcome in your world. You'd be ashamed of me."

She tore her gaze away, embarrassed by the truth and vehemence of those last words she'd never meant to utter.

Her childhood had been an agony of shame—something she had believed she'd put far behind her. Though it drove everything she did, even now, she seldom thought of those unhappy years in the States, before she met Etienne.

She tried to extract herself from Jean-Marc's grasp. "Please," she whispered. "Let me go."

"*Non.* I won't. It is you who are wrong, so very wrong, about me." He put his lips to her hair. "Age is of no consequence when you're past thirty. And I could never be ashamed of you, *mon ange.*"

His fingers sought the last buttons on her camisole. He opened them and brushed his hand over her yearning flesh. For a moment war raged within her: desire versus wisdom. She *wasn't* wrong. But he seemed so...sincere.

She knew what she'd have to do if she had sex with him again. Hell, even if she didn't. The moment she'd seen him standing at her apartment door she'd known what she'd be forced to do.

So what would it matter if she surrendered now? Gave in to the sheer insanity of this incredible, impossible attraction?

"We're not different, Ciara," he murmured, sliding the camisole off her shoulders completely. Taking her in his arms. Holding her. *Wanting her.* "I'm not who you think I am."

She sighed as he kissed her neck, melting into the pure joy of being with this man who was so wrong for her. Accepting that, despite everything, at this moment he was exactly right for her. For today, anyway. Until he realized what a monumental mistake he'd made....

"I'm not who you think I am, either, Jean-Marc," she whispered, letting down her guard completely. "But for now, I'll try to be just who you want me to be."

🔲 🔲 🔲

Jean-Marc gathered Ciara in his arms. He took her mouth with his and plundered, using his lips and tongue, thrusting deep. Tasting bliss.

He groaned softly. He was sunk, and he knew it. It was as though all the pent-up emotional need he'd suppressed for five years had busted loose at one time. Inconvenient. But probably past due.

She wrapped her leg around his knee, met his tongue with hers, opening to him completely, yielding her sweet favors to his demands. Her eagerness made him dizzy with desire; he wanted to feel her luscious body under him, to hilt his cock deep inside her.

Bon sang... No wonder he was feeling obsessed about this woman. What was it about her that had him crawling out of his skin to have her? Was it because he recognized her on some visceral, elemental level as being so much like himself? A fish out of water. Basically, thoroughly, insecure. Striving to be something he was not.

A fake.

But the emotions he was feeling right now were not false. And in her naked passion for him at least, he sensed she was being honest.

He backed her up to the bed and reached for her zipper. In two seconds he'd peeled off her skirt. Two more, and her panties were on the floor.

She groped for his shirt buttons as he tumbled her down onto the mattress.

"*Non,*" he growled, and tore his mouth from hers. He grasped her wrists in one hand, pulling them above her head as he pushed her thighs apart and lowered himself between them. He savored the sight of her nude body below. He'd wanted her like this last night, and now he had her exactly as he'd craved. Naked and panting under him. Open. Willing. Needy. And in his complete power.

He took her mouth again, hard, and skimmed his hand down her body.

Relishing the silken feel of her warm, undulating flesh, the taste of her tongue on his lips, the smell of her desire for him filling his nostrils.

Si bon. So good. So different from the counterfeit passion he'd grown used to. What had he possibly seen in the cool indifference?

"Take...your clothes...off," she moaned between eating kisses.

"Later." He liked being fully clothed, his shoulder holster in place, while she was so vulnerable.

He let her wrists go and slid down so he could feast on her breasts— another fantasy from last night. She cried out as he took one nipple into his mouth and sucked fiercely. Her body bowed in a crescent and her fingers tunneled in his hair.

"Please, Jean-Marc," she moaned. "Oh, God."

He fought for self-control. He'd never been with a more responsive woman. Every touch, every lick, every nip he gave her made her moan and writhe and plead with him to come inside her. But he had no intention of ending the pleasure so quickly. He wanted to make it last and last. All night.

He slid even further down her body. Over the dip of her belly to the joining of her legs. And he feasted there. Teasing and inflaming her with his tongue and teeth. As he did, he slipped a finger into her and sought the rough spot that would make her light up like Bastille Day.

He wanted her out of control. He wanted her helpless and boneless with need. He wanted her begging for his cock. For *him.*

She screamed. And came apart, sobbing his name.

He banked the immense gratification and kept at her, until she came again. Until she lay under him, trembling helplessly with the pleasure he'd given her, moaning in bliss.

Completely his.

He lifted off her and she watched with slumberous, half-lidded eyes as he slowly stripped off his gun and his clothes, and sheathed himself. Preening for her. Making her wait. Making her spread her thighs and whisper, "Hurry."

She reached for him as he mounted her, wrapping her arms and legs around her body. But he didn't enter her. Not yet.

"Who is your man now?" he demanded softly.

A shiver purled through her and her eyelids drifted closed. "You are, Jean-Marc."

"Open your eyes," he commanded. "And say it again."

She did as he bid. "You're the only man I want, Jean-Marc," she whispered breathlessly.

He thrust home in triumph, his male pride swelling along with his member. "You are mine, Ciara. Don't try to hide from me again."

He twined his fingers through her hair and held her still for his kisses. He pulled out and plunged into her again. She gasped. He hilted again.

"Mine," he murmured, thrusting over and over, claiming his right to her body, and imprinting his name on her will.

He didn't even want to think about why he was acting like this. Didn't want to think about anything but burying himself as deep as he could inside her. He had her now. And he would keep her. She was *his*.

Her body trembled and shuddered under him, filling him with an erotic sense of power. Of possession. She cried his name in climax once again, and he knew that she had surrendered completely.

With three final, powerful thrusts, he allowed himself to fall into the ecstasy. Sweaty and burning in the flames of their passion, he held her tight and flung himself into the pleasure of orgasm. Roaring his completion like a man possessed.

Because he was. For as much as he'd claimed and taken her tonight, she had claimed him just as surely.

And for the first time in many years, belonging to someone else felt like a good thing.

◙ ◙ ◙

The next morning in his office, Jean-Marc leaned his elbows on his desk, propped his chin in his hands and hummed in satisfaction.

Dieu, he felt great.

Exhausted, wrung out and emptied. But in a good way. A very good way. Thanks to Ciara he was alive again.

And he was *definitely* in love.

He hadn't left her place until practically dawn this morning, and even then he'd had to tear himself away from her delectable, awesome body. Ah, the things they'd done! Just thinking about them—and her—left him hard as a pistol and counting the seconds until they met again.

He would take her to his flat tonight. Where they'd have better wine, more horizontal surfaces to explore, and carpeted floors. A bigger bed, too, when they finally made it that far. His cock swelled with alacrity.

"You look like Hades on the second day of spring." He opened his eyes to find Pierre grinning at him with amusement.

"You should see Persephone," Jean-Marc said with a contented smile.

"Won over, sated and panting for more, eh?"

"Did you doubt it? Thanks for leaving the interview. I take it that was planned?"

Pierre shrugged and gave him a wink. "*Peut-être.*" Perhaps. "So, what's all this?" he asked, indicating the piles of file boxes stacked around Jean-Marc's desk.

"Archives sent them up. With a note for you." He handed Pierre a white memo slip.

"YOU OWE ME BIG-TIME, ROUSSELOT," Pierre read. "I'M THINKING SAN TROPEZ. AFTER THE FILES ARE RETURNED IN GOOD ORDER. HUGS, NICOLE." He looked up. "O la la. I've hit the jackpot."

"It's a scam," Jean-Marc assured him. "She just wants her damn files back."

Pierre chuckled. "Then she shall have them. And the sooner the better, in my view. Let's get to it," he said, and grabbed the top container, which happened to be Saville's box of files on *le Revenant*.

After going over the two dozen or so robberies attributed with fair certainty to the Ghost, they made a list of the things those cases told them about the thief. The list was topped by the time of month the thefts had been committed.

"I'll bet he's paying his mortgage with the proceeds," Pierre declared when Jean-Marc pointed out that nearly all of the thefts had occurred within the week before the first of the month.

"Or his rent," Jean-Marc agreed.

"Pretty high for the suburbs," Pierre said, studying the figures. "About right for a fancy place downtown, though."

"Or, he's living modestly but paying all his bills with his robbery proceeds, and just gets it over with all at once, with one heist."

"Makes sense."

"What would either of those options tell us?"

"That he's lazy?"

Jean-Marc picked up the neat list of columned statistics he'd written, and pondered the bigger picture: motive. "Or that he's not doing it for the thrill. If he's waiting until the last minute, I'd say stealing is not a lifestyle for him, but a necessity. And not one he particularly enjoys."

Pierre nodded. "I see what you mean. Thieving obviously doesn't scare him, but it doesn't turn him on, either, or he'd be doing it a lot more."

"And yet, he's very good at it. So why doesn't he go for bigger things? Knock over a store, rather than take one bracelet or necklace at a time? Pay the bills for a whole year in one fell swoop?"

"Because he's smart," Pierre said, with a shade of respect. "Staying small-time kept him low-profile and low-priority with the police for a long time."

"Exactly," Jean-Marc said, tapping his pencil on the list. "Very smart." He got the distinct feeling they'd all been underestimating this guy. "Which makes me wonder..."

"What's that?"

"If he's been working in other countries besides France. Maybe he only steals during the last week of the month here because he's working the other weeks in Germany, or Belgium, or Spain."

Pierre's eyes widened. *"Mon Dieu."* He sat up straight. "You mean like that serial killer who was murdering women for years all along the E50. Different months for different countries."

"Well, not quite that grim, but yes, like that." Jean-Marc lifted his phone. "Think I'll put in a few calls and check it out."

By ten o'clock he'd gotten promises from his contacts in the Dutch, Spanish, German, Belgian and Swiss authorities to look into things and call him back.

By lunchtime Jean-Marc had made his next major discovery.

"It's not just jewelry. He's stealing other things, too."

Pierre looked up from his fourth box of files and frowned. "How do you figure?"

"There aren't many, but—" Jean-Marc held up several pages of notes he'd made on unsolved cases from the past two years "—these robberies fit his pattern to a T."

"And they're not jewelry?"

Jean-Marc shook his head. "Paintings and silver. Plus..." He pointed to their master list of *le Revenant*'s known robberies. "The other thefts took place in months when his jewelry takes were lower than normal."

Pierre leaned back in his chair and whistled. "Paintings and silver. A lot harder to conceal than jewelry. Sounds like Plan B."

"He's stuck to small pieces, and he cut the paintings out of the frames. Even so, they're harder to get away with and probably tougher to fence than jewelry. So yeah. Plan B. Find anything like that in your stack?"

Pierre frowned. "I'll have to go back and check my notes."

"Here. Let me." Jean-Marc shuffled through the hand-written pages, skimming over the sea of dates and figures. "Look. Here's one more that fits. Another piece of silver."

His lieutenant gave him an incredulous look. "How the hell did you see that so fast? My head is spinning with all these facts and figures."

"It's a gift," Jean-Marc said with a grin. "I was a national math scholar in school. Statistics were always my favorite."

Pierre rolled his eyes. *"Merde.* It's unnatural." He gave him an appraising glance. "Remind me never to play poker with you."

Jean-Marc laughed. "Don't worry. I only gamble when I want revenge on someone. Well, actually, no one invites me to poker night any more. Sore losers."

"Don't bloody blame them," Pierre muttered.

By late afternoon, Jean-Marc had already gotten a positive response from the ever-efficient Germans, including an email with all the pertinent data on five matching robberies over the past three years in that country. So before quitting time he appropriated one of the incident rooms, then he and Pierre tacked up a large map of Europe and also one of Paris on the wall.

Using stick pins, they marked all the places where *le Revenant* had struck: red for jewelry, silver for silver items, and blue for the three paintings that fit the profile.

They stood back and looked it over for a moment. Suddenly they exchanged broad smiles.

"The train," they said in unison. "He's been taking the train."

◙ 5 ◙

"Are you all right?" Sofie asked for the fifth time since they'd sat down at an outside table at Café Constantinople, which was across the street from *Valois Vieilli*.

Ciara mustered a smile. She wasn't. It had been six hours since Jean-Marc had left her bed, and she was worried as hell. Emotionally, she felt like she'd been through a blender. But Sofie didn't need to hear about her problems. She had plenty of her own.

"I'm fine," she said. "How's your face today?"

"Better," the girl said softly, touching a finger to the largest bruise on her cheek. Despite the thick layer of disguising make-up, it still showed livid purple in a circling ring of blue and yellow. "I've been taking aspirin and it hardly hurts at all anymore." She picked up her pen and went back to doodling on a napkin.

Ciara watched the gentle brown eyes of the girl she had grown to love as a little sister and knew she was lying, too. Ciara wanted to kill Beck for what he'd done to her. Renewed anger welled up within her, and she embraced it. She'd brought Sofie along on her excursion to Valois's shop specifically to remind herself of the consequences of associating with cops.

A reminder she desperately needed after last night.

She heard the faint tinkle of a bell and glanced across the street. Valois had returned from his errand and was unlocking the shop's front door. She'd give him a few minutes before walking over for their meeting.

"You're glowing today," Sofie said, yanking her out of her thoughts.

"What?"

"Glowing. And yet, you look so incredibly sad. Why?"

Ciara lifted her cup and took a sip of the sweet Turkish coffee that was the specialty of the café. "I can't imagine," she evaded.

"It's a man, isn't it?" Sofie pressed. "That detective you said you met the other night," she concluded with a nod, shocking Ciara. "You've seen him again."

"Maybe," she said, schooling her expression. The girl was too perceptive by half. Or maybe the incredible night she'd spent making love with that detective showed on her face as plainly as Sofie's bruises. "But it won't happen again," she said. It couldn't. No matter how much it hurt to think about never seeing him again. "I'll have to move now. So he can't find me."

Which is why it was a mystery that she'd hit upon every excuse in the book not to look for a new apartment this morning....

"I see," Sofie said solemnly, putting a flourish to her doodle, which had transformed into her signature Hand of Fatima. Sofie signed all her paintings with the distinctive symbol instead of her name. "Better to be safe, I suppose."

"You'll have to paint me another Hand of Fatima, over my new bed," Ciara said with a sigh. "For protection." Not that the old one had protected her from the wicked charms of *Commissaire* Jean-Marc Lacroix last night. She'd been helpless as a babe against him and his masculine charms.

Sofie smiled shyly, pleased. "I'd love to."

"Paint me one, too," said the owner of the café, who was just walking by after waiting on another table. He picked up the napkin and admired the drawing. "A big one. Right there," he said, waving it at a blank end wall inside the café. "I'll pay you, of course."

Sofie's eyes lit up. "Really?"

"The *khamsa* is a Turkish symbol. This is a Turkish café. What could be more appropriate?"

Sofie looked to her for guidance, and Ciara could see how excited she was. Being paid for her paintings was Sofie's dream. Ciara leaned over and kissed her forehead, relieved at the change of topic. "You go for it, sweetie. I'll just step over and speak with Valois while you discuss your fee. See that you don't cheat her," she told the owner with a friendly warning smile.

Valois was expecting her. Hopefully he had good news.

As soon as she entered the shop, he ushered her into the back room. "It's a go," he said. "I have a buyer for the Michaud Picasso."

Lightheadedness swirled through Ciara and she dropped into a seat-sprung eighteenth century lounge that served as both file cabinet and guest chair. "Yeah?" she said, unsure whether she should be ecstatic or petrified. *One point three million euros.*

"Are you absolutely certain you want to do this?" he asked, seeming to sense her waver.

"Absolutely. I'm ready." Ready to get out of the thieving business. Ready to start a new life. The way it should have been from the beginning.

And this laydown would do it.

"Have you seen this?" he asked, and tossed her a copy of today's paper. "Page three."

She quickly opened it, and started in surprise. There was a picture of Jean-Marc. And a short article stating that this morning the *DCPJ* had announced he'd been put in charge of *le Revenant* case, replacing *Commissaire* Saville.

"Fuck," she whispered.

"This is not good news, *ma petite*. Saville is an average detective at best. Unimaginative. Lacroix is not. You must take extra precautions at the Michaud's to see nothing is left behind for him to find. Not so much as a stray hair."

"Fuck," she repeated. Because that pretty much summed up her whole situation. "*On est foutus.*" She was so fucked.

◉ ◉ ◉

That evening, Jean-Marc came to Ciara's flat earlier than she anticipated. It was late afternoon and she'd packed a few things in her oversized purse and was escaping down the stairs heading for the Orphans' when he caught her. Literally. He grabbed her around the waist and swung her up into his arms, taking her mouth and cutting off her protest.

"Mmm," he hummed when he finally lifted his lips. "Miss me?"

Her insides were a roiling mass of contradicting emotions. Elation to see him again, to feel his embrace. Desperation and anxiety because she hadn't meant to see him again. Didn't *want* to see him again. Shouldn't. *Couldn't.* For her own good.

But one look at his face and she knew there was no getting away from *Commissaire* Lacroix. Not tonight, anyway. So, she answered, "I missed you like crazy," because it was the God's honest truth. "I thought about you all day." Then she kissed him back.

Her bag dropped from her fingers and he broke the kiss, glancing down at it. "Going somewhere?"

"Um, just meeting the...some friends. For dinner."

"Forget them. You're having dinner with me," he said, but he grabbed the bag and started herding her back up the stairs.

"Wha—"

"After."

A coil of desire wound through her body at the single roughly spoken word. His dark eyes glittered with implication.

"Oh," she whispered, already lost to the erotic allure of him. Of his hard body and velvet technique.

What would one more night hurt?

She unlocked her door and they tumbled through it; he kicked it closed and her bag hit the bare wood floor with a dull thud.

"The chair," he said, shoving her around behind it. "Grab the back."

Before she knew what was happening, she was bent over the back of the easy chair with her skirt bunched up around her waist. He ripped her panties down and spread her feet wide apart with his.

And then he was inside her, deep and hard.

"God, you feel good," he groaned. His fingers sought her sex and strummed over her, making her gasp in pleasure. He pressed harder, and circled.

She came. Suddenly, and unexpectedly. She cried out, convulsing with the impact, her climax nearly buckling her knees.

He grunted low and withdrew, then scythed into her again, gripping her hips to keep her from falling. Over and over he plunged, so deep, so good, wringing wave after wave of agonizing sensation from her body until she could only cling to the chair and pray she wouldn't pass out from the sheer pleasure. Then he stiffened, and shouted out his own release.

When it was over, he lay bent over her back, panting with his exertion. She could feel his penis throb within her, still semi-hard. His depleted balls tickled her thighs as they quickened and refilled, readying themselves for another bout.

"You're...amazing," she whispered between gulps of breath, in awe of his easy mastery over her, over her body. She'd never met a man like him, who could make her come like that, and so quickly. Never wanted any other man so exquisitely that she was willing to give up everything to have him. Even with Etienne, it had never been like this.

Intellectually, she knew her turbulent feelings and chaotic longing for Jean-Marc had nothing to do with love, and everything to do with biology. But at the moment her heart couldn't tell the difference.

And really, where was the line? She wanted nothing more than to wrap her arms around him and never let him go. To spend the rest of her life kissing and making love to him. If that wasn't at least the beginnings of real love, what was?

He nuzzled her ear and withdrew, giving her butt a swat as he headed for the bathroom. "*Viens, chérie*, put on some lipstick. We're going out."

She straightened and managed to get her knees to work. The skirt of her flirty summer dress fell into place and she brushed the wrinkles out of the front. What on earth should she do about this untenable situation? Sex was one thing, but love...love was entirely different. She *couldn't* fall in love—not with Jean-Marc. Even if he did make her feel warm and wanted, and so good it scared her.

"Leave them off," he called as she was about to pick up her panties. "I want you bare under that dress."

"Why?" she said, suddenly irritated with herself for being so damn easy. "So you can push me into an alley and have me whenever you feel the urge?"

He appeared in the bathroom door wearing a wolfish grin. "Maybe. Would you like that?"

She shook a finger at him. But didn't answer. Because the awful truth was, she *would* like it. Which made her even more irritated. "Where are we going?" she asked instead.

"Nowhere in particular," he said cheerfully as he adjusted his trousers. "Just for a walk."

He beckoned to her, but she held back, struggling to get control over her wayward emotions.

"*Viens, mon ange,*" he murmured seductively. Luring her to him with a silken promise in his eyes. Impossible to resist.

She gave up the struggle, going into his arms, melting into another long kiss.

"Keep doing this and we'll never get out of here," she sighed.

"The thought has its attractions." He pulled back with a wink. "But I'm afraid you may grow tired of my carnal demands. I want to show you there's more to me than a hungry cock."

She tipped her head. "Ah, a hungry stomach, too? So like a Frenchman."

He feigned offense, covering his heart with a hand. "A true Frenchman hungers for romance, *mon amour.* To get to know his lover." His lip quirked. "But—" he gave an expansive shrug "—if that involves a good meal, so much the better."

She laughed and gave him a kiss, glowing inside because he'd called her his love. She was even more attracted to this playful side of him. "I'd better make myself beautiful, then. If I'm to compete with the entrecote."

"Entrecote? *Ah, non,*" he said. "No competition there."

She shot him an over-the-shoulder warning glance, and he broke into a grin. "Perhaps we should stay in, after all."

"Forget it, Lacroix," she said, taking a seat in front of the vanity mirror to freshen her makeup. Sealing her fate. "I'd like to see just how romantic a true Frenchman can be."

◨ ◨ ◨

As it turned out, unfortunately, very romantic.

Of course, it would be impossible for a twilight stroll along the River Seine on a warm summer's night not to be romantic. Paris, City of Light, was the most romantic place on earth.

And Jean-Marc was the most romantic of men, Ciara decided sometime later as they walked over the Petit Pont among the throng of lighthearted tourists jostling their way toward Notre Dame. He bought a sprig of purple stephanotis from a roving flower vendor, and tucked it behind her ear so the sweet scent floated about their heads.

He bent to steal a kiss and she sighed against his lips, loving the taste of him. Loving the way he smiled at her as he took her hand in his. Wishing...wishing he were any man on earth but the man he was.

She withdrew her hand and banded her arms over her abdomen, turning to gaze out over the Seine, at a glass tourist boat glittering in the sunlight as it glided along the peaceful water under the bridge.

Damn.

"Why are you avoiding me again, Ciara?" he asked, glancing over her defensive body position.

God, how she hated lying. How she hated deceiving him. How she hated that it was impossible for them to be together.

She needed distance. Somehow, she had to push him away.

She took a steadying breath, and asked, "Are you married?"

The air between them shifted. Bristled.

"Is that what you think?" he demanded quietly. Not a peaceful quietly— a dangerous quietly.

"Yesterday you asked me if I was a drug dealer or prostitute. Is that what *you* think?"

His mouth thinned. "That was different."

"Was it?" Suddenly, she wondered... "A man like you—respectable, handsome, sexy. Romantic..." She turned to him. "It doesn't make sense for you not to be married."

He regarded her. The muscle at the back of his cheek ticked. "I was married," he said. "But not anymore. We've been divorced for four years."

"Not separated?"

"Divorced," he repeated. "Why are you asking? Now, after it's too late?"

A warning buzz skittered up her spine. "What do you mean, too late?"

He grasped her upper arms, pulled her to his chest and put his mouth close to her ear. "I've fucked you, Ciara, more than once," he said in a low growl. "You gave yourself to me willingly, and I intend to keep you."

Her pulse kicked up. Everything in her wanted to surrender to the raw power contained in his murmured declaration, in the strength of his fingers on her flesh. To lie back night after dark night and let him take his fill of her, for as long as he wished.

But the very thought of it scared her to death.

"Why are you so determined?" she asked, baffled that he would want her this fiercely. "We hardly know each other."

He raised his hand to cup her cheek, looking both frustrated and menacing all at the same time. "I wish to God I knew."

"You have to know I want you, too. Jean-Marc. But—"

He showed her his palm. "Don't try to feed me that lame bullshit about us being too different, or you being too young for me. I don't give a damn about all that."

She swallowed at his expression. *Hot. Possessive.*

"What happened to your wife?" she asked.

His eyes narrowed. "You're testing my patience, woman."

"And you're pushing me too hard."

The frustration took over his eyes completely. He paced away and shoved his hands in his pockets. "I went through a rough patch about five years ago. There was this case—" He blew out a breath. "It went bad and I took a nosedive for a while. Got a little obsessed. Stopped trusting people."

She tipped her head. "Including your wife?"

"Including everybody. My ex-wife took the opportunity to move on. She has since remarried."

Was this the case Valois had told her about? That had nearly ended his career? Ciara wanted to ask more, but he obviously didn't want to talk about it. "I'm sorry," she said.

"Don't be. I'm fine. About that," he added pointedly.

She sighed, her insides filled with conflicting feelings that pulled her in opposite directions. "I still—"

"*Écoute,*" he interrupted. "Let us call a truce for tonight. We're here together in this beautiful place. Let's enjoy it. And later..." He smiled and gathered her in his arms. "Later, we can enjoy each other," he murmured, tipping up her chin for a kiss.

What was it about good sex that could turn a woman into a brainless, witless lump of clay, ready to be molded into anything a man wanted?

She opened to him and he took. Standing there in the fading golden light of the warm Paris evening, with the ripe green smell of the river and flowers, and the sweet spice of the cafes and food vendors surrounding them, the laughter of children in the air, and the cooing and rustling of pigeons underfoot. It was all too perfect to spoil.

Tomorrow she would do what she must. But tonight...tonight she would forget about all the reasons she shouldn't, and simply enjoy him.

She wouldn't feel guilty.

Not while they strolled past the incredible cathedral of Notre Dame, then to the Isle St. Louis and back, then further down the river to a small bistro on a dark, cobblestoned side street where they ate a simple meal accompanied by a sizeable carafe of hearty red wine and talked with their fingers laced and their heads bent close till the smiling proprietress finally shooed them out at closing time well past midnight.

And certainly not as they made sweet, languorous love for hours and hours, until the orange-rose sun peeked over the gray slate tile rooftops and the birds began to sing their morning songs and the church bells chimed five times.

Not until Jean-Marc reluctantly left her bed to get dressed and go to work did harsh reality once again intrude onto her haze of sated emotional bliss. Along with the guilt.

When he was gone she buried her face in the tousled sheets where he had lain. She wrapped her hands around the back of her head and fought the tears, breathing in the musky peach blossom scent of his body and his passion.

She had to leave him. She had no choice. But God, did it hurt.

Who would ever have thought the very worst consequence of her life of crime would be this?

Slowly, Ciara rose and dragged herself from the bed. And reluctantly started to pack her things.

◉ ◉ ◉

For Jean-Marc, the next day started out good and just got better. Making love to Ciara two nights in a row had him feeling happier and more content than he had in years.

At 36 Quai des Orfèvres, he and Pierre made excellent progress on the unsolved robbery cases they were going through, piecing together *le Revenant*'s early history of petty theft.

It was slow work. It took the whole day to get there, but by the time they'd gone back through ten years' worth of files, the matching thefts finally trickled to a stop.

"I think we've finally found when he started," Pierre said after they'd pored through the files for eleven years back and come up with nothing that fit. "Thank God."

Jean-Marc stretched his aching back muscles. A sense of satisfaction settled in his bones. Even if they were hitting dead ends everywhere else, their profile was yielding some great information.

"*Alors...* It definitely appears the Ghost started stealing ten years ago," Jean-Marc agreed. "That probably puts his age at this point between twenty-five and thirty-five. Which fits with his current level of sophistication."

He got up and perused the maps on the incident room wall. Yesterday they'd added a second one of Europe, and used a different color push pin to mark the robberies committed during each calendar year.

An unmistakable pattern had emerged.

"*And* we know where he's from."

Pierre tapped the pins for le Revenant's first year in business, one by one. Every one of them was stuck in the port city of Marseilles. He grinned at Jean-Marc. "I gotta tell you, *mon vieux*, this was one damned fine bit of police work, if I don't say so myself."

Jean-Marc grinned back. "May as well admit it, we're geniuses."

Pierre jerked his chin at the sheaf of notes and graphs by Jean-Marc's hand. "What else does your brilliant statistical analysis tell us?"

Jean-Marc's chair squeaked familiarly as he leaned back in it and contemplated the cracked plaster of the ceiling, ticking off on his fingers. "He moved to Paris nine years ago. He started out snatching purses and lifting wallets on the train and *métro*. Eight years ago he switched to jewelry, started refining his craft. Then he added silver and a painting or two, and began to escalate. Every year the items he steals get more and more valuable."

"And his robberies get progressively more skilled and more daring," Pierre said. "And yet still elegantly simple. To filch a diamond bracelet right off a heavily guarded princess's wrist, surrounded by two hundred people and the *commissaire* who is hunting him..." Pierre's words trailed off in a shrug and a puff of admiration.

Jean-Marc didn't need reminding of the man's preternatural abilities.

"There's something we're missing," he said, drumming his fingers on the desk blotter. "Something important."

"Like what?"

"That's the question," Jean-Marc said, and thoughtfully turned his gaze to the wall map. "Let's talk to the police in Marseille. I have an old friend there I can call. See if they're able to shed any light. Meanwhile we have to ask ourselves, is he finished now, for this month?"

"That diamond bracelet was pretty valuable. He's over his usual take. You really think he's going to pull off another job right away?"

"It's possible. He has been steadily escalating."

Pierre hummed in agreement. "Okay. So say he's not done. Where will he strike next?"

Jean-Marc turned back to him with a grimace. "That, *mon vieux*, is exactly what we must figure out."

◙ ◙ ◙

Jean-Marc glanced at his watch as he rang the outside bell to Ciara's flat for a third time. He and Pierre had gotten so wrapped up in their work on predicting le Revenant's next move that Jean-Marc hadn't noticed the time flying by. It was late. Well past 9:00 pm.

He hoped she hadn't given up on him. He'd wanted to call her earlier, to let her know he was on his way, but she didn't have a phone. Ridiculous, in this day and age.

He'd have to have one installed for her. Or better yet, buy her a cell phone. So he could get hold of her whenever he felt the urge. Which, if today was any indication, would be every other minute.

He'd just pressed the buzzer for the fourth time when a gray-haired old lady with bifocals poked her head out from the locked front entrance to the building.

"You're here about the apartment?" she asked.

"I'm here to see Ciara Alexander. Apartment 6B."

The woman opened the door wider and looked him up and down in the dim glow from the ancient courtyard corridor, her gaze snagging on the large bouquet of flowers he held in one hand.

"She's gone," she said with an accusing scowl. "This morning. Who are you?"

He stared at her in disbelief. "Gone? *Ciara?* What do you mean gone? Where?"

She lifted a shoulder. "How the hell should I know? Damn foreigners. Can't be relied on. I knew I shouldn't have rented to her. Nothing but tr—"

"You're telling me she *moved out?*" This had to be some kind of mistake. A misunderstanding.

"Packed her bags and had me call a taxi. Nothing left of her but that damn Arab demon symbol painted on the wall. Knew I should have gotten a bigger security deposit."

"Did she leave a forwarding address?" he demanded, his mind finally emerging from paralysis.

She narrowed her eyes at him calculatingly. "Who's asking?"

He whipped out his wallet and held his *carte* to her face. "*Le flic.*"

She backed up, eyes flaring. "Honest! I have no idea where she's gone—"

"I want to see the apartment," he snapped. "She must have left a note." Something to tell him where she'd gone. She knew he was coming tonight. They'd talked about it.

They went upstairs and he hurried through both rooms of her closet-sized apartment, searching for a letter or a piece of paper.

The furniture was all there. The ratty sofa they'd made love on the third time, the wobbly table where they'd shared a thrown-together meal, the dresser where his card had sat along with her hairbrush and a tiny bottle of perfume. The bed where they'd—

"Get out," he told the hovering landlady, and slammed the door in her face. He needed to be alone.

He threw the bouquet of flowers on the bed, staring at it for long minutes, trying to come to terms with what he knew he had to accept, but couldn't fucking believe.

She'd lied to him. The entire time he'd been with her. The entire time he'd been between her legs, deep inside her. She'd sworn she wasn't afraid of him because he was a cop. But he must have been right about her all along. There was no other explanation for her precipitous disappearance.

What the *hell* was she involved in?

He took one last look at the ornate blue design painted over the bed, the only thing left to show she'd ever lived there, turned, and walked out.

He should have known. Should have followed the visceral instinct that had screamed warnings at him to leave Ciara Alexander the fuck alone.

Damn Pierre for dragging him over here after he'd made up his mind.

But damn himself most, for his silly romantic notions. For falling for her.

Non, he thought, blinded by the bright summer sun as he marched out of the building. He slid his dark shades over his eyes. *Forget her.* He didn't need this. Didn't need her.

Now he could pour all his energy into the case he'd been handed. Closing it successfully would secure his job. Probably get him the promotion that had eluded him for so long. A raise. Those were the things that mattered.

Fuck Ciara Alexander and her soft, pliant curves.

From now on there was only one thing he wanted to concentrate on. And that was catching *le Revenant.*

◙ 6 ◙

Being picked up by the police was definitely not what Ciara had in mind when she'd let the air out of the tire of Davie's dad's Jaguar XJ-12 on this lonely stretch of country road seventy miles outside of Paris.

The week had ticked by slowly. Each morning she'd awoken in tangled sheets caused by nightmares that Jean-Marc had somehow tracked her down and come for her. To throw her in prison. And worse...

Seeing the distinctive white, red and blue radio car marked with the triangular emblem of the *police nationale* rolling to a halt behind the Jag reminded her just a little too much of those nightmares. She dabbed moisture from her upper lip and smoothed a hand down her dowdy brown gown.

It was the weekend of the Michaud's soiree. The day of her big job.

Davie had...borrowed...the Jag from his parents' country estate carriage house. "They'll never miss it," he'd assured her. "They're in Quebec for a few weeks."

Davie hadn't spoken to his parents in years, but he had lunch with his old nanny once a month, so he always knew what was happening with them. And on what days he could liberate the car.

Typical bad luck that a police patrol was the first thing to drive by after she'd deliberately deflated the Jag's back tire. She'd counted on someone else stopping on their way to the Michaud estate to help out a stranded fellow guest. And give her a ride to the exclusive end-of-season soiree. Thus solving her tiny problem of not having an invitation.

If she weren't about to have a freaking heart attack, she might have laughed at the cosmic irony. But at the moment she needed all her energy to maintain her composure and stay in character.

Chill, Ciara, they're not here to arrest you, she told herself. They were just doing what cops did, helping an old lady in distress.

Tamping down on her speeding pulse, she watched a uniformed officer emerge from the vehicle and approach her. For effect, she fanned her forehead with a bit of lace from her sturdy handbag. Praying her disguise would stand the test.

Of course it would. Disguises and slipping into different characters were her specialties. Between Davie's coaching and her own gift for languages, she could become anyone from an East End street urchin to an East European countess. Even looking carefully, no one would ever guess that the aristocratic old lady with a flat tire was really an American who'd just turned thirty-one. The uppity accent would throw off the cops once her robbery was reported, if by some miracle the old lady was remembered.

Yes, the disguise was perfect. And she could handle these cops, too.

"*Madame, vous avez besoin d'aide?*" asked the young, blue-clad officer, with a small bow.

Smiling at him, she daintily lifted the hem of her matronly gown and resisted the urge to scratch her cheeks. Masquerading as a sixty year-old woman might render her as good as invisible, but the fake wrinkles could be torture in hot weather.

"Why, thank you officer," she answered in flawless upper crust French.

"A flat tire?" he asked, glancing at the Jag.

"So it seems." She aimed for an air of pompous entitlement. "If the officer would give me a ride to the Michaud estate, I would greatly appreciate it. It is just up the road."

The man looked uncomfortable. "Taking passengers in the patrol car is against regulations, *madame*. But I would be happy to—"

"Young man," she interrupted haughtily, "Do you have any idea to whom you are speaking?"

The officer sputtered, but before he could reply, a deep voice came from the passenger side of the cruiser. "We're going the same place. Give the lady a fucking ride."

She froze in her tracks, every one of her nightmares swirling into terrifying reality.

That voice.

The officer glanced at her contritely and she drew herself up, mainly to hide her fear and dismay. "W-Well!" she stuttered, seizing onto the man's obvious belief that it was the crude language that had shocked her to the core.

"Don't mind the *commissaire*," the officer said. "He's in a foul mood. Come, *madame*." He extended a hand toward the radio car. "We will take you."

Yes, but where?

59

She forced herself to follow him, sliding into the back seat. Praying Jean-Marc would not turn around.

She couldn't see much of him, just his broad shoulders and dark hair as he leafed through a thick file in his lap. He didn't look up, but in the rear view mirror she saw the reflection of his left eye. Unmistakable porcelain blue. Outlined by the familiar sculpted brow, and a frown of concentration.

Another shower of nerves skittered down Ciara's spine. What business did Jean-Marc have at the Michaud soiree?

As if she didn't know. He'd predicted she'd strike at Club LeCœur, hadn't he? Somehow the man had gotten inside her head, knowing her next move almost before she did.

Okay. Okay. She was *not* going to panic.

She considered her options. She didn't have to do this laydown. There would be other paintings, other pieces of silver and jewelry. She could go to Spain, or Italy, so she wouldn't have to worry about Jean-Marc and his uncanny insight.

Except, Sofie was depending on her. Right now. Beck would not wait much longer for his blackmail money—he'd already threatened Sofie again. Ciara must protect her, and keep Beck placated until they could come up with a fail-safe plan to take care of him for good. No, she could not fail today. She must proceed.

The sun was just dipping below the horizon, painting a rosy pink glow over the rolling fields of green, heavy with ripening vegetables, neat, endless rows bursting with their fat bounty. Even in the stale confines of the police car, the French countryside smelled verdant and ripe. Expectant. Abundant.

She loved the country. If she ever got her million, this was where she'd live. Far from the ugly urban chaos where she'd grown up, the decaying towns that stretched on and on, one after the other without respite. Instead, she'd be in the clean, nurturing country, within a stone's throw of the most beautiful city on earth, Paris.

In just a few minutes, the fields gave way to stately trees, pristine lawns and the long, majestic entrance drive of the Michaud estate. Bypassing the valet, the officer parked the cruiser behind the manor house, next to a jumble of catering vans.

Ciara looked around, getting her bearings. Where was Ricardo? Davie had managed to get Ricardo hired on at the last minute as a waiter for the sizeable party. She didn't like giving the Orphans an active role in a laydown, but if the job was risky they usually insisted on one of them playing backup, to stage a diversion in case things went south. She just hoped Ricardo wouldn't give either of them away if he saw her being escorted into the house by the police.

The officer held open the service door and accompanied her through the kitchen into the public rooms, apologizing for not taking her in via the grand front entrance.

"Nowhere to park," he explained. "And valet service for a police car..."
He made a face. "Not a great idea."

"Don't give it a thought," she said, grateful the whole invitation issue
had been neatly skirted. "It's rather exciting having a police escort. I shall be
the talk of the party."

The pitying smile he returned assured her that unless she walked in with
Brad Pitt on her arm there was no way in hell she'd be the talk of anything,
let alone this gathering of the glitzy and glamorous.

For a split second old insecurities swamped over her. Her stomach
squeezed with nausea before she could remind herself that this was exactly
the image she'd striven for with her disguise.

She dared a peek over her shoulder at Jean-Marc, who was still following
them, a few paces behind. When he saw her glance, he gave her an absent
nod then continued to scan the other guests.

She wanted to jump for joy that he didn't recognize her. Or maybe fall
to her knees with relief. Her confidence returned with a surge. She was
really going to pull this off. If her own lover couldn't identify her, nobody
could.

Making her way through the crowded grand salon, she thought to rid
herself of her unwanted escorts by slipping through a set of double glass
doors outside to the sprawling courtyard. Even in the growing darkness, she
could see the gardens were spectacular. Flowers scented the cool evening
air and soft music wafted in from somewhere beyond the bordering box
hedge.

Suddenly, there was a loud crash. Behind her an explosion of glass
shattered on the paving stones. She spun, clutching at her overstuffed
bosom, and it wasn't all acting. Visions of Jean-Marc drawing his gun,
calling "Halt! Thief!" and firing when she tried to escape whirled through
her imagination.

Damn, she had to calm down. She was nervous as a cat.

In reality, a tray of drinks lay scattered on the ground in a glistening
puddle of crystal shards and still bubbling liquid that reflected the brightly
colored lanterns overhead. In the middle of it all stood Ricardo and a short
man dressed in white, both cursing and gesturing wildly. Ricardo's eyes shot
to her, dismayed. She gave him a smile of reassurance and shook her head
slightly.

"Oh, dear," she murmured to the officer, who seemed stuck to her like
glue and must have been the cause of Ricardo's consternation. She had to
get rid of him. "Perhaps you should do something about those two before
they come to blows."

With a grunt, the officer deserted her for the fray.

One down, one to go. She steadied her nerves and turned to politely thank

Jean-Marc and get the hell away from him. But he had disappeared.

Uneasiness crawled through her. She swept her gaze over the crush of people crowding the artfully lit gardens, seeking him out. He was nowhere in sight.

For a minute she stood paralyzed with indecision. Should she call it off? A minute turned into two, and then three, as she wavered between caution and necessity.

The hum of a dozen conversations buzzed in her ears but no one said a word to her. No one even looked at her. A handsome young waiter passed by with a tray of fresh champagne flutes, another with a plate of hors de oeuvres, but neither paused to offer her anything.

All of which served to make up her mind.

She would not change the plan. *One point three mil.* There wouldn't be another opportunity such as this. Not without weeks or months of research. Far too long. Sofie needed that money now. Jean-Marc or no, she wouldn't put this off. She couldn't.

"Right," she murmured softly. "Off to the trenches."

At a slow, dignified stroll, she crossed the elegant courtyard back toward the manor house, humming to an old melody that drifted in from a dance floor set up on the lawn behind the gardens. Under her sensible old lady flats, the paving stones winked up at her. They weren't ordinary brick cobbles, but granite, or porphyry, or some other natural stone that reflected the twinkle of lanterns and the hundreds of fairy lights adorning the trees and paths, as well as the matching sparkle of diamonds, sapphires and rubies hanging from the throats, ears and wrists of every lady there.

Jewelry worth a fortune...

Don't switch horses in mid-stream, Ciara.

She'd heard that expression more than once, in the old movies that had kept her company while her mom was out working her loser job waitressing at a local dive, and whatever the hell she did after closing time. Ciara had learned a lot from those old movies.

No, she wouldn't switch horses, as tempting as it was. The plan was set. The arrangements made. No changes.

She re-entered the house through a second set of mullioned double patio doors and found herself in a massive salon, also filled with partygoers dressed to the nines. Quickly she scanned the framed art crowding the walls. Valois hadn't been able to pinpoint her target's location, so she'd have to wander around the chateau until she spotted it. She recognized a pair of ornately framed old masters, several stunning impressionists, and a large Henri Rousseau. Gorgeous. There were a dozen others, mostly older paintings. But no Picasso.

She slipped unnoticed through the throng to a paneled door that led toward the rear of the house. Weaving past the guests she made her way to the narrow back servant's staircase, and up to the second level. There, the crowd thinned considerably.

It took her just a few minutes of searching to find the Picasso.

And less than two to make the switch.

◻ ◻ ◻

Five minutes later Ciara was settling into the back seat of the Jag, which Davie had re-inflated the tire on and driven to the front of the house, dressed as a chauffer.

"Got it?" he asked.

"Rolled up in my purse," she affirmed, closing her eyes briefly and easing out the pent-up breath it felt like she'd been holding since she'd spotted that police car earlier. Not to mention running into her lover, *le commissaire*.

She didn't even want to think about how wrong things might have gone tonight.

But they hadn't. Thank God.

Opening her eyes, she took one last look at the Michaud mansion as Davie pulled away from the front entrance.

Her heart stalled. High in a second floor window stood a man holding back the curtain and looking down. Watching her.

It was Jean-Marc.

▣ 7 ▣

"How could you let this happen?"

The Countess Michaud's voice screeched like nails on a chalkboard, making Jean-Marc wince.

Merde. As if he hadn't asked himself that very question a hundred times already. Last night he'd been so certain he'd foiled *le Revenant* and nothing had been stolen.

"What are you going to do to get it back?" the countess demanded. "That Picasso is irreplaceable!"

"It was insured, *non?*"

"Well, yes, of course, but—"

"*Voilà.* There you are, then." He didn't want to be unfeeling, but he had a job to do.

Before she could screech any more, he glanced at a uniformed officer and jerked his head at her. Peace thankfully descended on the room as she was led away, the echoes of her unhappiness bouncing off the walls.

Jean-Marc squinted at the neatly framed Picasso—*alors*, neatly forged Picasso—hanging on the wall. It was a decent likeness, actually. The artist was talented and captured the essence of the original without trying for a precise duplicate. It was more like an interpretation than a copy, really.

"It reminds me of something," murmured Pierre. "Something I've seen fairly recently."

Jean-Marc had had the same feeling when he'd first looked at the painting. But at the moment he couldn't focus on figuring out what it reminded him of. He could barely keep his anger in check. He was furious. Absolutely furious. At himself.

While he'd been busy watching over the guests' jewels, the hosts had been robbed of a Picasso valued at over a million euros. And he'd even known *le Revenant* sometimes targeted paintings. There was no excuse.

"This can't be the work of the Ghost," Pierre said, seeming to read his mind. "Sure, he takes the occasional painting. But nothing else fits our profile—the value of the stolen piece, leaving a copy in its place, no train nearby. All of that's wrong."

Jean-Marc contemplated the ersatz Picasso. "And yet..." Something niggled at the back of his mind. Something he couldn't put a finger on. "It feels exactly like him."

"How so?"

"The timing's right—last week of the month. And the painting is small, cut from the frame like he always does. Stolen in the midst of a crowd."

"But this Picasso is worth a thousand times the other paintings combined! Why such a jump?"

Jean-Marc shrugged. "Maybe he wants out. Or maybe he just wants a fancy new yacht."

"I still don't think it's him. Look at this thing! Our Ghost is a thief, not a goddamn painter."

"He may have found an accomplice. Or you may be right and it's not him at all," he conceded. "But whoever it is, he made a colossal mistake leaving that fake for us to analyze. With any luck forensics will be able to nail who painted it. And with the cameras the Michaud's have everywhere, we've definitely got the thief's picture. All we have to do is connect a face to the evidence."

If Belfort gave them the chance.

Pierre was right, the Picasso was in a whole different ball park than the modest jobs *Le Revenant* had pulled before. With the higher-ups breathing down Belfort's neck about the jewel thief, his boss might just take the easy way out and send jurisdiction of the Picasso investigation away from 36 *Quai des Orfèvres* and up the ladder, to a *juge d'instruction*.

Jean-Marc wasn't about to let that happen. He had a huge personal stake in solving both cases.

"Any fingerprints?" he asked the tech who was still nearby dusting.

"Two dozen or more in this room alone. The forgery will be processed by the chief at the lab, of course. But don't get your hopes up. Doesn't look promising."

"Hairs? Fibers? Anything?"

The tech chuckled. "You're kidding, right? This place is four centuries old. We'll probably find hairs and fibers belonging to Louis XV himself. There are bags of stuff to be gone through by the lab."

Jean-Marc turned back to the painting. "*Dieu*, there had to be three hundred people at this party. How did he manage the switch without being seen by a single one?" He rubbed his temples, fighting off the beginnings of a headache. "*Merde*," he muttered. "First the Ghost. Now the Invisible Man."

The corner of Pierre's lip rose. "Or Invisible Woman."

Pierre was always busting his balls about his tendency to assume the criminals they chased were male. Could he help it if they usually were?

"A woman? You think?"

"To Catch A Thief," Pierre said.

"Quoi?"

"Nineteen fifty-five, Cary Grant, Grace Kelly. The thief turned out to be a girl."

"Pierre. That was a film."

"Art imitates life. And the whole end of the month thing could just be PMS."

After rolling his eyes, Jean-Marc waved an impatient hand. PMS. Yeah, right. "Okay. *Une femme, c'est une possibilité*," he granted. Though not too likely, in his opinion. "Hollywood aside, women don't usually go in for this kind of elaborate, carefully planned scheme. They tend to do crimes of opportunity. Based on need rather than as a vocation. The Picasso thief was a pro. He came prepared with a fake painting, a utility knife and staple-pull to remove the real one, and fast-drying glue to attach the forgery to the back of the frame so the theft would not be discovered until well after he was gone."

"And may I ask where a man would hide all those things? A woman would have a purse," his friend said triumphantly.

Jean-Marc gave up. He did have a point. "Okay, okay. I'll keep an open mind." He sighed. "*Merveilleux*. You just doubled our number of suspects from half the world to everyone on the whole damn planet."

Pierre laughed and slapped him on the back. "We should probably start with the big cities. He's got to fence this baby somewhere."

OCBC officers had already been to every pawn shop and purveyor of previously-owned jewelry, as well as suspected fences, in Paris and beyond, asking about *le Revenant*'s stolen jewels. Now they could do it all over again, adding art galleries, antique stores and Picassos to the list.

"Swell."

"Guess this bumps our friendly Ghost down the priority ladder," Pierre said. "Pity. Just when we were getting somewhere."

"This changes nothing. The cases are similar enough we can work them together. We may even come out ahead."

When they got back to his office at 36 *Quai des Orfèvres*, Jean-Marc called the *Laboratoire de Police Scientifique* and talked to Dr. Terrance, chief of forensics. "I want you to run every conceivable test on that forgery," he said. "And I need the results yesterday."

Then he called the police video lab. "Do you have photos isolated of all the soiree guests from the Michaud's surveillance cameras yet?" he asked Renard, who was in charge of that department.

"Yes, sir. I'm just sending you a set."

"I want you to run them through the facial recognition software, compare them to the arrest and prison databases. All of them."

"Sure thing, boss," Renard said.

"And run the photos from the disco robbery last week through it, too." He was about to hang up when a thought suddenly occurred to him. "And while you're at it, run the disco photos against the Michaud guests. See if anyone pops."

He replaced the receiver and ran an excited hand over his mouth. Holy shit. If it was the same perp, they had him! What were the odds of anyone being at both crime scenes if he wasn't the thief?

For the first time since walking out of Ciara's empty apartment five days ago, he actually smiled.

It was too early to celebrate, he knew that. They could be dealing with two different perps and no one would pop.

But he didn't think so. Usually his cop instincts were pretty good. And right now they were doing the Snoopy dance all over his gut.

◻ ◻ ◻

"The Picasso is a fake."

Ciara's jaw dropped and she stared at Valois in disbelief. "A fake? But how is that possible?"

The old man looked nearly as upset as she felt. "I'm sorry. I wish I knew, ma cocotte. *Viens.*" He beckoned.

She'd pulled off the Michaud job two days ago, and had hoped for a speedy turnover of the painting, since the buyer was already in place. Obviously there was not going to be a turnover. A fake? Jesus. Beck was already rattling his chains at the delay in getting his blackmail money and it had only been four days. This was nothing short of a disaster.

Ciara went with Valois into the back of the antique store, then through a narrow corridor to a storage room. He scooted aside a large trunk, under which was a trap door in the floor. She helped him grab the ring and lift it, revealing a crude brick stairway that descended into blackness.

Even as distracted as she was, it always gave her a thrill and a tingle up her spine when she followed Valois down into his little piece of the ancient Parisian sewer system. This was not from the modern, post eighteen-hundreds sewers, but part of the much older Medieval or even Roman works. There was a sense of history, and mystery, unlike anywhere else she'd ever been in the world. Something like she imagined she'd feel in the chambers of an ancient Egyptian pyramid, or an old Roman catacomb.

Valois's father had discovered the tunnel under his shop quite by accident while digging out a hollow under the floorboards to hide a Jewish friend in during World War II. They'd ended up hiding a whole lot more than one friend, as well as most of the shop's valuable pieces. Now it served as a secure repository for Valois's illegal fencing activities.

Using flashlights, they quickly made their way through a crumbling, deserted section to what looked like a solid brick wall. After Valois pulled a hidden latch it swung away to reveal a much larger slice of the tunnel. Clean and neat, the area had a wooden floor and electric lights installed by Valois Senior. They switched off their flashlights and swung the wall closed behind them.

The Picasso was set up on an easel in the center of the room. A large nearby desk was covered with a scatter of photos.

"The buyer's appraiser was here this morning," Valois said, wiping his moist brow with a delicate hankie from his pocket. "A professor from Canada. He was able to obtain these authenticating photos from Dufour Auction House, where the Michauds bought the Picasso." He handed her a magnifying glass from the desk. "It's not the same painting. The strokes are similar but not identical. A very clever copy. But a copy nonetheless."

She roused herself long enough to focus the glass on a section of painting, comparing the brush work with a close-up photo from the same spot. Her eye wasn't as well-trained as Valois's, but even she could see a subtle difference. "Oh, my God. It is a forgery!" Her heart sank. "I can't believe I stole a fake."

"How could you know? The Michauds bought an authenticated Picasso from the most renowned auction house in France less than three years ago. God alone knows what happened to the real one."

"God and the Michauds, I'll bet," she muttered. "The lying cheats! They're probably ecstatic about it being stolen. They undoubtedly sold the original under the table, and now they can collect insurance, too. And they have me to blame its disappearance on! If I'm caught—"

"You won't be. You and Sofie were very careful, non?"

They had worked out the switch together, Valois suggesting Sofie paint a substitute so the robbery wouldn't be discovered until after Ciara was long gone. It had been a good plan. They'd both worn gloves at all times and taken every possible precaution against leaving any kind of traceable evidence. They'd bought their original materials from an art supply store that was part of a large European chain, using cash. Ciara had made sure to remind Sofie not to sign the copy with her usual Hand of Fatima signature. And she had gotten rid of her old lady disguise immediately after the job, as always.

There was no way anything could be traced to them.

So why was she so damned nervous?

One word.

Jean-Marc.

He was in charge of her case now, and he'd been there at the Michaud's. Why had he been standing in the window as she left? Had he recognized her?

She squeezed her eyes shut. "I hope you're right, Valois. I hope to hell you're right."

◧ ◧ ◧

For the next several days Jean-Marc and Pierre interviewed the Michaud's soiree guests who lived in Paris, and dispatched officers from the various regional police departments to speak with the out-of-towners, of which there were quite a few. A team was assigned the task of identifying and locating those people the countess couldn't put names to. Other officers re-canvassed the major art galleries around the country, carrying photos of the forgery so they could ask about artists who might have painted it.

Unfortunately, no one turned up anything new. Nor did a re-interview of the discothèque patrons and *le Revenant*'s more recent victims.

In frustration, Jean-Marc put out the word with his informants among the demi-monde that it was now *Commissaire* Lacroix who was looking for *le Revenant* and the Picasso thief. He still had some street cred from his youth—he may have been a math whiz, but he'd also been very good with his knife—so the effort might actually pay off. Some of his best friends growing up were now deep in the criminal element of Paris. You never knew what kicking over a few old stones might turn up.

One afternoon a few days later, the phone on Jean-Marc's desk rang. Ever hopeful of a break, he snatched it up. "Lacroix."

"It's Renard, down in the video lab. I've got something you should see."

Excitement buzzed over Jean-Marc's scalp. "Tell me you've got a match."

Renard coughed. "Well. Sort of. Better get down here and see for yourself."

Jean-Marc leapt from his chair and grabbed his jacket, stopping only to call Pierre. "Facial recognition software has turned up something. Let's check it out."

They met at the elevator. On the way down to the video lab, one of the forensics techs got in and rode with them for a couple of floors. "Still haven't unearthed anything useful on your Michaud case," he told them. "No fingerprints or any other physical evidence. Sorry about that."

Disappointing, but not unexpected. "What about the painting?" Jean-

Marc asked.

"The chief is still working on it. We'll let you know."

Jean-Marc thanked the tech as he got off, then he and Pierre continued on to the video lab.

"Who've we got?" Jean-Marc asked, striding up to the oversized flat screen monitor Renard was peering at.

"Well..." Renard turned the screen toward them.

Jean-Marc blinked. Twice. It was the snooty old lady with a flat tire he and his driver had picked up on the way to the Michaud's soiree.

He gave a bark of laughter. "Is this some kind of a joke?"

"Not really. You see—"

"She was in prison?" he asked incredulously.

"Non, not exactly."

"Then why the hell did the software spit her out? You were cross-checking arrest and prison files, right?"

"Yes, but also the disco patrons from Club LeCoeur."

He stared. "Club LeCoeur. Now you really are kidding me."

"*Alors*. She's a facial match for someone who was there that night."

Jean-Marc started to laugh for real. Pierre was already chuckling. "Renard. There were no old ladies at the disco. I'd have remembered that, believe me."

Renard looked slightly offended. "This is a very reliable computer program. Not always a hundred percent accurate, but fairly—"

Jean-Marc held up his palms. "All right. Show me the match."

Renard punched a few keys and all at once Jean-Marc was gazing at the last face he'd ever expected to see again.

▣ 8 ▣

Ciara!

Stunned, Jean-Marc felt his jaw slacken and every thought flew from his brain. What the hell?

Staring at the video monitor, Pierre started to laugh madly. "She's your match with the old lady? Ciara Alexander?"

Renard spread his hands. "The facial structures are a sixty-eight percent match. Not perfect, admittedly, but pretty darn—"

"In other words, there's a thirty-two percent chance it's wrong," Pierre pointed out, wiping his eyes. "*Mec*, when the weather man says thirty-two percent, I always bring an umbrella."

Renard's chin rose. "If I had a sixty-eight percent chance of winning at the roulette wheel you can bet I'd be packing for Monaco."

Jean-Marc shook himself mentally and interrupted. "Thanks, Renard. This is very interesting, and you did exactly right to call me. But I fear Pierre is correct. This is not a match. Continue to run the program, though. And keep me informed."

They managed to hold it together until they were back in the elevator. Then they looked at each other and Pierre burst out laughing again. "My God. Ciara Alexander and some old lady!"

"The wonders of modern technology," Jean-Marc said with a dry smirk. "Computers are never a substitute for good police work."

"They have their uses, but not this time," Pierre agreed. "Although..." he added teasingly, "no one seems to know who the old bat is. And she did have a big enough handbag to hide the canvas in...."

Oh, for chrissakes. "Shut up, Pierre," he said, but in the back of his mind he was mentally measuring the purse. It was big enough... And there was something else about the old lady. From an upstairs window he'd observed her leave the party within half an hour of arriving, and remembered thinking there was something odd about that. Or her car. Or...something.

Non. He gave himself a silent upbraiding. This was completely absurd. The old lady was not *le Revenant.* Or the Picasso thief. The thought was totally ridiculous. She was a woman. And she had to be at least seventy! A couple of the jobs *le Revenant* had pulled involved climbing in second and even third story windows and balconies. No way could an old lady do that.

"How about some lunch?" Pierre asked, glancing at his watch. "It's nearly noon."

"You go ahead. Think I'll hit the last of the art galleries and rattle the owners a bit."

"In that case," Pierre said with a wink, and grabbed one of the boxes they were done with, "Maybe it's time to return these files to Archives."

"Just remember, no San Tropez until both cases are solved," Jean-Marc warned, a spike of unexpected envy jabbing his chest. Pierre had been smart to be drawn to a woman who was actually obtainable. He, on the other hand...

Merde. Not going there.

Jean-Marc decided against taking a cruiser, instead fetching his own car from the parking garage. His Saab was forest green and some would say old enough to be seriously out of style. He preferred to think of it as pre-vintage. He'd owned it since he was a teenager—his first major purchase, bought used with the winnings of a nationally televised high school math competition. His mentor and teacher had been thrilled with his win, but Jean-Marc had been astounded...mostly by the windfall. That anything other than extortion or selling drugs could make him money had opened his eyes—to a lot of possibilities he'd never considered before.

His green Saab reminded him of that, of the potential often hidden in unexpected places. Especially on the days he needed reminding.

Today was one of those days.

It seemed like every time he took one step forward in the investigation, he landed two steps further back.

And then there was the shock of seeing Ciara's photo on Renard's screen. That had really jolted him. He'd almost managed to forget her over the past week, along with the betrayal and anger he'd felt over her disappearance. But now the feelings returned in full force.

Where the hell were the hidden possibilities when he needed them? Locked in his anger, he decided, as he strode into the first gallery on his list.

So he used that anger. To put the fear of God into those shady characters who were buying and selling stolen merchandise. And let them know if they chose to do it on his watch, he'd take them down so hard their heads would crack.

By the fourth art gallery, he'd had enough. Frustrated and hungry, he resolved to make one more stop, then grab a bite to eat somewhere before returning to headquarters to see how Pierre's lunch date had gone. He needed a pleasant distraction to get him back on track.

He happened to be just up the street from Valois Vielli, the unassuming antique storefront for France's most infamous fence. *Alors*, alleged fence. Valois had never been convicted—hell, he'd never even been arrested, although everyone on both sides of the law knew exactly what he was up to. Valois was a legend, as Valois Sr. had been before him. Even over sixty years later, the heroicism of the last war clung to the family name like a tricolored cloak of protection, far outweighing the fact that that same war had also given birth to the other, less honorable family business.

Jean-Marc didn't give a damn how many refugees the old man had saved during World War II; if Valois was helping *le Revenant*, or had anything to do with the Picasso's disappearance, he was going to jail. Period.

"Ah, *Monsieur le Commissaire!*" Valois greeted him as he came into the cave-like shop, removing his dark shades. "*Enfin de retour!* I understand congratulations are in order."

Which only confirmed his involvement in illegal activity, in Jean-Marc's mind. Why else would a civilian know or care about his promotion to lead detective?

"Thank you," he said, folding his sunglasses into his breast pocket. "I need your help, Valois. There seems to be a Picasso missing. And you know where it is."

Naturally, the old man denied all knowledge. With a smile, of course. They had a very civilized conversation. Unproductive. But the old geezer knew something. In fact, at one point Jean-Marc was certain he was about to give him a morsel of information, but at the last moment he clammed up. Interesting.

This was as close to a lead as Jean-Marc had gotten in weeks. The man bore watching. He'd assign one of his officers to sit in the small café across the street and snap photographs of everyone who went in and out of Valois Vielli.

That should send a message. And with any luck might even yield something useful.

He left his card with a cordial request to be notified if anyone turned up at the shop trying to sell a Picasso. Valois smiled and bowed and said he most certainly would.

Right.

The bell above the door tinkled as it shut behind Jean-Marc. The warm afternoon air was redolent with the scent of strong, sweet coffee. His stomach growled in response. Slipping on his shades, he glanced across the street at the Café Constantinople. Its specialty was Turkish coffee. Perhaps they also had sandwiches.

He strolled over and took a seat at one of the white iron bistro tables on the sidewalk outside. After placing his order with the owner who came around to greet him, he sat back to think about his next move.

But before he could, his attention was caught by a slim, dark-haired girl inside the café. She was on a ladder, painting the wall. Or rather, she was painting a large design onto the wall. It was ornately beautiful, and blue.

A Hand of Fatima.

Exactly like the one above Ciara Alexander's bed.

Before he was aware of what he was doing, he found himself inside the café, standing below the ladder, hands on hips.

"Where is she?" he demanded.

"What?" Surprised, the girl quickly turned, grabbing the ladder to keep herself from falling. Taking him in at a glance, for a split second she looked terrified.

"Ciara Alexander," he said, pressing his advantage. "I want to know where she is. And you are going to tell me."

▣ ▣ ▣

The girl's eyes shuttered. "I have no idea what you're talking about," she said, and turned her back to Jean-Marc. She continued to paint, but the brush strokes came out wavy. Her hand was shaking.

She knew exactly what he was talking about.

She appeared to be very young. Middle Eastern by the look of her olive skin and long brown-black hair. Algerian, probably. And by her reaction, well used to male intimidation. Strong-arming her wouldn't work, Jean-Marc realized. But the opposite might.

He sat down at a table below the ladder and let out a sigh, chin in hand. "Sorry," he said. "Ciara had a design like that over her bed when we... Anyway, I miss her and just thought..." He sighed again.

"This guy bothering you, Sofie?" the owner said, frowning as he came over.

She didn't look around, but shook her head. "No," she said softly.

"Just admiring the painting," Jean-Marc said. "She has a very unique style. Thought I recognized it. Guess I was mistaken."

The owner grunted, and went back for Jean-Marc's coffee, bringing it to him with a suspicious glare. "He bothers you, *habibi*, let me know."

"I will, Ghalil."

Jean-Marc took a sip of the thick, aromatic liquid and smiled. "Damn, that's good." He looked up. The girl—Sofie—had turned on the ladder and

74

was watching him.

"You're the cop, aren't you?" she said.

He tipped his head, mildly surprised. "Ciara, she talked about me?"

The girl gnawed her bottom lip and studied her paint brush silently for a moment. Finally, she said, "She liked you. A lot. She's been sad since..." Her words trailed off into more silence.

Sad.

A ripple of disbelief, or maybe renewed anger, sifted through his chest. *Sad?*

He wanted to challenge the girl. Make her tell the truth. But he knew that would only shut her up again. So he said, "I've been sad, too." And waited.

His sandwich came, and she went back to painting. Her strokes were flowing and sure now, skimming over the white wall, turning the blank space into a delightful work of art. Curlicues and intricate designs surrounded the elegant blue fingers of Fatima's hand.

Suddenly, she turned and said, "She trusted you, you know. That's not why she left."

He bit back the urge to ask the obvious, and asked instead, "Why wouldn't she trust me?"

The girl snorted delicately and went back to her painting.

"Because I'm a cop?"

"What do you think?" she said, a wealth of information contained in her soft drawl. More curlicues appeared.

All at once it hit him. Maybe Ciara had not been afraid of him being a cop because of something she'd done. Maybe she was afraid because of what some other cop had done to her.

Outraged at the thought, he tore a bite from his sandwich to keep from demanding to know what had happened.

"People like us," the girl said, glancing over her shoulder at him, as though she could sense his turmoil, "we have little reason to trust *le flic.*"

"Sofie," he said, meeting her gaze head-on, "I'm not so unlike you. I grew up in *les banlieues.* I know all about bad cops. And I'm not one of them."

She gnawed on her lip again, and a bleak smile broke through. "Yes. She said you were different."

He couldn't read the girl. Couldn't figure out if she thought that was a good thing or a bad thing. He was more confused than ever.

"Sofie, please. Where is she?"

She turned back to her wall. "I can't tell you."

His blood bloomed with impatience. Fine. He'd have her followed. Eventually she'd lead him right to Ciara.

Though why he wanted to know was beyond him. He had no desire to renew their affair. She'd made it clear where he stood with her. Why push it?

But he couldn't let it go. He had to know where she was. Had to see her again. To find out why she didn't want him. It was like an obsession, his need to find her. A sick obsession.

What was wrong with him?

"She takes care of us, you know," the girl said solemnly. "All of us. I don't know what we'd do without her."

The quiet statement brought him back to reality. "How?" he asked, interest piquing. He felt instinctively that in the answer lay a key to the puzzle that was Ciara Alexander.

Sofie's lips parted, as though he'd caught her off guard. She shook her head, dipping her brush into the Aegean blue.

"I want to understand," he said. He also wanted to know who "all of us" were, but one thing at a time.

The design on the wall was nearly complete. He followed her graceful movements as she filled in the thumb and put finishing touches on the curls and flourishes surrounding it. When she was done, she climbed down from the ladder.

"Aren't you going to sign it?"

She looked at him, startled, then back at the wall. "That is my signature," she said.

He frowned, not understanding. But before he could question her meaning, she slid into the chair opposite him. Wiping her fingers on a bright orange cloth, she studied them like she had something to say.

Her hair fell over her eyes, making her look extremely young. How old was she? Fifteen, sixteen, max. He thought about what she'd said, and wondered why Ciara was taking care of her, and not her parents.

"Ciara has very little money," Sofie said, barely above a whisper. "But what she has she shares with us. Without her help, we would all be living on the streets instead of having a decent place to sleep and food in our stomachs. She keeps us on a good path."

After a pause to digest that unexpected information, he gently asked, "We?"

"The Orphans. There are five of us."

What the hell? "Street kids?"

She nodded at her hands.

He leaned back in his chair, slightly taken aback. His vivacious, sexy Ciara was caring for five young runaways? Of all the things for her to be doing, of all the reasons for her to avoid him, that was one he'd never seen coming.

"She's afraid to get involved with me," he deduced aloud, "because she thinks I'll contact social services. Take you all away from her."

Sofie swallowed but didn't look up. "Something like that."

Was she right? Would he?

He was a sworn officer of the *police judicaire*, bound to uphold the law. If the kids were underage, he'd have no choice but to report the situation, regardless of his personal feelings on the matter.

He blew out a breath. *Merde.* Had Ciara pegged him so accurately after three nights in bed? He didn't know whether to be flattered or insulted.

Across the street, the bell above Valois Vielli's door tinkled and he realized he'd completely forgotten about calling for an officer to keep watch over the place. A sophisticated woman with short black hair and large sunglasses emerged from the shop, looked both ways down the sidewalk, then over toward the café. High heels clicking smartly, she crossed the street and came in, seating herself at a table on the other side of the room.

Jean-Marc turned back to Sofie. It was time for him to go. Before he overstayed his welcome and she got suspicious.

"Thank you for explaining," he said, and rose. "Next time you see Ciara, would you tell her—"

Tell her what? That she'd been right in her assessment of him? That he was a heartless bastard who saw life in black and white, with no room for extenuating circumstances? That it was better she had made the choice than he? Because although in his heart he admired what she was doing more than he could say, he'd always be a cop first.

"Tell her I still want her," he murmured. Because that much was also true.

Ignoring Sofie's blush, he tossed a ten on the table and started to walk away. But before taking two steps, he went back and handed her a hundred euro note. "Buy her something pretty," he said, "Something she'd like." Then he turned and strode out of the café.

As soon as he'd rounded the corner, he pulled out his cell phone.

"Pierre?" he said when his partner picked up. "Send me an officer. I need someone watched."

▣ 9 ▣

Ciara averted her face and held her breath as Jean-Marc's tall frame disappeared through the café door. Her heart beat like thunder. She couldn't believe he was here! Talking with Sofie! But how?

He'd walked right past her table, close enough to reach over and touch. She hadn't done it, but she'd been tempted. Oh, so tempted.

The faint smell of his cologne lingered in his path, triggering a deep yearning, way down inside her. Sometimes when she thought about Jean-Marc, the physical craving was almost unbearable, God help her. She took a deep breath and shuddered it out. She was so messed up.

Lowering her sunglasses, she met Sofie's large, luminous brown eyes. They were filled with sympathy.

"What did he want?" Ciara asked, blocking out the insane feelings assaulting her insides.

Sofie came over to the table. "To find you."

Ciara's pulse sped. "But...how? How did he know?"

Sofie glanced toward her painting, then back. "Fatima's Hand. He recognized it. From over your bed."

"Oh, sweet Jesus." Ciara's mind scrambled. She'd never thought of that. What other details had she not thought about that could give her away? "You didn't tell him where I moved, did you?"

"Never," Sofie assured. "Never, ever."

"Thank God," Ciara whispered, relief pouring through her. For as much as she longed to be with Jean-Marc, it would be pure disaster if he found her again. That kind of complication she did not need.

"He seemed nice," Sofie said. "I liked him."

"Yes. I liked him, too," Ciara murmured. *Unfortunately.*

"Too bad he's a cop, and not a gangster, eh? Like Etienne."

She smiled wearily. "Too bad I didn't meet him before I met Etienne. Our lives might have been very different."

Sofie's dark brows tilted. "If you'd met him first, you'd never have bothered with us Orphans."

"Don't be silly." Ciara stood and gave her a heartfelt hug. "I'd be the same person inside. And I'd love you just as much as I do now. How could I not? You're my family."

Sofie's smile glowed. "I love you, too." She reached up to touch Ciara's short black wig. "I can't believe he didn't recognize you when you came in."

"I'm not. He didn't at the Michaud's either. Nobody sees through my disguises."

"A lover should."

"I guess that tells you something, then."

"You're wrong. He loves you, Ciara."

She let out a weary laugh. "Sweetie, we've only seen each other three times. He couldn't possibly love me."

The young girl shook her head slowly. "*Non*. You didn't hear his voice. He loves you. And you love him. Why didn't you tell us?"

Good Lord. How could a child who'd gone through such hell still have such a ridiculously romantic view of life?

"Honey, there's nothing to tell. Yes, I'll admit, I have a wicked terrible crush on the man. But...it's impossible, and we both know why. End of story."

Sofie shook her head. "There must be a way."

"There isn't." Ciara gestured to the painting equipment by the far wall. "I'll help you clean up. It looks gorgeous, by the way. Your best one yet."

Sofie stood mulishly for a moment, stubborn in her optimism. Then she pushed out a sigh and joined her in picking up the paint and brushes. "Thanks. I'll paint another over your new bed tomorrow. Perhaps it will bring you a miracle, just like Fatima's. So you can be with your man."

She kissed Sofie on the forehead. A miracle. That's exactly what it would take for that to happen. And if there was one thing Ciara had never believed in, it was miracles. The things she believed in were hard work, determination, and having realistic goals. And right now, her number one goal was to get enough money to pay off Beck so she and her kids could get on with their education, and ultimately their lives. Just a few more years and they'd all be able to support themselves. But until that happened, it was up to her to keep things afloat.

The only miracle Ciara needed right now was another job to pull off. And soon.

◊ ◊ ◊

"I'm returning the Picasso," Ciara told Sofie as they strolled the half kilometer from the café to the *métro*. The day was beautiful and they weren't in any hurry.

Sofie's eyes widened. "Return it? Are you serious?"

Ciara shrugged. "It's a fake, not worth a fraction of what we need. If I let the cops have it, that should redirect the investigation back onto the Micheauds and take the heat off me. Long enough to lift something else, anyway."

"Give it to the cops? Sounds dangerous."

"I just have to be sure not to leave any traceable—"

Suddenly, an iron grip latched onto her wrist and her arm was yanked practically from its socket. She was dragged off the sidewalk through a broken outer doorway and into a garbage-filled courtyard.

"*Putain!*" the stocky man attached to the grip spat out. "You think you can protect my whore?"

Beck!

Sofie yelped, looking wild-eyed, welded to the spot as the heavy wooden door swung back at her. "Stay there!" she called. She didn't want her anywhere near Beck or what was about to happen.

Beck jerked Ciara's arms painfully, slamming her back against the filthy alley wall. "The little whore missed her deadline. She's mine now," he hissed. "To do with as I want. Nothing you can do about it." He raised his fist.

Ciara forced herself not to react or resist. Men like Beck got off on a woman's fear and struggles. "We'll get your money. We just need more time."

A vicious slap stung her cheek. "How much time? A day? A month? A year?" A backhand to her other cheek whipped her head back against the hard brick.

She cried out in pain. "A week! Give us a week."

"That will cost you five thousand more," Beck snarled. His face twisted into an ugly smirk. "Unless..." He grabbed at her breast, ripping the buttons off the pretty silk blouse that she'd spent an hour bartering down at the *Puce de Montreuil* flea market. "You'd rather take it out in trade...eh, *morue?* You and the little whore together." The smell of cheap red wine scorched across her nostrils. His fingers squeezed into her flesh.

Bile filled her throat. She wanted to knee him in the balls so hard he'd stay doubled over for a year. But she resisted the urge. That satisfaction wouldn't be worth what Beck would do to Sofie in retaliation.

"You'll get your fucking money," she gritted out, twisting her body away from his hands. "Now *let me go.*"

He narrowed his black eyes, breathing heavily into her face. She almost gagged.

"Fifteen thousand. One week, *connasse*. Or—" he jerked a thumb at Sofie, who cowered at the courtyard entrance, tears streaming down her face "—after I'm done with her she'll be back in the loving care of her dear old daddy. And you, little bitch—" he jabbed his finger into Ciara's breast "—you'll be wishing you were dead."

The last thing she was aware of was a sudden horrible, blinding pain in her kidney as she stumbled for the outer door. Then everything went black.

◉ 10 ◉

"Ciara? *Ciara!*"

The frantic sound of Sofie's weeping finally penetrated the excruciating, twisting void Ciara was being sucked into. She groaned and tried to move, gasping at the sharp pain in her side that resulted.

"Please, Ciara. Wake up!"

"*Mademoiselle,* are you all right?" A concerned male voice mingled with Sofie's soft sobs.

"I'm fine," she whispered, her voice cracking. She opened her eyes and immediately wished she hadn't. The man bending over her was dressed in civvies, but his haircut and official demeanor immediately identified him as some kind of law enforcement. *Great.*

"Really, I'm okay," she said, ignoring her pain and sitting up. She had nearly made it back to the sidewalk before collapsing.

"What happened here?" the cop asked, lifting a cell phone from his jacket pocket.

Quickly, she put her hand on his. "No need to call *le flic,*" she said, smiling past her stinging cheeks. "It was just a misunderstanding. My fault. Honest."

The cop scowled down the street in the direction Beck had disappeared. "Was that guy a police officer?"

Beck had covered his uniform shirt with a light nylon windbreaker, so Ciara feigned surprise, waving off Sofie's alarmed mewl behind her back. "No, of course not. Just my neighbor." She did her best to look embarrassed. "I, um... My dog messed on his doorstep. Again. It was the third time, and he stepped in it. I don't blame him for being angry."

The cop didn't look the least bit convinced. "What about her?" he asked, indicating Sofie. A thin trail of blood trickled from her nose.

Ciara sent him a beseeching look. "He was really mad. My friend accidentally got in the way. Please, we're all right. Honestly." To illustrate her point, Ciara climbed to her feet, hiding a wince and swallowing a groan. Straightening her skirt, she surreptitiously smoothed a hand over her wig to make sure it was still in place. Sofie took her arm.

He looked dubious, but relented at their united front. "Where do you live? I'll walk you there."

"That's very sweet, but we're on our way to my friend's place. It's some distance."

"I'll hail you a taxi then," he insisted.

"You're very kind," she relented, just to be rid of him.

In less than a minute he'd flagged down an empty cab and helped them inside. With a grateful wave at the cop, she gave the driver the Orphans' address on rue Daguerre and leaned back against the seat with a groan.

Once the car rounded the corner she turned to Sofie. Her heart sank. Along with the bloody nose, the girl's left eye was swelling black and blue.

"The fucking bastard," Ciara gritted out.

She'd never been a violent person, but right now she truly wanted to kill Beck. With her bare hands. Right after she'd castrated him with a pair of pliers.

"Are you okay, sweetie?"

Sofie nodded, eyes swimming with tears, which she dashed at ineffectually. She wasn't okay. That was obvious.

Ciara could almost hear the cogs turning, circling some terrible idea in her desperate mind.

"Don't even think about it, Sofie," she said, pulling her into a hug, ignoring the rip of pain in her side. "Whatever it is you're contemplating, don't. We'll take care of Beck. I swear to you."

"I'd rather die than go back to my father," Sofie whispered. "I couldn't."

"That's not happening. I promise."

"But Beck—"

"Beck is a horny, greedy animal. He wants you out here on your own, where he can use you and manipulate you with fear. Not hidden away behind your father's eight foot walls. Trust me, he's not going to your father."

Sofie swallowed, more tears cresting. "Oh, Ciara, what are we to do?"

"We're going home and washing our faces," she said, somehow mustering up a firm voice from behind the lump lodged in her throat. "And then we'll figure out who I have to rob to get this scumbag off our backs. Until we can take care of him once and for all."

◘ ◘ ◘

*D*amn, *he needed a drink.*

Already. And it was barely lunchtime.

Jean-Marc hadn't been able to shake the weird feeling he'd had in the pit of his stomach since leaving the café yesterday. The unbidden reminder of Ciara Alexander had not been a welcome addition to his week. He'd dreamt about her last night again. For the hundredth time.

What was it about the fucking woman that had her embedded so firmly under his skin? He'd never reacted this way to a one night—okay three night—stand before. It was making him nuts! Why couldn't he just forget about her? His male pride had been wounded before—hell, his ex-wife had practically put it through the shredder—and he'd emerged unscathed. Well, relatively unscathed.

He didn't need this strange obsession. He had enough to worry about.

Another day, and no closer to catching either *le Revenant* or the Picasso thief. Belfort was getting impatient. So was Jean-Marc. He needed a break.

And then there was that weird incident reported by Gerard, the undercover guy he'd had follow Sofie home yesterday. Gerard said she'd been attacked. By a neighbor of some friend she'd been walking with. Actually, the friend had borne the brunt of it, but both women had been bloodied. Jean-Marc had been furious when Gerard admitted he hadn't done anything about it.

"They refused to let me call for help," he'd contended. "Insisted they were fine. Besides, *Commissaire*, I found out where the girl lives, which is what you wanted, *non?*"

True. But the incident still bothered him. Men beating up women made him furious. And Sofie had seemed so fragile.

Pierre popped his head into his office. "Delivery for you."

Jean-Marc shook off his residual distaste, and asked, "What is it?"

"Not a bomb. They checked it." Pierre grinned and handed him a long cardboard tube.

He glanced over it. No markings or delivery stickers. "Came by messenger?"

Pierre nodded. "No return address, and the kid had no idea where it came from."

Curious, Jean-Marc used a pen to pop off the plastic end cap.

"What—you think it's some kind of evidence?" Pierre asked with hiked brows, indicating the precautions Jean-Marc was using not to mar any possible finger prints.

"Never know." He gingerly slid the contents onto his desk. It was a rolled up piece of cloth. A...canvas?

"Jesus!" Pierre exclaimed as Jean-Marc unrolled it. "It's the fucking Picasso!"

Shock stuttered through him. It *was* the Picasso. Along with a note, which said, in all its simplicity, in block letters, "IT'S A FAKE."

He stared for a long moment before tipping the note to Pierre. A laugh escaped him. Then another. And another. *Oh, God, the irony.* He tipped his head to the ceiling as laughter rolled out of him. This was just too fucking weird.

Pierre gaped. *"Tu est fou?"*

Was he crazy? Maybe. Getting there, certainly.

"Alors. Guess we'd better let CD Belfort know the case has taken a bit of a bizarre twist," he finally managed.

"Ho-kay," Pierre said carefully. "Meanwhile, what should we do with that?" He jerked his thumb at the Picasso.

"Evidence bag. The insurance company will want a good look."

"Putain. This leaves our investigation kinda up in the air."

Jean-Marc hitched out a breath. "No shit. God knows what the boss will want to do."

"Drop the case, I'd guess. Looks better for the OCBC to stamp the file, 'Closed. Goods Recovered and Returned.'"

The phone rang and Jean-Marc snatched it up. "Lacroix."

"This is Terrance over in Forensics. I found something you'll want to see."

It took a moment for him to switch gears. Terrance was the chief of the Forensics Lab, and had spent the past week analyzing everything possible about the forged Picasso. Hell. The *other* forged Picasso.

"You got something on the painting?" he asked Terrance.

"Yep."

"We'll be right there."

His face must have given him away because Pierre looked at him and hopped to his feet. "What?"

"Not sure. Forensics found something."

"Merci, Dieu." Pierre lifted the two sealed bags containing the cardboard tube and the painting. "What do we do with those?"

"We'll log them into evidence on the way," Jean-Marc said, grabbing his jacket off the back of his chair. "And deal with it later."

Which they did, then made tracks for the forensics lab. An assistant led them into an ultra-modern glass-enclosed cubicle where Dr. Terrance greeted them and offered them seats. Precisely mounted in a clear frame, the forged Picasso sat in the middle of his desk.

"As you know," he said matter-of-factly, "we haven't found anything about the painting that can be used to pinpoint either the specific sources of the materials or the actual artist."

"So what *did* you find?" Jean-Marc asked when the chief hesitated.

"Even though everything indicates it was painted very recently, using brand new materials, I decided to do an x-ray of the canvas. To see if there was a mark indicating a store, or anything else underneath the paint itself."

Jean-Marc straightened to attention. "And?"

"And I found a ghost."

He froze at the unexpected word. "A...what?"

"A ghost. That's what experts call an image painted over by another. Like when an artist reuses an old canvas, or makes a mistake and covers it up."

His breath whooshed out. "No shit?"

"Look." Dr. Terrance reached over to a light frame and switched it on. Two x-ray images were mounted there, side by side. The first was the visible part of the painting, reversed in the confusing black and white way of a typical x-ray, showing the design as it appeared on the canvas. The second film showed the same thing, slightly out of focus. But there was a bright blotch on the bottom right corner. The ghost.

Jean-Marc squinted, but couldn't make out the design. "A mistake, perhaps?" he suggested.

"Perhaps." Terrance clipped a third x-ray to the light frame. "This is a deeper close up, better focused."

Jean-Marc's whole body clenched in shock. There, staring him right in the face, was an all-too-familiar image.

"I don't believe it," he muttered, sinking into a chair. "I don't fucking believe it."

"You recognize it?" Terrance said, puzzled.

"What?" Pierre asked sharply. "*Med* What is it?"

"It's a goddamn Hand of Fatima," Jean-Marc answered through gritted teeth. *To think he'd felt sorry for the duplicitous little urchin.* "And I know exactly who painted it."

◙ 11 ◙

"I say we slit his throat."

Ciara glanced at Hugo, who was pacing once again. The kid was cocked tight as a trigger. Back and forth in front of the window he strode, fists clenched and knuckles white. He looked positively murderous. Ricardo watched nervously from the sofa next to Davie, whose arms were around a downcast Sofie.

They had all gathered at the apartment for dinner the day after the Beck incident to discuss what to do about the escalating situation.

"God, don't even think about it, Hugo," Ciara said, striving for a level-headedness she didn't actually feel. "We need to find a way to make Beck spend the rest of *his* life in jail. Not you. He's not worth throwing away your future."

Not now that her beautiful, volatile boy finally had one. His job at the garage didn't pay much, but it was legit. And a start. More than he'd had four years ago when, at CoCo's pleading, Ciara had practically dragged him off the docks of Marseilles. Cocky as hell and good-looking as sin, he'd been well on his way to a life of violence and addiction. It had taken some fast talking by both of them—and the graphic reminder of Etienne's death—to convince him, but they'd finally managed to make him see the light. But there were still times he reverted to his old ways of dealing with trouble.

"Then what do you suggest?" he asked, his young eyes blazing with fury. "I'm supposed to just let him beat you? What kind of a man would I be? And Sofie, what of her, if he takes it in his mind to—" His words cut off with a slash of his hand. "*Sale enculé*," he ground out. "Etienne would have—"

"And that's why Etienne is dead!" she snapped, lurching to her feet, feeling like a broken record. The boy's hero worship of his late older cousin was a constant battle between them. Etienne had been cocky and good-looking, too. A man's man who loved hard and lived harder. In the end his over-confidence had cost him his life, taken down by a cop's bullet—from the gun of a man he'd been sure was his friend.

CoCo rose from the arm of the easy chair where Ciara had been

87

perched, went over and put her hands on Hugo's shoulders. "She is right, *mon cher*. We're smarter than he is. Let's use our heads." She pushed a fallen lock off his temple. "We all loved Etienne, but he wasn't much of a role model, eh? What will happen to us, to Sofie, if you are put in jail for murder?"

Ciara watched the siblings with a hitch in her heart. How she admired CoCo's ability to tame her tempestuous brother, to set aside her bitchy firecracker façade and unabashedly show him the love and tenderness he so badly craved. The love and tenderness they *all* craved, because those things had been so completely lacking in their lives. CoCo and Hugo were lucky to have each other.

She had used exactly the right words with her brother. No one could miss the gentleness with which he always treated shy Sofie, nor the way he looked at her when he thought no one was watching. Even if he'd made no outward claims on her affections, there was no doubt Hugo considered himself Sofie's protector.

Ciara tamped down her anxiety, and sat down again.

She had loved Etienne with the fierceness—and utter blindness—of an abandoned, forgotten seventeen-year-old girl for the man who had rescued her and showered her with love. She had married him without hesitation and followed him across the sea, taken up his life of crime without looking back. After all, what had she to lose? She'd shared her body and her dreams, and he'd shared his skills at pick-pocketing and second-story work. A match made in heaven, she'd thought.

His strength had turned her on. His intensity had excited her. His recklessness she'd mistaken for *joie de vivre* , his brutality had been well-hidden and never directed against her. She'd conveniently denied its existence. Until the violence of his life had caught up with him and her eyes were forced open.

Etienne had taught her a difficult lesson. One she was working hard not to forget.

"Valois is helping to find a job that will pay enough to keep Beck away for now," she said, pushing aside the chaotic memories. "Meanwhile, we need ideas. How can we catch Beck in his own trap? Without implicating or endangering any of us?"

Suddenly, there was a loud knock. Ciara glanced at the mantle clock as everyone else turned to the door. Seven-ten p.m..

"Anyone expecting company?" she asked, already knowing the answer by the uneasy looks on everyone's faces. Her pulse leapt.

"Beck?" Ricardo whispered, cautiously rising.

The fist banged again. "*Police Nationale!*"

She gasped. Jean-Marc's voice!

"*Merde.*" Davie leaped up from the couch. "What do we do?"

What the hell was Jean-Marc doing here? She met Sofie's panicked eyes and silently questioned her. The girl shook her head, a little desperately, as the pounding continued. No, she hadn't given him the address.

Now everyone was on their feet. Jean-Marc yelled out again, angrily, like he would bash the door in if someone didn't come soon.

"Answer it," Ciara told CoCo in a low murmur. "They've got nothing on us." She turned to Sofie. "Whatever he says, deny any involvement. If he gets specific, you were here, with all the others as witnesses. Right?" She glanced around the circle of worried faces and they all nodded in solidarity. "Hugo, keep your hands in your pockets, *no matter what*," she ordered as she started for the back bedroom. "I'll go out through the attic as we planned."

They'd practiced this a dozen times over the past years, but she'd prayed they'd never have to use their emergency plan. So much for prayers *and* fantasies.

Swiftly, she ran down the hall and into the bedroom, reaching the closet as she heard CoCo open the front door. Her heart quailed at the sound of Jean-Marc's harsh demand to speak with Sofie.

God *damn* it. Why hadn't she delivered the Picasso to him a day earlier? The investigation into its theft surely would have been halted by now.

Gritting her teeth against the pain that still twanged in her side from Beck's beating, she hoisted herself up through the trap door in the closet ceiling and into the attic.

Despair flooded through her. She'd *known* something like this would happen. As soon as she'd seen Jean-Marc in the café talking to Sofie she'd had a terrible premonition, that somehow he'd figure it all out. That Sofie was the artist who had painted the fake Ciara planted at the Michaud's. That Sofie could tell him where she was hiding.

Fuck.

Silently, she slid the square wooden trapdoor back into place behind her. The attic was steaming hot, bisected with shafts of sunlight poking through the roof vents and the dirty round dormer portholes. Dust motes danced around her as she teetered quickly along the thick wooden beams which traversed the length of the entire attic that served all four contiguous apartment buildings on the block. Stopping at one of the back dormers overlooking the inner courtyard, she unlatched the window, whisked off her pumps, and gingerly climbed through it, clinging to the sill as her bare feet gained purchase on a narrow decorative ledge. Hunching down, she grabbed the ledge and lowered herself to an iron balcony attached to the story below.

Her imagination filled with awful pictures of what was happening back in the apartment as she made her escape. Was she being a coward? Should she have stayed and faced the music instead of bailing and leaving the Orphans at the mercy of...

Don't be ridiculous, she told herself. Jean-Marc may be her own personal nemesis, but he wouldn't mess with her kids. Not without any kind of evidence against them.

Would he?

You could tell a lot about a man by the way he made love. Jean-Marc had been domineering, sometimes even rough. But he'd always made sure she got hers first. And she knew his reputation on the street, from Valois and others who'd dealt with him. *Commissaire* Lacroix was tough but fair, had been the verdict all the way around.

On the other hand... She recalled the case Valois had told her about. The one where the thief had disappeared, leaving Lacroix holding the bag. It had nearly ruined his career. Jean-Marc had himself admitted that it *had* ended his marriage. *Le Commissaire* hadn't been the same since, it was said.

Lacroix was definitely tough. But was he still fair?

Maybe. But maybe not. Especially when it concerned a thief who betrayed him personally.... If Jean-Marc ever learned who she really was, she had a sinking feeling the word mercy would not be in his vocabulary.

Which was why she'd better get the hell out of here. The Orphans could take care of each other. They had a plan to follow. But she was in no state to be looking into Jean-Marc's eyes, answering lies to his questions.

Tossing her shoes, she swung from balcony to balcony, making her way to the other end of the block. There she found the fire escape ladder, grasped it, and climbed down the rest of the five stories to the postage stamp inner courtyard below. She hurried through the covered entrance passageway and cracked open the outer door to the sidewalk.

Catching her breath, she peered through it and down the street. Half a block away, two *Police Nationale* radio cars were still parked at angles to the entrance of the Orphans' apartment building, yellow lights flashing.

Was that really necessary? And what was taking them so long, anyway? Surely, they weren't searching the apartment, or—

Suddenly, the building's wooden entry door banged open and a uniformed officer held it open for Jean-Marc's partner, Pierre, who strode through, followed by—

Sofie!

No!

Sofie had her hands behind her back and Jean-Marc walked close behind her, his fingers gripping her shoulder, guiding her toward one of the cars.

"What are you doing?" Ciara cried without thinking, launching herself out of her hiding place at a run. "You can't arrest her! Let her go!"

The officer spun and took up a defensive stance. "*Arrêtez!*" he shouted, putting his hand on the butt of his gun.

Pierre glanced at her but kept walking around the car. Jean-Marc ignored her completely, opening the rear door for Sofie and handing her into the back. But he must have said something to the officer, because he also relaxed and went to the car.

"Hey!" Ciara's feet ate up the pavement despite the burgeoning pain in her side and the heels she'd slipped back on. "Why are you arresting her? She's done nothing!"

Jean-Marc continued to disregard her until he slammed the car door closed, locking Sofie inside. Ciara appealed to Pierre, who had leaned against the car roof on folded arms. His shoulders and brows lifted. The uniformed officer got into the driver's seat at Jean-Marc's signal.

"I demand—!" she began, but the words choked off when Jean-Marc finally turned to her.

His eyes were flinty. *Merciless.*

"You are in no position to demand anything, *Madamoiselle* Alexander," he said coolly, then jerked his chin at Pierre, who nodded and got into the car, too. The engine came to life and the tires squealed as it took off down the street.

Instinctively, she took a step to go after it, but was yanked to a stop by Jean-Marc's steely grip. "Where do you think you're going?"

"Where are they taking her?" she demanded, attempting to shake her arm free.

"36 Quai des Orfèvres. Would you like to come along?" His tone was not amiable. It was more of a dare. His grip was relentless.

Jesus. Straight into the lion's den.

"What have you charged her with?"

"Nothing. She's not under arrest."

"Then why the handcuffs?"

"No cuffs. I simply asked her to hold her hands behind her back."

"Why?" she asked, outraged. He'd tricked her!

"To flush you out," he said. His blue eyes were almost black, more intense and penetrating than she'd ever seen them. The harsh angles of his face held no sympathy whatsoever. Not even a hint of a smile. "Even if you weren't watching, I knew you'd hear about it."

"And?"

"And come to me."

Her stomach knotted. "What do you want with me, Jean-Marc?" she asked, struggling to keep her voice even. Fighting not to recall the times when the power of his will had made her melt in his arms, the times his firm, strong touch had opened her body to his every whim. The times she'd come to him—for him—more than willingly.

His gaze went to her breasts, almost insolently. "What do you think?"

Her traitorous nipples tightened, but before she could think to respond, a scowl sketched across his face. His eyes had dropped below the hem of skirt, to her knees, scraped and scabbed from her scuffle with Beck. His gaze whipped up to her cheeks. She swallowed. She'd forgotten all about her bruises.

"What the hell happened to you?" he asked angrily.

"I, um...I fell."

His eyes flared in surprise, as though he'd suddenly remembered something important, then narrowed dangerously. "I'm growing tired of your lies."

She straightened. "Then let's talk about Sofie."

His hand curled around her neck, holding her in place for a closer inspection. "It was you with Sofie last night, wasn't it? Who hit you, Ciara?" he asked softly. Too softly. A shiver traced down her spine.

"I'd rather not discuss it," she murmured. "It's complicated." She met his simmering gaze. "But it wasn't anything...personal."

"A man hitting you wasn't personal?" He let her arm go, and ran his hand clinically over her torso. When he got to her tender kidney she did her best not to wince, but he was a trained observer. His jaw clenched.

"Please, Jean-Marc, leave it alone," she whispered. "I need to get to Sofie. She has to be scared to death."

He traced the very tips of his fingers over her cheek, barely grazing the skin. The aching gentleness of his touch contrasted sharply with the stone deadly look on his face. "Why the fuck don't you trust me?" he growled, nearly under his breath.

"I do." Her head wobbled. "I wish..." She shook it. "I can't do this now. Please. Take me to Sofie."

He stared down at her for a long moment, then dropped his hand and turned to the second police car. "Get in."

Self-consciously, she slid into the front seat as he stalked around to the driver's side. In the apartment building, up in the fifth floor window, four anxious faces pressed together, peering down at her. She gave them a wave she hoped was reassuring.

And prayed she wasn't making the biggest mistake of her life. Okay, the second biggest. Right after sleeping with the man who was taking her to national police headquarters—the last place on earth she wanted to be.

But she couldn't abandon Sofie. Would never abandon her. Not even if it mean sacrificing her own freedom.

She just prayed it wouldn't come to that. She just prayed this was all a misunderstanding.

But most of all, she prayed for the strength to resist Jean-Marc. Resist his probing questions. Resist his brooding regard. And especially, resist the promise of his touch.

She had to be firm. Or face the consequences.

Because those consequences could easily prove her undoing.

◙ 12 ◙

Jean-Marc gripped the steering wheel hard, turning his knuckles white. That way he couldn't grab Ciara and do any of the things that were parading through his mind. Like strangling her. Or shaking some sense into her. Or ripping her clothes off.

Putain de merde.

What was happening to him? To his objectivity? Hell, to his sanity? The line between professional and personal was blurring dangerously on this case, because of Ciara. He didn't like it. Not one bit. Last time that had happened—

Non. Wasn't going there. Thinking about the past would only make him crazy furious. As would thinking about how she'd gotten those bruises....

He eased his white knuckles from the steering wheel at a red light. *Business, Jean-Marc.*

"Your friend is in big trouble. If you know anything, now's the time to spill. Before it gets official and I can't help her."

"In trouble how?"

He curbed his temper. Naturally she'd go for the innocent routine. "You know the Picasso that was stolen a few days ago?"

A hesitation, then, "I heard about it."

"The thief left a fake in its place. Sofie painted it."

Her head zipped around. "How do you know that?"

Not a denial, he noted grimly. *Just as he thought.* "We'll get into that during the interrogation. For now, let's talk about why you moved out of your apartment so suddenly."

She blinked at the swift change of subject, then her gaze swiveled back toward the windshield. "I had to go. You wouldn't take no for an answer."

He snorted. "*Non?* Gee, I don't recall that part. What I remember is a

93

whole lot of yes. 'Yes, Jean-Marc. Oh, God, yes. More, harder, faster, *yes*.'"

His tight imitation of her love cries hovered in the air between them. A flush ripped across her bruised cheek.

His jaw muscle ticked. Damn, he was being an asshole. Normally that would bother him. But by this point he figured they were pretty evenly matched.

She eased out a slow breath. "That's not fair."

"Oh, and you were being fair when you left without a word?" He pulled a left-hand turn into the *Palais de Justice* parking area, showing his *carte de requisition* to the guard.

"I—"

"This doesn't have to be complicated, Ciara. I like fucking you and you like being fucked. We can play it that way if you don't want to get more involved than that." Though, God knew he did. Still. For some frustratingly unfathomable reason.

"Jesus, Jean-Marc." The red flag of her blush deepened.

"I can be good to you. And I can be useful," he said reasonably as he pulled the car into an empty spot and set the brake. He grasped her chin and forced her to look at him. "For instance, I can arrest the bastard who hit you."

"No," she whispered.

Alors. But to which part?

If they hadn't been surrounded by a score of police cars, a half dozen cops and two guards witnesses he would have leaned forward and kissed her. Thoroughly. To prove she still wanted him. To convince her to surrender again, as she had before.

"Why are you being so stubborn?" he gritted out.

"Just because I don't want to be your whore?"

He jerked back. "I offered you more. You ran away."

"Take a hint, Lacroix."

He set his jaw and let her go. "*Va te faire foutre*." He reached for the door handle. Fuck you.

Her hand on his arm stopped him. "I'm sorry. You didn't deserve that."

"Forget it. I'm obviously barking up the wrong tree."

After a slight hesitation she said, "Yes. But not for the reasons you think."

"And you're not going to enlighten me, are you?" he said mockingly. Frustration surged through his veins.

She shook her head, having the grace at least to look miserable.

"*Bon*." He didn't need this crap. Whatever was going on, he didn't want to know. As of now he was washing his hands of the whole *merdier*. "Let's go. Sofie's waiting."

He led her through security, and then on to the reception desk where he handed her a pen and made her fill out a personal info sheet.

"I want *Mademoiselle.* Alexander's street address verified before she leaves today," he told the desk officer as she started to write. "She's given me false information before," he added when she looked taken aback, and returned a flat what-did-you-expect-? smile.

He might never darken her door again, but he wanted her to know he knew exactly where her door was, and that he could walk through it and fuck her anytime he wished.

Because regardless of her outraged glare, they both knew she wouldn't stop him.

Jamming his hands in his trouser pockets, he kept the cold front going the whole way up to the interview room, refusing to meet her gaze.

Dieu. He wasn't sure he liked this new side of himself that she was bringing out. This obsessive, domineering bastard, determined to assert his power over her. He didn't approve of hypothalamic macho behavior, especially in himself. But with Ciara it was purely instinctual. Whenever he was within two meters of the woman he was reduced to a single-cell testosterone-driven beast.

Whatever. As soon as they were done with this interview, with any luck, he'd be quit of her forever and could get back to his uncomplicated paid companions. The sex might not be as good, but at least they could be relied upon.

He allowed her to sit in on the interview with Sofie. After Pierre got the tape rolling—all interviews were recorded—and took care of the preliminaries, Jean-Marc opened the folder in front of him, extracted a photo of the replacement Picasso and slid it in front of Sofie.

"Tell me about this."

"Wh-What about it?"

He folded his hands on the table and raised his voice—just slightly. He could do bad cop. "I want to know who you painted it for."

Her eyes got a little wild. "I-I didn't."

"Don't lie to me, Sofie," he said harshly. "I'm really sick of being lied to today."

Her eyes filled with tears. "Why are you doing this? You were so nice at the café." Her voice wavered convincingly.

Silently, he counted to five. "I *am* being nice. I'm giving you the opportunity to come clean." He bent forward, gazing at her earnestly. "I'm not interested in arresting you. I want the man you painted this for. Help me and you walk out of here, no other questions asked."

"But I didn't—"

Before she could get the words out, he slammed his palms on the table. She practically jumped out of her chair. Swiping up a print of the x-ray of the ghost signature from the file, he slapped it down in front of her. "Talk before I lose my patience!"

Her eyes got wide as saucers, then she turned desperately to Ciara, who was staring at the image, mouth open.

"What is this?" Ciara asked.

"It's a ghost."

The blood drained from her face, leaving it porcelain pale. "A...a what?"

Jean-Marc's eyes narrowed. This was not the reaction he'd expected.

"A ghost. Of Sofie's signature on the painting." He explained briefly what that meant. "It was discovered by our forensics team under the fake Picasso left at the Michaud's the night of the robbery. Any comment?"

Ciara glanced up at him nervously, then back to the x-ray. "It's obvious, isn't it?" she said after clearing her throat. "He's a thief. He must have stolen the picture and painted over this part himself."

"You think?" Jean-Marc said dryly. She was good on her feet, he had to give her that.

"He must have."

"Are you by any chance missing a painting?" he asked Sofie.

The girl swallowed and shook her head, looking more and more desperate to bolt. *"Non."*

"Tell me, Sofie. How many artists besides yourself do you know sign their paintings with a Hand of Fatima?"

He guessed none.

But Ciara cut in before Sofie could answer. "The Hand of Fatima is a common talisman among Middle Eastern women. Women who are often bullied and cowed by the men who think they own them." She glowered at him for a moment, then continued, "There are probably dozens of immigrant women in Paris alone who hide their talent by not signing their work. Or using a symbol such as this instead of her name."

For a moment he studied their bruises, weighing the possibilities. "To avoid a beating?"

"What?" Her eyes flared in surprise. "Yes. Or worse."

The slow burn that had simmered in his gut since seeing her battered face flared hot. "Is that what happened?" he asked.

Ciara blinked. Sofie looked puzzled.

"No. Because Sofie didn't paint this picture," Ciara repeated. "And you can't prove she did, or you'd already have arrested her." She got to her feet, pulling Sofie up by the elbow. "We're done answering your questions," she said.

With that, she marched Sofie out of the room.

◙ ◙ ◙

Ciara's high heels clacked decisively on the linoleum as they retreated to the elevator. With a sigh, Pierre formally ended the interview and punched off the recorder. "That went well."

"The girl's guilty as hell," Jean-Marc said consideringly.

"Yeah, but as the lady said, proving it might be difficult."

Jean-Marc grabbed the phone and called downstairs. "The two women I interviewed are on their way out. I want them tailed. Both of them."

"Yes, *Commissaire.*"

"You verified *Mlle.* Alexander's address?"

"Yes, sir. I did quick background checks on them, too. I put the files in your incident room."

After ejecting the cassette from the recorder, he and Pierre went directly there. He made himself pick up Sofie's file instead of Ciara's.

It was pretty thin. She'd been hauled in to a Paris nick once at age thirteen for solicitation, at which time her parents had been called, but by the time her father and uncle arrived she'd managed to slip out a side door. The reporting officer had not been impressed with her father. "A first-generation Algerian with a nasty temper who wanted his daughter back solely to punish her for disobeying and bringing shame on his name. The uncle looked like a professional wrestler. She'll probably live longer on the streets," was his conclusion. Which explained why there'd been no follow-up with Social Services.

"Wow," Pierre muttered, flipping through the other file.

"What?"

"You know she was married?"

Jean-Marc glanced up with a frown. "Sofie? She's sixteen."

"Ciara."

For a second he couldn't breathe. "What are you talking about?"

"Some petty gangster. French. Married her fourteen years ago in New York City. That's why she came to France."

Ciara was *married?* "Thirteen years?" *To a gangster?* His mind scrambled back to her apartment, before she'd skipped out. No men's things. He'd made special note of that. "I thought she was here on a student visa."

Pierre flipped some more. "Nope. Says here permanent resident permit thanks to marrying a French citizen."

She'd lied.

Oh, what a shock.

"Not exactly a model citizen, though. He was part of the Alexander crime family down south. I didn't make the connection before, her being American and all."

Jean-Marc suddenly remembered her bruises. "Where is the prick now?"

Pierre pursed his lips. "Dead. Killed ten years ago in a shoot-out with the local constabulary in Marseille."

Well, that explained her aversion to cops.

All at once, the impact of Pierre's full statement registered. Jean-Marc glanced over to the map of France on the wall. The one full of colored push-pins. He stiffened. "Marseilles?"

"Mmm-hmm. He had quite a rap sheet. Robbery, extortion, car theft, assault."

Robbery... Theft.

"Marseilles?"

And we know where he's from...

A horrible thought crept into Jean-Marc's head. His brain spun with it, making him dizzy. Ten years ago in Marseille... A petty criminal being killed by the police could easily make that man's wife start down the same path....

I'm not who you think I am.

Non. This was crazy. Insane.

Pierre looked up. At once aware. "Yeah, Marseille. What about it?"

I'm barking up the wrong tree. Yes. But not for the reasons you think.

Jean-Marc's whole body went weightless, as though he'd just jumped out of a jet with no parachute.

Airless. Suffocating.

Shaking.

Two plus two always adds up to four. Now tell me what you're doing that's illegal.

"Does it say when she moved to Paris?" he asked. Praying just once his cop instincts would be wrong.

That it wasn't what he was thinking.

She was a woman, he reminded himself.

He'd fucked her.

She couldn't...

"Hmm."

He stood boneless while Pierre looked through the papers in the file.

"She has to register every year with immigration," Pierre murmured, drawing out the words. "Here it is. First mention of Paris was...nine years ago."

Nine years ago.

Jean-Marc's disbelieving gaze was drawn inexorably back to the map of Europe.

He moved to Paris nine years ago. Started out snatching purses and lifting wallets on the train and métro. Eight years ago he switched to silver and jewelry, started refining his craft.

Jesus.

"At the apartment this evening," he said in a controlled voice. "Did you ask the landlord when Sofie and the other kids had moved in there?"

Pierre consulted his pocket notebook. "Ciara's the one on the lease. She rented it four years ag—" Suddenly his eyes widened and darted to Jean-Marc's. "Whoa. *Mec.* Surely, you don't think—" Pierre swore softly at his expression.

Putain. Putain de fucking merde.

But he *did* think.

The bottom fell out of his stomach. Totally.

He was so screwed.

"Pierre. It's her."

"*Non.* Seriously, *mec.* It's not possible."

But it was possible. It all fit. The timing. Her lowlife husband giving her the skills. The Orphans giving her the reason. Her being at the disco. Even the old lady. The facial recognition software had been right all along. Suddenly he realized what had been bothering him about that old lady. He'd seen her leave the soiree soon after arriving...in the same car that moments before had had a flat tire. Driven by a chauffeur who looked amazingly like one of the boys at the apartment on rue Daguerre.

Jean-Marc had been played for a fool. Again.

"It's her," he growled. "I'd bet my life on it. Ciara Alexander is *le Revenant.*"

▣ 13 ▣

Words couldn't begin to describe the rage that burned in Jean-Marc's chest at Ciara's betrayal.

Duped. By a thief. *Again.*

How the hell gullible *was* he?

He bowed his head and gripped his temples with unsteady fingers, unable to look Pierre in the eye.

"It's not your fault," Pierre said, ever the faithful friend.

"What's not my fault? Fucking my prime suspect?"

"She wasn't a suspect when you fucked her. Wasn't even on the radar."

"But I should have known."

"How?"

He dropped his fingers and drilled them through his hair. "I didn't have to pay her."

Pierre regarded him long and hard. "That is so screwed up I'm not even going to address it. Get a grip. You really think Ciara's *le Revenant*?"

"Not a doubt in my mind."

"So what are you going to do about it?"

The fury in his heart prodded him like tiny demons with sharp pitchforks. The woman was toast.

He swiped up his suit jacket. "Think I'll go and pay our illusive Ghost a little visit."

▣ ▣ ▣

It took a couple of hours to calm Sofie down to the point where Ciara could leave the Orphans' apartment. The girl had been hysterical from the time they'd left 36 Quai des Orfèvres until Davie had finally managed to

100

coax a half tumbler of cognac down her throat a while ago.

"I'm so sorry I signed the picture by mistake and painted over it," she'd wailed over and over. "I had no idea they could do that with x-rays. And now he knows! He knows it was *me* who painted that fake Picasso!"

"It doesn't matter what he knows," Ciara maintained patiently. "What counts is what he can *prove*. And he can prove nothing. As long as we stick to our story we'll be fine."

Eventually she'd convinced Sofie that Jean-Marc could not arrest them.

Now all she had to do was convince herself.

Damn.

She dragged herself up the six flights to the top floor apartment on rue Germain Pilon in the Pigalle she'd rented a few days earlier. She'd vowed never to live up here again, but unfortunately it was the only place she'd been able to find on such short notice. She waved tiredly to the landlady who lurked in the shabby doorway watching her with a suspicious frown.

She should have paid more attention. But her face had started to throb and her lower back ached and all she could think of was the ancient claw-foot bathtub that had been the only bright spot about renting the dilapidated walk-up with peeling wallpaper and rotting window frames she now called home.

She sighed with relief as she reached the door and inserted her skeleton key into the ridiculous sham that passed for a lock and turned it.

"That was some performance," a familiar male voice said behind her. A voice crackling with the kind of white-hot anger that could incinerate a body in its tracks.

She whirled, barely stifling a scream as he stepped out of the shadows of the hallway. "Jean-Marc! What are you doing here?"

He didn't answer. Just smiled. Like a serpent.

She took a step back. "What do you want?"

The smile stretched. But not to his eyes. Not even close.

Something was different about him. He seemed harder. Sharper. More...ruthless. He looked like he wanted to take her apart and eat her for supper. Or...maybe kill her.

Fear, sudden and immobilizing, zinged through her.

Oh, God.

He knew. *About her.*

"Are you going to invite me in, Ciara?"

She shook her head. Unable to utter a word.

No. Not inside. *Not inside her apartment. Not inside her.*

He tugged the key from her trembling fingers and unlocked the door, swinging it wide. Silently he held it open for her and waited.

She didn't move. How had he found her?

"What's the matter, *mon ange*? Afraid of something I might find?"

"L-Like what?" she stammered.

He shrugged easily, but it was far from a casual gesture. Every muscle in his body was tense, his gaze on her hawk-like. "Jewelry. Silver. Paintings. Money."

Her heart literally stopped in her chest. Stupid as it was, she'd hoped she was wrong. But his description left no room for doubt.

When her heart started up again, it felt heavy, painful, in her chest. She wanted to sink to the floor and weep. Not because she'd been found out. But because it was Jean-Marc who'd done it.

She forced a laugh. "Hardly," she said, gathering every bit of strength within her. As much as it would kill her to lie to him, she had to deny everything. It would do neither her nor the Orphans any good if she just rolled over and meekly went off to prison. "If I had jewels and money, would I be living in a dump like this?" she asked, gesturing at the surroundings. It was a definite step down, even from her postage-stamp Latin Quarter apartment.

Something flitted through his eyes. Doubt?

Yeah, right.

"In that case," he said, "you won't mind if I have a look around?"

She took a deep breath and strolled into the single room of the studio. "Knock yourself out."

He wouldn't find anything. There was nothing to find. Certainly none of the stuff he was looking for. After switching apartments the other day, she'd even rented a locker at a local gym to keep her wigs and makeup and disguises in. This place was clean. As had been the Orphans apartment on rue Daguerre when they searched it earlier.

Even so, her nerves were nearly in shreds by the time he'd finished examining every nook and cranny of the three-hundred year-old artist's garret—every cupboard, behind every piece of furniture, even popping the windows open to look around outside them.

If possible, he was even more furious when he ran out of places to tear apart. Luckily she didn't have a lot of possessions to put back in place.

He stalked up to where she was nervously sitting, planted his hands on the chair arms and leaned into her face. "You're a very clever woman. But I take betrayal very personally. I *will* find evidence and put you behind bars, if it's the last thing I do."

She shrank away from the disgust in his tone. "Who's betraying whom here?" she muttered.

His eyes narrowed. "Nice try, baby. But if you thought seducing me would keep you out of prison, you've made a big mistake."

"Jean-Marc, it was you who seduced me," she reminded him, stilling her shaking hands. "If you'll recall, from the night we met I did everything I could to stay away from you."

His jaw clenched. "And now I know why. Because you are *le Revenant*."

There it was, out in the open. Her pulse sped.

"No. Because I knew we would end badly. Please believe me, Jean-Marc. Whatever you think I've done, betraying you was never part of the plan. I would never betray someone I...like."

He wheeled back. "Do *not* pull that crap on me, Ciara. This situation is bad enough without pretending we're any kind of friends."

She gave up and closed her eyes, leaning her head back on the uneven stuffing of the easy chair. "No. And I guess lovers doesn't count."

She could hear his breaths, shallow and harsh, and felt the air crackle with tension around them. He was still standing close, practically touching her knees. The musky, acrid smell of him, of his anger, nearly choked her with the need to reach out to him.

But it was over between them. Now that he knew.

Wasn't it?

She opened her eyes and saw him staring down at her, his expression savage. Desire, potent and irrational, raced through her.

"Are you insane?" he spat, eyes flaring. "You think I'm going to fuck you again? When I know who you are, *what* you are?"

"Do you?" she softly challenged. "Know who I am?"

Did anyone? Anyone on earth?

Bald disbelief washed through his expression. He spun and paced away, then turned back to her. The skin of his throat was mottled red beneath the black stubble. "I do. You're a thief! And that's all that matters."

But...he was getting hard.

The fine wool fabric of his suit trousers stretched and distorted over his lengthening arousal. She felt herself grow damp between her legs.

Okay, yeah. She *was* insane.

"Is it?" she managed. "All that matters?" She stood, and mutely dared him to come closer. Taunting his outrage.

Playing with fire.

"You don't care—" *his wrath was woven tight with incredulity* "—that I'd throw you in jail in a hot minute?"

"I wouldn't respect you if you didn't do your job," she said.

And suddenly she realized it was true. She would hate him if he turned out to be another Beck, corrupt and immoral. Better to land in prison than fall for scum.

God, was she falling for him? She attempted a smile. Failed.

His mouth opened, then snapped shut. "I don't fucking believe this."

Frankly, neither did she.

He shook a finger at her. "You," he said, stalking past her, "can forget it." With that, he swept out the door, slamming it behind him.

She stood perfectly still for a long time, half expecting him to come crashing back in, grab her, fling her to the floor and...

Wishful thinking, obviously. Or mental illness.

Well, at least now she didn't have to come up with any more lame excuses. She wouldn't have to avoid him. Because next time she saw him he'd probably be putting her in handcuffs.

And unfortunately, it wouldn't be for a night of kinky sex.

▣ ▣ ▣

As it happened, the next time Ciara saw Jean-Marc was the very next morning. She was astonished to find him propping up the building across the street, watching her door. And although his handcuffs were displayed prominently in their case on the front of his belt, he didn't make a move for them when he spotted her coming out.

"What are you doing here?" she asked, marching across the narrow street to confront him.

"Waiting for you." His sharp-angled face was neutral, his fury from last night gone. Or at least carefully hidden away.

"Why?"

He unpropped himself. "I'm tailing you."

"Tailing me." She regarded him with a spike of annoyance.

"Everywhere you go, I go." He smiled. The serpent was back. "I happen to know your last job didn't come off quite as expected. And it's still your time of month."

"Ex*cuse* me?"

His teeth gleamed in the morning sun. "To steal something. Rent due? Bills piling up? Eh?"

His smug, arrogant attitude made her want to kick him. Good thing she wasn't a violent person. She thought about Beck's threats and clenched her still-tender jaw. *He was a cop*, she reminded herself. He wouldn't care about that.

"*Va te faire foutre*," she suggested tartly, raising his eyebrow.

She turned on a toe and stalked off toward boulevard de Clichy, the main tourist area in this arrondissement. She had things to do, but not with Jean-Marc's shadow glued to her ass.

Half an hour later, she emerged from the maze of souvenir shops, triple-X theaters and sex boutiques minus one arrogant tail. *Take that*, she thought, sliding on the hat and pair of sunglasses that she always kept in her oversized handbag. She trotted down the steps of the entrance to the *métro*. Luckily she'd put on heavy make-up that morning to disguise her bruised face. Nothing made a woman more noticeable to others than potential abuse.

Making a quick decision, she got off at the la Chapelle stop and walked through the tunnel to Gare du Nord. Around the corner there was a no-questions-asked business that did mail-forwarding and rented out lockers. There she kept with an envelope of fake IDs, a wig, extra tools and a small amount of money, again for emergencies. After extracting a driver's license with a different name, the tools and a hundred euro in cash, she used her Swiss account's debit card to buy a ticket for the Thalys train going north to Brussels.

As annoying as he was, Jean-Marc had hit the nail on the head. Rent and tuition were due in a few days, taking up nearly all of the money the princess's bracelet had brought in. Hugo's new job barely paid for food, let alone make a dent in Beck's blackmail. Neither Valois nor Davie had come up with anything more profitable yet. Fencing few good pieces of jewelry would hopefully stave off Beck for now. She needed a fast lay-down—outside of Jean-Marc's jurisdiction.

A favorite with daytrippers from Belgium and Germany, the high-speed Thalys train to Brussels was usually liberally sprinkled with ladies toting newly-acquired Hermès luggage stuffed with expensive designer fashions—jewelry included. Not that train work wasn't tricky. Most people kept their real valuables in the overhead compartment by their seat, only leaving their larger, unwieldy suitcases in the communal rack by the door. So striking on the train itself was unproductive. Instead, she'd pick out a couple of promising targets and hang around the taxi stand to overhear where they were staying in Brussels, then hit one of the hotel rooms later in the afternoon or evening while the lady went out for a meal or more shopping.

Unless you had an inside accomplice, hotel jobs were only slightly easier than the train. Which was why she almost always avoided them. Hotels had plain clothes security and cameras; maids and maintenance people were everywhere. It was a real measure of her desperation that she was taking the risk now. But she had no choice.

Settling into her plush seat with a good view of the communal luggage rack, Ciara surreptitiously studied the single women who stowed cases there as they came onboard, looking for a likely candidate who matched her own size. The pretty boho skirt and blouse she'd put on this morning were cute, but she'd stand out like a sore thumb in the rarified atmosphere of the upscale Brussels hotel her potential mark would no doubt be staying in.

There. A slim blonde wearing this season's Donna Karan. Nothing too flashy, but definitely classy. Ciara watched with satisfaction as the blonde stowed her Louis Vuitton rolling bag and sashayed down the aisle to the far end of the car where she had a club seat facing the opposite direction. Perfect.

After waiting until the blonde had settled in, Ciara nonchalantly went and pulled the suitcase off the rack, and slipped into the tiny restroom across from it. Moments later she came out wearing the wig she'd grabbed from her locker, along with a soft lilac silk suit from Chanel and matching kitten heels that were only a tad loose. From her fingers dangled a gold handled Ponte Vecchio shopping bag which contained her own clothes and purse. Sliding the Louis Vuitton back into the luggage rack, she casually made her way through the connecting door into the next car. Easing a breath from her backed-up lungs, she took her time strolling through the other first class cars, scoping out the ladies most likely to have jewelry worth stealing.

She wasn't disappointed. By the time the train pulled into Bruxelles Midi station, she'd picked out four older, obviously wealthy candidates.

One was met on the platform by a husband and whisked off. One hurried toward another track and got on a connecting train. But the other two went straight to the taxi stand. One of them gave the driver the name of a grand, aristocratic old hotel—which still used real keys instead of cards with magnetic strips.

Ciara's choice was made.

◙ 14 ◙

After following the woman's taxi to the hotel, Ciara perused the brochure rack until she'd registered, then preceded her into the elevator and got out on the same floor. Exchanging a friendly nod, she noted the woman's room number, then as soon as the door was closed went back to the elevator and returned to the lobby, carefully checking the locations of the security cameras as she went.

In the lobby she cast about for a lounge bar with a good view of things, where she could sit and read the novel she'd picked up on the train and wait for the woman to come down.

She'd just finished a quick lunch when her mark rushed into the lobby and straight into the arms of a grey-haired, distinguished-looking gentleman. The woman had changed into a gorgeous Roberto Cavalli day dress, which probably meant a leisurely luncheon for the couple, and enough time for Ciara to safely complete her task.

She had one more cup of coffee just in case the woman had forgotten something, then strode purposefully back to the elevator and went straight up to the room, keeping her head down and face averted from the security cameras. She pulled on her gloves. The lock wasn't an easy type to pick, but Valois had taught her well. After several pulse-pounding moments she heard the distinctive *snick* of the cylinders yielding. She slid into the room and closed the door behind her, heart thundering with nerves and adrenaline.

Turning on the light, she went for the suitcases. Nothing but clothes. Lots of them. Expensive. She quickly checked the dresser drawers. Bingo. Bottom drawer. A small jewelry case was tucked in back. She grabbed it;

emptied it onto the bed. And let out a low whistle.

Jackpot. The real thing. Emeralds and opals. Antique mine-cut rubies. Several high quality pieces of amber in thick gold settings. A magnificent pair of diamond earrings with matching pendant.

She lifted the pendant. It was a huge pear-shaped diamond, as were the earrings, in a surprisingly plain setting. Newish.

Ciara tamped down a prickle of guilt. Normally, she carefully researched her jobs in advance so she only took recently acquired pieces. People tended to make a lot bigger fuss over missing heirlooms than impulse baubles. She could be fairly certain this woman was insured to the hilt, but...some of her pieces were obviously old. No doubt treasured possessions.

After a minute of inner struggle—conscience against necessity—she sorted the jewelry into two piles. Old and new, according to style. Dumping the pile of old pieces back into the case, she snapped it shut and surveyed what was left.

A nice set of emeralds in modern settings, a gorgeous fire opal ring and, thankfully, the diamonds. She scooped the lot into her handbag, then put the case back into the drawer. With luck the woman wouldn't notice anything was missing until the next day. Or the day after.

Steeling her pulsing nerves, she slipped out the room and strode from the hotel at a businesslike clip. Hailing a taxi, she checked her watch. If she hurried, she'd be home well before *Valois Vieilli* closed for the day.

After which she'd have to face the wrath of a frustrated *Commissaire* Lacroix. She couldn't help a grim smile. He didn't know her very well if he'd thought following her would intimidate her, or deter her from what she had to do.

Next time it may prove a bit more difficult to elude him. But she still had a few tricks up her sleeve. Meanwhile, he'd likely be waiting for her when she got home, prepared to give her the third degree.

Whatever. He could ask all the questions he wanted, and search her from head to toe. But he wouldn't find anything.

When the train pulled back into the Gare du Nord in Paris, she carefully threw her ripped up train tickets into a trash basket several tracks down from where she'd arrived, and her thrift store gloves in another. Then she found a phone and called Valois.

"The shop is being watched," he warned before she could say anything but hello.

Damn. "Can you meet me?"

"The usual place?"

"How soon can you get away?"

"Right now."

She let out a sigh of relief, and silently blessed Valois's father and the war for providing him with the secret tunnel along with a hidden grated entrance several blocks away. He rarely used it, but it did occasionally come in handy.

She had a feeling it would be coming in handy more and more as Jean-Marc increased the pressure.

She really had to get out of this business.

For the millionth time she went over in her mind how much longer she'd have to maintain her illegal activities. Hugo was already working and contributing to the household. Next would be Ricardo, who'd be graduating from cooking school this fall, and CoCo, who was finishing up her nursing assistant courses in the spring. Between the three of them, at that point they would be able to take care of all the Orphans' expenses, except for Sofie and Davie's tuition. Which would be a tremendous burden lifted from Ciara's shoulders.

If only they could somehow make Beck go away, she might actually have a shot at a normal life soon.

After returning her ID, wig and tools to the locker, she found a restroom, peeled out of the beautiful lilac Chanel suit and shoes, and put her own outfit back on. Using a tissue, she wiped the slick gold bag of fingerprints, then folded the suit into it. She washed her hands at the sink, then walked back to the station. It didn't take her long to find what she was looking for.

A young woman about her own size wearing a threadbare dress sat on a wooden bench next to a battered suitcase. A small child played with a rag doll at her feet. Ciara went over and held out the gold bag to her.

"Please," she said. "I'd like you to have this."

The woman looked up uncomprehendingly. "*Pardon?*"

She answer, but smiled brilliantly, patted the child on the head and walked away, heading for the *métro*. Once there, she found a seat, gave herself and her handbag a thorough check, just to make sure no evidence remained of her day's work—other than the jewels nestling at the bottom of the purse.

Valois was waiting for her on their usual bench by the Pompidou Center. He rose as she approached, and greeted her with a hug and a kiss on each cheek. She slipped the jewels into his jacket pocket.

"If we make this quick," he said with a grin, "the idiot watching the shop will never know I'm gone."

"Sounds good," she said, returning his smile. "Well, I guess we'll have to be careful contacting each other from now on. For some reason, *Commissaire* Lacroix has gotten it into his head that I am *le Revenant.*"

Valois's eyes registered shock. "He accused you? To your face?"

She nodded, and he gave a low curse. A flock of pigeons at their feet took wing, flying in a circle before swooping down on the other side of the square.

"You should probably deposit my whole cut into the Swiss account this time," she said. "I don't want to be caught with a lot of cash."

"*D'accord.* I'll leave a message at Café Constantinople for you when it's done."

She sat down on the bench. "Beck is getting nasty about his money, Valois. Have you come up with anything yet?"

"I think so. How do you feel about Italy?"

"Good food and disorganized cops," she said wryly. "Works for me. Tell me about it."

He sat next to her and talked in a low voice as she closed her eyes and tipped her face into the fading sunlight. It was still warm, a perfect late summer day in Paris. The job sounded good. A small but outstanding collection of silver items, collected for a nouveau riche novelist by her greedy, but discerning, interior designer.

Valois handed Ciara a slip of paper with an address written on it. "I've arranged for shipment to Paris by a colleague in Milan."

"Excellent." That would make the train ride home much less stressful. She took a moment to memorize the address, then tore up the paper and tossed it into the silver metal basket next to the bench.

She rose. "Thanks, Valois. You're the best."

He shook his head. "You be very careful, *ma petite. Commissaire* Lacroix could be a big problem."

He had no idea.

She said more firmly than she felt, "Don't worry. I can handle Lacroix."

She just wished she truly believed that. But the truth was, she was starting to feel the walls close in on her. Jean-Marc was smart. He was persistent. And he had a bug up his butt about her. Not a good combination.

She couldn't go to jail. If she did, what would happen to the Orphans? Somehow she had to think of a way to knock Jean-Marc off his game. Mislead him. Or distract him.

Maybe she should reconsider enlisting his help in dealing with Beck. If Beck went away, maybe, just maybe, she could quit while she was still ahead, and officially retire *le Revenant.*

Life wouldn't be easy if she stopped stealing. Nor would she be able to finish her own education. She could forget about her dream of being a translator. Unskilled with no degree, she'd have to take what she could get. But at least she wouldn't be in jail.

And since when had life ever been easy?

Suddenly, she wondered how she'd ever gotten sucked into this loser lifestyle... Why had she never questioned it before? While Etienne was alive, it had all seemed natural and inevitable—after all his whole family was involved in criminal activity. But after he was gone, why had she taken the easy way out instead of doing what she knew in her heart to be the right thing? Sure, her motives were pure—keeping the Orphans on the straight and narrow. Without stealing, there would have been no way to help them as she had. But was that really an excuse?

She walked home deep in thought. And came to a decision.

At their inevitable confrontation tonight, she'd bring it up with Jean-Marc. See what he had to say. Ask if he could help her deal with Beck. Help her find a better solution.

It was with a much lighter step that she skipped up the steps from the *métro* and walked the few blocks to her apartment.

He would help her. She knew he would.

As she approached her building, she spotted a police car parked at the curb; a lone figure sat behind the wheel. Her heart leapt. She ran the last few steps and thrust her head down to the open window.

"Jean-Marc! I'm so glad you're here. I need to—" He turned toward her and her words choked off with a gasp.

The man was not Jean-Marc.

▣ 15 ▣

"There's a call for you, *Commissaire*." The bored voice of the dispatcher crackled across the police radio in Jean-Marc's Saab. "A woman. She sounds a bit hysterical if you ask me."

Irritated, Jean-Marc stretched his back, wincing at the sharp bite of muscles popping. Hell. Whatever this was, he did not want to deal with it right now. It had been a long, frustrating day and it didn't appear to be ending anytime soon. "Isn't there anyone else who can take it?" he asked. "What about Pierre?"

"She asked for you by name, sir."

He sighed in resignation. "Fine. Patch it through."

"Jean-Marc? Are you there?"

He ground his jaw at the sound of Ciara's voice. But his initial anger was stalled by the fact that something was obviously wrong. She *did* sound hysterical.

"Are you all right?" he demanded. And immediately regretted it. Her welfare was of no concern to him. Especially after what she'd put him through today.

"You've got to get over here! Please, Jean-Marc, right now!"

And yet, he couldn't help himself. "Where are you? What's going on, Ciara?"

"He's after me. I'm afraid—" There was a loud pounding in the background, and a man yelling. "I'm hiding in my landlady's apartment. He's trying to break down the door!"

Jean-Marc was already turning the Saab in the direction of her apartment. Not exactly the way he'd envisioned picking up her trail again

112

after she'd ditched him that morning. "Is it the guy who beat you up?"

"Yes," she said. "Hurry!" Then the line went dead.

Putain. He grabbed a portable cherry and reached up through the window, smacking it onto his car roof at the same time he hit the siren. With the crazy Paris rush hour traffic it would take forever to get to her place. He hailed the dispatcher again and yelled at her to divert any nearby police units to rue Germain Pilan. Hopefully someone would get there in time to catch the bastard before he did any harm.

Fifteen harrowing, stress-filled minutes later Jean-Marc roared up to her building. Three police cars were already pulled up front, yellow and blue lights flashing off the smooth sand-colored stone. He sprinted out, seeking Ciara's blond hair among the knot of policemen. He finally spotted her standing to one side, ramrod straight, lips pressed together and arms tightly banded across her midriff.

"Let me through," he commanded, pushing his way past the curious neighbors and passersby. He flashed his carte at the officers. "Did you get him?" he asked without taking his sights off Ciara.

At his voice, her head jerked around. Relief flew across her face for a brief second, then her eyes filled with uncertainty. She didn't move.

"No one to get," one of the cops replied in answer to his question. "Whoever it was, he was gone before the first car arrived. The old lady—" he pointed at the plump landlady with salt and pepper hair who was talking a mile a minute, gesturing animatedly to another officer "—she doesn't know who it was. The young one—" he pointed to Ciara "—isn't talking. Says she'll only speak to you."

For a moment Jean-Marc let the war rage freely within him. He wanted to shake her and shout at her at the top of his lungs, he wanted to slap her in handcuffs and throw her in jail for a hundred years. He wanted to murder the man who was doing this to her.

He wanted to take her home and fuck her.

He never wanted to see her again.

"All right," he said to the first cop. "You guys write it up and do your thing." He bobbed his head at Ciara— "I'll take her statement and—"

"But she's *our* witness," a third officer, a swarthy, plug-shaped man, protested.

"She's not much of a witness if she's not talking," Jean-Marc shot back, not in the mood for interdepartmental bickering. "I'll forward her statement to you." He handed the first cop a business card and took one of his. "Get in the car," he ordered Ciara.

She obeyed without saying a word, keeping her eyes to the sidewalk. The swarthy officer made a move to follow, then halted with fists clenched when the other man put a restraining hand on his shoulder.

Jean-Marc pulled the Saab out with a squeal of tires and blasted his siren to stop traffic so he could get away from there.

She winced, but still didn't say anything. Not until a good five minutes later when they were stuck in the choke of rush hour traffic on boulevard de Clichy and he did nothing to extract them from it. He had no idea where to take her, so he was just driving, letting the flow of traffic carry them along as he tried to compose himself and quell the voices in his head.

"You're angry with me," she murmured.

He glared at her but didn't reply. Angry didn't come close.

"I'm sorry about this morning," she murmured.

He bit his tongue. How many years would he get for strangling her? Hell, a judge would probably go easy on him. Catching *le Revenant* had to count for something. Did the courts do dead or alive anymore?

"Thank you for coming for me," she murmured.

Coming for her...

Fuck.

He knew *that* wasn't remotely what she meant, but already he could feel his traitorous cock lengthen and harden. His capricious member could care less that she was a notorious felon wanted by every law enforcement agency in France. It still wanted to ram itself into her wet heat and take its pleasure between her silken thighs. Come for her. Fuck.

He swallowed, gripping the steering wheel tighter.

"Thank God the other cops got there quickly," she said. "I don't know what he might have done—"

Jean-Marc made a concerted effort to focus. "I want his name," he interrupted. His voice came out as a harsh, low growl.

She blanched. He watched her pretty lips part a fraction, then close again.

The same lips he'd laved with his. Lips that had kissed him back with such ardor. Lips that had glided slowly up his cock and taken him between them, and—

"Beck," she said reluctantly. "Louis Beck."

He shifted in his seat in frustration. Scowled. "What does he want?" he gritted out. Praying it wasn't her. Because then he really would have to strangle them both.

"He wants money."

That finally pried his attention off his dick. He turned to her. "Explain."

She fiddled with her purse strap for a moment, as though deciding what or how much to tell him.

"Damn it, Ciara. Tell me *everything* right now or I swear I'll tie you to a stake and let him—"

"Jesus, Jean-Marc. Don't even joke about that."

"Who's joking?"

His expression must have convinced her just how close to the edge he was. "All right," she said. "All right. He wants Sofie. He didn't appreciate it when I took her off the streets."

"Where does the money come in?"

"He's threatened to tell her father where she lives if she doesn't spread her legs for him. Either that, or pay him an outrageous blackmail. Fifteen thousand. The first is not an option. And the second..." Her words trailed off.

"Have you reported this to the cops?" was his first reaction.

Again she hesitated.

He hit the steering wheel with his fist and swerved the Saab out of traffic and to the curb. "Fuck it, Ciara! You're the one who called me. Spill it—all of it—or get out!"

His anger echoed through the small confines of the vehicle and she seemed to sink deeper into the leather of her seat, looking unhappily down at her fingers.

"I can't," she said quietly. "He *is* a cop."

◘ ◘ ◘

Outside the car, horns blared, delivery vans rumbled, pedestrians clattered along the sidewalks speaking loudly to each other to be heard above the din of traffic. Inside, the silence was absolute. At least for the handful of seconds it took for Jean-Marc to respond to Ciara's obviously unexpected confession.

She flinched when his snort of disbelief finally came. "You're telling me a *cop* beat you up? That a *cop* is blackmailing a sixteen year-old girl for sex or money?"

She should have known he wouldn't believe her. Hell, who could blame him? It wasn't like she had the highest credibility on the planet. Especially with him. Still, he might at least listen to her story.

"Yes," she said. "That's exactly what I'm telling you."

He stared at her, his eyes narrowing slightly in blatant skepticism.

He really *didn't* believe her.

How would he react if she told him Beck had been there, pretending to be one of the responding officers, and had even spoken to him? He'd probably turn the car around and confront him. And believe Beck's lies when the bastard claimed complete innocence. And if she thought Beck was angry now, that would really set him off. But not until later, when Jean-Marc couldn't help her. Or Sofie.

Lord, how could she *ever* have thought Jean-Marc would help her expose a fellow cop's corruption? Cops were cops, and they stuck together. She must be completely delusional. With a sigh, she reached for the car door handle.

"*Don't,*" he said, the single barked word making her jump. She jerked her hand back.

He studied her cheeks, his gaze penetrating below the layer of makeup that covered her bruises. His hand snaked over and lightly drew the hem of her skirt up over her knees. His fingers hovered above the scabs there. Her body shivered, knowing his touch wasn't sexual but wishing to God it were. She squeezed her eyes shut. *Insanity.*

"What *préfecture* is he in?" he asked.

Damn, she regretted calling him. Why hadn't she listened to Hugo and Valois? No good would come of pulling Jean-Marc into this. He'd admitted he hated her for what she did, for who she was. God...maybe he'd even join up with Beck, in order to force her to turn herself in! He knew how she felt about Sofie, and could easily use that knowledge against her.

Because of her misguided feelings for this man, she'd left herself totally vulnerable to him, in nearly every way.

"Maybe," she said uneasily, "it would be better if you don't get involved. We can deal with Beck ourselves."

"How?" His gaze bored through her misgivings. "How are you going to deal with Beck, Ciara?" His voice was eerily soft.

She licked her lips. She could practically hear the possibilities running through his head. Would le *Revenant* steal even more so she could pay Beck off? Or maybe she'd sacrifice Sofie...? Perhaps sacrifice herself?

Damned if she did, damned if she didn't.

Hell, she was damned no matter what, and she knew it.

"I'll find a way," she said, and reached for the door again. "I shouldn't have called you. I'm sorry."

His firm grip halted her escape. "Ciara."

She looked up at him. For the first time that day truly looked at him. The fury was still there in his eyes, but it was tempered by something else. Something that gazed back at her with frustration and...longing?

Could she be wrong about him?

"Where did you go this morning?" he asked coldly. Smacking her right out of that nice little fantasy world.

She lifted her chin. "I had errands. I didn't want company."

"What kind of errands? Where?"

She didn't think so. Her chin went up even more. "Am I under arrest?"

He didn't answer. His face didn't move a muscle.

"In that case, I'll be going," she said, but then added, "Thank you for the rescue, Jean-Marc. I know..." She shook her head and this time succeeded in opening the door. She unclipped her seat belt.

He took it from her and clipped it back in, reaching over her to slam the door shut. "I'm driving you home."

Despite her misgivings, she didn't argue. She recognized his tone of voice. It was the one that didn't brook any compromise.

Against her will, her nipples spiraled, her body turned on by his almost casual air of power and authority. She looked away from him, mortified by her unbidden reaction.

Neither of them spoke during the stop-and-go return trip to her apartment. The other police had left by the time he pulled up to the curb in front of her door. She hurried out of the car as fast as she could. So she wouldn't make a fool of herself. Maybe invite him up.

The passenger window glided down and he called after her, "Ciara." She stopped and looked over her shoulder, heart beating fast. "Don't think," he said, "that this changes anything. I'm going to be all over you like a bad smell. Eventually I'll catch *le Revenant* red-handed, and then I'm going to put you in jail. Don't doubt it for a minute."

How could she when he kept reminding her?

She felt the sudden hot sting of tears behind her eyes, and turned away again. Walked away from him, hurried into the building, and ran up the stairs.

She knew her time had run out. It was too late to change her fate.

She'd made her bed. And now she had to lie in it.

Alone.

◨ ◨ ◨

Jean-Marc met with Pierre in the office at 7:00 am the next morning to talk strategy.

"We're changing priorities," he told him. "Now that we know who *le Revenant* is, our main goal is obtaining good, hard evidence to prove it."

Pierre regarded him. To his credit, his face held only concern, not skepticism...or all-out incredulity. "You're that sure it's her?"

Jean-Marc sighed. "She didn't deny it, Pierre. Didn't even try. If I accused you to your face of being this thief, wouldn't you tell me I'm wrong?"

Pierre pursed his lips. "Daresay I would."

"There are too many connections to her. They can't all be coincidence."

"Okay. So let's assume it's her. What do we do? How do we get evidence?"

"I've put a tail on her. Day and night. And I'm going to make myself visible, so she knows I'm watching her. Crank up the pressure. Sooner or later she'll slip up and give us something to work with."

"Like a clue to where she gets her intel, or the fence she's working with?"

"Exactly that kind of thing. She's too smart to let me catch her in the act. But we're smart enough not to need that for a conviction. I want you to find out everything you can about Ciara Alexander. Friends, family, jobs. Financials, school records. I want to know about every place she's ever been, every person she's ever spoken to, every breath she's ever taken."

Pierre raised a brow. "Every lover she's ever had?"

An unexpected coil of possessiveness tightened around Jean-Marc's groin, but he ignored it. "Only if she speaks or breathes when she's with him."

"Marc, are you sure about—"

"I'm sure," he bit out savagely. "This one's not getting away."

Not like that other thief who'd made a fool of him. Catching *le Revenant* would do much to erase the blight on Jean-Marc's professional reputation the incident five years earlier had left. But if he didn't get her... Well, a photo of them together had already been splashed all over the tabloids. He may as well retire to the South Pole now, as go through the professional humiliation her escape would engender for him, both within the ranks of the DCPJ and among journalists seeking a sensational story. That would *not* happen again.

Pierre nodded. "I understand how badly you want this." He paused. "There's another way we could try, you know," he said, glancing up. Looking just the slightest bit uncomfortable.

Jean-Marc stilled. Somehow knowing in his gut he wasn't going to like what Pierre was about to suggest. Whatever it was.

"Yes?"

"Those kids of hers," Pierre said slowly. "We could get one of them to flip on her."

◻ ◻ ◻

Jean-Marc was still chewing over Pierre's suggestion an hour later as he climbed the stairs to Ciara's apartment.

He'd gaped at his partner after he'd spoken, letting the distasteful idea float disembodied about the office for several seconds before forcing himself to face it head on. Then he'd said just two words before stalking out the door.

"Do it."

It was a totally fucked up plan, even if it was standard police procedure. He knew how Ciara felt about those Orphans, as she liked to call them. They were like her own children. They were her good reason and her bad excuse for doing what she was doing. She loved those kids. And he was a fucking prick for even contemplating deliberately turning one of them against her. She'd take it hard. She'd feel incredibly betrayed.

Kind of like him.

Alors, merde. He was a cop, he reminded himself. And she knew the goddamn score. He'd be a fool not to use every bit of ammunition at his disposal to put *le Revenant* behind bars.

And he would. Better believe he would.

He raised his fist and banged on Ciara's door, adjusting the bag under his left arm. And waited. He knew she was home from the officer doing surveillance. Jean-Marc checked his watch. Late sleeper. He banged again.

After several minutes, her groggy voice asked, *"Qui est là?"*

"C'est moi."

He heard a sigh. "Go away."

"Let me in, Ciara."

"I'm not dressed."

"Since when does that matter? I've brought coffee."

Another sigh. But this time the door opened. "You really are annoyingly persistent."

"That's why they pay me the big bucks," he said, attempting to step past her into the apartment. He felt surprisingly calm. Not at all like he was there to ruin the life of a woman he'd much rather be getting to know better.

Correction: she'd already ruined her own life. He was just there to dole out consequences.

She blocked his way. "What makes you in your wildest dreams think I'll let you in?" she asked grumpily. She looked delightfully sleep-rumpled, all warm, wrinkly pajamas and tousled hair. "You've made it abundantly clear what you have in mind for my future. I'd have to be a fool—"

He steeled himself against her homey girl-next-door image. *She was a thief. He was a cop.* "During my search I noticed you were out of coffee," he said calmly, lifting the bag from under his arm. "I brought Costa Rican. Best in the world."

She blinked at the shiny silver package, then gave him a wan smile. "Nice try, Lacroix. I'm going back to bed."

The door closed in his face.

So much for *that* strategy.

Just as well. Distance was undoubtedly a better option.

He trotted back down the stairs and went out to the Saab, which was parked a bit down the other side of the street, but still had a good view of her windows and the front door to the building. Waving the surveillance officer over, he got in and made himself comfortable, rolling down all the windows and loosening his tie. God knew how long he'd have to wait until she decided to come out.

The rookie officer who'd drawn surveillance today came up to the driver's side and hunched down. "What's the plan, boss?"

"Gonna be a long day," Jean-Marc answered. "When she comes out, I'll follow her. I want you to stay at your post. Monitor all activity at her apartment—photos and times of everyone coming and going. Never know who might turn up."

The other officer patted the small digital camera sticking out of his breast pocket. "Will do, sir."

There were plenty of comings and goings at the building that morning, but it wasn't until just after ten that Jean-Marc finally spotted Ciara emerging.

She looked around and saw him immediately. To his surprise, she waited patiently until he got out of the Saab, then she took off at a brisk walk down the sidewalk.

He followed easily for several blocks, wondering if she'd try to lose him again this morning. But when she went into a local branch of the Zurich National Bank, she glanced back, as though to make sure he was still there. Strange. Writing the specifics down in his notebook, he waited outside the entrance, leaning against a bus stop where he had an unobstructed view through the glass front. She conducted her business at a teller's window, then strode back out the door and came up to him. She had something in her hand.

"Hold this a moment, will you?" she asked, thrusting it at him.

He took it and looked down, seeing to his astonishment that it was a bundle of hundred-euro bank notes.

"Christ, woman, what the hell is this?" he demanded angrily, and glanced quickly around to find whoever was pointing a camera at them for blackmail purposes. He didn't quite believe it when he saw no one.

Meanwhile she had withdrawn a largish manila envelope from her shoulder bag, and now she waved it in front of his face. "Observe," she said.

On the outside was written *"Brigadier Louis Beck." What the--?*

The name distracted him from his avalanche of conspiracy theories. She snatched the packet of bills back from him, stuffed them into the envelope and licked the flap, gluing it shut. By the time his cloudy thinking had cleared and his mouth dropped open in disbelief, she had marched halfway down the block.

"Ciara!" he shouted. She didn't turn. Or even slow.

He ran to catch up, but didn't make it in time. The eighteenth arrondissement police station was right around the corner. She halted just outside and leaned close to his ear, hissing, "For godsake, stay out of sight. You don't want to be seen with me." Then she disappeared through the door.

Christ. She was paying off Beck with that stack of hundred-euro notes! Right at the *préfecture!* For once the cop inside Jean-Marc was in complete agreement with his much beleaguered male side. Neither one liked what she was doing a damn bit.

He wanted to rush into the station and do something. But what? Jean-Marc was not usually an impulse kind of guy. Accusing a fellow law enforcement officer of corruption was a serious thing, with far-reaching consequences. Before he did anything at all, he had to think through his actions. He needed to be absolutely sure of his facts.

Because what if he was wrong?

He slashed a hand through his hair as something even worse occurred to him. His stomach sank at the very thought.

What if she was actually telling the truth?

What the hell would he do then?

▣ 16 ▣

Ciara felt a certain amount of satisfaction at Jean-Marc's horrified face when she came out of the police station and her meeting with Beck. It almost made up for emptying her Swiss account in order to make up the difference for the blackmail money. Almost.

It had been a stroke of genius coming to Beck's own station to give him the payoff. He had been furious—both over her showing up there, of all places, and also over her paying the blackmail at all. He'd obviously never expected them to come up with the money; his real motive had been getting Sofie under his thumb again. But what could he do when Ciara presented him with the envelope of cash? Make a scene at his work place? Arrest her for bribery?

From the look on Jean-Marc's face as she emerged, he finally believed her about Beck.

Not that it mattered. The bastard would leave them alone now that he had his fifteen thousand. Besides, she had no illusions Jean-Marc ever would have done anything about him anyway. Still, on the off chance that something bad ever happened to Sofie, or even to herself, she now had a reliable witness who knew about Beck. She trusted Jean-Marc that far. If it came down to it, he would do the right thing, she had no doubt about that much, at least.

"Are you *nuts?*" he demanded, falling into step next to her. "Do you realize I'm bound to report this?"

"Report what?" she asked innocently. "I went to see *Brigadier* Beck as a follow-up to yesterday's incident. There's nothing to report."

She could actually feel his scowl on the back of her neck. "Yeah. I so believe that."

She turned and looked at him impassively. "Believe what you like, Jean-Marc, but if Sofie or I turn up dead or beaten to within an inch of our lives, you'll know who to look for."

She left it at that, and started walking again. It was just past ten-thirty, and the morning had gone well so far, but now she had a train to catch. She didn't want to miss it. Before he could argue, or even comment, she said over her shoulder, "I'm going to the Orphans' now. Spending the day there, and probably the night, too. Hope you brought a book."

Sneaking out of the apartment wouldn't be difficult, but keeping Jean-Marc at bay for twenty-four hours while she went to Italy might prove tricky. With any luck, CoCo strolling past the fifth story windows in a blond wig every so often would keep him from becoming suspicious.

"Why spend the night?" he asked.

"Sofie's not feeling well. It's been a rough couple of days." Which was true enough to satisfy him.

From the corner of her eye she saw his hands shove into his trouser pockets and his face go serious.

They didn't talk any more. In fact, Jean-Marc dropped back and walked several paces behind her. He didn't sit next to her on the *métro*. Didn't say a word when she went into the Orphan's apartment building and left him standing there, watching her with an unreadable expression. He looked so forlorn, she almost felt sorry for him.

Damn, this thing between them was weird.

How could you be friends and enemies at the same time? How could you feel bad about lying to the cop who was systematically hunting you down? How could you still want to kiss the man who had sworn to send you to jail?

Hell. Insane didn't come close.

◙ ◙ ◙

Unlike her relationship with Jean-Marc, the Italian job went like clockwork.

Leaving the apartment on rue Daguerre almost immediately via the attic escape route, she took the high-speed train which put her in Turin just after sunset. That gave her two hours to make her way to the hilltop villa and back before the last train back to Paris.

If all went according to plan, she'd be home around eight the next morning, and with any luck Jean-Marc would be none the wiser. But if he should knock on the Orphans' door before that and demand to see her, they would tell him she'd taken the night train to visit her relatives in

Marseille.

In Turin, Valois's contact from Milan met her as promised and after the laydown took charge of the antique silver items, making the return trip to France far less dangerous for her

She got back to the train station in Turin in plenty of time, and sat down with a cup of coffee to settle her nerves. Idly she watched the electronic departure board cycle through to the next set of trains, the small number and letter tiles flipping like mad. When it stopped, at the top of the list was a train to Marseille.

Her coffee cup halted halfway to her mouth as she was suddenly hit by an unexpected wave of nostalgia. It had been several years since she'd visited her old stomping grounds and her old friends and family. Or Etienne's grave.

Maybe she actually *should* go to Marseille.

She looked at the clock again and made some quick calculations. A detour to the coastal town would add at least half a day to her trip. Possibly more, once she met up with family and former compatriots, all of whom would want to lift a glass and reminisce about the good old days.

So why not? She could use some uncomplicated company and a strong drink about now. Maybe even several strong drinks. And she'd like a chance to talk to Etienne again. He never answered, of course. But sitting by his grave, pouring out her troubles, it was like he was sitting there with her. She could always feel the love they had once shared, wrapping itself around her like a warm, ghostly hug. Feeling Etienne's spirit always gave her the strength to make the tough decisions.

Maybe she'd tell him about Jean-Marc. She wondered what he'd have to say about that little fiasco. Hell, he'd probably laugh his ass off. Maybe he'd be jealous. Maybe he'd tell her to stop being an idiot and get on with her life.

She just wished he'd tell her how.

Maybe he would, if she listened hard enough...

Hell, it was worth a try.

◻ ◻ ◻

The sun was just peeking over the mismatched riot of rooftops that made up the Marseilles skyline that surrounded the rundown, ancient graveyard in the worst part of town where Etienne was buried.

Ciara could smell the salty brine of the sea on the crisp dawn breeze, hovering beneath the pervasive stench of fish, refuse and diesel fuel that always choked the harbor district. Sea gulls cried out in their distinctive voices, swirling overhead in their never-ending quest for survival among the detritus of mankind.

She shivered, pulling her sweater closer to her body as she picked her way through the sagging headstones and unkempt graves. The churchyard was a tiny square of greenish brown in an otherwise cement-gray world, clinging to the side of an eighteenth-century stone chapel which looked like it might tumble to the litter-strewn ground at any minute. This was the chapel Etienne's family had worshipped in for three hundred years. Those who were still alive continued to attend every Sunday...despite its outward state of decay, and despite their seedy professions. Inside, the chapel was all polished wood and gleaming stained glass, immaculate in its humble homage to its Lord. This was where Ciara had gone through her second marriage ceremony—the civil one in New York didn't count to his family— where she had first met CoCo and Hugo, and where she had buried Etienne just a few short years later.

When she found his grave, she sat down on the dew-laden grass beside it, curling her legs under her. She didn't worry about her safety, or about prying ears. In this place, there really *was* honor among thieves. She was one of them; she belonged. She would be protected. And so would her secrets.

"Hey, sweetheart," she murmured, placing the bunch of tiny roses she'd purchased at the train station at the foot of his already weathered headstone. "How are you?"

The wind whispered through the tall, dry weeds, rustling dead leaves and lifting the ends of her hair.

"Me?" she said with a sigh. "I'm fucked."

It was silly, she knew, to talk to ghosts, but she let the whole long, miserable story pour out of her. She reminisced about the dreams she'd had as a young bride making a brand new start in a new country with him. How much she'd had to look forward to back then. How little had actually come to pass...

She told him about her present life and asked him how she could have ended up where she was. It was a rhetorical question. They both knew. It would have been a miracle if she *hadn't* ended up doing what she was doing.

Looking back, she realized her life had been doomed from the start. Her mother had been such a sterling example. Drug addict, occasional prostitute, loser. She'd never wanted a child, and nothing Ciara did had ever changed her mind. By comparison, Etienne had been like a fairytale prince come to rescue her on his white steed.

And yet, how had she ever thought marrying a petty criminal, no matter how handsome, loving and kind to her, would lead to anything but heartache?

Yes, they *had* been happy. In spite of it all, those years had been the happiest of her life, before or since. Would she ever find that kind of blind cheerfulness again? A snort of humorless laughter escaped her and wafted into the balmy glow of dawn. Hardly. By now she knew too much about the world's possibilities—and lack thereof—to be quite that stupidly naïve.

Could happiness make up for Etienne's profession, or the path he'd inevitably led her down? It wasn't as if her life up until that point had been all roses and angels... And yet, until then she had managed to survive without systematically turning to crime. She'd wanted to be a translator. She'd wanted to be a good wife, and eventually a mother to a couple of kids whom she'd shower with all the love and affection she'd never gotten from her own. Modest enough wishes.

But ones never destined to come to pass. Especially not now. She'd been found out. It was only a matter of time before Jean-Marc put her in jail. God knew for how long.

The thought was so depressing, she curled up next to Etienne and let her eyes drift shut. She was so tired. Tired of fighting. Tired of losing. Tired of hoping for more and getting less.

The one bright spot in her life was what she had done for her Orphans. They were her redemption. If she saved them, kept them from making her mistakes, the loss of herself would be bearable. She turned to let the rising sun warm her tear-streaked face.

She could do it. She *would* do it. They were almost there.

She had to hold on, keep Jean-Marc at bay, just for a few months more. Then the Orphans would make it on their own. She knew they would.

Then come what may, she would finally be at peace.

◙ ◙ ◙

Jean-Marc's train pulled into the Marseille St. Charles station and he hopped off the outside step where he'd been hanging on, anxious to get where he was going. Striding quickly toward the exit, he flipped open his cell phone and dialed the same number he'd already called twice today— once this morning before leaving Paris, and again during the brief stop in Lyon.

His friend at the local Marseille constabulary picked up on the second ring. "Cheveau."

"Anything?" Jean-Marc asked after his greeting.

"Still no thefts matching any of your parameters reported for last night," Cheveau said. "Sorry."

Jean-Marc asked to be contacted if anything showed up later, then hung up feeling acutely frustrated. He didn't know whether to be glad, or more furious than he already was. Was Ciara playing some kind of game with him? Or had she really left the Orphans apartment last night to visit her late husband's family, as CoCo had insisted when he'd stormed in this morning demanding to know where she was? He'd finally seen through CoCo's blond wig routine, kicking himself soundly for not twigging to it sooner.

Damned if he bought this in-laws ruse for a nanosecond. Ciara could have told him about that kind of visit. Never mind she'd never actually told him she'd been married... *Non*, renewing family ties was not why she was here, he'd bet a year's salary on it.

Well, he'd know soon enough. Cheveau had told him the whole shady Alexander clan lived within five square blocks of St. Antoine's, north of the docks. He'd checked to find out where Etienne Alexander was buried. Same place. Which was as good a place to start as any. If she was even in Marseille....

Jean-Marc hailed a taxi and had the driver let him off close to St. Antoine's. As soon as he got out, a group of tanned, whipcord-strong men hanging out in front of a seedy building threw him suspicious looks. A weathered brass plaque by the building's front door read DOCK WORKERS LOCAL XXVIII. Jean-Marc glanced down at his impeccably stylish suit. Maybe Dries van Noten wasn't the right look for the slums of Marseille.

Ah well, let them come. If the flash of his badge and gun didn't stop them, his blade was tucked in its usual spot against his right ankle. The black stiletto was sharp as a razor, and he knew how to use it.

Hell, the situation might even turn to his advantage. There was no better way of gaining respect among thugs than winning a knife fight.

He got as far as the stark, unwelcoming square in front of the church before they surrounded him.

He went into a relaxed stance, prepared for anything, making sure his shoulder holster was visible. "What can I do for you gentlemen?" he asked calmly.

"*Keuf*," spat out the gorilla who appeared to be their leader. "This is *our* neighborhood. What are you doing here?"

Jean-Marc tilted his head, unoffended by the insult. He'd been called far worse by respectable people. "Just out for a morning stroll."

"It's afternoon. So fuck off."

He made a show of checking his watch. Just after twelve. "So it is. No wonder I'm hungry. Know any good places to eat around here?"

A long, lethal knife appeared in the gorilla's hand. "You can eat this, *poulet*."

He hiked a brow. "You do realize I have a gun," he said conversationally.

The gorilla grinned. "So do I."

Jean-Marc also allowed a slow grin to spread across his face. "Well, then. In that case..." In a twinkling his stiletto was balanced in his hand, at the ready. "Looks like we're even."

A murmur went through the five or six other men who surrounded him.

At the gorilla's signal, they moved backwards in a circle to give them room to maneuver. Jean-Marc slid off his suit jacket and tossed it over a nearby bench. "Touch the jacket and I will shoot you," he said to no one in particular.

The gorilla's first lunge came quickly. This was going to be easier than he thought. The guy was strong as an ox, but his technique sucked. Jean-Marc stepped aside, feigning surprise. The other man whirled and lunged again. Jean-Marc spun away, pretending to be worried. *Like candy from a baby*. The gorilla gave a sneering laugh and closed in on him. Jean-Marc's blade sang through stiff cotton fabric and slashed soft flesh. The other man's arm spurted blood. His face registered shock. Outraged, he roared and came at Jean-Marc, who easily avoided his thrust. The ring of muttering men tightened around them. They didn't sound happy. This could get interesting. Jean-Marc turned and held his ground. Knees bent, knife ready.

His opponent bared his teeth and started for him.

"Hey! What's going on here?" came a sharp female cry from the direction of the church. "Stop it right now, you fools!"

All eyes except Jean-Marc's turned to her. His didn't have to. A flare of anger mixed with gratification zinged through him. He'd found her. okay, she'd found him. Either way, when he got out of this she was so busted.

"Let him go," she said, quickly broaching the circle of men.

"*C'est un keuf*," the gorilla protested. "Got no business here."

"Yeah, he's *un keuf*, but—" to Jean-Marc's shock, she wrapped her arms around him and gave him a kiss "—he's *my keuf*."

For a second the men surrounding them were as stunned as he was. He recovered first.

He wrapped his hand around her hair at the nape of her neck and held her there. He did his best not to notice the hot surge of desire in his groin.

He was angry. She was his suspect. This was just business.

"Appreciate the rescue effort, doll, but I can take care of myself."

"I could see that," she said with mild sarcasm. "What are you doing here?"

He wound his hand a bit tighter in her hair. "*Mon ange*, you know how much I hate it when you disappear on me." He kept his gaze cool, unforgiving. He wanted her to know she was in big trouble.

Her chin rose. "I got homesick."

"Ciara," the gorilla asked incredulously. "Are you really saying this cop belongs to you?" In disbelief, he looked from Ciara to Jean-Marc and back again.

Jean-Marc wasn't about to quibble over semantics. Still holding the stiletto in his right hand, he turned her in his arms and pulled her back against his chest. "You have a problem with that?" he growled.

There was complete silence as the shuffling group of men decided how to react.

"And before you ask," Jean-Marc said impassively, "yes, I know who she is and what she does." He could play dirty cop as well as the next guy. Maybe the thugs would take him into their confidence. Let something slip about her.

"Don't believe him," Ciara said with a defiant edge to her voice, turning to face him again and drawing her tongue across the seam of his lips in a blatantly erotic gesture that nearly did him in. "He just likes to fuck me."

"Well," the gorilla finally said, somewhat uncertainly. His long knife disappeared from his hand. "Since Etienne's woman vouches for you, guess I won't kill you. Just yet."

Jean-Marc refrained from snorting. Instead he looked at her like he owned her, "I've had a long trip chasing you down, woman. Where can I find something to eat?"

Her brow rose infinitesimally at his imperious tone, but good ol' Etienne had apparently trained her well. "Right across the square," she said, jerking her thumb at a sleazy hole-in-the-wall bar a few dozen meters down the block. A knot of customers had gathered in front, drawn out by the prospect of a knife fight in full daylight.

"Let's go," he said. He beckoned to the group of men who'd just moments earlier had every intention of killing him. "*Allez*. Let me buy you all a drink. In memory of Etienne."

◙ ◙ ◙

If possible, the inside of the bar was even seamier than the outside. Dark, with low ceilings stained black from the smoke of countless Galois, and once-white walls smeared with the prints of thousands of dock-filthy hands, the room smelled thickly of onions, potatoes and rue. An ancient American juke box in the corner poured out an endless stream of Piaf oldies through tinny speakers. Small, round wooden tables with uncomfortable wooden chairs were crammed into the entire space, most of them occupied by sweating men and bearing an assortment of chipped china and plain but surprisingly appetizing food.

Jean-Marc felt right at home.

Choosing a free table on the far wall, he emptied the pockets of his jacket, putting everything in his pants pockets before slinging it over a chair and sitting on top of it. He left his weapon where it was—didn't matter, by now everyone in the place would know he was a cop. He signaled the bartender and ordered a round of Pernod for the men who'd come in with them.

"To Etienne. *Santé*," he said.

They all lifted their glasses, downed them, and he ordered another round.

Ciara watched him with an odd expression. "Not nervous being in this kind of place?" she asked.

He tilted his chair casually onto its back legs and leaned his shoulders against the wall behind him. "*Non*. Should I be?"

"The only cop in a room full of gangsters?" She shrugged and gave him a lopsided smile as she moved her chair close to his. "What the hell, except for the badge—and the suit—you could be one of them."

"Hardly surprising," he said impassively. "since I *was* one of them for my first eighteen years."

"Tell me," she encouraged, resting her elbow on the table with chin in hand. "What were you like growing up?"

He took a sip from his second Pernod and let it roll around in his mouth, as though that could take the foul taste of memories away. "I was a rough-edged bad-ass, heading for prison like all my friends in the *banlieue* where I lived. But I had a gift for math so a teacher took pity on me. I managed to escape."

"Lucky you." She studied him for a long moment, then picked up her drink and looked away. "But I got news, baby, you're still a hard-edged bad-ass."

He gave a bark of humorless laughter. "So my boss keeps telling me."

That earned a smile. Hers, not his.

"No wonder you like me so much," she said.

"I don't like you," he denied. Desperately wishing it were true. Scrabbling to hang onto his anger.

"Right." She surprised him by swinging a leg over his knees and straddling his lap, face to face. She slid her hands over his shoulders and up, pushed her fingers into his hair. She rubbed her thumbs back and forth along his jaw. "You're trying so hard not to like me," she murmured.

"Yeah," he agreed, the entire lower half of his body coming to life under the warm weight of hers. "I am."

"Is it working?"

He eased out a breath. And fought not to put his hands on her. She was wearing soft, well-worn jeans today, and a tight black T-shirt which left little to the imagination. He lost his battle and stroked his fingers up her thighs. "What do you think?" he drawled.

Under her T-shirt her nipples quickened, turning to hard little points that poked out at him. He found himself licking his lips.

She watched his tongue disappear, then leaned down and kissed him.

He closed his eyes and tried to talk himself into resisting. But it was no use, and he knew it. He opened his mouth and let her plunder it. Softly, sensually, thoroughly.

For a moment the buzz of conversation around them halted, then it started up again accompanied by chuckles and off-color comments. But nobody seemed particularly concerned. Which was good, because he didn't feel like pulling out his knife again. Or shooting someone.

What he felt like was having sex.

Hard, fast, raunchy, mind-blowing sex.

And she knew it.

Her kiss deepened even more and her bottom ground erotically into his thick erection. He groaned softly.

"*Commissaire* Lacroix?" she whispered into his mouth.

"*Oui, le Revenant?*" he whispered back, feeling like he was falling, spinning at the speed of light down a black, bottomless pit toward... He had no idea.

But wherever it was, when he landed he wanted her there.

"Are you really hungry?" she murmured, dragging her tongue across his lips. Pressing herself down onto his cock so he thought he'd explode.

"Oh, yeah," he said, tugging her tight to his body. Giving in to the sensation. "Hungry for you."

▣ 17 ▣

"I know a place," Ciara whispered, though she shouldn't. This was the stupidest, most ill-advised thing she'd done in a long succession of stupid, ill-advised things.

She didn't care. The pull to Jean-Marc was too strong. The attraction too explosive. The need too intense. She wanted him.

She wanted him.

She wanted him.

He drew back and searched her eyes. His own were dark, midnight blue, glittering with desire. Filled with conflict.

"*C'est fou,*" he murmured. "*Foutrement fou.*"

Fucking insane. Yeah, that about covered it.

She put her forehead to his. "No one will know."

"I will."

Her heart squeezed. How could you not love a man with such honor?

"I could seduce you," she ventured softly. "Then it wouldn't be your fault." She kissed him again. Savored the taste of him. The strength. The goodness. She wanted to meld her body with his, absorb that strength and goodness for her own. So she could be just as strong and as good as he.

Somber, he asked, "If I make love to you, will you confess?"

She smiled faintly. "To what? Being madly and completely in love with you?"

The words just slipped out. She certainly hadn't meant to say them aloud. He froze. In horror? She dropped her gaze, unable to watch his rejection.

He wrapped a large hand around her jaw and lifted her face back up. In

132

his eyes she saw sympathy and sorrow where she'd half expected disdain. He looked as though he wanted to say something, then changed his mind.

Abruptly he rose, bringing her with him and setting her on her feet. "Let's get out of here."

She let him guide her through the mass of beefy bodies in the dim bar, out into the blazing light of afternoon. Temporarily blinded, she reached for him. His arms went around her. Suddenly, inexplicably, she realized she was trembling.

He kissed her. But she could feel the tension in his muscles, in his whole bearing. She wished she could take back her words.

"You said you know somewhere to go?" he asked.

Wordlessly, she took his arm and walked the three blocks to a place she knew would welcome them without asking any questions. When they got to the old red brick building, she knocked a one-three-one pattern on the plain and unremarkable front door. It opened a crack and she heard a feminine gasp, then it was flung wide.

"Ciara! *Chérie!*" gushed the handsome woman dressed in silk who answered, gathering her into her arms. "Where have you been all these—" Then she spotted Jean-Marc and her eyebrows flew up. "*O, lala, p'tite chatte! Mais, viens! Bienvenue, Commissaire!* Come in, come in."

Ciara quelled her sudden panic and stepped inside to a lush, sweetly fragrant confection of a room totally unlike the bland outside façade. It overflowed with ivory lace and red satin, plush furniture and scantily clad women. Jean-Marc held himself ramrod straight beside her, jaw tight, but didn't blink once. Apparently nothing she did shocked him anymore.

When introduced, he politely greeted Madame Felicité—a distant aunt or cousin of Etienne's whom Ciara had been friends with since the old days—and brought out his wallet when Ciara asked if they could borrow a room for a few hours.

"*Pfft!*" Felicité said, waving the money away. "Don't be silly. You are family. It is my pleasure." She eyed Jean-Marc appreciatively. "Or...perhaps yours. *Chérie*, we really must talk more often. Victoire!" she called to a young girl in a diaphanous robe. "Show Ciara and *le commissaire* up to the blue room." She urged them toward the stairs with a hand on each one's shoulder and spoke between their heads. "Take your time, darlings, it is early. We won't be needing the room until after supper—hours from now."

Ciara's face blazed with embarrassment but Jean-Marc's remained impassive. Not a good sign. Whenever his expression went carefully blank he was usually furious with her.

With every eye in the place following them up, it felt like it took forever to climb to the top of the stairs. Etienne had occasionally brought her here, just for fun and adventure, and the ladies had been all teasing giggles and indulgent laughter as they cheered them upstairs. But this was different.

Now everyone was wide-eyed and mute with disbelief.

Tell her about it. She'd had no idea her old family kept such close tabs on her. News traveled fast.

Victoire showed them to the very last room at the end of the hall. Ciara went in and stood uncertainly as Jean-Marc stepped in, shut the door and locked it with a decisive twist of his wrist. He leaned his back against the door, tossed his jacket and tie onto a nearby chair, and gazed at her.

Her knees shook. "You're angry with me again."

"Whatever gave you that idea?" he said deceptively calmly.

The clenched teeth and hands? The steam rising from under his collar? The daggers from his eyes?

"Um, lucky guess?"

"A *brothel?* You really are trying to get me fired, aren't you?"

"I'm sorry, Jean-Marc. I never thought she would recognize you."

His eyes narrowed. "And the stack of hundred-euro notes on the street in broad daylight yesterday? Didn't think anyone would notice that, either? Or sneaking out from under my surveillance? *Twice?* Never thought my superiors would catch that tiny detail, eh?"

"Jean-Marc—"

"It won't matter, you know," he cut her off. "If I get thrown off the case, Pierre will just take over. He knows as much about you as I do."

"That's not—"

"And as for what you said in the bar, you can't possibly think—"

"I meant that," she interrupted stubbornly, fending off a wellspring of hurt that he'd think she could lie about her feelings for him. "Though under the circumstances, I probably shouldn't have said it," she admitted. "I...I'm sorry."

The slashing angles of his face grew severe and his half-lidded eyes burned darkly from beneath a scowl. Lace-patterned shadows danced on the wall behind him as he regarded her.

"Fine. You meant it," he said. "Prove it."

A tingle of apprehension wrapped her in goosebumps. "Wh-what?"

"Prove you love me. Take off your clothes," he ordered roughly. "Now."

◫ ◫ ◫

Ciara's cheeks heated as a surge of sexual desire slammed through her body at his growled command. She swallowed heavily, unsure of what to do. What to make of the sudden change in him.

Or was it a change?

"Not what you had in mind?" he asked, tilting his head arrogantly.

She took a deep breath. She wouldn't lie. Not about this. "Yes. It is."

"I'll give you what you want, Ciara. But we're doing it my way."

She finally understood. Jean-Marc was a man who needed to be in control of his world. With her, he wasn't. He had to reestablish his dominance. If nothing else, at least in bed.

She could live with that.

"All right," she whispered.

"Go on, then."

Haltingly, she toed off her sandals, then unsnapped her jeans and unzipped them. She hazarded a glance at him. Not moving from his spot propping up the door, he was watching her with a hard expression. She almost faltered completely, except he jerked his chin impatiently at the jeans. She quickly shimmied out of them.

Dropping the blue denim to the floor, she reached for the hem of her black T-shirt.

"Panties first," he ordered.

She hesitated, because for some reason that felt far more vulnerable— her T-shirt reached only to her navel. But his expression was growing even more impatient, so she hurriedly slid off her panties.

"Now your bra."

She bit her lip. And reached for the hem of her T-shirt.

"*Non!*" he barked. "Just the bra. Leave the shirt on."

For a second she was confused. "But—"

"Do it."

She found and fumbled with the hook of her bra. It took her a moment to slip the straps off from under the sleeves, but somehow she managed it, even with her hands shaking badly.

How well did she know him? Had she pushed him over the edge by bringing him to a place like this? How could she be so sure he wouldn't hurt her? Her thoughts strayed briefly to Beck, and she closed her eyes.

"Look at me!" he snapped. "Don't ever stop looking at me. I want you to know who you're with."

"I know who I'm with, Jean-Marc. I told you that I—"

"*Arrête!*" He held up a palm. "Do not say you love me, *mon ange*. I know you mean to betray me, so I don't want to hear it."

He stood there with his back to the wall, looking so bad-tempered she forgot all about her fears.

She walked up to him and put her hand on his cheek. "*Mon amour,*" she whispered.

The scent of his cologne, subtle, expensive, masculine, wrapped itself around her. She felt her body quicken. Heat. Melt.

And that quickly she wanted him again. That desperately. She moved closer and drew her fingers down his chest, the silky-fine cotton of his white dress shirt hot and slippery under their tips. Like she would be, if he touched her.

His harsh breaths scorched over her temple. She leaned into him, rubbing her nipples against his chest. A low rumble sounded deep in his throat. Like the warning growl of a wolf. But he didn't touch her.

She reached for his shoulder holster and slid it off, laying it over his jacket on the chair. Then she went for his shirt buttons.

Slowly, one by one, she undid them. She could smell him now...the strong, musky odor of light sweat and potent lust. He didn't utter a word, just watched her with wary, carnal eyes.

Pulling aside his shirt, she raked her fingers deliberately across his chest, sifting through the thatch of black hair, pausing over his tight, flat nipples erect with need. Like he would be, if she touched him.

She put her nose to his jaw, his throat, inhaled the erotic scent of his skin, the unique scent of her lover. Her insides clenched in recognition, twisting with the nearly unbearable desire to be united with him.

She was wet. Slick with need. Trembling with a tumult of sensations and emotions. Wanting him. Wanting him. She touched the button on his waistband.

He grabbed her wrists. "*Non*." Then with strong, powerful hands he urged her down. Down to her knees.

He was hard, the bulge in his trousers long and thick. Excitement zinged a path through her body straight to her center.

His cruel, sculpted lips curled up at the corner. "Shoes," he ordered softly. "My shoes and socks."

With a moue of disappointment, she complied, quickly ridding him of the nuisances.

"Now get up," he said. "Up on the bed."

She blinked.

"*Now!*"

She scrambled to obey. Tucking her legs under her on the mattress, she sat self-consciously on her heels, awaiting his next command.

At last pushing away from the door, he took his time closing the distance. He halted at the edge of the bed.

She shivered, freezing cold in the hot, close room. Terrified. Electrified. Excited beyond reason.

He put his fingertips on her knee and she nearly jumped a foot in the air.

"Nervous?" he asked softly.

"What are you going to do to me?"

He smiled. The knowing smile of a devil. "Anything I want." He paused. Raised a black brow. "*D'accord?*"

Her pulse went into hyperspace. What exactly did he have in mind? Did she trust him...to do anything he wanted?

She felt like she was about to jump off a cliff. But the amazing part was, she *did* trust him. To jump with her.

She fought not to gnaw her lip, and nodded. "Yes."

His eyes glittered like black obsidian. "*Bon.* Kneel up, and spread your knees." She did. "Wider." She did.

Even kneeling on the bed, she was shorter than Jean-Marc. His broad-shouldered body towered above her, making her feel overpowered and helpless. Surprisingly, it wasn't an unpleasant sensation. The fact was, she'd had to take care of herself for so long, it came as an unforeseen relief...to be under his complete control. To give herself up to his will.

Dangerous, a part of her warned—the sensible part. *Don't lose yourself to him. Don't give in.*

But she was beyond reason and beyond warning. She wanted this.

His fingers skimmed up her thighs and she shivered harder. His touch was light, illusive, as he explored the curves of her lower body, almost teasingly. Then they dipped under her T-shirt, more insistent as they reached for her breasts. The fabric was taut around her, so he had to shove his hands under it to get to them.

Her breath sucked in as he roughly seized her. His eyes never left hers; probing, analyzing, calculating. His thumbs rubbed over her sensitive nipples. She swallowed a cry as he did it again. And again. All the while watching her, his devil's lips curved in their infuriatingly knowing smile.

"Unbuckle my trousers," he finally said, rolling one nipple between thumb and forefinger.

She could barely stay upright. Moisture trickled down her inner thighs and there was an unbearable pressure clamping her sex in a vise of craving. She wanted to be filled.

But her fingers refused to cooperate. They fumbled with the button of his waistband and struggled with his zipper until she nearly screamed with frustration. But at last the trousers slid to his ankles, followed quickly by his boxer briefs.

Her breath caught. She'd seen him before, of course. Knew intimately how large and finely-proportioned his cock was. But today it seemed even bigger. Thicker. *Angrier.*

Her quivering hands reached for him.

He stepped back. She wanted to groan.

Removing his pants, he set them aside. His smile, such as it was, disappeared. "Get down on your hands and knees," he ordered.

Her heartbeat stuttered. "Jean-Marc—"

"*Do it!*"

Haltingly, she dropped to her hands and knees along the length of the bed. Head up, she awaited his next move. It seemed like an eternity before it came.

Coming close to the bed, he gathered her long hair in his left hand and wound it around his fist until the knot rested tight at the back of her head. The pull on her hair was almost painful, the strength of his muscles as he held her there immobilizing. His right hand he placed on her naked bottom.

"Spread your knees," he ordered her again. This time she spread them wide apart, desperately wanting him to touch her there.

Which he did. With almost clinical interest, he moved his hand down her bottom and along her cleft. Touching her with his palm and his fingers, gliding, squeezing, probing.

"*Dieu. Tu es en feu.*"

She was panting by now. Definitely on fire. "Jean-Marc—"

A sharp slap stung on her backside. "*La ferme!*" Quiet!

A cry escaped before she could stop it. Not so much of pain as pure surprise. And shock. He had spanked her!

His palm rubbed over the sore spot, soothing the sting on her derrière. Then his long finger slid into her, making her gasp in pleasure. She moaned, undulating against his hand.

"*C'est bon?*" he asked, his voice like the crunch of gravel under a car tire. "You like that?"

Though barely able to move her captive head, she decided just to nod, mindful of his last command. She was looking down at the pillow and wished she could see his face, but he stood too high above her back.

He withdrew his finger. She whimpered. He shoved her T-shirt up, tugging it off her breasts so they hung down ripe and begging for him. She had never felt so completely exposed in her life.

At least until he exerted pressure on her neck and urged her head to lower to the pillow. She wanted to drop her bottom too, but his hand between her legs prevented it. Her pulse thundered at her position.

"Stay like this," he said, voice low. "I want you just like this."

"Jean-Marc," she began, and again a sharp slap stung across her ass. "Unh!" she cried.

"Do you understand?"

She swallowed and nodded quickly. But he spanked her anyway. Not hard, but fast and stinging. And again. And again. Her ass burned and she cried out to him. But all at once she realized she was crying out in pleasure. It didn't hurt, it felt...arousing. He spanked her, and every agonizing sensation shot straight between her legs and throbbed there, increasing her desire for him.

Suddenly her hair was released, the bed dipped, and she felt him behind her. His fingers gripped her and his thumbs spread her apart and in one powerful thrust he mounted her.

His roughened voice caught on a roar as his cock pushed deep inside.

She came apart. She shuddered and shook as he scythed in and out twice, then swiftly joined her. He wrapped his arms around her and pressed his chest tight to her back as he spasmed, his hot essence spurting into her with each jerk.

He swore. Even before he was finished, he swore.

She was too wrung out, too sated, too filled with heated pleasure, to wonder why.

When he stilled, he held her even tighter, groaned, and whispered, "*Merde*. I forgot the condom."

◙ 18 ◙

Ciara didn't move.

"I'm sorry," Jean-Marc murmured, his addled brain swamped with consternation. "I don't know what happened. I *never* forget."

Collapsing onto the bed, he turned her in his arms, gathering her into an embrace. She wouldn't look at him. Twin flags of scarlet dotted her pleasure-flushed cheeks. She appeared slightly shell-shocked.

Inwardly, he called himself every kind of name.

"Ciara, *mon ange*, I swear I'm— Don't worry, I haven't given you anything." At that, her eyes darted to his. "Except..." he added with a blown-out breath, "of course, maybe, depending on if you..." He braced himself. "Do you take the pill?"

The flags grew redder. "No," she whispered.

Merde.

He wanted to curse long and hard. But then something very peculiar happened. A sudden feeling of intense pride blazed through him, and for one stark, unreal moment he wanted nothing more than for her to be carrying his child.

"You *spanked* me," she whispered incredulously, breaking the uncharacteristic spell.

He cleared his throat, more than a little embarrassed. "Seemed like a good idea at the time," he murmured, a bit defensively. The woman brought out things in him he'd never— *Dieu.*

"Is this some kind of clever new law enforcement strategy?" she asked with obvious pique, but settled her head on his shoulder. "Confess or I'll spank you..."

Thank God she was regaining her sense of humor. Sort of. She seemed more dazed than upset. Denial? Denial worked for him.

"Well, you *have* been very naughty..." he ventured, testing the less daunting waters.

She didn't whack him, so he raised her chin with his fingers and kissed her.

Her lips were soft and warm...and reluctant. But she didn't pull away. A reprieve? He cradled her body and deepened the kiss. The tension in her limbs slowly seeped out and she wound her arms around his neck, letting him take his fill of her mouth.

"My God, Jean-Marc, you may have gotten me *pregnant*. Seems to me *you're* the one who's been naughty," she murmured when their lips parted. "I should get to spank you."

He swallowed and managed a half smile. "Wouldn't want to assault an officer of the law. That's a federal offense."

"And what kind of offense is getting your prime suspect pregnant?" she asked pointedly.

He grimaced, growing somber. "A damn serious one."

She held his career, as well as any chance at a conviction for *le Revenant*, in the palm of her hand—or the curve of her belly—and they both knew it.

He put his lips to her temple. "You going to report me?"

She lay quietly in his arms for so long he started making plans for what he'd do when he got kicked off the force. Unfortunately, everything he came up with involved bringing her and the baby along.

"I could never report you Jean-Marc," she said at last, surprising the hell out of him. "That wouldn't be fair. I seduced you, remember?"

"Which time?" he asked sardonically. A rhetorical question. It didn't matter. He'd screwed up. Royally. Even if she didn't report him, he'd have to report himself. Be removed from the case. Let someone else arrest her so the evidence wouldn't be tainted by his monumental stupidity.

But the worst part was, he didn't regret a thing he'd done. Not a single fucking thing.

He tipped her onto her back and canted his body over hers. He placed his hand between them, splayed his fingers over her belly. He felt the smooth dip of her abdomen, where his child might already be growing. And his passion bloomed. He kissed her, then lowered himself between her thighs and slid into her heat.

She made a noise and broke the kiss, gazing up at him uncertainly. She looked frightened, happy, hopeful...wary...all at the same time.

"Ciara," he said, pushing himself deep inside her. "Let me take care of you. You don't have to do what you're doing. Quit, and come and live with me. I have plenty for all three of us."

Her lips parted in disbelief, and again surprising him, her green eyes slowly filled. Then she tightened her arms around him and pulled him close. He couldn't see her face, but her breath shuddered.

"Ciara? I'm serious—"

"Don't," she whispered. "You know it can never happen."

She hooked her legs around his hips and took him deeper still. He was acutely aware he wasn't sheathed, but this time it had been deliberate. He sensed she was equally aware. Had they both gone completely crazy?

He was teetering on the edge of...something he didn't understand. But for the first time he had found something more important than his job.

He wanted her with him. And he wanted their child.

"We'll find a way," he said. "But you have to turn yourself in."

She let out a watery laugh. "Jean-Marc, if I turn myself in I'll be having your baby in jail, whether or not I'm guilty."

"*Non.* I'll get you the best lawyer in the country. We've got no evidence—"

She put her fingers over his mouth and gave him a heartrending smile. "*Shhh,*" she whispered. "You mustn't say these things, my love. It would never work. For either of us. But I love you even more for asking."

His heart squeezed so hard his chest hurt. "What if there really is a baby?"

Her head gave a tiny shake. "There's probably not. Wrong time of month."

Searingly disappointed, he buried his face in her hair, inhaled the sweet scent of her. Fought to keep his emotions in check. He pulled out and drove back into her.

No baby would be a *good* thing. At least he could keep a modicum of dignity when he resigned from the case. And he wouldn't have to explain to the *Préfet* why *le Revenant*'s baby had his DNA.

"This is so fucked up," he muttered.

"Yeah," she agreed.

He thrust into her again.

"I want you with me."

"I want to be with you, too."

Pulled and thrust.

"There has to be a way."

"Maybe in another lifetime," she said with a moan as he scythed in deep, deep.

"Turn yourself in," he urged again.

"I can't," she panted. "Who'll take care of the Orphans?"

"I will," he promised, astonishing both of them. He paused.

She looked up at him. Met his eyes. "And Beck?"

"I'll keep Sofie safe. He won't ever get close to her."

"Jean-Marc...what if there's *not* a baby?"

He gazed down at the face of the woman who had turned his world on its head. For whom he had compromised everything. The woman who would surely end his career and negate everything he'd deemed important in life up until this very moment.

"Then we'll keep trying," he whispered.

◙ ◙ ◙

They made love.

For the first time.

Sweet and tender, with both laughter and tears, their lovemaking transcended anything Jean-Marc had ever experienced. Sure, he'd had more creative sex. But never more emotionally satisfying. It was so much better this way. It made him happy from the inside out, clear to his toes happy.

He brushed it off when Ciara wouldn't be pinned down to a specific date to move in with him; he concentrated instead on how beautiful she looked pinned down under him, calling his name as he brought her to orgasm. He didn't worry when she still wouldn't admit she was *le Revenant*, nor speak again about agreeing to turn herself in. His only thought was that she'd agreed to have his child—if implicitly, by allowing him to make love to her unprotected.

He was too busy falling in love to notice those things.

Too busy being happy, learning her body and her responses to his touch. Too busy listening to his heart, not his head.

When she finally, hours later, fell asleep in his arms, he was as content as a man could be. He would think about it later—all the problems, all the obstacles they'd have to overcome to be together. Right now there were only two things that mattered.

She was his. And he wasn't going to let her go.

◙ ◙ ◙

"Jean-Marc." Ciara shook him reluctantly. He looked so at peace. "Baby, we should go. We'll miss our train."

His eyes fluttered open, and immediately she was gifted with a blinding smile. My God, he was handsome when he smiled. It happened all too rarely. At least when he was around her.

"*Mon ange*," he murmured, and reached for her. "So it wasn't a dream."

Guilt swirled through her insides as he took her in his arms. He'd be a lot better off if it had been.

"That depends on what you dreamed," she said teasingly. Better to keep it light. Avoid the agonizing emotion they'd shared while making love. She'd start to cry again if she gave herself time to think about everything he'd offered her. Everything she must turn down.

His smile widened. "It was one hell of a dream."

"Yeah?"

He rolled on top of her and she felt his cock slide home.

"Oh, yeah."

She wrapped her arms around him. Oh, how she wished they could stay here in their satin and lace cocoon forever!

"Did it involve a brothel and a magic wand?" she asked, waggling her eyebrows. Wishing she really had a magic wand. A powerful one that could change the past...and the future.

His teeth flashed white in a fading sunbeam. "Oh, it's magic, all right. It's amazing the things it can do."

"Mmm," she purred. "Show me."

So he did, and she was able to lose herself in him for just a little while longer, lovers wrapped in ivory satin and bathed in the last orange-gold light of day. Then, after the moans had quieted and the kisses trickled to a stop, they rose, got dressed and headed to the cavernous train station, where the harsh electric lights were just coming on.

Loudspeakers blared out delays and track changes, busy travelers bumped them with overstuffed suitcases, porters hawked their services, and local gendarmes stood with crossed arms scrutinizing every passenger for anything suspicious.

Back to reality.

"We shouldn't sit together," she said. "You're supposed to be tailing me. Official police business and all."

"Fuck that. You're not getting rid of me so easily." He gave her a kiss on the nose.

She shook her head in resignation. He was not in the mood to listen to reason. She was a thief. He was a cop. Couldn't he see there was no way that could ever work? No matter how much they wanted it to?

The fact that she might be pregnant with his baby terrified her. And thrilled her. It was too incredible. She'd never thought about having children before. But suddenly it felt...right.

She had a lot of thinking to do when she got home. About her life. About her future. About the choices she had to make.

Could they really find a way, as Jean-Marc insisted? Or was it all just an impossible fantasy, and her heart destined to be broken...?

Or worse, could he be lying?

A man he called his friend had once betrayed him badly. Might he have learned that lesson a little too well?

Jean-Marc was a shrewd police officer—*un grand flic*—who'd many times admitted he'd stop at nothing to put Ciara in jail. Could this just be a clever ruse to get her to turn herself in? To close the case?

Could she be trusting him, surrendering her heart to him, only to lose everything she held dear—including him?

⬚ ⬚ ⬚

Jean-Marc was worried about Ciara. For the past three hours on the Paris express train, she'd been too quiet. The closer they sped toward home, the wilder the look in her eyes had gotten. It was a look he'd never seen there before. Panic?

He didn't blame her. He was a bit panicked himself.

"I could use a drink," he said, and got up to walk to the bar in the club car. "How about you? Anything?"

She shook her head absently. "No thanks. But you go ahead."

He hesitated for a second, watching her turn her gaze unseeingly out the window into the blackness beyond.

Did she already regret what they'd done? Was she planning to run out and get a morning-after pill so she didn't have to deal with the consequences? Or was she possibly considering his plea to turn herself in?

Hell, was *he* regretting what he'd done? Was he mad to think she would reform just to be with him? And what if she really was pregnant...?

Jesus. What *had* he done?

Doubts assailed him...until he remembered what it had been like last night. How close he'd felt to her. How he'd felt for the first time ever that someone had truly gotten to the core of him. Understood what he was all about, the hidden insecurities, the desperate need to be loved unconditionally, and had instinctively met every need. Given of herself as no woman ever had before.

She'd said she loved him. He just hoped she loved him enough to take it all the way.

He found a seat at the bar and ordered a bourbon. He didn't usually go for the hard stuff, but he'd acquired a taste for good shot of Kentucky during the week-long profiling seminar he'd attended at Quantico last year in the States. He tossed it back and ordered another. Why not? It wasn't every day a man celebrated blowing up his own career.

He'd just relaxed and gotten to the point where he was mentally placing baby furniture in his sleek, modern bachelor pad when his cell phone rang. A look at his watch told him it was nearly ten pm. A glance outside told him they must be on the outskirts of Paris.

"Lacroix," he answered.

"Thank God," came Pierre's excited voice. "Where the hell are you?

Why haven't you answered your phone?"

He sighed. Was one uninterrupted afternoon of bliss really too much to ask? "I was busy."

"Never mind." Pierre rushed on. "We got a tip. I know where she is. And we've got her, *mec*. She's as good as ours."

Alarm blazed through Jean-Marc, raising the hairs on the nape of his neck. "What in hell are you talking about?"

"*Le Revenant, mon ami*. I'm on the way to arrest her right now."

◙ ◙ ◙

"Jean-Marc? Are you still there?"

"Wait."

Jean-Marc vaulted from his seat at the bar and stalked to the rear of the car where he whipped open the door and stepped into the observation deck at the end of the train. Two young, starry-eyed lovers stood in each other's arms, watching the scenery whiz by.

"Move it," Jean-Marc ordered brusquely, opening his jacket to reveal his weapon and flashing his DCPJ *carte*. When he was alone, he hissed into the phone, "Pierre, there's something I need to explain."

"Later, *mon ami*. Right now you need to meet me at the Gare du Lyon. Make it fast. The train from Marseille arrives in ten minutes. She's on it."

"I know, damn it. I'm with her. But—"

"Fucking perfect. Don't let her out of your sight. We—"

"Pierre! Would you stop for a minute and—"

"We're home free, *mec*. She was down there pulling another job. And this time she's got the goods on her."

Stunned, Jean-Marc reeled back against the hard wall of the train car. "*What?*"

"A ruby necklace and matching earrings. Worth a mint. Stolen late last night from a yacht moored off one of those trendy new restaurants on the bay."

"It couldn't have been her."

Pierre paused. "How do you know? Were you with her last night?"

His mouth thinned. "No."

"Did you at least have eyes on her?"

"No."

"Well, then. My information says she was in Marseille and she pulled this job. And my information is reliable."

Jean-Marc slammed his eyes shut and fought the roiling knot that twisted in his stomach as he listened to his partner systematically crush each and every one of the hopes and dreams he'd so recently entertained about the extraordinarily talented Ciara Alexander.

She hadn't lied to him. Not exactly. But God help him, he'd never asked.

Putain de merde!

All the time they'd been making love...had she been laughing at him the whole time? Knowing she had a fortune of jewels sitting right in her purse, practically within plain sight of the detective superintendent in charge of bringing her to justice? Did it turn her on knowing she had duped him so thoroughly? Did she have a hard time keeping a straight face as he'd begged her to move in with him and have his baby?

Putain de fucking *merde.*

Did he fucking *never* learn?

Obviously, this was why she'd kept saying no to his pursuit. She had no intention of stopping her illegal activities. She would never reform. She was just using him. As she had from the very first night at the club.

"All right," Jean-Marc bit out. "What's the plan?"

◘ ◘ ◘

Ciara woke with a start. She looked around swiftly, disoriented from her bad dream. She'd dreamt Beck had locked her in a tiny, filthy cell then beaten Sofie in front of her, laughing as they both screamed for him to stop.

Ciara took a deep breath. She was safe. On a train. With Jean-Marc. She glanced around again. Where was he? Her purse was sitting on his seat next to her and she grabbed it, jumping to her feet. It looked like they were coming into Gare du Lyon. She remembered he'd gone to the club car for a— There! She spotted him leaning against the wall by connecting door to the next car, watching her.

She smiled and waved, and started toward him. But he didn't smile back. She faltered at his dark expression. Something was wrong.

The loudspeaker announced that the train was approaching the Paris station and suddenly everyone got up from their seats, blocking her path to him.

Heart pounding, she fought her way through the crowd, tripping over luggage to get to him. *Something was wrong.* She had reach him! She wanted to be safe in his arms again. Needed that terrible look on his face to go away. Dregs of the awful dream swirled through her mind as the crowd jostled her, but Jean-Marc's pitiless expression was the worst of all. Terror crawled through her veins.

Something was terribly wrong.

"Jean-Marc!" she called.

She saw him hesitate for a split second, then he raised his outstretched hand to her.

"*Oui*," he said. "Come to me, Ciara."

The train slowed, metal wheels screeching like giant fingernails on the steel rails of the track. She covered her ears, her pulse screaming just as loudly. Every instinct shrieked at her to run. *Run from him. Run from whatever was about to happen. Save yourself and run like hell.*

"Come to me, Ciara," he repeated, eyes cold as ice, his hand still outstretched, steady as a hangman's.

Tears stung, blurred her vision.

She was betrayed.

Oh, God, Jean-Marc had taken her love and betrayed her.

When she reached him at last, she looked up into those impenetrable eyes. And knew the bitter truth.

The train jolted to a stop. The door flung open. But she would not run. She would not give him the satisfaction.

She took his hand.

The sound of heavy boots clattered up the steps. Shouts. Whistles. And the familiar timbre of his partner, *Lieutenant* Rousselot's voice saying, "Ciara Alexander, I have a warrant to search your purse. Please surrender it at once."

She didn't protest when he ripped it from her shoulder, jammed his big hands inside and groped around. Wasn't even surprised when one hand instantly reappeared holding something shiny and gold, sparkling in blood red.

She searched Jean-Marc's impassive face with tears trickling down her own. And found nothing but contempt staring back at her. He let go of her hand.

She ripped her gaze from his, swiped the moisture from her cheeks and faced *Lieutenant* Rousselot with head held high. She didn't even blink when he said the words she knew were coming.

"Ciara Alexander, you are under arrest."

◙ 19 ◙

There wasn't a trial.

Ciara didn't have the heart to fight the charges. Of which, ironically enough, she was innocent. She'd had nothing to do with stealing those rubies. And Jean-Marc, the fucking bastard, must have known it all along.

The pain of that nearly brought her to her knees.

At first she'd thought it was Jean-Marc who'd actually planted the stolen necklace and earrings in her purse. But when *Lieutenant* Rousselot let it slip at the preliminary hearing that their informant had been a Paris beat cop, she'd had the belated realization that it must have been Beck. Beck or one of his minions must have gotten onto the train at the last stop before Paris, put the jewels in her purse as she slept, then called the DCPJ on her. She had to give the little shit credit—she had truly underestimated his cleverness.

On the other hand, she had given Jean-Marc far too much credit. Her heart had blinded her to his true colors. Jean-Marc had believed the lying Beck without reservation. He hadn't confronted her, hadn't asked to hear her side. Not once during the interrogations had he even spoken to her. It had all been *Lieutenant* Rousselot.

That spoke volumes about how much her lover really cared about her.

He didn't. It had all been lies.

Ciara thought she didn't have any more tears left. She'd cried a river that first night in jail when Jean-Marc didn't come to see her. In the morning, when she realized he wasn't *ever* going to come, she dried her eyes, straightened her spine, and determined to put the manipulating bastard out of her mind forever.

She didn't cry at the pitying looks during questioning when she claimed Beck had framed her; she didn't cry when the Orphans came to see her and Sofie broke down and Ricardo and Davie said they had to tackle Hugo to keep him from bursting into 36 Quai des Orfèvres and slashing Jean-Marc to ribbons; she didn't cry when her lawyer threatened to quit if she didn't use her personal relationship with Jean-Marc to force all charges against her to be dismissed even though the prosecutor wasn't charging her with anything but the rubies for lack of concrete evidence on her other thefts.

She didn't cry when the judge sentenced her to eighteen months in prison.

Only once did she give in to her feelings and cry. It was three-and-a-half weeks after her arrest, in the lonely confines of her cement cell. On the day she got her period.

◙ 20 ◙

Eighteen months was a hell of a lot of days—five-hundred-forty-seven-and-a-half to be exact—to hold onto your anger.

Jean-Marc did his best. He managed to make it through Ciara's arrest and interrogation.

Just.

He'd naturally expected her to cry rape, or at least drag out all the sordid details of their spectacularly ill-advised affair for all of France to snicker over. He was holding his breath waiting for her to announce that *Commissaire* Lacroix was the father of her unborn child.

He'd been so disillusioned by her deception in Marseille, he'd barely been able to look at her during Pierre's interrogations. Convinced of his impending professional disgrace and dismissal at any moment, Jean-Marc didn't even bother to formally resign from the case. Instead he handed it all over to Pierre and waited stoically for the boom to fall.

But as days went by, and then weeks, and it still didn't happen, Jean-Marc grew more and more uneasy. And finally on a crisp autumn day in early October, looking like a beautiful fallen angel, Ciara stood wordlessly in the courtroom at the *Palais de Justice* on the Ile de la Cité and listened to her sentence, and was quietly led off to prison.

And that was the precise moment when Jean-Marc was struck by a creeping, horrible certainty.

He'd been completely wrong about Ciara Alexander.

◙ 21 ◙

EIGHTEEN MONTHS LATER
11:59 AM, FEBRUARY 14
OUTSIDE LA MAISON D'ARRÊT DES FEMMES, PARIS, FRANCE

Jean-Marc lounged against his Saab, arms crossed over his stomach, eyes closed and face tipped up to catch the stingy warmth the winter sun. He'd been standing like this for close to twenty minutes when a soft beep sounded from the fancy wristwatch he'd given himself this past Christmas.

Finally.

He opened his eyes, unpropped his butt from the front fender and turned to face the prison's entrance. Five seconds later, the front gate swung wide and a woman walked through it carrying an oversized purse.

Ciara.

A jumble of conflicting emotions wrestled in the pit of his stomach as he watched her stride purposefully out to the sidewalk and glance around. She was wearing the same jeans and T-shirt she'd worn when they arrested her. A stab of guilt hit him square in the gut, followed swiftly by a punch of arousal a bit lower. *Dieu*, she looked good.

She spotted him.

Halting abruptly, she threw him a glaring scowl, then just as abruptly resumed striding down the street.

He pushed out a sigh, walked over and stepped in front of her, ready to do battle.

"Ciara—"

"Get out of my way, Lacroix."

"We need to talk."

"What part of leave me alone don't you get?" She attempted to move by him, but he wasn't about to let her escape.

"We need to talk," he repeated. He had things to say. Answers to get.

"I wouldn't talk to you in prison," she said tartly. "What makes you think I'll talk to you now?" She tried to shove past him more forcefully.

After his unsettling revelation at her sentencing, he'd gone to the prison to see her. To find out the truth. And ask about the baby. But she wouldn't see him. Twice a month like clockwork he'd gone to see her, for eighteen months. Each time she'd refused his visit.

He didn't really blame her. But enough was enough.

"Because you don't have a choice," he ground out, and grasped her arms.

Her brows shot up. "Police harassment? Not really your style, Lacroix. Or...maybe this is stalking?"

He clamped his jaw. "Neither. This is a man picking up his lover who just got released from prison."

Her jaw dropped. "His lover? Are you kidding me? You put me in there, in case you'd forgotten!"

"You put yourself in there, Ciara. Not me. And you were lucky to get away with as little time served as you did," he reminded her pointedly. "Real lucky."

They glared at each other for a long moment before she looked away. "I suppose it was you who arranged for my release a day early," she said resentfully.

"Tomorrow was going to be a media circus. Thought I'd spare you the ordeal."

She snorted, studying the ground beneath her sandals. She rubbed her arms. "Let me go, Jean-Marc. I have nothing to say to you, and I'm cold."

He took off his jacket and put it around her shoulders. For a second he thought she might toss it to the sidewalk and stomp on it. But she just jetted out a breath and said a clearly reluctant, "Thanks."

"*C'est rien.* Now get in the car before you catch pneumonia."

"I don't want to go anywhere with you, Jean-Marc. I don't want to have anything to do with you. I hate you," she said, attempting vehemence, but the fight had gone out of her. The words came out breathy and petulant.

Like a lover's.

"No, you don't," he refuted calmly, squeezing her shoulders. "You love me. You told me so yourself."

"In your dreams, Lacroix."

"Not what I recall. Ciara, what happened to the baby?" He waited for an endless silent moment. *Putain.* "Did you...?"

Under his hands her shoulders fell. She shook her head. "There was no baby," she whispered.

He slowly let out the painful breath he'd been holding. Sweet relief flooded through him, washing away the last of his uncertainty. She hadn't gotten rid of it. *Dieu merci.* He didn't think he could have forgiven her for that.

"*Viens,*" he said, wanting badly to take her in his arms. To take comfort in her arms. "Come home with me now."

"Not a chance."

"You've nowhere else to go."

"I'm going to the Orphans'."

"And spoil the surprise party tomorrow? They've been working on it for weeks."

Her eyes shot to his, narrowed. "How do you know that?"

"I promised you I'd take care of them, Ciara. I always keep my promises."

That took her by surprise. He'd had kept in regular touch with the kids while Ciara was in prison, even attending Sofie's graduation, as well as CoCo's, and Ricardo's just last month. He'd also kept a close eye on Beck as promised.

"But..."

He guided her to the Saab and opened the passenger door. "You've nothing to fear from me, *mon ange.* If you don't want me to touch you, I won't. I promise."

He met her gaze and waited for her to make up her mind whether or not to trust him. With a huff she relented, and at last she slid into his car.

Kneeling down, he snapped on her seat belt for her. And said, "But if you feel like touching me, *chérie,* you go right ahead."

◻ ◻ ◻

Ciara was jumpy as a frog who'd made a wrong turn into La Tour d'Argent restaurant.

"Relax," Jean-Marc said, taking his jacket and her purse from her and hanging them in the hall closet. "There's a bottle of wine breathing on the bar. Pour us a glass and I'll start a fire."

Arms clamped tight across her abdomen, she scanned his living room. "Nice digs."

Jean-Marc's apartment occupied half of the penthouse level of one of the few modern apartment buildings in the Opera district. Actually, it was from the thirties, complete with sleek curved windows, ship-like balcony railings and stylized cornices. He owned the whole top floor, but had divided the penthouse into two separate apartments and rented the other to a divorced government official. He'd bought the place years ago, at a time when many Parisians turned up their noses at modern architecture, and had gotten quite a good deal.

Ciara leveled him an openly suspicious gaze. "I'm surprised a cop can afford this kind of address."

"Most can't," he said, unperturbed, heading for the fireplace. "Years ago, in my misspent youth, I got lucky in Monaco. Made several good investments with the winnings. This apartment was one of them."

Early on, he'd discovered that his uncanny ability at math gave him an unfair advantage in card games. One summer just after applying to the DCPJ he'd decided to test that ability to its fullest at the blackjack tables all along the Riviera. He'd won an obscene amount of money—for back then, anyway—before wisely deciding to decamp back to Paris lest he be thrown out for card-counting and barred from the casinos for life—not to mention losing his chance with the DCPJ. To this day, he wasn't sure how much his winning had been due to skill or just pure dumb luck.

But he had not stepped foot in a gambling establishment since. He'd decided that was one addiction no cop needed.

Ciara was looking at him with an indecipherable expression. "Lucky break," she said neutrally.

"Nah. My real lucky break came five years earlier when my math teacher took an interest in me. He yanked me out of that viper pit called my childhood and showed me there was a different way to live life. If it weren't for his influence, when I discovered those gambling abilities I wouldn't have stopped. I'd probably be in jail right now. Or some lowlife barfly hustling people like your friends in Marseille out of their ill-gotten gains."

She chuckled and wandered over to the bar. "Somehow I doubt that." She picked up the wine bottle he'd opened earlier and whistled at the label. "You sure you've stopped gambling?"

With a smile, he lifted a shoulder. "Like I said, I made some good investments."

She poured a glass of wine and leaned back against the granite edge of the bar, perusing his expensive but minimalist furniture and bare walls. "A decorator wasn't one of them, I see."

"Smart ass." He pushed a button and flames leapt to life behind the glass doors of the fireplace. "My ex-wife decorated it. When she left she took everything, and I had the whole place painted white. New décor, new life. That was the theory anyway. I never quite got around to following through, though"

"How long has it been?"

"Five years."

She nodded and poured him a glass of wine as he walked over to her. "You could use some art on your walls. Liven up the joint." She held out the glass. "I know where you can find a Picasso cheap."

He gave her a withering glance as he took it. *"Très amusant."* He tapped his glass to hers and the ring of crystal tinkled through the room, clear, pure, sweet. "Welcome home, Ciara." He bent down and kissed each of her cheeks in the traditional French greeting.

She stiffened. He was oh, so tempted to kiss her on the lips, too. If only to rile her even more. But he resisted. After all, he'd promised no touching.

"This isn't home, Jean-Marc," she murmured, turning away.

He just smiled and drank to his toast.

"Hungry?" he asked. "I stopped at Fauchon for a little something for lunch. Figured you're probably sick of macaroni and cheese."

"Pretty sure of yourself, aren't you, flic?"

"I usually get my way," he said with a modest smile. "Now, would you like to eat before or after your bath?"

Her glass stopped dead halfway to her mouth. "Excuse me?"

"Whenever I've been to prison," he said, strolling over to the windows, taking in the incredible view over the rooftops of Paris, "in a professional capacity of course—the first thing I do when I get out is take a nice relaxing bubble bath. Relieves the stress of all that noise and ugliness. I imagine you'd like to wash away your whole experience." He knew that she hadn't had anything untoward happen to her in prison—he'd made sure of that with several well-placed bribes. French women's prison wasn't exactly Sing-Sing, but it still couldn't have been pleasant.

She stared at him as though he'd lost his mind. "You honestly think I'll take my clothes off in your apartment?"

Again he shrugged. "Keep them on, then. But I just want to remind you that getting wet jeans off can be murder. Bring your wine," he said, and walked the length of the living room into the master suite without looking back. She'd follow. It might take a minute or two, but he'd been inside enough times to know she'd probably kill to be able to scrub the prison stench from her skin and hair.

He went into the master bath and turned on the taps that filled water into the luxurious spa tub like a waterfall. "Vanilla or jasmine?" he called, pausing over a couple of ornate bottles of bath beads he'd picked up yesterday. "I have some of my usual citrus blend left, too."

He sensed her in the doorway. "You take bubble baths often, Lacroix?"

"Comes from having spent much of my childhood fetching water from an apartment down the hall, I guess." He smiled wryly. "Our landlord wasn't terribly responsive. Of course, who could blame him when my mother was always a year behind on the rent?"

She studied him silently for a moment, then said, "Jasmine, please."

A tiny curl of victory spun through him. He poured the sweet-smelling beads into the steamy, roiling water. "I've set out towels and a robe for you." He nodded to a tall pile of white fluff on the counter. "Take your time. Lunch will wait."

She nibbled on her bottom lip and he nearly weakened. Damn, he wanted to be in that tub with her! But he just smiled and closed the door behind him as he went out.

After half an hour of putzing around the kitchen getting the lunch things together, he picked up the open wine bottle and headed for the bathroom. On second thought, he set it down, unbuttoned his dress shirt, rolled up the cuffs and pulled the tails from his waistband. Then he grabbed the wine bottle again, knocked on the bathroom door and went in without waiting for an answer.

Ciara was stretched out in the tub under a mound of bubbles, her head resting on a plastic pillow, her wet hair curled in a tangled halo about her face. Her eyes popped open, startled, when he walked in.

Before she could react, he breezed over and picked up her wineglass. "Brought you a refill," he said, pouring. "How's the water? Still hot enough?" He handed her the glass and dipped his fingers into the bubbles. She gasped. But he was careful not to touch her. "Feels good. But don't stay in too long or you'll turn into a prune," he warned with a smile. "Though, I'll admit I've always been partial to prunes." He winked. "Especially when they're soaked in wine."

Her eyes widened even further.

He stood and set the bottle on the sink. "You don't mind if I change, do you? I thought we'd eat in front of the fire and I don't want to get carpet lint on my suit."

"As a matter of fact—"

But he'd already peeled off his shirt and was tossing it into a hamper hidden under the sink. Her words cut off when he unbuckled his belt. He unzipped his trousers. From the corner of his eye he saw her take a large gulp of wine.

Hiding a smile, he opened the door to the large adjoining walk-in closet and went in. There he stripped off the rest of his clothes, set the shoes in their place on the rack and hung the trousers on their hanger. Picking up his discarded things, he walked back into the bathroom. Naked.

He heard her intake of breath and the splash of water as it sloshed onto the marble floor. "Jean-Marc..." she said in a warning tone.

"I'll put your clothes in the wash with mine, eh?" he said, and grabbed her jeans and T-shirt from the floor.

"That's not necessary," she protested, but again too late. The things were already in the washing machine, which was conveniently located in a recessed alcove with folding doors between the bathroom and closet.

He spun the dial. "Fresh clothes, fresh start," he said, and leaned casually against the polished stone vanity counter.

"You're just full of pithy little sayings, aren't you?" she muttered, avoiding looking at his body. She sighed. "Why are you doing this, Jean-Marc? Why did you bring me here?"

He, however, had no such qualms. She'd sat up when he'd walked in, exposing her breasts above the water. Her plump wet flesh was rosy from the heat of the bath, her cheeks flushed from the wine—or maybe it was from the sight of his body?—and trails of soap bubbles trickled down over her lush curves. A blob of white had fastened to one nipple, looking so much like whipped cream he had to physically restrain himself from licking it off.

He felt his cock rise.

"Look at me, Ciara," he ordered softly.

Grudgingly she did so. Her gaze wavered at his growing erection, then rose to his eyes. "You have to be out of your mind."

"Possibly," he admitted. "But I still want you. You've got a clean record now, you've paid your debt to society. There's no reason we can't be together."

Her mouth dropped open. Then it snapped shut and she shook her head. "You really have gone over the deep end."

"Surely, you've forgiven me by now. I never made it a secret I intended to put you in jail."

She gave a humorless laugh. "True. But I have to hand it to you, Lacroix, your method of closing the case was ingenious. Your seduction was singularly effective."

He frowned. "You surely can't mean— If you think I used our relationship to—" He ground his jaw. "For the record, I had nothing to do with your arrest. I didn't even know about it until minutes beforehand. If it had been me—"

He cut himself off before he blurted out that he'd have waited to arrest her until they had solid evidence on all her thefts, so she'd have spent a whole lot longer than eighteen months in jail. Unless she'd turned herself in, as he'd implored her. In which case he'd have done everything he could to help her plead out and come back to him as soon as possible.

"Yes, I know," she said quietly. "But for the record, I really didn't steal those rubies. Beck had them stolen and planted in my purse, to frame me. I'm sure of it."

He sighed. "I figured that out, too, eventually. The whole thing was just a little too convenient."

"Not that it matters," she said even more softly. "I was guilty of all the rest. I am a thief, Jean-Marc. I am *le Revenant*. Which is reason enough we can't be together."

His breath caught in his lungs. It was the first time she'd admitted her guilt out loud to him. Admitted who she'd been. But no more.

"You were *le Revenant*," he corrected firmly, pushing off the counter. "But *Le Revenant* is dead and buried now in a closed case file at the bottom of a locked cabinet in the basement of 36 *Quai des Orfèvres*. Your slate is clean, Ciara. You can do anything you want with your future."

She looked unconvinced, but didn't say anything as she watched him slip on a pair of black linen drawstring pants.

"*Viens*," he said. "I'm starving, and that water's got to be stone cold by now. Hop out and let's have some lunch."

He swiped up the wine bottle and wagged a finger at her. "Five minutes, *chérie*. Then I'm coming back to get you."

◙ ◙ ◙

He wasn't serious. He couldn't be.

Clean slate. Right. Who was he kidding? If *Commissaire* Lacroix took up with her, a convicted felon, the DCPJ would fire his ass so fast it wouldn't be funny.

Still, he looked so sincere...

He probably just wanted to fuck her again.

Hell. She was tempted to let him.

Except he'd no doubt end up fucking her over again.

Ciara didn't know what it was about the man, but every time she got within five meters of Jean-Marc, her brain seemed to vaporize.

Every time she told herself, don't listen to him, don't let yourself fall for his pretty promises. But every damn time she ended up in the same damn place. Under him with her legs spread.

Last time she'd believed his promises she'd also ended up in jail.

So, no. Not this time.

She'd just spent eighteen months hating *Commissaire* Lacroix and studiously avoiding him, with damn good reason.

She thought about him naked.

Damn good reason.

And she'd remember what it was any minute now.

Fuck.

She glanced down at the long, soft terry cloth robe he'd left for her and pulled the belt tighter. Then walked out of the bathroom to face him.

She found him sprawled on the floor in front of the fireplace, his bare chest cast in tones of red and bronze from the glow of the flames. A feast of delicacies was spread out on a low table in front of the sofa. Her mouth watered.

She told herself it was because of the food.

"There you are," he said as she took a spot on the floor next to him.

He sat up, refilled her wineglass, and they began to eat. She didn't know what was more orgasmic, the taste of the incredible gourmet morsels he plied her with, or the sight of his virile male body clad only in those semi-transparent linen pants. Everything he possessed was clearly visible, but enhanced by the intriguing play of shadows and firelight through the gauzy black cloth.

"You look beautiful," he said when their eating had slowed to nibbling. Breaking into her thoughts about how beautiful he was. "I hate to say prison must have agreed with you, but..."

She smiled, distressingly pleased by the unexpected compliment. He had lolled back, elbow bent and head resting on his hand, one knee bent up, clearly showing her exactly how beautiful he thought she was.

Unconsciously, she licked her lips. "I, um..." She tore her gaze away from the tempting sight. "It did agree with me, actually. As far as it goes. I hadn't realized how stressed out I was, about the Orphans, money, Beck's blackmail. Everything. When I was inside and social services told me a benefactor had come forward as a result of the trial, to pay the Orphans' rent and tuition, that they weren't going to split them up...it was like a reprieve."

"I understand you took some classes. In interpreting?"

She stared at him. "You checked up on me?"

"Of course. You're my lover, Ciara. I never stopped caring about you."

A spiral of desire curled through her center, immediately crushed by a slash of hurt. Suddenly she remembered why she'd hated him for eighteen months.

"Not your only lover, from what I understand," she said acerbically. "You can't have cared all that much."

"Checked up on me, too, eh?"

"Not me. But I was in prison, Jean-Marc, not the Antarctic. The rumors—" She shook her head. "Let's just say my fellow inmates delighted in showing me the tabloids every time you graced the centerfold, I couldn't help noticing you had a new woman on your arm in every photo. Catching *le Revenant* made you quite the eligible Paris bachelor, I must say."

"I was invited to a lot of functions," he said evenly. "The boss made me go. It was good publicity for the OCBC. But you weren't the only one affected by the rumors. I had no choice but to be seen with other women."

"Kicking and screaming, I'm sure."

"Most of them were paid escorts, *chérie*."

She rolled her eyes. "That makes it so much better."

"May I remind you, you wouldn't even see me? For eighteen months you wouldn't see me. You were the only woman I wanted, Ciara, but I'd have been a fool to turn into a monk for eighteen months for a woman who didn't even want me."

She snorted derisively. "Eighteen months is a long time for a woman, too, *mon cher*."

She realized her mistake immediately. She slammed her eyes shut. The ensuing silence was thick enough to slice.

"Well," he finally said with classic Gallic insouciance, "I could help you out with that now, if you like."

"They gave me fifty euro to get started. I could pay you," she threw back.

He chuckled, unoffended. "Fifty? I usually charge more, but I guess I could give you a break, considering your dire need."

"You're a riot, Lacroix," she ground out.

He rolled onto his side and regarded her. He was fully, flagrantly aroused. His brow rose. "Well?"

At some point her belt had come loose and her robe gaped apart. She didn't bother to pull it closed. She had the sinking feeling she'd already lost this battle. Had lost it the moment she'd seen him outside the prison, lounging there against his Saab like some modern-day French James Dean.

Jesus, how had this happened again?

He reached over and tugged her belt all the way off. Her robe fell open and his gaze caressed her body, from the top of her head to the tips of her toes. She felt ravished by it, by him, and he hadn't even touched her.

Damn, damn, damn.

"What do you want me to do, Ciara?" he asked, his voice rough as sandpaper, husky as a lion's purr.

She gave up. Gave in.

What the hell. She'd been eighteen months without a man. And Jean-Marc was the only man she wanted to be with. Would probably ever want to be with.

"Let me touch you," she murmured, reaching for him. "Let me touch you and smell you and taste you. Let me kiss you all over, and make love to you. Then let me do it all again."

▣ 22 ▣

Jean-Marc met her halfway but Ciara pushed him back onto the floor. "I'm paying," she said. "I get to do what I like to you."

A corner of his lip curved up. "Hmm. Sounds a bit backwards. Shouldn't I be pleasuring you?"

"Oh, you will be," she assured him, climbing onto his big, muscular body.

She grasped his broad shoulders and stretched her body out on top of him. Putting her nose to the crease of his neck, she breathed deeply of his dusky, male scent, enjoying the rough scratch of his chest hair on her breasts. She wanted to rub herself all over him until the smell of him surrounded her like a blanket. She wanted to lick his body until she drown in the rich, erotic taste of him. She wanted to touch and meld with his flesh until she didn't know where he stopped and she began. She wanted to kiss him until she forgot the pain and loneliness of the past year-and-a-half, and once again believed in him.

He reached for her and she caught his wrists. "No." She tucked them above his head. "I don't want you to touch me."

A shadow of uncertainty flitted through his eyes. But he obeyed. "There are condoms in my pocket," he murmured.

"You won't need them."

His pupils flared, so she leaned down close to his ear, and whispered, "I'm not going to let you come."

And she didn't. Not for an hour or more, until after he'd made her climax at least three or four times. Not until she'd tortured him with her lips and her tongue and the hot passage between her thighs, keeping him on the edge, pleasuring herself by pleasuring him to the brink of explosion, only to stop and start all over again. He groaned. He pleaded. He begged.

She felt immensely satisfied.

And he roared like a beast when she finally allowed him completion.

"*Mon Dieu*," he swore when he could speak again. "*Bon Dieu de merde*. I think you've killed me."

She rolled onto her back next to him and smiled at the ceiling. She was floating on a sea of delighted gratification. The torture had done the trick. Revenge was sweet; prison had receded to an indistinct blur. She was back to loving him.

She didn't dare think about tomorrow. Tomorrow was too complicated. But in prison she'd learned to live each day on its own, one day at a time.

Tonight she loved him. And that was enough.

But the next morning...

The next morning, everything changed.

Ciara and Jean-Marc slept in, happily exhausted from their long night of making love. She awoke in his arms, content, optimistic, and dimly aware of a faraway chirping sound. His cell phone.

"Damn Pierre," he muttered. "I told him I wouldn't be in today."

"Probably should get it," she said with a yawn and a stretch. "Must be important or he wouldn't call."

Jean-Marc grunted, sighed, and slid out from under the massive goose down quilt. "Don't move. I'll be right back."

Thirty seconds later he walked back into the room, cell phone to his ear and a worried look on his face. "Ricardo, slow down. I don't underst— Speak French, Ricardo! For chrissake—"

Ciara was already on her feet. She grabbed the phone from him. "Ricardo, it's me. What's happened?"

"Sofie!" came the boy's almost hysterical reply. "*Dios mio*, Ciara. Sofie's been—It was Beck. He raped her."

◘ ◘ ◘

"Hell of a homecoming," Davie murmured, and kissed Ciara on the cheeks. "Sorry, darling. We had a big party all planned..."

Ciara gave him a squeeze. "Yes. Jean-Marc told me."

Ciara, Davie, Ricardo and CoCo were sitting in the waiting room of the Hôpital la Rochefoucault while a forensic nurse did a rape kit on Sofie. Jean-Marc had stormed off earlier to question Beck. Hugo was doing his usual pacing back and forth, looking like he would murder the first thing that moved. Thank God Jean-Marc had read him the riot act before leaving, telling him to stay put on pain of death. And Hugo had actually heeded the order, to Ciara's everlasting wonder.

For herself, she was so angry she prayed she didn't see Beck anytime soon or she'd do Hugo's murder for him. "How did this happen?" she asked them, despising what Sofie must be going through.

CoCo shook her head. "She went out for a few last-minute things for the party. We could hear her singing all the way down the stairs. We were all so happy you were coming home today..." She glanced up, and Ciara could see the mild question in her eyes.

"Jean-Marc arranged for me to be released yesterday. To avoid the media," she explained, feeling incredibly guilty. "If only I'd gone straight to rue Daguerre."

"How could you know? There was nothing you could have done, anyway." CoCo gave her a crooked smile. "So you spent the night with the man who put you in jail?"

"Seemed like a good idea at the time," Ciara muttered. *Damn.*

Davie choked. "That is so wrong."

Hugo halted and glowered at Davie. "The *commissaire* is a good man, and you two know it very well," he snapped, then resumed his pacing. "Ciara could do a lot worse."

Ciara's jaw dropped in astonishment at his supportive outburst. Davie and CoCo looked suddenly uncomfortable. A red flag went up at the speed of light.

"All right," she demanded, "what are you not telling me?"

Everyone studied their hands.

"Come on you guys. No secrets. I mean it."

"Lacroix paid the rent while you were gone," Hugo said almost belligerently, raking the others with a glare.

Momentarily stunned, she regarded at them one by one.

"And our tuition," Ricardo said when she got to him.

"*Jean-Marc?*" She could scarcely believe it. "*Commissaire Lacroix* was social services' mysterious benefactor?" Except...it made perfect sense. He'd promised, hadn't he? Why should it surprise her that the most honorable man she knew would take his promise seriously? She should have guessed immediately.

"He also kept Beck away," CoCo said, then glanced toward the room where Sofie was being examined. "At least until now."

Which explained why he'd been on such a tear when he'd taken off after Beck. Ciara wasn't sure what she should think of it all. But she didn't get the chance to decide. The forensic nurse emerged from the exam room and gathered them all together.

"The good news is that Sofie is doing just fine. No lasting physical trauma. Psychologically?" She frowned. "Only time will tell. The bad news is that the man left no evidence behind to nail him with."

"Nothing?" Ciara asked, dismayed.

"I'm afraid not. No fluids, no fibers, no hairs. Nothing at all."

Ciara's heart sank. "So it's her word against his. There's no way to convict the bastard."

"Not unless he confesses. Physically, he was too careful. I'm so sorry."

Everyone's mood was subdued as they collected Sofie and took a taxi home. The colorful decorations festooning the Orphans' apartment seemed grotesquely out of place.

As CoCo and Davie ripped them down, Ciara gave Sofie a long hug.

"I'm sorry I've spoiled your homecoming," Sofie whispered with a hiccough in her voice. "I hope you don't mind, but I think I'll go to bed now."

Feeling helpless, they all watched her go into her room and softly close the door. Ciara wanted to scream and throw things and rage against the injustice.

"We need to get him," Hugo said savagely. "We need to make him pay."

Ciara agreed. So did the others.

A knock sounded at the door. "That'll be Jean-Marc," Ciara guessed, and went over to answer it.

But it wasn't Jean-Marc. It was two police officers. And one of them was Beck.

"Good evening," the first officer said politely. "The hospital informed us someone at this address reported a rape. We'll need to get the victim's statement."

Beck stood behind the first officer, wearing a bland expression, as though his presence here weren't the most perverse insult Ciara could possibly imagine.

She forced herself not to leap on his filthy carcass and tear his eyes out. That wouldn't help Sofie. Instead she ground out, "No, I'm afraid it was all a misunderstanding. My friend doesn't wish to press charges. Sorry to have wasted your time." She was proud of herself. Her voice barely shook at all.

Beck's mouth twitched into a smile as the other officer tried to change her mind. "Please reconsider. If she doesn't report this man, he'll only do it again," he argued sensibly. He seemed sincere enough. Obviously he didn't have a clue.

"It's true," Beck said with smarmy false civility. "Next time it could even be you..."

Ciara gripped the door jamb so hard her fingernails dug gouges into the wood. "Let him try, the coward!" she spat out, and felt Davie's restraining arm come around her shoulder. "See what happens to him if he does!"

"Taking the law into your own hands is no solution," the first officer said with a frown. "The best thing your friend can do is help put this animal behind bars."

"Thank you, officer. We'll think about it."

He nodded and, disappointed, went to leave. Beck waited until after he'd started back down the stairs, then turned to Ciara.

"Hope you liked my welcome home present, bitch," he hissed under his breath. "I've been waiting a long time for this day."

"Get out of my sight, Beck, before I really do kill you," she warned. Davie grabbed her arm before she could take a swing at him.

"You don't want to do that," the bastard returned with a menacing chuckle. "In fact, the only thing you'll want to do is exactly as I say."

"You're completely delusional if you think—"

"Or things could go badly for your lover-boy."

She narrowed her eyes. "What the hell are you talking about?"

"I just had you locked up for eighteen months without anyone being the wiser. What do you think I could do to your precious *commissaire*'s career? Think *he'd* have a good time in prison? With all those felons he's put in there for company? Good looking guy, your Lacroix..."

She went for Beck's throat. But got all tangled up in Davie and CoCo. Behind her she heard Hugo curse at Ricardo and furniture go flying.

"I want more money," Beck growled. "Or you can kiss his pretty ass goodbye. Another ten thousand by the end of the month. And *get him off my back*. If he comes around me one more time, he'll be wearing stripes." Beck leaned in, baring his teeth. "And dare breathe a word—*to anyone*—and he'll be a dead man." With that, the little shit slithered away and down the stairs.

"Goddamn it, Beck! You won't get away with this!" she screamed after him.

His parting laughter echoed up the stairwell, followed by the front entry door slamming.

It sounded eerily like prison bars clanging shut.

"God damn you," she screamed as Davie and CoCo forcibly hauled her inside. "God fucking *damn* you!"

Hugo finally managed to wrestle free of Ricardo and came lunging toward the door. "Let me at him!"

"No!" Davie said, barring his way. "No. Sofie's hurt and we just got Ciara back. We're not losing you, too. *Either* of you."

"But you heard him! He *raped Sofie*, and threatened to do it to Ciara! Are we just going to stand here and take it?"

They all looked to her for direction. But her mind refused to function. She was still back at the part about Jean-Marc being a dead man. She put a shaking hand to her mouth.

Beck meant what he'd said. She had no doubt about it.

"Oh, God," she moaned, seeing every one of her hopes and dreams evaporate before her eyes.

All that time in prison for nothing! A clean slate? Ha. Just another impossible fantasy, as always. Beck would never let her stop stealing. *Never.*

"Oh, God. Jean-Marc..." she whispered in despair. "What in God's name am I going to do?"

◉ ◉ ◉

An hour later, Jean-Marc climbed the stairs to the Orphans' apartment in a foul mood.

After dropping off Ciara at the hospital, he'd chased down Louis Beck at his *préfecture* and questioned him about his whereabouts earlier that morning. It was perfectly obvious to Jean-Marc that Beck knew exactly what his questions were in reference to, even though Jean-Marc was very careful not to make any direct accusations. To make any charges stick, he needed proof. Beck blithely told Jean-Marc that he'd been at the station all morning doing paperwork, and any one of his colleagues would back him up. Unfortunately, they did. Every one Jean-Marc could find.

He came away with worse than nothing. Sofie's rapist had a solid alibi and there was nothing he would ever be able to do to crack it.

Today he was ashamed to be a cop, and didn't know how he'd face Ciara.

The apartment door opened, and there she stood. Looking shell-shocked and...he could swear, nervous.

His bad mood and the terrible situation couldn't quite overpower his somber pleasure at seeing her. "*Mon ange,*" he murmured, and pulled her into his embrace, even more furious with Beck for spoiling their reunion in this awful way, on top of his horrific cruelty. He kissed her hair. "I'm sorry. Beck wouldn't admit anything, and somehow he's gotten his whole squad to say he was at the police station all morning. There was nothing I could do."

"It's not your fault, Jean-Marc." She stepped back and held him at arm's length. "I'm sure you did your best." She looked down at the floor and fell silent.

He glanced around the room. CoCo, Davie and Ricardo were also looking anywhere but at him. Even Hugo, who had become his staunchest supporter in the bunch, was gazing determinedly out the window. Suddenly, Jean-Marc became uneasy.

"What's going on?" he asked sharply.

"Nothing," Ciara said, giving him an unconvincingly weak smile.

"Then give me a kiss." The Orphans wouldn't be shocked. It was pretty clear they knew where Ciara had spent last night.

The blood drained from her face. "Jean-Marc, um..."

"Something wrong?" he asked mildly, but his pulse had already started to pound. *Something was definitely wrong.* He gripped her arms to keep her from slipping away from him.

"Of course not," she said. And kissed him. A pathetic attempt. Short, dry and self-conscious.

"*Alors*," he said, temper rising. So that's how it was to be. He turned to leave before hurt could trump his anger.

"Jean-Marc," she said, grabbing his hand. She dropped it again. Then turned and swiped up her purse. "Let's go somewhere and have a drink. We need to talk."

That clinched it. In the movies, whenever a woman said "we need to talk," the man was about to eat shit.

Confusion swirled through his chest. What had happened to the affectionate, adoring lover who had shared his bed last night? He didn't understand. True, they hadn't spoken of the future, but...he'd taken it for granted they had one.

They'd only reached the third floor landing on their way down the stairs, but Jean-Marc couldn't take it anymore. He pulled her to a stop.

"*Non*," he said. "I don't want a fucking drink. We can do this right here and now." He set his mouth in a thin line and regarded her. "What the hell is going on, Ciara?"

"Here?" She glanced around at the apartment doors in consternation. "But people can—"

"*Now*, Ciara." He wasn't waiting another goddamn minute to hear the bad news. "You dumping me, baby? Is that it?"

"Jean-Marc, this isn't the place—"

"I knew it! Why?" he demanded. "Last night—"

"Last night was amazing," she interrupted, keeping her voice low. "Utterly amazing," she said, finally meeting his gaze— "I...I wish..." —but it slid away again. "God, Jean-Marc, this is happening too fast!" Her hands went up to hold her temples. "*We* are happening too fast. And now this thing with Sofie." Ciara's green eyes appealed to him. *Lied to him.* "She needs me, Jean-Marc. Beck isn't going to leave her alone, and I don't want you involved."

"Why not? I can—"

"No!" she said vehemently. Too vehemently. "No. Really. You said it yourself—he has an unbreakable alibi, and they found no physical evidence at all. Accusing him will only get you in trouble."

"The man's a slimeball. He needs to be stopped."

"I agree, but— I can't think about that now. I can't think about *us* now. Sofie's so fragile. She needs me. Do you understand?"

"*Non*," he growled. He didn't understand anything. His lover was giving him the brush-off and he had no idea why. Fuck Beck. And Sofie could share. "*I* need you, Ciara."

Her face fell and she looked like she would cry. Good. He was not feeling charitable at the moment. He was feeling selfish and slighted and once again betrayed.

"*Mon amour*," she murmured, and put her arms around him. He held himself cold and stiff. He didn't need her pity. Didn't want her lousy excuses. But when she whispered, "I love you, Jean-Marc," he couldn't help himself.

He pulled her into a tight embrace. "You have a fucking strange way of showing it, *chérie*."

"I just need some time. To sort things out. I'm not leaving you. Just...until Sofie is better, and I decide what to do with my life."

Something about the way she said that last part struck a chord of panic in his gut. Surely, she wasn't considering going back to her old ways? "You don't need to do anything with your life other than love me," he said quickly. "I got my lucky break when I was fifteen. It's about time you got yours, Ciara. I want to take care of you. Don't go back to the past, *mon ange*. Move in with me and we can have a future. Please, let me take care of you."

She nuzzled her face deep into the crook of his throat and sighed. She didn't say anything for a long time, and when she finally did, he tipped her chin up and saw tears shining in her eyes.

"I can't," was all she said. "I'm sorry." Then she slid from his embrace, looked at him one last time, turned and fled up the stairs.

Moments later, the apartment door slammed above his head.

And she was gone from his life.

▣ 23 ▣

"Lacroix is watching us. He's having me tailed!" CoCo declared, flouncing into the apartment one afternoon several days later. She flung her purse onto the sofa next to Davie as he and Ciara glanced up from the map they were studying on the coffee table. "Yesterday I caught him lurking about in his Saab," CoCo continued, "just down the street. He didn't even try to hide his face. It was definitely Jean-Marc."

"Yes, I've seen him too," Ciara said, worried by his cool persistence. Over the past few days, with Valois's help, she and the Orphans had decided on one last, big laydown. It was huge, complicated, and would take extremely careful planning to pull off. But it would settle their business with Beck once and for all. It was that big.

However, she hadn't counted on Jean-Marc keeping tabs on them day and night. What was he up to?

And what if Beck found out about him?

"Then today," CoCo continued, "guess who I just happened to run into on La Mouffe at the vegetable market? Why, none other than that sexy partner of his, *Lieutenant* Rousselot. Bought me a coffee at Le Verre à Pied, he did. As if I couldn't see through that ploy. Tried to pump me for information!"

"Is that all he tried to pump?" Davie asked, his brow raised over CoCo's uncharacteristic girlish flutter while speaking of Pierre.

CoCo sputtered in indignation, but Ciara tipped her head and looked at her consideringly. "What information?" she asked.

CoCo made a rude gesture at Davie, who chuckled while she answered, "About you, Ciara, *naturellement*. Jean-Marc is afraid *le Revenant* is about to make a comeback."

Ciara froze in consternation. "What did you tell Pierre?"

"That it's all nonsense, of course. That you've learned your lesson and would never, ever do anything illegal again."

"Good," she said with relief. "Keep telling him that."

This time both of Davie's brows went up. CoCo also looked startled. "*Keep* telling him?" they said in unison.

Ciara pursed her lips. "Time honored tradition with *le flic.* Divide and conquer. I shouldn't be surprised, the way I hurt his pride."

They both frowned. "Eh?"

"Jean-Marc. He's using Pierre to recruit you. To spy on me."

CoCo gasped. "I would never—"

"You like Pierre, don't you?" Ciara pressed. "You think he's handsome...sexy..."

"The man's a pig!" CoCo stated emphatically. "A big, fat ugly swine!"

Ciara smiled. "I thought so. Next time you *accidentally* run into him, let him invite you to dinner."

CoCo blinked. Perked up. "Really? You wouldn't mind?"

Ciara shook her head, an idea growing. "Let Jean-Marc have his spy."

"Oh, but my lips will be sealed! I swear—"

"No, you should tell Pierre exactly what we're doing. Not right away, you understand, but eventually... I'll tell you when to break down. But first you must make him pay dearly for the information. Take your time. Wrestle with your conscience. Otherwise Jean-Marc will know we're on to him. He has to think Pierre's dragging it out of you against your will."

"Hey! Who's dragging my little sister against her will?" Hugo asked, coming in from the kitchen eating an apple.

"*Lieutenant* Rousselot," CoCo said coyly. "I'm to be his Mata Hari."

"Who?" Hugo scowled at Ciara. "You're selling my sister to a *flic?*"

Ciara grinned. "Don't worry, Hugo. The lieutenant will survive unscathed." She and Davie shared a wry glance at CoCo. "Well," she amended. "Probably."

She just hoped this was the right decision. It was risky. Jean-Marc and Pierre were smart. Very smart.

And if things didn't go according to plan, *she* was the one who might not survive. She...and Jean-Marc.

◙ ◙ ◙

Ciara was up to something. Jean-Marc could feel it in his bones. Every cop instinct in his body screamed that she was not the innocent she pretended to be, spending her days caring for Sofie and slowly easing back into civilian life after prison.

She didn't move into her own place, didn't get a job. When she left the Orphans' apartment at all, she went to the shops, took quiet, arm-in-arm walks along the Seine with Sofie, sat in the afternoon sunshine on a bench in front of the Pompidou Center feeding the pigeons, reading and chatting to an old man who wandered by.

She didn't do a single suspicious thing.

Which was exactly what made Jean-Marc suspicious.

Pierre thought he was crazy. But hadn't objected too strenuously when he suggested they implement Pierre's old suggestion and try to flip one of the Orphans. They needed an inside source, and Jean-Marc hadn't missed how his partner cast admiring glances at CoCo every time they'd run into the feisty girl over the past two years. She was now eighteen, had blossomed into quite the young woman, and started casting her own glances back. A match made in cop heaven. Jean-Marc didn't even feel guilty. Much.

A rap of knuckles tapped on the car window. Jean-Marc reluctantly looked up through the driver's side of the Saab, which today he'd parked directly across from the Orphans' front entrance. Ciara stood there holding a Styrofoam cup. She made a circular motion with her fingers, indicating he should roll down the window, which he did. He kept his expression carefully neutral.

"Hi," she said. "Been sitting here a while. Thought you might like some coffee." She held it up to him.

"*Non, merci.* I'll just have to piss."

"Charming." Her lip curled infinitesimally. "You could come up to the apartment. The kids are all gone."

He knew that. He'd watched as one by one they went off to their jobs, and Davie to his photography class. He also knew that none of them would be home for several hours.

"*Non, merci,*" he said coolly. "Was there anything else?"

She squatted down and folded her arms across the window opening. He could smell her hair. Her perfume. He wanted to plug his nose.

"Why are you watching us, Jean-Marc?"

"I'm watching *you*," he corrected harshly.

"Why? I haven't done anything."

"To make sure you don't," he said. He was having a difficult time controlling his anger. And his hurt. He needed her gone. Far away from him.

"Jean-Marc I swear—"

In a flash he had his hand firmly around the base of her throat. The foam cup tumbled from her fingers and splattered on the pavement.

"Don't lie to me, Ciara. *Never* lie to me again."

She licked her lips. Then slowly leaned toward him. He could smell the spilt coffee, and the scent of her skin. Helpless, he watched her come closer and closer. For some reason his hand felt paralyzed and wouldn't stop her.

Her warm mouth settled on his. After a moment her tongue slipped between his lips. He tasted her. And battled back a groan.

Her hand was on his cheek, her thumb on his chin. She tugged down and his mouth opened, letting her in.

Non!

Too late. His senses swirled and he started to weaken.

"*Je t'aime*," she whispered. "*Aie confiance*. Please, Jean-Marc. Trust me."

He jerked back. Stunned. Only a fool would believe she loved him. And *trust her*? He saw red. How *dare* she!

But before he could lash out, she straightened and started to back up. "Go away, Jean-Marc. Please. Leave us alone, I beg you."

Slamming his eyes shut, he wiped his mouth with the back of his hand, controlling his fury. He counted to ten, then opened his eyes and shouted after her, "I will not go away, Ciara! So think very carefully before doing whatever it is you're planning. Because I *will* put you back in jail. And that's a goddamn promise!"

◙ 24 ◙

Ciara believed Jean-Marc.

The man was as tenacious as a junkyard dog and just as incorruptible. So it was a damned good thing she didn't plan on letting Jean-Marc catch her doing anything illegal. She would keep her activities innocuous and her fingers idle. Right up until the big laydown. And then forever afterward.

Her only hope was that someday he would forgive her for deceiving him. And for what she was about to do. She truly had no choice. Louis Beck was not going away. But everyone had their price. And she was counting on twelve million being Beck's.

Half an hour after kissing Jean-Marc, she checked the drab second-hand dress Davie had picked up for her at Guerrisol yesterday, patted her unfashionable mousy-brown wig, picked up her string grocery bag and shuffled through the front gate. Without sparing the Saab a second glance, she moved at just the right unconcerned pace for a downtrodden housewife out to buy ingredients for supper, until she was around the corner. Then she hurried straight to the *métro* and made for Valois's antique shop. This was one time she didn't want Jean-Marc following her. She'd be back within an hour, well before he'd notice she was gone.

"*Ma petite*," Valois greeted her, grinning. "I hardly recognized you."

She grinned back. "Admit it, you *didn't* recognize me. Not until I started tapping my foot because you were ignoring me for so long."

He made a face and ushered her into the back, then down through the tunnel into his secret rooms. "You do have a gift for disguises."

"Maybe I can get a job as a costume designer with the movies when I go straight."

174

He chuckled. "Or your CIA."

She choked. "Now, why didn't I think of that?"

"Too sensible? *Et voilà*," he said, spreading out a set of blueprints on the work table. "Plans for the Casino Palais d'Or in Cannes." He sighed. "And may I go on record as saying I think you are completely out of your mind?"

"So noted." She pulled three color brochures from her string purse and unfolded them on top of the blueprints. "Okay, next month during the film festival in Cannes there are going to be several important exhibitions. But the ones that interest us are these." The first brochure bore a photo of a lavish painting in shades of blue and purple. "One of Monet's famous nymphea series will be displayed in the salon area of the Casino Palais d'Or. The canvas is small, with only two men guarding it in a very crowded room. Value: twelve million dollars. And it's blue." She looked up with a grin. "Sofie's favorite color. She's already practicing water lilies on the bathroom walls."

Valois rolled his eyes. "You'll never get close to it."

"We'll see," she said. "Next—" she opened up the second brochure "— the infamous so-called Anastasia Faberge Egg. Discovered two years ago by a movie crew in an old barn while filming in Poland a few kilometers from the Russian border. A mythology has sprung up around the fabulously beautiful egg that it was left behind by the Russian Princess Anastasia on her flight from the evil red army after they killed her parents and family, and left her for dead, too."

"Complete nonsense," muttered Valois. "She was shot just like the rest of them. The egg was no doubt dropped by some unfortunate Jew fleeing from the Nazis."

"Probably," she agreed. "Or even salted by the film producer himself, looking to cash in on some great publicity."

"You're even more cynical than I am," he chuckled. "Where would he have gotten such a treasure?" She darted him a wry look and he threw up his hands with a grin. "Ah. Of course. Silly me."

"Anyway, it is, coincidentally, also valued at twelve million dollars. Though the producer refuses to sell it. This setup is even easier. Locked in a bullet-proof, bomb-proof polymer display case, it has only one guard."

He picked up the third brochure and asked, "So what's the third option? I see nothing to steal in this one."

It was a list of the visiting celebrities and VIPs slated to attend the various festival events. She pointed to a name listed next to the reception for the South American film contingent.

"Look. Here."

He peered at the name, then sucked in a horrified breath. "Jose Villalobo!? The Columbian drug czar? You must be joking! What could you possibly—" His eyebrows disappeared into his scalp—or would have if he hadn't been almost bald. "*Non*. Do not mess with that man—*or* his wife's jewels. At best, you'll end up as shark bait in the middle of the Atlantic. Villalobo is dangerous. As ruthless as they come. He's a psychopath!"

"True. But he's a psychopath with diamonds. Unmarked conflict diamonds. Worth...wait for it...twelve million dollars on the open market. It's a sign, Valois."

"Ciara! You're planning to steal *blood diamonds* from Jose Villalobo?" Valois actually crossed himself. "How do you know about these diamonds?"

"Etienne's family runs a couple of the docks in Marseille. I remembered they worked with Villalobo in the past when he first started gaining notoriety, bringing in his drugs off the freighters when his regular channels were too hot. When I saw his name on the guest list for Cannes, I made a few phone calls. Seems he acquired a large stash of conflict diamonds in a turf takeover recently. He's looking to exchange them. Thought I'd save him the trouble." She winked.

"*Non! Non, non, ma petite*. I cannot allow this." He shook his head vigorously. "*Mon Dieu*. I'll turn you in to *Commissaire* Lacroix myself if you persist with this insanity. Better for you to be safely in prison than..."

He didn't finish. His face had gone white as the paper the blueprints were printed on, and the veins pulsing in his temples matched the blue of the drawings. His hand shook as he rubbed it over his forehead.

She felt such a rush of affection for the old man she pulled him into a heartfelt hug. "It's okay, Valois. I know what I'm doing. Trust me."

That was the second time within as many hours she'd asked a man she loved to trust her, she thought ruefully. And the second time she'd lied. By the time this job was over, she'd have done a lot worse than lie. Did the end justify the means? She sure as hell hoped so.

Valois sighed, looking bleak. "I do trust you, *ma petite*. It's Villalobo I don't trust. If you value my health...and your own...you'll stick with the Monet."

◘ ◘ ◘

Sofie was doing much better. Over the next week she came out of her shell more and more, talking and even smiling as Ciara took her on walks and encouraged her to practice painting water lilies. It seemed to be therapeutic. All four walls of the bathroom were now littered with the beautiful lilac blossoms. Even Sofie's Hand of Fatima signature above the bathtub had a lotus flower blooming in its palm. She really was very talented, Ciara thought proudly. Nobody would mistake the mural for a real Monet, but Sofie's lilies were just as gorgeous in their own unique way.

While Sofie painted, the rest of them studied the blueprints of the Casino Palais d'Or and meticulously formulated several working scenarios for each of the three job possibilities.

Before deciding for sure, they had to visit the casino in person, to get the lay of the land. Ciara knew one could never rely on blueprints. Things changed during construction. Things changed after a business opened. Layouts changed. Decorating changed. Security changed. She'd learned never to take anything for granted. And with their whole future riding on this one night, she wasn't about to start now.

"Tomorrow morning, you and CoCo leave for work as usual so Jean-Marc doesn't get suspicious, but take the early flight to Marseille," she told Hugo. "Talk to your uncle about Villalobo and the diamonds. Find out everything you can. Dig deep."

Hugo and Etienne's Uncle Jacques was the current leader of the Alexander crime clan—the godfather, as it were. Nothing happened in Marseille that he didn't know about...and probably had a finger in. He'd know all about Villalobo, and she trusted Jacques completely. He was family.

"Should I tell him what we're planning?"

"Best you do. But not a word to anyone else," Ciara said. "Villalobo undoubtedly has informers everywhere. Even within the clan."

Hugo nodded uncertainly. "Are you sure about this Ciara?"

The only thing she was sure of was that she was scared to death she wouldn't be able to pull it off. But the Orphans didn't need to know that.

"We'll all make the final decision together when we've gathered our information," she said confidently, then turned to the others. "Meanwhile, Davie, Ricardo and Sofie should take the morning bullet train to Marseille, then go directly on to Cannes. I'll take the noon flight to Marseille. I assume Lacroix will be tailing me, so I'll lead him back to Madame Felicité's place. He's been there before and won't be surprised. CoCo, you have everything ready, okay?"

CoCo gave her a lopsided grin. "Oh, never you worry. The girls will take good care of him for you."

"We're just locking him up, CoCo. Nothing else."

He'd be mad as a hornet by the time the girls let him out. But she couldn't have him following her to Cannes. If he found out their plans, it would be all over.

Nope. He was not going to like being taken prisoner one bit. Unless of course, when she returned, she found a way to soothe the sting of his anger....

◨ ◨ ◨

The next morning, everything went off without a hitch.

It was a lovely April day, warm and sunny after the gray, rainy days that had gone before, so Ciara decided to wear a sassy little vintage YSL sundress she'd picked up at a flea market on one of her morning wanderings with Sofie. Classic, yet sexy. Just the thing to warm Jean-Marc's arctic gaze. Well, right up until the part where they locked him up for the day.

She sashayed up to the Saab, which was parked out front as usual, knocked on the passenger door for him to unlock it—cops, always so security-minded—and when he did, she got in, sliding her case onto the floor.

"I'm going to the airport," she said with a brilliant smile. "Why don't you save us both some time and give me a ride." She crossed her legs, making sure the dress slipped way up her thigh.

"Leaving the country?" he asked, giving her outfit a clinical once-over, ending with the small case by her feet.

"Marseille," she said evenly. "Family reunion. I'll be back tonight. You could pick me up if you're really that worried." She flashed him her e-ticket, and he took it from her. "Surely, you aren't going to follow me all the way to Marseille?"

"Why wouldn't I? You can steal as easily there as here."

Genuine irritation spiked through her. "You really must not think very highly of me, Jean-Marc."

"On the contrary. I think very highly of your skills. Perhaps not of your intelligence at the moment..."

"On second thought, I'll take a taxi," she said stiffly, reaching for the door."

He grabbed the handle and slammed it shut. It was becoming a ritual with them.

"Forget it. I'm going with you."

"To Marseille?" she asked, feigning incredulity, then huffed at his steely nod. "Fine. Whatever."

She ignored him for the entire drive to the airport. It stung her to the quick that he would so easily believe she'd reverted to her old life the day after she got out of prison. That she had learned absolutely nothing. From prison. From him...

She reminded herself that she'd given him every reason to think that. *Wanted* him to think that. But unreasonably, illogically, it still hurt. She was not the same woman as when she'd met him. Couldn't he see it? Feel it?

"So. How much does he want this time?" he asked, breaking the prickly silence as he pulled into a parking spot at the airport reserved for police.

"How much does who want?"

"Beck. For his blackmail."

She picked up her case, fighting butterflies in her stomach. "What makes you think—"

"Cut the crap, Ciara. You've got no other motive to steal now. And don't even try to tell me you like it. How much?"

As harshly as the words were spoken, they were like a sweet salve. Maybe there was a hope he'd understand...

But no way could she could tell him. Not yet. Not until the job was done and she'd sent Beck away forever with twelve million reasons never to return.

"Nothing, Jean-Marc," she said. "There's no blackmail. I'm not going to steal anything. It's a family reunion. And by the way, you're not invited."

◙ ◙ ◙

When the plane arrived in Marseille, Ciara was collected by one of Madame Felicité's girls driving a chartreuse Smart Car the size of a sardine can on wheels. Jean-Marc had apparently called ahead for a local cop friend to chauffer him around, because they spotted the white police car behind them almost immediately.

"I wonder what excuse *le commissaire* will give for spending the entire day at a brothel?" the girl said with a giggle.

Ciara gave her a wry smile. "If he doesn't like it, tell him to go back to Paris. I'll be on the flight tonight, as promised."

It turned out to be ridiculously easy to lure him upstairs, into the same room they'd shared so many months before. She simply went up, sat on the bed and waited for him. He appeared a few minutes later and stood in the doorway looking grim.

"Come in," she said.

"My rate's going to be considerably higher than fifty euro this time," he said.

"Ah. Too rich for me, then," she said, leaning back against the silk and lace pillows. Morbid curiosity got the better of her, and she asked, "How much more?"

He wandered into the room, casually examining the contents. The rich fabrics, a bouquet of wildflowers on the dresser, framed erotic prints on the wall. "More than you're willing to pay." He cocked an elbow on the mantel and crossed his ankles in a negligent pose. "You must give up your life of crime, forever."

She smiled. If only he knew...

"What if I *am* willing," she ventured, "and I do that, give it all up?

179

Would you actually believe me? Could you ever truly trust me, Jean-Marc, without following me around all day, every day, to be sure?"

The muscle in his cheek twitched. He remained silent.

She sighed, and rose from the bed, more depressed and hurt than ever. "I didn't think so." She turned from him, but in the door she glanced sadly over her shoulder. "Well, make yourself at home, *chéri*. I have a reunion to go to."

With that, she walked out, closed the door and with a decisive *snick* turned the key, locking him in.

She let out a sigh. He'd be mad, but he'd get over it.

No doubt just as easily as he'd gotten over her.

Pasting a smile to her face, she pulled the key from the lock and placed it in the hand of the waiting girl.

A shame she couldn't do the same thing with her heart.

◙ ◙ ◙

"Ciara?"

Jean-Marc frowned when he heard the door lock behind her. *What the hell?*

"Ciara! Let me out of here this instant."

"I am sorry, *monsieur le commissaire*," came the reply—*not* Ciara's-- "I cannot do that just yet."

He strode to the door and rattled it. Hard. "Do you have any idea what the punishment is for kidnapping a police officer?" he growled, the situation finally penetrating his thick head. How stupid could he be?

There was an exchange of hushed voices. Then, "Do not be silly, *Commissaire*, you are free to leave any time you wish. Unfortunately, we seem to have misplaced the key. Just relax *un petit moment*, while I find the extra one."

Monumentally stupid, apparently. When he got his hands on Ciara...

He rammed his fists into his pockets and had a sudden, erotic vision of what he'd done to Ciara last time they'd been in this room and she'd angered him. Her bare bottom, the sharp slap of his hand on her flesh... The blinding pleasure that had followed.

He swallowed heavily. The woman had deliberately deceived him and trapped him, and all he could think of was seizing his pound of her delectable flesh any way—and every way—he could. He was beyond salvage.

"If that door is not open in fifteen minutes," he called through gritted teeth, "I *will* break it down."

IN HIS CONTROL

◙ ◙ ◙

It took half an hour. But by that time Jean-Marc knew Ciara was long gone, so it really didn't matter. He also knew that not a single soul in Marseille would ever tell him where she'd gone or what she was doing. This was her turf. Her family knew they were lovers, but they also knew he'd put her in jail.

Frustrated as hell, he phoned his friend Cheveau to come pick him back up and return him to the airport. Despite his friend's amused smirk, he just rolled his eyes and didn't bother explaining.

When he got back to 36 Quai des Orfèvres, CD Belfort immediately summoned him to his office.

"What the fuck are you up to, Lacroix?" he demanded. He slammed a copy of an evening tabloid onto his desk and whipped it open.

A photo of Jean-Marc sitting in his Saab graced the center of the page. Ciara was leaning into the driver's side window. Kissing him.

Jean-Marc swore under his breath. *Putain de Merde.* He'd never even seen the damn paparazzi that morning.

"If I'm not mistaken, that's Ciara Alexander you are kissing. The woman convicted as *Le Revenant.*"

"Yes, sir. That is, no, sir. She was kissing me. A bribe, to leave her alone. I'm doing surveillance on her," he explained before he dug a hole so deep he'd never get out.

Belfort's eyes narrowed. "Why? She just got out of jail a few weeks ago!"

"Yes," he said. "And she's already back to her old tricks."

"What are you talking about?"

"She's planning a robbery. A big one."

"And you know this how?"

He hesitated. "A hunch."

He winced as Belfort pounded his fist on his desk. "*Putain*, Lacroix! I am not spending valuable OCBC funds financing a wild goose chase! What evidence do you have of this robbery?"

Jean-Marc straightened his spine. "Nothing concrete yet. But she's been acting—"

"Acting? *Acting?*" Belfort exploded. "I heard rumors during the trial, Lacroix," he ground out. "Rumors I refused to believe because, given your history, I knew for a fact you would never again allow yourself to become personally involved with a suspect!" He slapped at the newspaper so it flew off the desk. "This photo calls me a fool. Tell me the truth, Lacroix! Are you involved with this woman?"

Myriad emotions flooded through Jean-Marc as he struggled to come up with an honest answer. "No," he finally said. "I'm not."

Belfort's jaw clenched, and he regarded Jean-Marc with a long glower before saying, "I will do you a favor and *not* start an internal investigation into why *le Revenant* was only charged with one theft instead of dozens, or why she only served eighteen months instead of eighteen years, or into what, exactly, your relationship with her was and is. The important point remains, the OCBC caught and convicted *le Revenant* under your watch."

"Yes, sir. Thank you, sir," he added grudgingly.

"Stay *away* from her, Lacroix. I mean it."

He jerked to attention. "But, boss—"

"You have plenty of other investigations to work on. *Le Revenant* is a closed case, and I want it to remain that way. Do I make myself clear, *Commissaire?*"

"I'm telling you, boss, she's planning—"

"*No more surveillance!*" Belfort roared. "Get over your obsession with this woman, Lacroix. That's an order!"

Jean-Marc clamped his mouth shut, turned and stormed out.

If only he could, he thought dourly.

If only he could.

◙ 25 ◙

Jean-Marc had never disobeyed a direct order from a commanding officer. Before now.

It felt strangely liberating. In a Kafkaesque sort of way.

But he just couldn't stay away from Ciara.

Pierre shook his head sadly when he showed up at 36 Quai des Orfèvres each morning for the next two weeks looking more and more frustrated and drawn from putting in a full day's work, then sleeping in his car as he kept watch over her—if you could call reclining the seat amid the litter of file folders and take-out cartons and staring up through the sun roof all night, wired from too many espressos, sleep. The times he couldn't be there himself, he hired two buddies with different shifts than his to watch for him. He paid them well to keep their mouths shut.

"You don't need to be doing surveillance on her. It's killing you," Pierre said from the visitor's chair in his office. "Let me get the information from CoCo. All those dinners are finally paying off. She's starting to trust me."

Jean-Marc ground his palms into his gritty eyes. "Great." That made him feel so much better. Especially since he was fairly certain he knew what they were doing *after* dinner. Pierre had gotten painfully chipper in the mornings.

"Last night she let something slip."

"Besides her panties, you mean?"

Pierre vaulted to his feet. "Hey!"

Jean-Marc held up his hands, surprised at the vehemence of his partner's reaction. "Sorry, *mec.*" *Merde.* He'd fallen for the girl. This was getting way more complicated than either of them had anticipated.

Pierre straightened his jacket and sat back down. "I don't feel good about deceiving CoCo," he said grumpily.

"Oh. Like I do?" Jean-Marc sighed. "It's for her own good, *mon ami.* You don't want her involved in anything illegal. Have you tried having her speak to Sofie and Ciara about pressing charges against Beck instead of paying his blackmail?"

His mouth thinned. "Subject's off-limits. She won't talk about it."

Big surprise there. "Keep trying. So, what did she spill?"

"She told me she couldn't meet Friday night because they were all going out of town."

Jean-Marc perked up. "Where?"

"She wouldn't say. But she seemed a bit miffed, so I asked why, and she made a face, and said because some of them had to take the train like peasants while others got to drive there in a ritzy Jaguar. Then she realized she'd said too much, and clammed up."

Jean-Marc steepled his fingers and sat back in his office chair which, *d'habitude*, squeaked in protest. "Hmm. Did she say what they were all doing?"

Pierre shook his head. "Something about a reunion."

Jean-Marc's chair almost toppled backwards. "A reunion? A *family* reunion?"

Pierre glanced up, lifting a shoulder. "I suppose, though I didn't think they were all related. Why?"

Slowly, a grin spread across Jean-Marc's face. He tipped his head back and laughed. "Pierre, *mec*, you are a fucking genius."

◙ ◙ ◙

Thursday night Jean-Marc let one of his off-duty buddies watch the Orphans' apartment. The next day would be a long one, and he needed sleep. In a real bed, for a change.

Unfortunately, he was too wound up to get more than fits and starts, and when he did actually fall asleep he was besieged by dreams. Of Ciara, *naturellement*. Hot, erotic, naked dreams, which always ended up with him behind bars, and her walking away scot-free laughing at him.

It did not make for a good mood when he awoke at dawn on Friday morning and relieved his buddy.

Driving straight to rue Daguerre, Jean-Marc's nerves hummed with adrenaline. He felt cramped in the Saab, itching to spring into action. But two hours of pacing and swearing later he was rewarded when Ciara, Sofie, Ricardo, CoCo and Hugo all clattered out through the front entry door. He gritted his teeth when they cheerfully waved to him and started walking toward the *métro*. Davie was nowhere to be seen. Jean-Marc figured he'd be along later. So he followed the others. On rue Froidevaux, the quartet split up. Sofie and Hugo went right toward their usual *métro* stop, Denfort-Rochereau, the others turned left to Gaîté.

Jean-Marc gave a humorless chuckle. Nice try, kids. Both lines me up at Montparnasse.

He stuck with Ciara, even when CoCo and Ricardo branched off a block later. He figured they'd head for the *métro*, and Ciara for the car.

He kept a tight leash on her, curious to find out where she would pick up the Jag. After the Michaud robbery, he'd tried every which way to track down the mysterious old lady with the flat tire, but—not surprisingly—had found neither her nor her Jaguar. Now, of course, he knew she was Ciara. But the Jag was not hers. It would give him a certain amount of gratification to get closure on that bit of frustration, even if it was too late. You never knew. Maybe the little shit who did own it had a stack of parking tickets he could put a warrant out on.

Which was why it really pissed him off when she managed to give him the slip.

When he realized she was gone, he ran straight to the *métro* and barreled down the steps, shouldering his way through the thick morning throng of commuters crowding the platform.

She wasn't among them.

He wanted to hit somebody.

How the hell did she *do* that? One minute she was there, the next she'd vanished into thin air. She may be good with disguises, but disguises took time. She had simply disappeared.

Fuck it; it didn't matter. He knew where they were headed.

He pulled out his cell phone and punched in Pierre's speed dial. Pierre was waiting at the Gare de Lyon, to visually confirm that the Orphans took the express to Marseille.

"They there yet?" Jean-Marc asked.

"Yep. All four present and accounted for. Traveling first class all the way."

"Four? Ciara didn't show up?"

"No. Why?"

He grimaced. "I lost her. What about Davie?"

"No sign of him, either."

Jean-Marc grunted, and hung up. *Damn.* He made his way back to the Saab, trying to decide what to do next. Catch a flight and intercept the quartet at the Marseille train station was probably his best option. They'd no doubt meet up with Ciara there. But it really burned him about the Jag.

Or maybe...maybe she was going by air, and would pick up the car down south. It was, after all, at least a nine hour drive by auto to Marseille.

Then he remembered. At the Michaud job, when the old lady was leaving...a man dressed as a chauffeur had picked her up. A young, sandy-haired man.

Davie.

Damn, damn, *damn.*

On his way to the airport Jean-Marc called Pierre back.

"Get over to the office right away. Find out who Davie's known associates are. And family. The others, too, just in case. See if any of them own a Jaguar."

There was a pause, then Pierre swore softly. "Sure, boss. I'll search all the little blighters' backgrounds and let you know if anything pops."

By the time Jean-Marc's flight was taxiing in at Marseille, Pierre had called back. Davie's father turned out to be a certain Comte de Figeac, who owned no less than two different models of Jaguar. Jean-Marc jotted down the particulars and plate numbers. Then he called Cheveau in Marseille.

"I just landed at the airport. How about picking me up?"

"Oh, la la, *mec,*" Cheveau said with a hearty chuckle. "Another brothel visit so soon?"

Jean-Marc bit his tongue and took the good-natured ribbing, then explained what he needed.

"No problem. I'll put out a description of the two Jags and have anyone who spots either of them radio in their position."

"Thanks, *mon ami.* Now, any chance I can borrow one of your radio cars for the day?"

◳ ◳ ◳

When the express train pulled into Marseille, Jean-Marc was there. But the Orphans weren't.

"I cannot believe this," Jean-Marc growled after searching the train from one end to the other. He then questioned the conductor and porters. Four people matching the Orphans' descriptions had gotten off at Aix-en-Provence, one stop before Marseille.

He slammed his eyes shut and took a long, deep breath.

He would *not* explode.

He would go about this calmly and rationally, as befitted a *commissaire* of the DCPJ conducting a routine investigation.

He would not think about throttling Ciara.

He would not think about shaking her until her teeth rattled.

He would *definitely* not think about spanking her until she begged for mercy.

He dug his fingernails into his itchy palms and let his breath out slowly. There. Better.

Which was good. Because he needed every ounce of patience he could get for the next eight long, frustrating hours, while he and the every law enforcement officer within a hundred square miles searched for any trace of the Jag.

When word finally came, it was from the Aix-en-Provence train station. At 11:13 pm, *le Compte de* Figeac's Jaguar was spotted in the parking lot.

And the slow overnight train to Paris had just pulled out of the station.

◙ ◙ ◙

"Stop that train!" Jean-Marc barked at the officer who had called it in.

"I'm afraid it's too late, sir. It's well past the yard limits. Can't be stopped until the next station, unless there's a side-track somewhere along the line where it can be detoured."

"Find one," he ordered. "I'm on my way. I want to be *on that train*. Am I understood?"

"Yes, sir!"

It took him twenty minutes at breakneck speeds with lights flashing and sirens screaming to reach the train, which had been diverted to an old, abandoned depot to await his arrival. He jumped up into the caboose and shook hands with the two onboard rail security agents who were there to meet him. This was not one of the ultra-modern bullet trains, but an old-fashioned slow-moving local.

"What's going on?" they asked with obvious concern after they'd exchanged credentials.

"I'm chasing a thief," he explained, knowing he had to tread carefully. His boss had out-and-out forbidden him from pursuing Ciara, and he had no real evidence that she had even committed a crime. Other than his roiling gut.

"A thief? Not a terrorist?" The two agents looked relieved.

"A woman. Not dangerous. And I'm not even certain she's on the train," he hedged. "But she probably has stolen valuables with her if she is. I'd like permission to search for her, and if I find her to search any compartment where she's been."

The two agents glanced at each other and shrugged. "Sure, why not. Will you need our help?"

He shook his head. "*Non, merci.* But I'll need a porter's key."

Further relieved that a key was all that would be required of them, the agents quickly produced one of the long, silver hex tools that opened all doors and sleeping bunks on the train. "Good luck," they said as they handed it over.

But Jean-Marc was pretty sure his luck had deserted him nearly two years earlier, on the day he'd met Ciara Alexander.

He didn't find her on the train. Nor did he find the Orphans.

He'd stalked slowly forward through all twenty-three cars, and now he turned around and searched them all again, twice as carefully. He checked every bathroom, every luggage rack, every connecting area between cars, the dining car and every damn sleeping compartment in the wagons-lit—much to the resentment of several sleeping passengers—and studied the face of every female in every seat.

No Ciara.

He thought of her disguise at the Michaud's, as an old lady, and despaired. Short of yanking on every head of gray hair, there was no way to tell if she was lurking somewhere under a wig and a pound of theatrical make-up. And if she could do an old lady, why not a man? She could be disguised as a fat guy with a bad rug.

Merde.

He needed a drink.

Since he was already at the rear of the train, he made his way to the bar behind the closed restaurant car and ordered a bourbon. A double.

And brooded about how she had outsmarted him. Again. It was really starting to irritate him.

This had never happened before. He'd always been completely in control of his investigations. Always smart enough to track the bad guy one way or another, and bring him down. Every time save one—when he'd been personally betrayed.

And now.

Ciara was messing with his head. Making him crazy. She was as unpredictable as he was. She played dirty, like he did. Always found a way to outwit her opponent, as he always had. Until now.

But he *would* catch her. If he had to sell his soul to the devil, he would. And he was going to make her pay dearly.

He slammed back his double and raised his hand to the barman to order another. His fingers grazed the arm of a woman walking by.

"*Ah, pardon,*" he mumbled.

"*Ce n'est rien,*" she politely returned in a silky, smoky voice. She had the pampered, smooth accents of a woman who'd been to a Swiss finishing school, and shared her bed with barons and princes.

Mildly intrigued, Jean-Marc spun his stool and watched her walk past. Model tall and thin, she had henna-red hair cut in a sleek style straight out of the pages of some fancy fashion magazine. She wore a dove gray couture suit—a short jacket and shorter skirt—with black silk stockings and breathtakingly high heels. Red high heels.

Every eye at the all-male occupied bar followed her sultry stroll between empty restaurant tables toward the exit. When she reached the middle of the deserted dining area she paused, and took a last, lingering glance over her shoulder.

Right at Jean-Marc.

Unexpected arousal bolted through his body. The woman was unbelievably sexy, and for a second—okay, two or three seconds—he actually thought about accepting her fairly blatant offer. He was definitely in the mood for some hot, mind-numbing sex. A quick, anonymous fuck with a princess appealed to his bad-ass street side. Two years ago he wouldn't have hesitated. What the hell was wrong with him now? Not that he really had to ask... Despite the acute differences, she only reminded him of Ciara.

He sighed with regret as she continued to walk away, her long, long legs and shapely hips swaying like a samba.

Non, he couldn't. Not in this foul mood. Even an anonymous princess deserved to be fucked for herself, not because she reminded him of someone else. Hell, the woman even *walked* like Ciara....

Suddenly, he frowned. And launched to his feet.

His heartbeat stopped dead, then went into hyperdrive.

Non. Impossible.

Could she...?

With a virulent oath, he tossed a ten on the bar and went after her.

He tore through the first car, scanning the heads of the passengers for the woman. She wasn't there. He ran through the second car, and the next, and the one after that. Finally he saw her, just a glimpse, disappearing through the connecting door to the car just ahead.

A large lady suddenly stood up in the center aisle and blocked his path as he rushed to catch up. Impatiently, he squeezed past her. The next car was a wagon-lit, consisting of a claustrophobic passageway in aging wood veneer and several closed doors to sleeping compartments. She was already at the other end. Just before vanishing around the corner, she glanced over her shoulder again. Their eyes met.

He started to run.

When he got to the next car, also a wagon-lit, she was gone.

He stood for a moment to regroup, breathing hard and leaning back against the cool glass and metal of the outer connecting door. *She was here.* He could feel her presence, like...a ghost, haunting him. Calling to him.

The sideways motion of the train rocked him side to side, side to side, his knees bending in rhythm to the *kachunk-kachunk-kachunk* of steel wheels passing over rail joints. The shadow of a scent, exotic and alluring, *unfamiliar*, teased his nostrils.

Was his own mind playing tricks on him? Did he want it to be her so badly he was letting his imagination run rampant? Or was the woman really Ciara, cleverly disguised...

He drilled a hand through his hair and studied the four closed, presumably locked, doors to the individual sleeping compartments.

Which one?

A subtle movement drew his attention to the floor below the doors. There was only one compartment with a tiny strip of light showing beneath. Suddenly, it went out.

His instincts centered. His blood surged.

Without giving himself a chance to think, he stalked forward and rapped. *"Police. Mademoiselle, ouvrez la porte!"*

A moment later the door opened, and she stood there in the darkened compartment. Still dressed in her cloud gray skirt and jacket, she looked impossibly sensual with her flame-colored hair and scarlet lipstick. Her large eyes were heavily made-up, rimmed by black kohl in the Arab way, with long thick lashes framing startlingly turquoise eyes. Turquoise, not green.

He faltered. Suddenly uncertain.

"Oui?" she whispered in that sweet, breathy princess accent.

He gathered himself and showed her his *carte.* *"Commissaire* Lacroix of the DCPJ. I would like to search your compartment, if I may, *mademoiselle?"*

She held his gaze for an instant, then bowed her head in graceful acquiescence. "If you wish," she said, voice still hushed. She stepped aside to let him in.

His body brushed against hers as he stepped past. He smelled a hint of her intoxicating perfume. Goose bumps cascaded over his skin.

The compartment was from another era. Narrow, with plush seats and wood appointments. A tiny bathroom with a folding door was squeezed into one corner. A pull-down bunk was folded up and locked above the bench seat, which could also be turned and made into a bed. All excellent hiding places for something small, like stolen jewels.

"Luggage?" he asked brusquely. She indicated a silver bag on the red velveteen seat. "Is that it?" he asked.

She nodded. "I travel light."

He emptied the bag. It contained a bottle of fifteen-year-old cognac and a sheer black teddie. He fingered the silky barely-there fabric and sent her a look.

She raised a shoulder and her scarlet lips curved.

His heart pounded. His cock grew stiff. His rational mind tried to decipher clues. Was she Ciara? Or was she a stranger?

Returning the things to the bag, he set it aside and ran his hands over the rest of the seat and between the cushion and the back.

"Shall I turn on the overhead light?" she asked.

"Don't bother." The moon shining through the compartment window was plenty for his purposes.

He wasn't going to find anything. He already knew that. But it annoyed the hell out of him. Out of sheer stubbornness, he brought out the porter's key and unlocked the sleeping bunk, pulling it open. He ran his hands over the cold, crisp sheets under the pillow, and between the mattress and back wall. Nothing, of course.

Jetting out a breath, he straightened and turned to her.

The breath fastened in his lungs.

She had closed the door. And unbuttoned her jacket.

Slowly, she pulled it open. She wasn't wearing anything under it. Anything at all.

Her bare breasts glowed creamy white in the dim moonlight; lush, round, just big enough to overflow his cupped hands, tipped with rose-dusky nipples.

Ciara's breasts.

Raw desire detonated through his veins, fed by his anger at her, amplified tenfold by the erotic game she was playing.

"As long as you're searching...*Monsieur le Commissaire*," she said, low and sultry, "you should search everywhere, don't you think?" The jacket slipped off one pale shoulder.

He...he was almost certain...

"What is your name?" he asked.

"What would you like it to be?" she whispered.

In an instant he closed the distance between them. With an unsteady hand, he reached up and touched her breast. She mewled softly and her nipple spiraled to a tight bud.

He touched the other, watching her extraordinary turquoise eyes darken. And noticed she was wearing contact lenses.

The tension of uncertainty unfurled into the tautness of desire. He took her breasts fully in his hands, a little roughly, and listened with gratification to her moan of pleasure. Yes, his own lover's moan. Unmistakable in its timbre of hushed need.

He bent and took her nipple in his mouth. *Her* nipple, pert and responsive. *Her* taste, the flavor of midnight spiced with the musk of her desire for him. He sucked hard, bringing her to her toes and her hands to reach for him blindly.

He grabbed her wrists and stopped her, peeled the jacket down her arms and flung it aside. He pinned her wordlessly against the door, breathing hard, his chest squashing her breasts, sensing the want build in her body.

His was already beyond reason.

She reached up to kiss him. He turned his face from her.

"*Non*," he said harshly. "I'm going to fuck you. Not kiss you."

Her breath sucked in. He went for her skirt zipper and pulled it down. Then he yanked her skirt over her hips.

She wore nothing under that, either. She stood there trembling in a pool of shimmering moonlight, naked but for her black, thigh-high stockings and high heels, waiting for him to take her.

He put his face close to hers, close enough to smell her nervousness, close enough to feel her warm, staccato breaths on his throat. He took hold of her shoulders. Then slowly, deliberately, drew his hands down her quaking body, feeling the velvet heat of her skin, the wild beat of the pulse at her throat, the erotic weight of her full breasts. His fingers traced the arousingly elegant curve of her waist and hips, tested the tempting wetness between her thighs. Slipped between swollen lips and plumbed the depths of her woman's center.

She whimpered softly, and tried to move.

"*Non*," he said, and splayed his hand again on her shoulder, holding her in place. He shoved one knee between her legs and spread them wide. And kept touching her.

She moaned, grasping at his arms for purchase, her breaths now coming in gasps. He didn't stop until she came apart. She shuddered and cried out, threw her arms around him and held on as he relentlessly wrung every last quiver of pleasure from her body.

Then, when she was boneless and helpless, he took the handcuffs from the case at the back of his waistband and clipped one end to her wrist.

She looked at it in shock. "Wh-what's this?"

"What does it look like?" he said calmly. "Now, get on the bunk."

She swallowed. "*Commissaire?*" she said in a shaky whisper.

"*Do it!*" he ordered.

She hesitantly obeyed. Her red high heels fell to the floor as she climbed up onto the narrow bunk. Ignoring her reluctance, he snapped the free end of her handcuff to the metal bar holding the bunk to the outer wall.

"There," he said with velvet resolve. "You won't be going anywhere tonight."

She tugged at her firmly shackled wrist, then glanced up at him, her expression a telling mix of fearful apprehension and aroused expectation. "What happens now?"

He slipped off his suit coat and unbuckled his shoulder holster. "Now, princess, you do exactly as I say."

◙ 26 ◙

Ciara hadn't counted on Jean-Marc being so angry.

She should have known.

She should have cared. But the truth was, his anger and her longing for him were like flame to oxygen. Both fueled their passion so a single look, a mere brush of fingers, ignited the conflagration.

Their bodies were the battlefield, and the bliss.

She surrendered to him, as she always did, in the kinetoscopic light of passing scenery, in their silvery moonlit compartment of forbidden pleasure.

She gave. He took. He gave. She took.

And in the rough slide of his skin, the firm touch of his hand, the slick insistence of his tongue, she found her place in the world.

With him.

At Lyon he rose and pulled the window shade down tight, plunging their secret hideaway into complete darkness.

They barely spoke, save his husky murmured commands and her breathless moans of encouragement. With her wrist shackled she felt bound, frustrated when she reached for him and her movement abruptly halted. She wanted to hold him.

"Turn me loose," she complained.

"*Non*," he said, and shackled her other wrist to the first.

He ravished her. Slowly and methodically taking his pleasure in her helpless, hopelessly thrilled flesh.

Hours later, when he had finished with her, he removed one handcuff and clipped it to his own, binding them, captor and captive, together. Then he stretched his tall, powerful frame over her sated and trembling body. And fell asleep.

She lay there in the darkness as long as she dared, savoring the weight of him as it pressed rhythmically into her to tune of the clack-clack-clacking of the train's ambling forward progress. Loving the musky bouquet of their spent bodies and earthy lovemaking. Comforted by the steady beat of her lover's heart and the soft burr of his breaths.

He would be even angrier when he awoke.

But it couldn't be helped.

When he was deep in dreamless slumber, she gently eased out from under him, skimmed the floor for his trousers, and found the key to the handcuffs.

▣ ▣ ▣

"It's actually going to work!"

Hugo's excited words boomed through the apartment. It was the next afternoon and they had all gathered to discuss how the previous day had gone. The others nodded in enthusiastic agreement with Hugo. Ricardo slapped Davie a high five, and CoCo hugged Sofie close.

Ciara smiled broadly, but held up her hands. "We still have a few critical pieces to put in place," she reminded them. "Without those, our plan is as good as useless. Yesterday's goals and run-through went well. But next Friday everything must come together perfectly, or we fail."

Again they nodded. More somberly, but no less optimistically. It was only Saturday. They had time.

"We won't fail," CoCo said firmly.

"My copy of the Monet is almost finished," Sofie said, her mood brighter than Ciara had seen it in a long, long time.

CoCo hugged her again. "And it's beautiful. Absolutely gorgeous."

"How is the box coming along, Davie?" Ciara asked.

He grinned. "Looks just like the real one. The photos I took yesterday of the Faberge Egg to mount inside it should fool anyone. For a few minutes, anyway."

Ciara grinned back. A few minutes was all they needed. "And the Jag?"

"My parents won't be back from Rome for two weeks. We're all set."

"That's great." She turned to Ricardo. "How did your job interview go?"

His hands swirled in an enthusiastic Italian gesture. "The manager of the Casino Palais d'Or kitchens was very impressed with my culinary experience." He blew his fingernails and polished them on his shirt. "*And* my considerable charm, of course. Hired me for the whole two weeks of the film festival."

"Excellent!" Ciara said, feeling a rush of relief. Getting someone inside the casino, with access to door codes and security badges, had been a concern. She hoped they wouldn't need them, but extra escape routes were imperative, just to be safe. "When do you start?"

"Monday," he said, laughing as everyone descended on him with hugs and backslaps.

After a moment Ciara pulled Hugo aside from the chattering knot. "What more did you learn about Jose Villalobo and his conflict diamonds?"

Hugo folded his arms and watched the others with a smile. "Uncle Jacques was able to confirm that Villalobo has not yet exchanged the diamonds. He says they are only of medium quality—but unmarked."

Ciara nodded. "Which makes them perfect for low-end designer jewelry that won't attract unwanted attention. Easy to sell, and high profit."

"According to Jacques' sources, the diamonds are in a high-tech safe on his heavily guarded luxury yacht. Right now it's moored off Monaco, but he'll be sailing to Cannes on Wednesday."

She nodded thoughtfully. "Good."

"Ciara, you're not thinking of breaking into Villalobo's safe, are you?" he asked worriedly. "It would be suicide."

"I know. Luckily, there's an easier way."

"How?"

"Valois. I'll have him set the exchange in motion for Friday."

The others were listening again, and at the outsider's name they all looked surprised.

"You mean Victor Valois?" Davie asked. "What does he have to do with this?"

Ciara sat on the arm of an easy chair. "I approached him a couple of days ago with our plan, and he has agreed to help us. Valois works with precious gems all the time. And he is known throughout Europe as a completely reliable fence. Villalobo won't be suspicious of his offer to exchange the diamonds for money."

"But why would he do this for us?" Davie persisted with a frown.

"He's my mentor," she reminded him. "He taught me everything I know. He likes all of you, and he hates Beck."

"You'd think a fence would be sympathetic to a corrupt cop."

"Corrupt, maybe. But not a sadistic animal."

Her harsh words sliced through the quiet apartment. After a moment Davie nodded. "*D'accord.*"

"Speaking of which..." Ricardo ventured.

Ciara bit her bottom lip at the final item on their agenda. "Right. Beck."

They all traded somber looks. One by one their expressions turned hard. Sofie went white.

"How do we deal with him?" Ricardo asked.

"I'll take care of Beck," Ciara said grimly.

"But the blackmail deadline is Monday."

"Which is why you can bet he'll be coming around soon. I'll talk to him when he makes contact."

Hugo glanced at Sofie, his expression softening. "I'm not leaving her side until Friday is over."

"Probably a good idea," Ciara agreed.

"Are you sure he'll give us until Friday?" Hugo asked.

"For twelve million, wouldn't you?"

That was the beauty of the plan. She would promise him five million. Beck was cruel and brutal, but he wasn't stupid. He would figure out what they were planning, and come up with a way to take it all. And they'd let him. Because a cop who'd stolen twelve million had only two choices: leave the country fast and never return, or go to jail.

"For twelve million," Hugo said wryly, "most people would probably sell their own grandmother."

Which was what she was counting on. And when Beck fell for it, his hold on Sofie would be over forever.

Pulling it off would be tricky. Timing was everything. They had to lure Beck to Cannes on Friday. And they had to make sure he knew exactly where and when the exchange would take place. Ciara wanted him to pull his double-cross right afterwards. No way did she want blood diamonds in her possession any longer than absolutely necessary. Jean-Marc would just love catching her with *those*.

Davie went to the fridge and fetched a bottle of champagne. "I think this calls for a celebration." He popped the cork and grabbed some glasses.

"Make mine a small one," CoCo called to him. "I'm meeting Pierre tonight."

Ciara winced inwardly at the reminder of what she'd set in motion with that part of the scheme. Pierre always plied CoCo with good food and drink. Ciara didn't want to think about what else he plied her with.

Early on, she'd changed her mind and begged CoCo not to see him again. Warned her not to get involved in something that would only hurt her in the end.

CoCo hadn't listened. "He's important to our plans," she had maintained, despite Ciara's insistence that they didn't really need Pierre. They could feed misinformation to Jean-Marc a different way. "Besides, Pierre won't hurt me. He's a good man."

Ciara wanted to believe that. But in any case she had no real say in the matter. CoCo was of age, and had made her own decisions since she was in diapers.

"Are you ready for his questions?" Ciara asked with real concern. "Under no circumstances can you tell him what we're really doing."

CoCo nodded. "Don't worry, I'm ready for him. I've got the cover story down."

Pierre was the wild card. Ciara had thought to use him only for the setup, to keep Jean-Marc from getting too close. She had no idea what Pierre would do if CoCo really let her guard down and something important accidentally slipped out. Would he guess their real plan? Would he interfere or stop them? Or would he get greedy? Ciara had made contingency plans either way. But it was still nerve-racking.

"*Alors*," CoCo said, lifting her champagne. "Here's to Friday." They all drank, then she rose from the sofa. "I'd better get ready to meet Pierre."

Ciara watched her walk from the room with a sudden spurt of uneasiness. CoCo was acting perfectly normal. And yet...

Ciara gave herself a mental shake. No. CoCo was fine. Pierre had not gotten to her. And would not get to her, no matter how much good food and drink he plied her with. Or...anything else, for that matter.

CoCo was completely loyal. As were all the Orphans. None of them would ever betray her. Or Sofie, for whom they were all doing this.

Ciara would bet her life on it.

◫ ◫ ◫

Jean-Marc called Cheveau first thing Saturday and found out no robbery had been reported in the Marseille area anytime within the last twenty-four hours which even remotely fit Ciara's MO.

Merde.

He was so fucking tired. Tired of getting nowhere. Tired of seeing Ciara run circles around him. Most of all, he was tired of having his heart stepped on.

Waking up alone on that train, naked and handcuffed to the sleeping berth, had been the final straw. He needed some time away from this. From her. He had to get his professional objectivity back.

The woman was a thief. Her actions since being released from prison had as much as proven she was planning another robbery. She wasn't going to change. Not for him. Apparently not for anything.

He'd set aside his feelings and put her away the first time, restoring his reputation and redeeming his professional pride. He'd risked all that by warning his boss she was up to her old tricks again. He'd put his very career in jeopardy again by disobeying Belfort's orders to leave it alone. He was oh, so tempted to let her pull this stupid job and let someone else have the case---and the fallout.

But that would be giving up. And Jean-Marc may be a lot of things, but a quitter wasn't one of them. Nor would he trade his integrity for emotional comfort.

He did, however, recognize when a strategy wasn't working.

So for the entire weekend he went into Zen cop mode and put Ciara Alexander out of his mind. He entrenched himself in his office at 36 Quai des Orfèvres and caught up on all the other work he should have been doing for the past few weeks. And firmly ignored the urge to drive out to rue Daguerre and sit in his car waiting for a glimpse of her.

In his zeal, he solved two open cases.

On Monday morning Belfort called him into his office to congratulate him.

"Good work, Lacroix. See what happens when you follow orders and devote yourself to solving real crimes?"

"Yes, sir."

"It pleases me you've given up your ridiculous notions about that woman, *le Revenant.*"

He bit his tongue and accepted two new case files. Then quickly went back to his office before steam started coming out of his ears.

"Hey, *mec*, what's up?" Pierre said, plopping himself in the visitor's chair with a grin. "Heard a rumor you met some hot babe on the train back to Paris Friday night. About time you stopped pining over your lady thief."

"I'm not pining. And it was her."

"Who?"

"Ciara."

"*Non*, this was a redhead. Sounded like a princess, I hear. Sexy as... Oh."

"Yeah. Oh. Who ratted?"

"When I didn't hear back after you jumped that train, I got worried. Called railroad security. They did a little investigating."

"Thanks. I appreciate that."

"Hey, what are friends for? So, um, anything? I assume you conducted a thorough search." His grin broadened.

Jean-Marc gave him a withering glare, then sighed. "Nothing." Head in hands, he leaned his elbows on the desk. "Pierre, I'm losing it. I don't know whether I'm coming or going, she's got me so twisted around. Why am I not seeing what she's up to?"

Pierre clucked his tongue. "Emotions, *mon ami*. You are letting your emotions for the woman interfere with your usually logical policeman's mind."

He snorted. "You know me better than that."

His partner gave him a sympathetic look. "I used to."

"There's never been a choice, here, Pierre. I'm a cop. First, foremost and always."

"You want to put her away again?"

"Have to, if she's doing something illegal."

"What if she's not?"

"Give me a break."

Pierre tipped his chair back and studied his fingers. "I don't know."

"Pierre," Jean-Marc said, studying his friend just as intently. "Is there something you're not telling me?"

His partner swiped a hand over his face. "I'm not sure."

"Spill, buddy."

"It's CoCo. She's acting...different."

"Like?"

"One minute she's all sweet and happy. The next she's a million miles away, looking like she's wrestling with the weight of the world."

Jean-Marc made a dismissive gesture. "Sounds like guilt to me."

"Maybe. I've tried to get it out of her. But she just rolls on top of me and insists I'm imagining things. Very distracting."

Jean-Marc didn't like that image. Didn't want to think of CoCo on top of Pierre. Because it conjured too-vivid, too-recent memories of Ciara.

He clenched his jaw. "Do you think we're being played? Both of us?"

Pierre chuckled. "*Mec*, I think we've been way out of our league from day one."

Jean-Marc winced. That was so true it wasn't even funny. "No more, Pierre. It's time to turn this bus around."

"How?" his friend asked in an interested, if unconvinced, tone.

"Stop chasing after Ciara. Get in front of her instead. Predict her next move."

"I thought that's what we've been trying to do?"

"But in all the wrong ways. We need to go back. Do the same things we did the first time we caught her. We have enough information on her new behavior." Jean-Marc stood and leaned over the desk, slamming his hands on the top. "Hell, Pierre, let's do another profile."

▣ ▣ ▣

Beck was furious when Ciara asked for another week on their deadline. Right up until she told him about the five million. That got his attention real quick.

"You're offering me five *million? Euros?*" he asked incredulously.

"In unmarked diamonds."

"Why the fuck would you do that?"

"To keep you away from Sofie. Permanently." Ciara flexed her fingers, readying herself for his reaction. "Either take the diamonds and get out of France, or we'll keep them ourselves and go where you'll never find us. Your choice."

Beck's mouth flapped like a beached cod. Then his eyes narrowed. "You think I'll fall for that bullshit? I'm no fucking idiot!"

She shrugged. "Fine. You don't want five million in untraceable diamonds. You'll get your ten thousand cash in a week, then. Look for it in a package mailed from Rio." She turned on a toe, heading for the mouth of the grungy courtyard where they'd met.

"*Arrête*! Bitch!" She felt him lunge for her.

God, how she'd been waiting for that. She whipped the gun from her jacket pocket—a Sig Sauer 9mm 2022 borrowed from Valois specifically for this meeting—and jammed it into his forehead. His fist came to a screeching halt, mid-swing.

"Don't. Even. Think. About it," she growled.

His eyes bugged and his hands raised above his head. "You are a lunatic!"

"Are you telling or asking?" she sneered.

He backed off, arms held carefully out from his body. "I'm reconsidering."

"Too late, asshole. I've decided you're not worth five million. Think I'll kill you instead."

Sweat popped out around the red mark the gun barrel had pressed into his forehead. "A cop? In broad daylight in the middle of Paris? You'll never get away with it."

"Who said I'll do it here?" she said. "I can wait. Until you least expect it. Then--" She aimed the gun at him and mouthed a silent, "Pow."

"I'll take the money," he rushed to say, his voice hoarse with swallowed fear. "I'll disappear. I swear."

She laughed. And put the gun back in her pocket. "I thought you'd see it my way."

"Where are you getting five million in diamonds?" he asked, his shoulders notching down slightly. Even scared shitless, his gaze had turned calculating.

She laughed again. So damned transparent. "You don't want to know. This guy's South American, a drug lord. He'll slit your throat as soon as look at your ugly mug if you mess with his diamonds."

"And yet, you're willing to take the chance? Just for me?" Beck's smarmy face wreathed in a smarmy smile. "I'm touched."

She smiled through her teeth. "Nah. I'm hoping you'll get greedy and pull something stupid, so he kills you. That way I'll get your five million as well as my seven."

That brought him up short. While he wallowed in speechlessness, she walked away. She had to physically restrain herself from laughing out loud.

Damn, she was good.

◙ ◙ ◙

Jean-Marc and Pierre had spent the morning working on their revised profile of Ciara, master thief and ex-con, trying to predict what she was planning next.

"Something's changed with her," Pierre said. "Something meaningful to her crimes. Today's the last of the month and she hasn't pulled a single job."

"Which means paying the rent is no longer a motive."

"So why is she still doing it? What's driving her?"

"The reason is personal now. Compelling."

Pierre nodded speculatively. "She wants the money for herself. To have her own life."

"More likely Beck's blackmail. He raped Sofie to show how serious he is."

"That would be compelling." Pierre shifted slightly. "Then there's you, of course."

Jean-Marc frowned. "Me? What do you mean?"

"Your relationship. Your pursuit of her. You, Jean-Marc, are bound to be a factor in Ciara's change of criminal behavior."

Jean-Marc stared, then laughed. "I seriously doubt it. Other than that she's gotten a lot more devious, maybe."

Pierre shrugged. "Which is a factor."

"Granted," he conceded, making a face. "Okay, so other than me, what do we have?"

Pierre held up one finger. "Motive? Likely Beck's blackmail."

Jean-Marc nodded. "I'll go along with that."

Pierre held up a second finger. "Means? Three trips to Marseille in the past weeks. That has to be significant."

"Definitely. Unfortunately, what we don't have is opportunity. Whatever she's planning to steal, it's got to be in the area around Marseille. But what to look for?"

"What would your profile say?" Pierre asked.

"Well, statistically," Jean-Marc mused, "a person who has been to prison does one of two things. Give up crime, or escalate."

"So," reasoned Pierre, "since we don't think she's given it up, we should assume she'll go for something bigger than before."

"Right. The Picasso being the biggest. Well, the real Picasso, the one she meant to steal." He thought for a moment. "Maybe this goes beyond Beck's blackmail, after all. Surely, he can't be asking that much."

"Living expenses? Like before?" Pierre suggested. "Except maybe she wants to get it all done with one big job?"

Jean-Marc considered the idea. "The Orphans are all self-sufficient now, except for Davie. So, all right, maybe this *is* about her giving up crime. Sort of. One big job, then she quits?"

"Except Beck will never let that happen," Pierre pointed out. "Not if she keeps paying his blackmail."

Their gazes met and locked.

"*Merde, mec,*" Jean-Marc murmured, the hairs standing up on his arms. "She's *not* going to kill him. She's a thief, not a murderer. She won't escalate *that* much."

"You sure?"

"I'm sure."

"It would explain why CoCo goes pensive on me."

"She's *not* going to kill him," Jean-Marc repeated vehemently.

"Okay, we'll assume she's not a murderer, she's out to pay him off. Big. Judging by the Picasso, she's comfortable going for over a million. So, what's worth that much in Marseille?"

"Are you kidding?" Jean-Marc said, relieved that Pierre had dropped the murder thing. He could deal—just—with his lover being a thief and his prime suspect. But a murderer.... *Merde.* He got to his feet, unable to sit any longer.

"The docks run by her in-laws are teeming with import-export stuff," he suggested, pacing behind his desk. "And the whole region is dotted with ritzy houses filled to the rafters with pricy art and antiquities. Hell, the Riviera is just a stone's throw away, too."

"You mean the casinos?" Pierre looked amused. "You think she's robbing a *casino?*" A lopsided grin curved his lips. "Ocean's Six. I like it."

"Don't be an ass, Rousselot."

"Well," Pierre said, still grinning and watching him pace, "It's a good bet she isn't pulling anything in her own family's territory, or anywhere she can catch flak from them. So we should rule out the docks, *non?*"

"Yeah. And unless she's been secretly hanging around George Cluny while I wasn't watching, I think we can rule out the casinos, too."

"Cash really isn't her style."

Jean-Marc agreed. "Which only leaves a couple thousand potential targets."

"All those ritzy homes, full of art and jewelry."

"Not too many pieces can be worth over a million. Are you sure CoCo hasn't let slip a hint? We could really use a clue here."

Pierre shook his head. "No, but I'll put the pressure on when I see her tonight."

"*Non.* We don't want her to tip off Ciara."

"Then how do we figure out the target?"

After a moment, he said, "We search their apartment."

Pierre's brows shot up. "You think we'll get a warrant based on pure conjecture? You're dreaming, *mec*."

Jean-Marc halted his pacing and looked his partner in the eye. And calmly murmured, "Who said anything about a warrant?"

◙ 27 ◙

No time like the present, Jean-Marc decided.

He talked Pierre out of going along on the illegal search of the apartment. "If Belfort finds out, no sense in both of us losing our jobs."

Being mid-afternoon, when Jean-Marc knocked on the Orphans' door nobody was home. Just as he'd hoped. He showed the landlord his *carte* and the man let him into the apartment without a second thought.

Jean-Marc went through every room thoroughly, inch by inch. To his immense frustration, he found nothing useful.

No notes, no plans, no maps, no drawings. Nothing.

Just Sofie's paintings, which were hanging everywhere, along with a collection of black and white photos he assumed had been taken by Davie for his photography course. Thinking of Sofie's Picasso, he examined all of the artwork carefully, including the large Hand of Fatima she'd painted on a bedroom wall over the bed—that one gave him a bad moment or two— and the incredible flower mural covering the ancient bathroom, floor to ceiling. He started to write down descriptions of everything in his notebook, but changed his mind. Going back to Davie's bedroom, he grabbed a small digital camera he'd spotted there earlier, and proceeded to fill the empty memory stick with pictures of Sofie's paintings and Davie's photos. Then he replaced the camera, pocketing the memory stick. He'd return that later, after copying the images to his computer. You just never knew what might turn out to be important.

He wasn't sure why Ciara hadn't gotten her own apartment yet, but she was still occupying a corner of Coco and Sofie's room. Expecting to go back to jail soon, maybe? A mattress lay on the floor, surrounded by a pair of cardboard boxes, a few plastic grocery bags, and a soft-sided suitcase, filled with the sum total of her belongings. Jesus, how depressing.

Guilt stabbed him in the gut. Though why he should feel so, he couldn't decipher. She'd chosen her own fate.

Sitting down on the mattress, he lingered for a long time over her things. Checking pockets. Leafing through her few books. Putting a scarf to his nose...

She had so damned few possessions. Why should it be that he had so much, while she had so little? They'd started out practically the same in life. At the bottom of the dung heap. But he'd been the lucky one.

He owed that math teacher more than he'd ever realized....

Perhaps she'd never really had the opportunity to choose anything....

It could so easily have been him in this position. Just out of prison, broke, continuing the downward spiral of a damnable childhood. Feeling the net close in.

At heart, Ciara was such a good person. Look what she'd done for five street kids who wouldn't have stood a chance without her help. He wasn't sure he'd have been as noble or generous with the fruits of his ill-gotten gain, had their places been reversed.

Hell, he knew he wouldn't have. His whole life, he had never thought of anyone but himself. Not before Ciara Alexander came along and made him see he didn't want to live as an island, a solitary fortress against the world, viewing life in black and white for fear he would slide back into the quagmire of his early years. Terrified to feel real emotions lest he be hurt again. When the truth was, the only real hurt he'd ever felt was to his pride.

Why the hell hadn't she accepted his offer to get out? To come and live with him and leave her unhappy, unsettled past behind?

He just didn't get it.

The tinkling chime of a mantle clock brought him back to the present. Time to go. Filled with frustration on too many levels to count, he stood and took one last look around.

He hadn't found anything. Not a single thing that implicated Ciara in any kind of illegal activity.

Could he be chasing something that just plain wasn't there?

Could she have changed?

Was it possible he was wrong about her?

Again?

◻ ◻ ◻

"You look like hell," Pierre remarked, sweeping into Jean-Marc's office and flopping into his usual chair.

"*Va te faire foutre.*" Another night spent tossing and turning had not left Jean-Marc in a particularly good mood.

"What's that?"

He looked up from his computer screen. "Photos I took yesterday at the apartment. Of Sofie and Davie's pictures."

Pierre got the connection immediately. "Anything?"

Jean-Marc flung his arms in the air. "How the hell should I know? I'm practically illiterate when it comes to art. If it's not the Mona Lisa, I'm lost. What about you?"

"Not much better, I'm afraid. Have you sent the images to an expert?"

"Sure. She'll get back to me. In a week."

Pierre puffed out his cheeks. "Very useful. What about Davie's photos? Anything look familiar?"

"Pretty much everything. All the typical tourist hangouts. Artsy shots of the Eiffel Tower. The Arc de Triumph at night. Le pyramid."

Pierre chuckled. "I doubt she's planning to rob the Louvre."

"I'm beginning to doubt she's planning to rob anything," Jean-Marc grumbled.

At that his partner froze. "*Pardon?* Do I detect a change of heart?"

"Maybe," Jean-Marc said more than reluctantly. "Face it. We've got nothing. Zip. Nada. I may be forced to admit Belfort could be right about Ciara."

Pierre blinked. "Jeezus, Marc. Are you feeling okay? You look a little flushed."

"Fuck, Pierre. We've tried everything to figure her out. I don't know what else to do." He closed his eyes and leaned his head back against the wall.

His friend's chair creaked and Jean-Marc could feel himself being studied and evaluated. "Perhaps you should give it a rest for a while. Work on other stuff. If it happens, it happens. Otherwise..." Jean-Marc opened his eyes to see Pierre shrug expansively.

"Yeah. I guess."

For several minutes they watched his monitor scroll slowly through yesterday's photos, each deep in thought.

"Sure there was nothing on their computer?" Pierre asked idly. "Sometimes files can be well-hidden."

"They don't have a computer. You know that from the last search."

"A printer?"

"Nope."

"Hmm. Then how does Davie process his photos? Didn't you say he uses digital cameras?"

Digital. Jean-Marc couldn't think for a full ten seconds of kicking himself mentally. "*Putain,*" he finally said.

"I'll look for it," Pierre said, rising. "Somehow I don't think you're in the right frame of mind."

"Thanks," he said, wondering how he could have missed something so basic. Just proved how far off his game Ciara had driven him. Jesus, he was so screwed up.

"Oh," Pierre said, stopping in the doorway. "I'm taking Friday off, okay? CoCo asked me to Cannes with her for the weekend."

Jean-Marc glanced up in surprise. "Cannes? Didn't the film festival start today? Where on earth are you going to stay?"

"Apparently Ricardo got a job cooking at one of the big casinos for the duration. They arranged a room for him. He's letting us use it Friday and Saturday nights since he'll be working round the clock those days."

Cannes... Wasn't that only a stone's throw from Marseille?

A tingle of excitement shivered over Jean-Marc's scalp. "Are all the others going, too?" he asked quickly.

"Nope."

The spark of hope quickly faded. *Damn.*

"No problem, take Friday," he said, realizing Pierre was still waiting for an answer. "Let me know about the computer, eh?"

Not that he thought there'd be any more clues in it than they'd found elsewhere.

Pierre left, and Jean-Marc sighed, reaching for one of the files Belfort had given him yesterday. Maybe solving a few more cases would put him in a better mood.

And let him think about something else—anything else—than the problematic Ciara Alexander.

▣ ▣ ▣

"You did *what?*" Ciara couldn't believe her ears.

CoCo was uncontrite. "I invited Pierre to Cannes. Now, before you blow up, listen to me. We all know Jean-Marc has stopped his surveillance of you. We need a backup, in case he doesn't show. He might not put it together in time."

"He'll put it together. The man's as smart as they come."

"But what if he doesn't?" CoCo insisted.

Ciara ground her jaw. "The place will be crawling with cops. We just use one of them instead."

"Too risky. Trust me, Pierre will never know what's going on," CoCo said confidently. "My only role in the job is creating a distraction. He can help with that, even unaware."

Ciara drove her fingers into her hair and tugged. "Jeezus, CoCo. I wish you'd consulted me first."

"And what would you have said?"

"No, of course!"

"I rest my case."

Ciara did her best to remain calm. Well, as calm as possible, considering her whole future was on the line here. And Sofie's.

"Okay. Obviously you can't tell him to get lost now or he'll get suspicious. I guess he could be useful. Just please, for godssakes, keep his attention firmly below his neck. If he starts seeing things, or heaven forbid, thinking, we're done for."

A furtive smile creased CoCo's face. "He won't. That's a guarantee. He'll do exactly as I say."

For some inexplicable reason, that didn't comfort Ciara as it should have.

"Sofie's counting on you, CoCo," she said softly. "She's counting on all of us. We can't let her down."

"I understand that," CoCo said, and without looking at her, turning away to go to her room. "We won't let her down."

Ciara refused to let the thought form in her mind that was threatening to break through.

No, CoCo was fine. Everything would be just fine. There were only two days to go and everyone was nervous. Most of all Ciara. But there was no reason the plan shouldn't work perfectly.

CoCo was probably right. Pierre need never know what was going on. And he'd help to establish their alibis. That was critical. The only thing better than one cop to establish an alibi was two cops.

All right. So Pierre was in.

And everything was good. She wouldn't panic.

At least not yet.

◐ ◐ ◐

By Wednesday morning Jean-Marc had solved the two cases Belfort had given him on Monday. This was way too easy.

And not nearly distracting enough.

Luckily, Pierre walked in with a thick file of computer printouts right before Jean-Marc did something drastic, like ask Belfort for more cases. Or drive the Saab to the rue Daguerre.

"Whatcha got?"

"I found the computer."

Jean-Marc sat straight up. "Yeah? Where?"

"The school where Davie takes his photography courses."

Within him, elation warred with despair. Jean-Marc's professional side was certain he was right about Ciara, and this could prove it...and yet, for the past day or two, the thought that his suspicions about her might actually be wrong had felt strangely...compelling.

"Any hidden files or secret photos?" he asked.

Pierre blew out a breath. "Well. Yes and no." He dropped the heavy file onto Jean-Marc's desk. "No hidden files, but lots of photos. *Tons* of photos."

"And?"

"And...they all look like student stuff to me. Portraits, close-ups of birds and flowers, every monument in Paris." His nose wrinkled. "A whole folder of naked guys. Yuck."

Jean-Marc laughed. "Well, he is gay."

"Just my luck," Pierre muttered. "Anyway, the only picture of anything that looked remotely like a possibility was some weird, fancy egg-shaped thing. Porcelain, maybe? Covered in jewels and gold embellishments."

"Egg-shaped?"

Pierre made a face. "Antique Easter ornament?"

Something in the back of Jean-Marc's mind triggered. He'd seen an object like that recently. But where? The image in his memory was black and white, but not sharp like Davie's photos. More grainy, like...newsprint.

That must be it. He'd bought *Le Monde* on the way home from work Sunday. Jumping up, he strode quickly down to the squad room.

"Anybody still have a copy of Sunday's paper?" he asked loudly, poking his head in.

Belfort's secretary motioned him over. He took the paper impatiently and swiftly checked the front page. Nothing. He whipped it open and went page by page, until he found what he was looking for.

"Here it is." The cover of the pull-out supplement for the Film Festival schedule had an article featuring non-film-related exhibits. He held up one of the pictures for Pierre to see. "Was it something like this?"

Pierre's mouth dropped open. "*Bon Dieu*, that's it! That's exactly the piece in Davie's photos!" he said. "What the heck is it?"

Belfort's secretary piped up with a slight tone of superiority, "Why, it's a Faberge Egg, of course. The Anastasia Egg. Very beautiful, and extremely valuable."

"How valuable?" he and Pierre asked simultaneously.

"*Very*," she pronounced with a nod of her steel-gray head.

Jean-Marc met Pierre's gaze, then snapped it back to the article, skimming for an exact figure. "*Sacrebleu*— It says here it's insured for twelve million."

"An egg?" Pierre said in pure disbelief.

The secretary just rolled her eyes. Jean-Marc could swear he heard a muttered, "Barbarian," under her breath, but her lips stayed tactfully immobile.

"May I take this?" he asked, dropping everything but the supplement back on her desk. She nodded. He jerked his head to Pierre and strode back out into the hall. When they were alone, he stopped and scanned the rest of the article. "Says here the egg will be on display for two weeks at the Casino Palais d'Or in Cannes."

Pierre frowned. "Palais d'Or?"

Jean-Marc glanced up. "What?"

"That's the casino where Ricardo is working."

This time the tingle in his scalp was stronger. "Yeah?"

They both let that digest for a minute. Could this really be it?

"But twelve million," Pierre said finally, shaking his head. "*Non*. I don't believe it. That's too far out of her range."

Jean-Marc was inclined to agree. "Still, it's quite a coincidence. And you know how I feel about coincidences."

"Same as I do. But get out. *Twelve million?*"

They stood there mired in indecision, letting the unreality and unlikelihood of the proposition versus the coincidence factor filter through their cop radars.

"*Non*," Jean-Marc said, reluctantly embracing the unlikelihood. "You're right." He gave the article one final glance, letting the newspaper fall to his side in one hand. The page fluttered and flipped over. And there, in full, living color, was a different photo.

A photo of a painting. Of flowers. Water lilies, painted by Monet.

Which looked so much like Sofie's mural in the Orphans' bathroom, he almost choked. Her inspiration was unmistakable.

Above the photo the headline read, RARE MONET ON DISPLAY AT CASINO PALAIS D'OR.

"*Merde*," he whispered.

Once might be a coincidence.

Twice was a pattern. And evidence that his worst fears had been correct.

Ciara was planning something. Big.

Bigger than Jean-Marc would ever have imagined.

◫ ◫ ◫

Jean-Marc felt almost oppressively calm.

He'd expected to be furious. To erupt in a black rage, wanting to beat someone bloody, to storm his way to Ciara, sirens blaring, and demand an explanation.

But when the grim reality finally hit him, he desired none of those things. What he really wanted was to curl up in a tight ball and weep. For her. For him. For what might have been.

He turned to Pierre. "Are you seeing CoCo tonight?"

His partner hesitated, eyes darting briefly to the supplement. "I'm not sure."

"When you do," Jean-Marc said, "do not tell her what we've found out. Not even a hint. Just make your weekend plans as though you have no idea about any of this."

"Okaaay. But—"

"*Not a word,*" Jean-Marc growled, then spun toward the elevator. "We'll talk tomorrow. Right now I have something to do."

With that, he went swiftly down and found the Saab. Tires squealing, he flew out of the parking lot and turned the car toward the rue Daguerre.

Halfway there, he changed his mind. Pulling over, he stared straight ahead, frowning as a new thought occurred to him.

Try as he might, it was not a thought he could ignore.

All right. Change of direction.

Fifteen minutes later, he pulled into the driveway of a squat, oil-soaked garage squashed between two old tenements in a part of town whose better days were probably several centuries ago. The garage, however, hummed with activity. Jean-Marc steered his car straight into an open bay, got out and strolled forward to lean casually against the Saab's front fender.

A man in greasy blue coveralls came forward, a nervous smile on his face. "Hey, Jean-Marc. What's up?"

"Hello, Hugo," he said quietly. "I think it's about time we had a little chat. Don't you?"

◙ 28 ◙

Ten pm Friday. It was time.

Ciara made a last-minute adjustment to her henna-red pageboy wig as Davie pulled the Jaguar up under the porte cochere of the Casino Palais d'Or.

"Stop fiddling," he admonished her, tipping his chauffer's cap to the valet who was checking in cars. "You look terrific."

"Sorry. I'm a little nervous," she confessed.

He grinned into the rearview mirror. "You? Nervous? The infamous *le Revenant?*"

"Oh, shut up." She grinned back, despite the adrenaline pounding through her veins like a herd of elephants on speed.

"You can do this, Ciara," he said, his tone gentling. "*We* can do this."

"I know," she said as he stopped the car in front of the impressive main entrance. "But there are so many things that could go wrong."

"None of which will happen," he assured her.

She hoped to hell he was right.

With a final adjustment to the plunging neckline of her backless Dior gown, she emerged from the Jag and swept toward the monumental entrance, smiling brilliantly for the gaggle of paparazzi who crowded in, furiously snapping photos of all new arrivals. The Palais d'Or was one of the hottest casinos in a city overflowing with celebrities. And she was a *princesse*.

As Jean-Marc had called tonight's disguise.

Had he known the princess he made love to on the train was really her?

A poignant stab of longing lanced through her, but she pushed it away. She couldn't afford to think about Jean-Marc now. There would be plenty

212

of time for that later. A whole lifetime.

Even in a room full of movie stars, heads turned to watch her regal, leisurely progress through the casino. She knew she looked good. She'd taken great care to look fabulously glamorous, matching hair and makeup to the magnificent sapphire blue floor-length Dior gown Valois had bought her for the occasion. She wore only one piece of jewelry, a narrow antique choker of emerald-cut diamonds, borrowed from his shop. He had insisted on both, saying she must look her best to impress Villalobo tonight at the exchange at midnight.

Her thumping pulse slowed, now that the lay-down had finally begun. Threading her way through the elegant tables and beautiful people, she stopped here and there to watch the action—and to get a feel for the room tonight. Eventually she spotted Hugo, looking youthfully attractive in his rented tux and poshed up hair, standing casually next to a roulette table with a low betting limit. He was her lookout tonight, and would always be near, even if unseen.

Steeling her nerves, she sat down in an open seat at the roulette table.

Davie and Ricardo had taught her the basics of the game, but she still felt like a fraud buying her chips from the croupier like she had a clue what she was doing. In her purse she carried a thousand euros—ashtray change to most of these people, but all the money she and the Orphans could scrape together. She had to make it last all night.

She lost on the first spin of the wheel. And the second. And the third. After fifteen minutes she'd only won once.

This was going well, she thought dryly, tempted to change the position of her next chip though Davie had specifically told her to pick one bet and stay with it. Even with the lowest ante possible, at this rate she'd be broke in less than an hour.

"Try betting the orphans," a gravelly male voice murmured from behind. "You might have better luck."

Her stomach zinged and her throat tightened. *Jean-Marc.*

His tuxedo-clad arm snaked around her, a stack of euro notes in his hand. He placed them on the table in front of her. "Black on full orphans *pour la princesse,*" he told the croupier. "*Pour moi,* the same on orphans split, *s'il vous plaît.*"

She dimly recalled Davie telling her about a complicated bet called an orphan, but as of thirty seconds ago her mind had gone totally blank.

He was here!

Jean-Marc had found her.

The croupier finished taking bets and spun the wheel before Ciara collected her wits enough to figure out Jean-Marc had just placed an eight hundred euro bet for each of them.

"*Dix-sept noir,*" the croupier called when the ball dropped into its final slot. "Seventeen black."

"We win, *Princesse*," Jean-Marc murmured in her ear.

The croupier efficiently raked the table and distributed the winnings. She almost fell over when she saw the color of chips he set in front of her. It was well over three thousand euros worth! *Four thousand dollars.*

She marshaled her worldly sang froid and inclined her head, turning slightly, "*Merci, Monsieur le Commissaire.* You are too generous."

"My pleasure." Still behind her, he stepped closer. The luxurious fabric of his tuxedo whispered against her bare back, radiating heat from his body. "Will you join me at the blackjack table, *Princesse?*"

Needing distance badly, she rose from her seat. By the time she'd gathered her purse and tipped the croupier, Jean-Marc had cashed them out. He pressed a stack of chips into her palm as they melted through the throng of people around the table.

"I couldn't possibly accept these," she said, trying to give them back. "It was your money and your bet that won."

"I got my stakes back and more. Keep it. Let's play blackjack."

She exhaled, recognizing his mulish expression, despite the urbane smile. "All right. But you play. I'll watch."

"You play. I'll kibitz."

They'd come to a halt between tables in a large, open area which contained several guarded displays, including the Monet and Faberge Egg. Her nerves shimmered. *Had he guessed? Was he angry?* It was always so difficult to tell...until it was too late.

Struggling to resist the urge to check the displays, she turned to face Jean-Marc. He looked more handsome than she'd ever seen him. The cut of his stark black tuxedo was straight from this year's runways, classic in a rebellious sort of way—like its wearer—nicely emphasizing the breadth of his shoulders. His strong, clean-shaven jaw appeared more angled, his cheeks leaner than usual, his expression more confident...and utterly relentless.

He didn't touch her, just gazed down at her with those all-knowing blue eyes. She got it. He had no intention of letting her leave his side for the rest of the night.

A shiver of anxiety—and something else—tingled down her spine. Would she be able to slip away from him when the time came?

Did she care?

She had the most foolish urge to throw her arms around him and tell him everything. Lose herself in the safe, secure strength of his embrace and his protection. Beg him to understand.

But she couldn't do that.

"*Viens*," he said, indicating the blackjack tables at the far side of the room. "Shall we?"

His fingers touched lightly at the small of her back as he guided her to the table he'd chosen, and bade her take a seat. Suddenly she didn't know what made her more nervous—the diamond exchange later tonight, or playing a game with Jean-Marc that she had no idea how to play.

Two games, if you counted blackjack....

As the dealer shuffled, Jean-Marc stood behind her and quietly went over the rules. Seemed simple enough. "If you should take another card, I'll squeeze," he murmured softly as he slid his hands onto her bare shoulders. "To hold, I'll caress."

She shivered again as his hands glided down her arms, raising goose bumps.

"Cold?" he asked, his voice low in her ear.

"No. Cut it out."

He chuckled deep in his throat. "Not a chance, *Princesse*."

"I won't be able to concentrate. You'll make me lose."

"You'll manage."

For a brief second she wondered if he was really here for the reason she'd hopefully led him to believe—to stop her from stealing the Monet and Faberge Egg. She and the Orphans had planted the clues. He was a great detective. He must have figured it out.

But his behavior seemed...incongruous.

Then it struck her. He hadn't used her name, only called her princess. Did he even know it was her under this disguise? The thought was so disconcerting she almost missed his signal for the first hand.

That, and his fingers gliding erotically down her bare back. Damn Valois for buying her a gown that had so little...gown...to it.

To her amazement, she won. And the next hand as well. And most of the hands for the next half hour. Which was even more of a miracle considering Jean-Marc kept up his steady torment of her body with his touch.

When she doubled her money, the crowd around her clapped politely at her excitement.

"You are my good luck charm, *Commissaire*," she told him, glowing with pleasure.

He smiled and lifted the glass of champagne he was sipping on in a salute. "I live to serve, *Princesse*."

Her smile faltered as she suddenly spotted CoCo standing in the throng, Pierre at her side. CoCo winked, and crooked her arm through Pierre's.

Damn. How could she have forgotten? While playing cards, she hadn't thought once about why she was really there. Jean-Marc had distracted her that thoroughly.

Appalled at her own lack of focus, Ciara slowly let out the breath that had backed up in her lungs. CoCo's appearance was a stark reminder she needed to concentrate better on the job at hand. She stole a glance at a neighboring man's watch.

Eleven-thirteen pm. Forty-seven minutes to go.

Villalobo had scheduled their meeting for midnight, in a private game room one floor up. CoCo's diversion with Pierre would come just before that, and Sofie and Davie would spring into action. In the ensuing chaos, Jean-Marc would leap up to direct the dozens of police officers he surely had waiting in the wings. He'd be taken by surprise when it wasn't her who struck, and with luck, would be confused enough to give her time to slip away for ten or fifteen minutes, meeting Valois for the exchange with Villalobo. The whole thing shouldn't take longer than that.

Ciara accepted a glass of champagne from a roving waiter and stood, clicking it against Jean-Marc's. "You take over, darling," she said with a smile. "I'm afraid my nerves are frayed from winning so much money."

He regarded her appraisingly. "Only if you promise to stay and be *my* good luck charm." His eyes told her she didn't have a choice.

Not that she wanted one. She had forty-five minutes and it was her turn to torment him. She could do arm candy.

"Or..." he added at a low murmur, "am I going to have to bring out the handcuffs?"

Her brow rose coyly. "I assume you recall what happened last time you tried that?"

"Vividly," he said, his voice deepening.

She blushed. "What exactly are you planning, *Monsieur le Commissaire?*"

"What I'm planning," he murmured, "is to win a lot of money, then either arrest you or take you upstairs to my suite for a repeat performance."

Her lips parted in wary surprise. She hadn't expected him to be so forthright. She feigned shock. "Arrest me?"

"Only if you're very naughty." He put his fingers to her collar bone and drew them lightly up her throat. The gesture was half caress, half threat. "And we both know what happens to girls who are very naughty."

She swallowed heavily. Her mind flooded with images of her and Jean-Marc on the bed in the brothel. *Just before he'd arrested her.*

"Jean-Marc..." she whispered, almost desperately.

"Ciara, listen to me very carefully. My men are watching us even now. The casino is surrounded by a hundred local police officers. Should anything at all be stolen here, the thief will not get past the door."

"Well---" Her voice cracked. She cleared it and tried again. "Then I'm very glad I'm not planning to steal anything."

The smile he gave her was enigmatic. "*Bon.* In that case I shall relax and play some cards. Stay close, *mon ange.* My men have orders to detain you should you attempt to sneak away from me."

She squeezed her eyes shut so he wouldn't see her mounting anxiety, and pressed her body seductively against his side as he took a seat. "How close would you like me to stay, *Commissaire?*"

Without looking up, he pulled a large bundle of hundred euro notes from his inside jacket pocket and placed it on the table. He put an arm around her hips and his hot breath tickled her breasts. "Right where you are," he murmured.

So she stayed there, distracting herself by playing the role of clinging mistress. Savoring, while she could, the feel of her body rubbing intimately against his, the smell of his cologne, the illusion that she was his.

She wanted to kiss him. Wanted to take his chin in her hand and pull his mouth to hers in a long, drugging kiss. Wanted to leave the table and drag him upstairs right now.

But she couldn't, so she ignored the noise and the card play and thoughts of the future, and contented herself with simply touching him.

Behind his back, every so often she spotted CoCo and Pierre blending in with the growing crowd. And suddenly, there were Davie and Sofie.

Jean-Marc's watch stared back at Ciara from his wrist. *Eleven forty-six.*

All at once he gave a luxuriant stretch. "Think I'll take a break," he said, making a signal to the dealer. "Cover me, *s'il vous plaît.*"

"No!" she said, instantly panicking. Not now!

He turned to her, brows raised in question. "*Non?*"

"You can't quit now," she blurted, hurriedly scanning the table for a plausible reason. If he left the game now, oh God, things would get complicated. "You—" To her shock, she saw a dozen or more large stacks of chips in front of him. "You're on a roll!" she stammered.

Around them, murmurs of agreement came from the rows of onlookers that had gathered to watch him play. Everyone loved seeing a player beat the pants off the bank.

Rolling his shoulders, he cocked his head at her. "I didn't think you were paying attention. To the game."

She felt her face heat. "You know I'm easily bored," she said with coquettish lightness.

He chuckled. "Most women would enjoy watching her lover win a small fortune for her."

She started— *for her?* —then covered smoothly. "Darling, it's only *you* I want. Not a fortune, small or otherwise." She finally gave in to her longing, took his face in her hands and kissed him.

She sighed with a heartfelt mix of pleasure and pain. This could be the last time...

"A noble sentiment," he murmured when, too soon, the kiss ended. An unreadable curve bowed his lips. "Shall we put it to the test?"

Puzzled, she answered, "I'm not sure what you mean."

He waved a hand over his stacks of winnings. "How much do you think

I have here?"

"No idea," she said truthfully. She'd memorized the colors of the standard chip denominations, but his were too many and too varied to begin to count. There were several piles of yellow—each a thousand euro—which alone must have been worth more money than she'd ever see again—after tonight.

"Dealer?" he asked.

The man gave a Gallic shrug, in-between dealing around him. "Four, five-hundred thousand, perhaps."

Her jaw dropped. *Half a million...* "Good lord," she breathed.

"Take it," Jean-Marc said. "I'll give it all to you, every *centime*." He paused for the exclamations from the onlookers to die down. "On one condition."

She went absolutely still. Inside she quailed at the icy chill in his blue eyes.

Suddenly she wanted to kill him. Why couldn't he have made this offer, along with whatever impossible condition he had in mind, a dozen years ago? When the money would have made a difference, and the condition be a possibility? Now it was too late.

Eleven fifty-four.

Far too late.

"What condition is that?" she asked, her pique cooling to sad resignation.

"You must leave with Pierre. Right now. This very minute. Go straight to Paris, stopping for nothing."

She stared at him. Somehow sensing the real blow was yet to come. "And you?"

His eyes met hers, black and remorseless. "You'll never see me again."

The crowd gasped theatrically. Hollywood stars and moguls of the silver screen, confronted by genuine drama.

Ciara straightened. And lifted her chin.

She didn't know what hurt more, the thought of never seeing Jean-Marc again, or the knowledge that he must think so little of her.

"An interesting offer," she said. "But why not make it even more interesting? Double or nothing."

He frowned. "What?"

"Bet it all," she said, gesturing back at the game, struggling not to let the deluge of emotions show. "Everything on one hand. If you win, I get both you *and* the money. If you lose, I leave, never to darken your door again."

His eyes flared in shock. "You'd risk that?"

"No risk," she said, throat aching. "Right now I have neither you nor money. What do I have to lose?"

He didn't answer.

They both knew he had the power to throw this hand by choice. Winning was less certain, but his record so far was testament enough to his skill at swaying the odds in his favor.

Which would he choose?

Eleven-fifty-seven.

"*D'accord,*" he said, face impassive, and turned back to the table. He nodded to the dealer. "All of it. Double or nothing."

The crowd cheered madly. The casino manager and pit boss, as well as two security guards descended to stand behind the dealer. The manager looked grim.

Ciara could barely focus as the cards were dealt, let alone have a prayer of counting up Jean-Marc's—even if he showed them to her. Which he didn't.

The onlookers groaned as the dealer turned up his cards. A four and a three. What did that mean? She squeezed her eyes shut. Hell. Why hadn't she paid more attention to the rules?

When it was his turn, Jean-Marc gave the signal to pass. Stone-faced, he watched the rest of the players complete the round, ending with the dealer, who turned up a five. The crowd groaned louder.

She tried to add up four plus three plus five, but her mind froze. Twelve? Thirteen?

Did it matter?

The dealer reached for his next card. Everyone held their breath. He turned an eight. A chorus of ambiguous exclamations came from the throng.

Ciara resorted to her fingers. Did that make over twenty-one? She couldn't think.

One by one, the other players showed their hands, winners happily, losers tossing them down in disgust.

All attention turned to Jean-Marc.

She couldn't bear it. "Please, for the love of God, turn them over," she pleaded.

The crowd hushed.

Eleven-fifty-nine.

He lifted his cards and started turning.

Abruptly, an earsplitting whistle shattered the silence. A claxon sounded, and a shout was heard. "The Egg! The Fabergé Egg! It's gone!"

Another yell came immediately after. "The Monet! It's also been stolen!"

Jean-Marc's hand froze in mid-air. His head whipped around and his eyes lasered in on hers. "*Non,*" he growled. "I don't believe it."

"Jean-Marc, I—" Her chest constricted with pain. She wanted stop the flow of time. So she could explain.

Then all hell broke loose. From nowhere, dozens of uniformed men appeared, converging on the nearby display area. The crowd roiled, straining at once to see Jean-Marc's cards as well as whatever was going on.

And still Jean-Marc's eyes drilled into hers, throwing sparks of fury. She shook her head.

"Pierre!" he yelled.

"*Oui?*" Pierre elbowed his way through the churning mass of humanity to his side.

Jean-Marc tossed down his cards, face up, then jabbed a finger at her. "Do *not* let her out of your sight."

Then he was gone, the multitudes parting in his path as though for Moses.

Pierre gave Ciara a hard look. She cringed. And noticed that everyone else was staring at her, too.

Suddenly she remembered.

His cards...

She spun. Looked at the two cards sitting alone on the table.

And her heart stopped.

▣ 29 ▣

Suddenly, CoCo appeared at Ciara's side.

"Go! Go!" she whispered urgently, then launched herself at Pierre, spinning him around. "Omigod, baby, this is too exciting! I want a drink!"

Ciara was still rooted to the spot. But at CoCo's frantic shooing motion, her wits returned and she slid away into the crowd. Straining against the rush of curious people, she worked her way to the other side of the room.

As planned, Valois was waiting for her at the elevator, holding the door open with a metal attaché case. They went quickly to the second floor and hurried toward the Palm room, where Villalobo was waiting.

"Any trouble getting in?" Ciara asked.

"No. Ricardo was at the catering entrance just as arranged. The diversion went well, I saw."

"Better than expected," she muttered, slowing her pace a bit for the old man. The Palm room was one of the furthest away in the huge upstairs labyrinth of private banquet and gaming rooms, and he was already getting winded. "Remind me to tell you about it sometime."

"Sounds ominous."

She refused to think about any of that right now. If she did she'd— She ruthlessly cut off the thought. "The room should be right beyond this—"

As she went around the last corner, she was forced to an abrupt halt. By a man in a tuxedo. Holding a large gun.

▣ ▣ ▣

Jean-Marc stalked grimly over to where the Monet and Faberge Egg were on display. Correction: *had been* on display.

Now, the ornate gilded frame was graced by one of Sofie's charming, but hardly masterful, stylized copies of Monet's water lilies.

He had to hand it to Ciara and her accomplices. The switch had been brilliantly executed. Not a soul had observed who the culprits were, and they'd gotten clean away. He thought with annoyance of his own unintended cameo role in their distraction. *Merde.* What would they have done if his blackjack game hadn't turned out quite so...fascinating? No doubt they'd had an excellent plan. Ciara always had an excellent plan.

The guards and casino manager crowded behind him, all talking at once. The owner was running around pulling his hair. Jean-Marc couldn't hear himself think.

"Silence!" he roared above the din. "And somebody shut off those damned alarms!"

Steeling himself for the worst, he peered closely at Sofie's Monet. The steel coil of panicked uncertainty in his stomach unwound slightly. Unlike with the Picasso, the fake Monet hadn't been stapled to the rear of the frame. In fact, it appeared to be sitting loose on top of it, just overlapping the inside edges. He reached up and yanked it off.

The men behind him gasped.

"*Voilà*," he said with an acute rush of relief.

They gasped again.

The real Monet in all its glory sat placidly in its frame. Unharmed. Untouched.

"*Alors*," he said, passing the fake canvas to one of his men. "And the egg?"

The group of security guards herded him over to a beautiful chest-high pedestal of clear fluted crystal, topped with an acanthus leaf capital and small square platform. On the platform sat a clear box, presumably of some bulletproof, tamper-proof polymer. Inside, photos of the egg had been inserted to line each side and the top of the box. A crude, but effective illusion. From a distance, the egg appeared to be there. Upon closer inspection, it was obviously photos. *Davie's* photos.

"Hmm." He gingerly touched his finger to the box. Then smiled and whipped it off. "*Et, voilà*."

The alarms suddenly stopped. The idiotic guards gasped again into the vibrating silence.

The real box, with the Faberge Egg intact, was right where it should be. The false box in his hand had merely been slipped over it. He gave it to another one of his men.

After a few stunned seconds, the manager erupted in an angry diatribe at the guards, who all started defending themselves at once.

Jean-Marc suddenly glanced at his watch. Five minutes after midnight. Why hadn't Pierre called? Had something gone wrong?

"You're in charge here," he told his ranking officer, who stood close by.

Then he made a beeline for the kitchens, taking off his tuxedo jacket as he went. A dozen armed, uniformed officers waited for him in the kitchen.

"Where's *Lieutenant* Rousselot?" he asked the cop who tossed him his shoulder holster and weapon, which he quickly slipped on.

"Followed the suspect upstairs, sir," the man replied.

He slid his jacket back on. "No one came in here looking him?"

"No, sir."

"Good. Send a man to see that the woman he was with stays in the casino. I don't want her showing up unexpectedly."

"Will do, sir."

Jean-Marc hated that he couldn't be upstairs for the sting. But he couldn't take the chance of blowing it. Ciara knew him too well. Even Beck would recognize him in an instant—almost breaking a man's nose would do that. For that matter, Villalobo may also; Jean-Marc's face was not exactly unknown on television and in the papers. So he'd had to send Pierre in his place.

Never mind. His partner was as reliable as they came. He'd see everything went down exactly as it should, leading right up to the final arrests.

In the meantime, Jean-Marc walked determinedly to the service elevator, folded his arms over his chest and took up his stance in front of it. *No one* was getting past him tonight.

"All right, men," he ordered. "Positions, everyone."

No turning back now. He thought grimly of Ciara, and the guilt and apprehension nearly overwhelmed him. But there was no calling it off, even if he wanted to. The trap was in place.

All he could do was pray his quarry walked into it.

◘ ◘ ◘

"Goddamn it, Beck!" Ciara sputtered angrily. She could not *believe* what was happening. "Only a fool would take the cash! Money is traceable. Besides, the diamonds are worth twice this amount. And they're unmarked!"

She had managed to talk Beck into lowering his gun, but the man was adamant. He wanted the cash, not the diamonds.

"How much is in the case?" Beck demanded for the fourth time. He whipped his gun up again, pointing at her face. "Tell me or I'll—"

"Six million euros," said Valois, who had been silent up until now. For a man about to lose a substantial chunk of change, he seem strangely unperturbed.

"For six million, I'll take my chances. Open the briefcase, bitch." Beck's gun jerked in warning.

Jetting out a furious breath, she snapped open the metal locks and raised the lid as Valois held it. Beck dug down to the bottom of the case and carefully inspected several bundles, fanning the bills to be sure they were legit.

Cackling like a hen who'd just been fed, he said, "Now close it up and hand it over."

"No." Her firm refusal reverberated down the hall, surprising both men. "Go ahead and shoot me. I'm not giving you the damn money."

Hell, paranoid as Villalobo was, if he thought he'd been betrayed, she was good as dead anyway.

Becks gun-slide cocked menacingly. "Hand it over, *connasse*, or you're dead!"

"You can wait for the diamonds like we agreed," she gritted out.

"Ciara, listen to the man," Valois pleaded softly. "I can handle Villalobo. Trust me, *ma petite*." He looked at her imploringly.

She ground her teeth together, trying to decide what to do. Hell, the old man had faced down Nazis. He could probably handle one slime bag drug dealer. And as for Beck, catching him with stolen cash wasn't as damning as blood diamonds, but he'd still go to jail. Which meant Sofie could press charges for rape without fearing for her life.

"Okay fine," she acceded. "But I'm warning you, leave the country tonight and don't ever come back. Or I'll tell Villalobo exactly who double-crossed his deal."

Beck snorted, grabbing the case from her. "If you live past tonight. Goodbye bitch. Give Sofie my love."

And with that he was gone.

Ciara spit out a choice oath, then turned to Valois. "God, I'm sorry. I can't believe Beck did this. All your money, gone."

"Not to worry. There's more where that came from."

"Like I could ask you to do that. Damn, I could *kill* him!"

Valois sighed, looking suddenly uncomfortable. "Listen, *ma petite*, there's something I must tell you."

"Later. Right now I need to find—"

"That won't be necessary," a voice said from behind her.

She spun. And was overjoyed to see Pierre Rousselot standing there. He didn't hold a gun in his hand, but one was tucked under his tuxedo jacket in a holster, clearly visible.

"Thank God! Just who I wanted to see," she burst out in relief. "*Brigadier* Louis Beck just stole six million euros from this man. He's getting away. You—"

"Yes, I know all about that," Pierre interrupted, a slight curl to his lip.

"You need to go after him! Call Jean-Marc. He'll tell you—"

"Forget Jean-Marc. He's busy downstairs."

"But Beck—"

"Forget about Beck, too. We have more important things to take care of."

Her jaw dropped. What was going on? Then suddenly, she faltered. Oh, God... *He and CoCo— She should have listened to her instincts.* Painful as they were.

"You want the diamonds," she said, her heart breaking in a million pieces. CoCo had been like a little sister. Her betrayal cut like a razor.

But the betrayers were going to be very disappointed.

"The buy will go as planned," Pierre said. "With one small change. I'll be accompanying you as a bodyguard. We're already late. Let's go."

"Sorry to disappoint you," she informed him acidly as he took her arm in a vise-like grip and towed her along the corridor toward the Palm room, Valois following along behind. "There's no money."

The news didn't faze Pierre, or slow him. "Not a problem," he said. "Monsieur Valois has kindly made available an equivalent amount in a bank in Switzerland. Villalobo prefers electronic transfer anyway. More cash is the last thing a drug dealer needs."

"You spoke to Valois about this?" she asked, stunned. "Before tonight?"

"I was trying to tell you," Valois murmured.

She wanted to cry. So CoCo and Pierre had deceived the old man, too, to gain his cooperation. And now he'd be out twelve million instead of six. Ciara had no idea what he was worth, but that had to be a good slice of it.

As they approached the Palm room, she hissed, "You'll never get aw—"

"Quiet!" Pierre ordered.

Two gorillas guarding the door saw them, and immediately reached for hidden weapons. "Private game," one said in broken French. "Get lost."

"*Señor* Villalobo is expecting *Monsieur* Valois," Pierre told them.

One guard opened the door, exchanged a few words with someone in the room, then jerked his head at Valois. "*Solo el viejo.*"

Over her dead body. "Not a chance," Ciara said firmly. "I'm his diamond expert. I have to go in, too."

"And I'm his bodyguard," Pierre said. "He goes nowhere without me. It's all three of us, or we walk away and there's no deal."

The guard glanced between them uncertainly, then stuck his head back in. "*Bueno,*" he finally said. "You can all go in, but I have to search you for weapons."

The search was unpleasant and very thorough. Ciara had to restrain herself from retaliating with a very thorough ball-kicking. But she knew that would get her real dead real quick. And she needed to live. Giving Pierre his due after all this was over would be far more satisfying.

He must have left his *carte* at home, because they were all admitted after the gun from his holster and one strapped to his ankle were confiscated.

They walked in, and Ciara almost gagged from the thick haze of cigar smoke. Villalobo sat at a green felt table in the middle of a poker game. A large pot of cash sat in the middle, surrounded by four or five other players. At a signal from Villalobo, they filed out of the room. The gorillas stayed.

"So you made it at last," he said in French heavily accented with Spanish. He took a drag from his foul cigar while studying them one by one with blatant distrust.

Valois stepped forward. "Our apologies for the delay. There was a bit of a fuss downstairs. The place is swarming with cops."

Villalobo's black eyes narrowed. "Were you followed?"

"Absolutely not. They have their hands full downstairs," Valois assured him.

Ciara was grateful for the long gown that covered her suddenly quaking knees. With his pinstriped suit, slicked-back hair and thick, menacing scar running along one jaw, the drug dealer looked exactly like someone straight out of a bad gangster movie.

"Shall we do this?" Valois prompted.

"I'll need to see the money first," Villalobo said silkily, beckoning over one of the gorillas, who produced a small wireless computer and set it on the green felt of the table.

"*Naturellement.*" Valois went to it and typed for a minute, until the screen filled with account information from a well-known Swiss bank. "As you can see, it's all there."

Villalobo jerked his chin at the other gorilla, who went to fetch a case sitting on the floor in the corner. When he poured the diamonds from their red velvet pouch onto the felt table, Ciara sucked in a sharp breath of awe.

The stones were absolutely gorgeous. Even in the low light of the smoky game room, they sparkled and shimmered like stars against a dark green heaven.

"They're larger than I expected," Valois said with a frown.

"That's a problem?"

"Diamonds of such size and quality will be much more difficult to dispose of. I'm afraid—"

"Enough!" Villalobo spat out, making Ciara jump and her pulse go into hyperspeed. "Not my concern. Do not try to renegotiate the price, *amigo*. You will regret it!"

To his credit, Pierre stepped forward as though to shield Valois. Villalobo's face turned so red, for a second she thought maybe he'd kill Pierre right here and save her the trouble.

But Valois waved Pierre back. "*Mademoiselle?*" In keeping with her role as gem expert, he handed her the jewelers loupe he carried on a chain like a pocket watch. "Your opinion?"

It was all for show, of course. But thankfully, he'd taught her enough over the years to look at the stones and pronounce a rough but respectable range of color, clarity and carats. Even if the terror-induced adrenaline made focusing difficult.

"Can we get twelve for them?" he asked.

She took a deep breath and said what they'd rehearsed. "Eleven to twelve. Perhaps a bit less. Of course, without a microscope..." She did her best to lift her shoulder casually.

Valois nodded, and told Villalobo, "Very well. You'll have your six million. "Pierre, gather the stones while I—"

"My man will do that," Villalobo snapped.

Valois swiftly transferred the money and shifted the wireless computer to Villalobo to check that it had been deposited to his own account. With a smile that sent chills down Ciara's spine, Villalobo then rose from his seat, took the velvet pouch from his man and tossed it to Valois.

Pierre reached out and caught it, offhandedly sticking it in his inside jacket pocket. "I'll need my weapons back."

The gorilla reluctantly handed them back under the suspicious eye of the other guard.

"See them out," Villalobo ordered, dismissing them with hardly a glance. "And send the others back in."

"A pleasure doing business," Valois said with a parting bow, then turned to her and took her arm. "Walk with me *ma petite*. All this excitement has quite taken the wind from my sails."

Alarmed, she helped him to the door, even more distressed to feel his arm was shaking. "Valois! Are you—"

"*Shhh.* Find me a comfortable chair and a cognac and I will be just fine."

So concerned she was with Valois that she forgot about Pierre and the diamonds, and everything else. It wasn't until they were well out into the corridor that she noticed the line of armed police officers pressed to the wall on either side of the door. *What the—*

Someone grabbed her, yanking her away from the opening. She landed with a thump against a solid wall of chest at the same time she heard Pierre say, "Jose Villalobo, you are under arrest."

She looked up just in time to see Jean-Marc pull out his handcuffs. Before she could exclaim, he spun her around and slapped the cuffs on her wrists—just as Pierre and a quartet of officers hustled Villalobo and his two gorillas out of the Palm room, also in handcuffs. The waiting phalanx of uniforms surrounded them, guns drawn. To her dismay, she saw another cop take hold of Valois' arm.

"Oh my God, Jean-Marc. You're not serious—"

But apparently he was. "You are under arrest," he shouted above

Villalobo's curses and threats at Pierre, who was reciting a litany of charges against him.

"Put your hands behind your back, old man," the other cop yelled at Valois over the din as Villalobo was led away, heading for the elevator. To her shock, right before disappearing around the corner, Pierre turned and gave her a wink.

What the *hell*...

She turned to Jean-Marc in confusion. "Wh-what's going on?"

"We're arresting the right-hand man of one of the world's most notorious drug lords. Thanks for setting him up for us. Couldn't have done it without you."

She gaped at Jean-Marc's serious face, more confused than ever. She had so many questions she didn't know where to begin.

"You *knew?*" she managed. "About the diamonds?"

"Of course I knew. You didn't think I'd fall for that old flowers on the bathroom wall routine, did you?" He honestly looked offended. "Really, Ciara. Give me a little credit."

He guided her over to the side of the corridor and tipped her chin up with a finger, inspecting her through narrowed eyes. "Are you all right?"

"Other than being arrested?" she muttered, still dazed by how this could have happened. "How did you know?" Then it hit her. Of course. "CoCo. Your spy strategy worked."

He looked pained. "No, actually, it didn't. She wouldn't tell Pierre a thing. Very loyal, that one."

She didn't know whether to be relieved or even more angry. Jean-Marc had beat her at her own game. She jerked her chin off his finger. "You were ahead of me every step of the way, weren't you," she said, disgusted at her own overconfidence.

Hell, she *deserved* to be put away. Her plan had failed on every possible level. Beck was free and a millionaire to boot, so Sofie was in more danger than ever. Valois would spend his autumn years in prison. And her—

"As a matter of fact, no," Jean-Marc said dryly. "I wasn't ahead of you."

She blinked. "Then...how did you figure it out?"

"Hugo."

She stared at him. "*Hugo?*"

Her face must have fallen, because Jean-Marc gave her a crooked smile. "For the record, he was very hard to convince. In the end, I took a page from your book. Made him an offer he couldn't refuse."

She was almost afraid to ask. "What kind of offer?"

"Immunity." He touched her cheek. "For you and Valois."

She gaped. Not believing her ears. "What exactly are you saying?"

"You're not really under arrest. That was just for Villalobo's benefit, so he wouldn't think you and Valois had betrayed him."

She blinked again. And darted a glance at Valois. He was laughing and slapping his cop on the shoulder like they were the best of friends as they turned to leave. Catching her gaze, he gave her a cheerful wave. "Come by the shop in a few days, *ma petite*. Right now, I have a date with a very large cognac."

With that, he and the cop walked off toward the elevator.

She was so stunned her only thought was, "He looks remarkably cheerful for a man who just lost twelve million euro."

"He didn't," Jean-Marc said.

"But..."

He clucked his tongue. "Twenty-first century rule number three. Never use wireless technology to do important transactions. Too easy for bad guys—or cops—to tap into."

"You stopped the transfer?"

"In mid-air."

Gladness soared for a split second, but then deflated. "That was only half the money. Beck took—"

"*Brigadier* Louis Beck was arrested on his way out of the casino." His eyes softened. "Don't worry, Ciara. Valois's money is safe and sound. And so is Sofie, now."

"Thank God," she said, closing her eyes against the flood of emotion that hit her at the news.

Could it really be over?

She battled back tears that threatened, and whispered, "Thank you, Jean-Marc."

He peered down at her, a funny little smile on his face. "My pleasure."

Suddenly, she realized they were all alone in the ominously silent corridor. Her heartbeat kicked up.

"Why didn't you tell me?" she quietly asked. "You could have trusted me."

"Why didn't you tell *me?*" he echoed. "You could have trusted me, too."

They gazed at each other for a long moment.

"Point taken," she whispered, properly chastised. "It won't happen again."

"No?"

"Never." She'd learned her lesson the hard way. When you loved someone you trusted them. Completely. No matter what.

"I'm going to hold you to that."

A warm, melting sensation burrowed itself into her heart. Did that mean they had a future?

"I'm really not under arrest?" she asked again, her voice coming out a bit breathier than she'd intended.

"You're really not."

She jingled her wrists. "Then why am I still in handcuffs?"

The corners of his lips curled up. "I could take them off." He stepped closer, raised a brow. "Or...not."

Her breath sucked in. The man was incorrigible. "Isn't there something we need to discuss first?"

She had to know. Now. Before this went any further. Despite the fact that her body was little by little dissolving under his slow, half-lidded perusal.

"Oh? And what would that be?" he asked.

He knew damn well what that would be. He was taunting her. Deliberately. The rogue.

"The blackjack game. Your final hand..."

He leisurely raised his fingers to the edge of her gown's plunging neckline and touched it. Not her. The fabric.

"You want to renege on that bet?"

She swallowed. As much as it killed her, she had to do this.

"Yes. Well, half the bet," she said. "I don't want—"

Her words choked off as his hand slid under the slippery silk, enveloping her breast. Goosebumps shimmered over her flesh, the nipple hardening and shrieking with pleasure.

She licked her lips. His eyes zeroed in on the movement. "You don't want...?" he prompted.

How could she ever live without this? Without his touch? Without his love? Her heart filled to bursting with the knowledge that everything she ever wished for, everything she ever needed, was right here, within her grasp. Jean-Marc. That's all that mattered to her.

But he had to understand how much he meant to her.

"The money," she whispered, her lips meeting his. "I don't want the money. All I ever want is you, Jean-Marc."

Under hers, his mouth curved. "That's good," he murmured. "Because I already gave it to the Orphans."

She laughed softly, happily. Her job was finally done. Her kids were taken care of, their futures secure. Now she could at last look to her own.

She leaned into his long, languid kiss. It went on and on, until her knees were jelly and her body was on fire for want of him.

"Jean-Marc?" she whispered, hoping his suite wasn't far.

He lifted his mouth to change angles. "Hmmm?"

"About these handcuffs..."

◙ The end ◙

ABOUT THE AUTHOR

New York Times and *USA Today* Bestselling author Nina Bruhns' adventurous romantic thrillers contain a unique blend of interesting characters and settings, twisty suspense and sizzling romance. To date she has published over 30 award-winning novels.

Awards and honors for Ms. Bruhns' books have included two RITA nominations, three Daphne du Maurier Awards for the Year's Best Overall Mystery-Suspense Book, two Romantic Times Reviewer Awards for Best Book of the Year, a National Readers Choice Award, an Eppie Award, and five Dorothy Parker Awards, just to name a few.

Read more about Nina Bruhns and her books on her website:
NinaBruhns.com

Please "like" Nina Bruhns' Facebook author page!
facebook.com/Nina.Bruhns.author

Don't forget to leave a review on Amazon!

NEW YORK TIMES BESTSELLING AUTHOR
NINA BRUHNS

Author of 30 award-winning novels

Over 1 Million copies sold worldwide

USA TODAY Bestselling Author
3-time Daphne du Maurier Award winner
National Readers Choice Award winner
3-time RITA Award nominee
4-time RT BookReviews Reviewers Choice Award

#1 Amazon Bestseller in Romantic Suspense,
Police Procedurals, Anthologies, and Movers & Shakers

Top 30 Amazon Most Popular Romance Authors

Top 50 Amazon Bestseller in Thrillers, Romance, Action &
Adventure, Mystery, Contemporary Romance, Thriller & Suspense,
Detective, Anthologies, and Women's Fiction

Amazon Germany Top 10 in Krimis & Thriller and Polizeiromane
Amazon Japan Top 100 in Police Procedurals and Romantic Suspense
Amazon UK #1 Bestselling author in Anthologies & Collections

NinaBruhns@aol.com   www.NinaBruhns.com

SIX MORE EXCITING NOVELS
BY NINA BRUHNS

W riting As Nina Bruhns...

Catch Me If You Can
Sweet Revenge
Warrior's Bride

W riting as Nikita Black...

Slave To Love
Cajun Hot
The Renegade's Woman

For details and excerpts please visit
www.NinaBruhns.com

CPSIA information can be obtained at www.ICGtesting.com
Printed in the USA
LVOW12s2105270714

396254LV00019B/564/P